W9-BRS-000

"Passion, peril, and plenty of medieval political intrigue . . . expertly crafted historical romance." —*Booklist*

Lord of Temptation

"Features a sinfully sexy hero who meets his match in a strong-willed heroine. . . . An excellent choice for readers who like powerful, passion-rich medieval romances."

—*Booklist*

"Quinn's lively romance . . . offers two spirited protagonists as well as engaging minor characters. . . . The sharp repartee and dramatic finale make this a pleasant read."

—*Publishers Weekly*

Lord of Desire

"4 Stars! . . . fast-paced and brimming with biting, sexy repartee, and a sensual cat-and-mouse game."

—*RT Book Reviews*

"Gloriously passionate . . . boldly sensual . . . Quinn deftly enhances her debut with just enough historical details to give a vivid sense of time and place." —*Booklist*

"An emotional and compelling story that brings together a strong but wounded hero and a spirited and determined heroine. The characters quickly immerse the reader into their lives." —*RomanceJunkies.com*

Also by Paula Quinn

Lord of Desire

Lord of Temptation

Lord of Seduction

Laird of the Mist

A Highlander Never Surrenders

Ravished by a Highlander

ATTENTION CORPORATIONS AND ORGANIZATIONS:
Most HACHETTE BOOK GROUP books are available
at quantity discounts with bulk purchase for educational,
business, or sales promotional use. For information,
please call or write:

Special Markets Department, Hachette Book Group
237 Park Avenue, New York, NY 10017
Telephone: 1-800-222-6747 Fax: 1-800-477-5925

Seduced
by a
Highlander

PAULA QUINN

FOREVER

NEW YORK   BOSTON

If you purchase this book without a cover you should be aware that this book may have been stolen property and reported as "unsold and destroyed" to the publisher. In such case neither the author nor the publisher has received any payment for this "stripped book."

This book is a work of fiction. Names, characters, places, and incidents are the product of the author's imagination or are used fictitiously. Any resemblance to actual events, locales, or persons, living or dead, is coincidental.

Copyright © 2010 by Paula Quinn
Excerpt from *Tamed by a Highlander* copyright © 2010 by Paula Quinn
Excerpt from *Ravished by a Highlander* copyright © 2010 by Paula Quinn
All rights reserved. Except as permitted under the U.S. Copyright Act of 1976, no part of this publication may be reproduced, distributed, or transmitted in any form or by any means, or stored in a database or retrieval system, without the prior written permission of the publisher.

Cover design by Diane Luger
Cover art by Franco Accornero
Book design by Giorgetta Bell McRee

Forever
Hachette Book Group
237 Park Avenue
New York, NY 10017
Visit our website at www.HachetteBookGroup.com.

Forever is an imprint of Grand Central Publishing.
The Forever name and logo is a trademark of Hachette Book Group, Inc.

Printed in the United States of America

First Printing: September 2010

10 9 8 7 6 5 4 3 2 1

*To knights and the ladies who love them . . .
and to Dan, my one and only.*

The Prodigal Son

Prologue

"Well, we all know that Tristan would have won the competition if not for what happened. No one can outrun him." Robert Campbell, Eleventh Earl of Argyll, turned to his nephew sitting beside him, smiled, and winked.

Sitting across from them in the earl's private solar, Callum MacGregor growled in agreement. "Aye, that's why the bastard Fergusson tripped him and provoked a fight. It should be his nose broken instead of my son's."

"I did manage to land a solid punch to his jaw, faither," Tristan defended. "Besides, it doesna' pain me anymore." He lifted his finger to his wounded nose. It still hurt like hell, but MacGregors did not whine or weep about broken bones. "'Tis Alex Fergusson's honor that will be more difficult to repair."

"Well spoken," his uncle commended, patting him on the shoulder. "You have the blood of knights in you and will grow to be a man of honor."

Tristan swelled with pride.

"I like the way it crooks slightly at the bridge." Kate

MacGregor set down her embroidery to aim her most loving smile at her son. "Now you look even more like your uncle. Does he not, Anne?"

Robert's bonnie wife looked up from her needle and agreed. "He's just as pretty. Even with the blackened eyes."

Tristan blushed and then pushed his shoulder into his sister when she laughed at him.

"I fear the boy's nose would need to suffer a few more breaks before it resembles mine." Robert Campbell picked up his nephew's hand, curled it into a fist, and then covered it with his own. "Remember, blocking is as important as the speed of your punch."

Sipping his ale by the fire, Graham Grant, closest friend to the MacGregors and the Campbells of Argyll, kicked the tip of his boot into the MacGregor Chief's ankle. "Callum, ye're not allowing Robbie to instruct yer son in the art of hand-to-hand combat, are ye?"

"Doubting my skill," Robert said smoothly, "only proves that you are a poor teacher, Graham."

"I admit yer skills have improved vastly under my training over the years," Graham replied playfully. "But had *I* been teaching Tristan, young Alex Fergusson would be missing a few teeth right now and mayhap an appendage or two."

Robert smiled and looked down at Tristan while the warriors around them all agreed that the troublesome Fergusson lad would someday find himself impaled on someone's blade—preferably Tristan's.

"Remember also"—he leaned down so that only Tristan could hear him—"that there are many moments in a man's life when the choices he makes will decide his destiny."

Tristan nodded. He understood that while warrior blood ran through his veins, it was not always necessary to do the most possible damage to his opponent—the fact that his father did not always agree with that sentiment sometimes made Tristan wish that the earl was his father instead of the Chief. He thought about his choice to fight Alex after he had picked himself off the floor. He wasn't expecting the boy's fist to fly as fast as it did. All he remembered after Alex hit him was the taste of blood in his mouth and his and Alex's fathers shouting at each other. After that, his mother would not let him compete in the rest of the games—three of which he knew he could have won. He'd changed his destiny all right, and come home with nothing but a bloody nose.

The sudden crash at the door brought the men in the solar to their feet. The shouts from beyond it drew their hands to the hilts of their swords.

"MacGregor!" Someone outside the keep roared. "Come out and face me, if ye have the courage! Ye will not insult me and my kin and live another night!"

Tristan barely heard his father ordering the women and children above stairs. He watched, all color draining from his face, as Graham and his uncle went to the door. It was Alex Fergusson's father out there. Had he come to kill his father over a child's fight?

"Tristan, go!" his father commanded, but Tristan could not move. He could barely breathe. This was his fault. The men were going to fight; his father could possibly die because of him. He reached out his hand, as if to stop his father when he strode toward the door. "Dinna' leave." He wanted to shout it, but the plea broke through his lips as quietly as a whisper. He was only ten and four. They wouldn't listen to him.

"Show yer face, Fergusson!" Callum shouted, pushing past his brother-in-law and his best friend and swinging open the heavy door. "Show yer face and I'll tell ye once again that ye're the son of a pig!"

More shouting ensued, but his mother pulling on his arm distracted Tristan. As he was led away to a room above stairs, he looked over his shoulder in time to see Graham and his uncle leave the keep behind his father.

"I should be with them." Tristan's eldest brother tried to push past their mother, but she blocked the door with her body and held up her hand to stop him.

"Your father will be fine, Rob. Sit down with your brothers. Please, my son."

Och, God, let him be fine, Tristan prayed. He felt sick to his stomach and a wee bit dizzy as wave after wave of fear engulfed him. His sister was crying in Lady Anne's lap. The sound of her weeping made Tristan want to run from the room and dash outside. Would Alex's father go back home if he apologized? He would do anything…anything to make the pain in his head, his guts, his heart go away. If anything were to befall his father…

A mournful roar pierced his gloom and stilled every other sound in the room. Graham's wife paled and drew her sword. "I'm going down there." Without waiting for anyone's approval, she pulled on the door and ran for the stairs. Her cries an instant later sent terror through the keep and into the hearts of everyone she left behind.

Tristan was not the first one to leave the room. When he stepped out of it, though, he wished he had remained and bolted the door, never to come out again. He had been afraid for his father's life. It hadn't occurred to him that someone else might die. And never, never him.

"They are goin' to die fer this!" he heard his father cry from somewhere deep in his chest. "They are all goin' to die."

Tristan descended the stairs so slowly it felt as if he wasn't really moving at all. Everything felt…unreal. It had to be. That could not be his uncle's limp body being set on the floor by his father's trembling hands, an arrow jutting from his chest. Robert Campbell could not be dead. He was too strong, too courageous and honorable to be struck down under cover of night, over a choice a child had made to fight. Too numb to cry just yet and too filled with despair and guilt to do anything but stand frozen in that terrible moment, he watched his mother and Anne fall to their knees, their anguished wails filling every corner of Campbell Keep.

The man he loved more than anyone in the world had been shot in the heart and was gone in a moment. A moment that altered the course of so many lives. Most of all, those of Tristan and the lass who would someday heal him.

Chapter One

*A*rrogant imbecile!" Isobel Fergusson pushed through the heavy wooden doors and entered Whitehall Palace's enormous privy garden with a dozen venomous oaths spilling from her lips. Finally, eleven years since her mother had died and ten since her father had left his seven children orphans, the full weight of taking care of her family had taken its toll on her. Her brother Alex was going to get them all killed. Oh, why had they come to England? And damnation, if they had to attend the Duke of York's coronation, it should be Patrick, her eldest brother and heir to their late father, the Fergusson Chieftain, here with her and not Alex. They were only supposed to stay for a sennight or two, but when the future king invited all his guests to remain at Whitehall for another month, Alex had accepted. She kicked a small rock out of her path and swore again. How could she have raised such an imprudent, thoughtless bratling?

It wasn't that Isobel was impervious to the lure of Whitehall's luxurious feathered mattresses, its grand galleries with vaulted ceilings where even the softest whispers uttered by elegant lords and ladies, powdered to look like living, breathing statues, echoed. It was all quite...unusual and beguiling in a queer sort of way. But Alex had accepted knowing the MacGregors of Skye were here! Oh, how could he? Had he forgotten the hatred between their clans? Or the trail of dead Fergusson Chieftains left by a devil bent on revenge a decade ago?

"Dear God," she beseeched, stopping at a large stone sundial in the center of the garden, "give me strength and my witless brother wisdom before he starts another war!"

A movement to her right drew her attention to a row of tall bronze statues gleaming in the sun. When one of them moved, Isobel startled back and bumped her hip against the sundial.

"Careful, lass."

He wasn't a statue at all, but a man—though his face could have been crafted by the same artist who had created the masterpieces lining the garden. Isobel took in every inch of him as he stepped out from behind the golden likeness of an archangel, wings paused forever in flight as it landed on its pedestal. He wore the garb of an Englishman, but without all the finery...or the wig. His hair hung loose to his shoulders in shades of rich chestnut and sun-streaked gold, almost the same blend coloring his eyes. He wore a cream-colored linen shirt belted to flare over his lean hips. The ruffled collar hung open at his throat, giving him more a roguish appearance than a noble one. He was tall and lithe, with long, muscular legs encased in snug-fitting breeches and dull black boots. His steps were light but deliberate as he moved toward her.

"I didna' mean to startle ye." The musical pitch of his voice branded him Scottish, mayhap even a Highlander.

"I thought ye were my sister. I am infinitely grateful that I was mistaken." His smile was utterly guileless, save for the flash of a playful dimple in one cheek, and as warm and inviting as the heavenly body perched behind him. But the way his eyes changed from brown to simmering gold, like a hawk's that spotted its prey, hinted of something far more primitive beyond his rakish charm.

For a moment that went completely out of her control, Isobel could not move as she took in the full measure of his striking countenance. Save for the slight bend at the bridge, his nose was classically cut, residing above a mouth fashioned to strip a woman of all her defenses, including reasonable thought.

She took a step around the sundial, instinctively keeping her distance from a force that befuddled her logic and tightened her breath.

Damnation, she had to say something before he thought her exactly what she was—exactly what any other woman with two working eyes in her head was when she saw him—a doddering fool. With a tilt of her chin that suggested she was a fool for no man, she flicked her deep auburn braid over her shoulder and said, "Yer sister thinks ye are an arrogant imbecile, also?"

"Aye," he answered with a grin that was all innocence and innately seductive at the same time. "That, and much worse."

As if to prove his statement true, a movement beyond the statue caught Isobel's attention. She looked in time to spy a glimpse of sapphire blue skirts and flaxen curls rushing back toward the palace.

"My guess," Isobel muttered, peering around his back to watch the lady's departure, "is that yer sister is likely correct."

"She most certainly is," he agreed, not bothering to look behind him. The cadence of his voice deepened with his smile. "But I'm no' completely irredeemable."

Rather than argue the point with such an obvious rogue when she should be thinking of a way to convince Alex to leave with her and Cameron, Isobel quirked a dubious brow at him and turned to leave. "As difficult as that is to believe, sir, I will have to take ye at yer word. Good day."

Her breath quickened an instant later when the stranger appeared at her side and leaned down toward her ear.

"Or ye could spend the afternoon with me and find oot fer yerself."

His nearness permeated the air around her with heat and the familiar scent of heather. He was definitely a Highlander, mayhap a Gordon or of the Donaldson clan, though he wore no plaid. She thought to ask his name, but decided against it. He might consider her interest in him an acceptance of his offer. She could not afford to allow her senses to be addled by a whole afternoon spent with him when her family's safety was at stake.

"Thank ye, m'lord, but I have matters to think on." She quickened her pace, but he would not be so easily dismissed.

"Do these matters have to do with the witless brother ye were prayin' fer?"

"Why?" Isobel asked, trying to sound unaffected by his boldness in following her. "Are ye worried he might have usurped yer title?"

She was completely unprepared for his laughter, or for the way it rang through her veins, coarse and carefree. A dozen other men would have scowled at her accusation, though she meant it only to show her lack of interest, but this charismatic stranger found it humorous. She liked that he had enough confidence to laugh, even at himself.

"Why must brothers be so difficult?" she conceded with a smile and began to walk with him. "Truly, if there is a title of witless brother, he has already taken it." She felt a tad bit guilty about speaking so about Alex with a man she didn't even know, but perhaps not knowing him made it easier. She needed someone to talk to about her dilemma. No, what she truly needed was a moment or two just spent *not* thinking about it. This man made her smile, and she hadn't done that all morning.

Beside her, he bent to pick up a rock and threw it into a small pond a few feet ahead of them. "And what has yer brother done that is so terrible?"

"He refuses to leave Whitehall and go home."

"Ah, unfergivable."

Isobel cut him a sidelong glance and found him smiling back at her. "Ye do not understand."

He raised a dark brow and waited for her to continue.

"All right then, if ye must know, our most hated enemies have recently arrived to pay homage to the king. My brother is cocky and prideful. If we remain here, he is likely to insult them and bring the barbarians down on our heads once again."

He nodded, leading her around the pool. "Now I see yer point more clearly. But why is it yer problem to ponder?" he asked, turning to her. "Where is yer faither that his son should make decisions that put his kin in jeopardy?"

"He is dead," Isobel told him, her eyes going hard on the palace doors and the beasts that strolled somewhere within. "Killed by these same enemies. I swear if I could get just one of them alone, I would slice open his throat and sing him back to the devil who spawned him."

She was a bit surprised to find both sympathy and amusement softening the man's features when she looked at him.

"It sounds to me like yer enemies have more to fear from ye, than ye do from them, lass."

Isobel shook her head. "I am not foolhardy like my brother. Our enemies have left us alone, and I wish it to stay that way."

"Wise," he said, and Isobel was glad she had told him. He agreed that she was correct in wanting to leave. "I could speak to him fer ye if ye'd like, mayhap talk some sense into him."

Isobel couldn't help shining her smile on him full force. He seemed to be listening in on her thoughts. She needed help and she was willing at this point to take it from anyone, even a stranger. "That is most kind of ye, but I could not impose—"

"Ye are no' imposin'. I wish to help ye if I can."

She stopped walking and looked up at him when he paused at her side. "Ye do not even know me. Why do ye want to help me?"

His dimple deepened, along with the honeyed hue of his eyes. "'Tis what I do best."

After he stole kisses and whatever else from ladies behind statues in gardens? He was crafty, this one, but immensely likable. "How verra gallant of ye."

He bowed slightly and crooked his mouth at her, setting her heart racing. "Ye see? There is hope fer me yet."

"Not according to yer sister, and she knows ye best."

"What would ye like to know?" He offered her his arm, and this time she accepted.

"I only have a moment or two…"

"Och, then ye'd best make yer question a good one."

She tapped her finger to her chin while they walked the vast lawns. "Verra well, I have it. Why does yer sister think ye are an arrogant imbecile...among other things?"

"Verra good," he commended her with a somewhat worrisome crease dipping his dark brow. "Ye're clever and bonnie."

She narrowed her eyes on him and cut him a knowing smile. "So are ye." She almost gasped at her own boldness, but his disarming candor made her feel at ease.

"How am I supposed to answer yer query truthfully after ye called me bonnie? Pick a different question."

She laughed, and it felt wonderful. "No. The same question. Answer, please."

"Hell, let's see then. Well, she thinks I am always reckless."

"Are ye?"

"Nae, I am simply less concerned with every consequence."

"Then ye are reckless indeed."

He nodded and held up a finger. "But no' always. I said less concerned, no' unconcerned."

She gave him the point, enjoying his shrewd banter. "Are ye less concerned or unconcerned with the consequences for a lady's reputation if she flees back inside a palace with her curls drooping against her flushed cheeks?"

He turned around slightly, as if just now remembering the one he had hidden behind the sculpture. "If she is eager to put her reputation in my hands after one day of knowin' her," he said, settling his gaze on Isobel again, "then I would be more inclined to be less concerned."

"I see. Well, ye are honest, at least."

"Go on," he teased. "I would much rather listen to ye list my virtues than tell ye my faults."

"Are there many more then?"

"That depends on who ye ask."

"I think in this instance I would prefer to make my own judgments."

"That is refreshin' to hear." He looked surprised and so sincerely relieved that for a moment Isobel wondered just how troublesome this man truly was.

She should go back inside and see to her brothers, but damnation, she was enjoying herself. What harm could come from just walking together? It wasn't as if she was going to let him kiss her behind the next structure they came to, although she could certainly understand why some stately, normally stuffy ladies at court would cast away their reputations for a few stolen moments with him. The more she looked at him, the more irresistible he became. She wasn't certain if it was his quicksilver smile or the way his eyes took in every nuance of her face when he gave her his full attention that beguiled her good sense. At the moment, she didn't care. She liked the way he looked at her, as if she was more than a mother, a nursemaid, and a cook to her brood of brothers. Not that she minded being those things. She loved her family more than anyone else in the world, but it was nice to forget her duties for a little while, especially knowing now that he would help her with Alex.

"What aboot ye?" he asked as they approached the west gate. "What would yer brother say aboot ye?"

"That depends on which brother ye ask." She smiled, thinking of the ones she'd left at home with Patrick. "I have six." She rolled her eyes heavenward and nodded in agreement when he gave her horrified look. "The three youngest would likely complain that I give them too many

chores to do, but it would be untrue, for they play much
more than they tend to them. Cam might tell ye I am too
soft, while Patrick thinks me as stubborn as our bull."

"Yer bull?" he asked, slanting her a wry grin. "Is there
one in particular that ye remind him of?"

"We have only the one, but he is all we need, since we
have only two cows." She was sorry she had told him the
moment after she spoke when his smile faded just a little.
She could tell by his clothes that he was not poor. Would
he look down his nose at her because she was?

"It must be difficult fer yer mother raisin' all those
sons with so few cattle to bring in any coin," he said,
proving that he was no more concerned with their stations
than he was about kissing ladies in public.

"My mother died giving birth to Tamas."

He stopped her as they came to a long stone bench at
the gate wall. "Ye raised them all on yer own then?"

"Patrick and I did. We still do. Tamas is only ten and
one. There have been difficult times, but wonderful ones,
as well." She smiled at him when he offered her a seat
before he gained his.

"Have ye gone hungry?" The concern in his expression was quite endearing now that she knew "what he
did best."

"Put away yer shining armor, knight. There is no need
to offer up yer aid. Patrick has always made certain there
is enough food on the table."

His charismatic grin returned and flashed across her
gaze, convincing her once and for all that no woman in
all of Scotland or England could likely resist him. "Armor
is too cumbersome a suit to don. Besides, mine would be
rather rusty."

"It can be polished."

She wasn't prepared for the way his eyes went soft on her or for the sudden silence that followed. "That is true," he said after a long moment that made her breath stall in her chest. "'Tis odd ye would speak of such things to me."

"No one else has, I presume."

They shared the same arcane smile between them before he answered. "My uncle used to speak of knights and their chivalrous deeds all the time. I have no' been reminded of his tales in a verra long time."

"Ye know the story of Arthur Pendragon then?"

"Of course. Would ye like me to tell it to ye?"

She really shouldn't. Alex and Cameron were probably already looking for her. "I would."

The few moments Isobel had intended to spend with her handsome stranger turned into hours, but it was only when the sun began its descent that she realized how long she had been gone. "I must go. My brothers are probably sick with worry."

"Meet with me tomorrow." He grasped her hand as she rose from the bench and turned to go. "In the garden by the stone dial."

She shook her head, acutely aware of his fingers leaving hers as she backed away. "I shouldn't. I do not even know what ye are called."

"Tristan," he told her.

She smiled playfully, feeling more lighthearted than she had in months...years. "I do not know the tale of that knight," she called out as the distance between them grew. "But ye may call me Guenevere."

"Nae," he laughed. "Iseult was Tristan's lady."

Turning back toward the palace, Isobel's smile widened. "Even better."

Chapter Two

Tristan watched her leave, enjoying the sway of her hips as she grew smaller in the distance. Who the hell was she? A Lowlander for certain. Briefly, he wondered which clan she belonged to. Despite the faded saffron of her gown and the fact that she had only one bull, she'd been invited to the coronation, so she couldn't be a peasant. Whoever she was, he found her utterly delightful. He was certain he'd never seen eyes as green or as wide as hers when he appeared from behind the statue and startled her. She wasn't as beautiful as some of the other women at court, but Tristan found the spray of freckles across her unpowdered nose and the blaze of her temper when she spoke about singing her enemy to hell quite beguiling.

His first thought, as was usually the case when he discovered a lass who piqued his interest, was how to get her out of her clothes the quickest way possible. Normally, he never pondered a woman past that point. Most didn't care what he was about. A few dashing smiles and well-placed compliments were enough to get him what he wanted. But this one challenged him with clever questions and replies almost as quick as his own. She offered him no coy smiles from her naturally coral lips. The soft blush of her cheeks was real and unguarded. She knew he was a rogue, thanks to Eleanor Hartley's leaving her cover and fleeing back to the palace, but quite astoundingly she pointed out his virtues instead of dwelling on his shortcomings.

He smiled to himself as he rose from the bench. She was an innocent, and the thought of seducing her made his nerve endings burn with thrill of such a challenge.

But hell, she called him gallant. No one had called him that, or anything even close to it, in ten years. She spoke about shining armor, and it stirred memories he'd locked away in a place he'd never thought to visit again. He didn't want to go there now. Whatever he had wanted to become when he was a lad was destroyed the day he fought with Alex Fergusson.

He set his gaze toward the Banqueting House, where supper was likely being served right now. His kin would be sitting at their guest table laughing over warm mead or ale, mayhap retelling an old battle story or discussing the news that their cousin Angus had brought them yesterday about Tristan's brother Rob saving a nun from a burning abbey. He didn't want to go there either. For while he could wield a sword as well as any warriors of Camlochlin, he had no desire to fit in with his kin's Highland code of pride, arrogance, and vengeance. He preferred disarming a man—or a woman—with his wit rather than with his blade. It was a distinction that, sometimes to his deep regret, set him apart from his father, a distinction he had perfected nonetheless, until there was no favor he could not win, no opinion of him he could not alter—if he had a mind to do so.

For a moment, he stood alone in the twilight, caught

SEDUCED BY A HIGHLANDER

between the two worlds he had rejected. His thoughts returned to the lass…Iseult…and the way she had smiled up at him when he offered her his aid. He could have stayed in that moment forever. But she was wrong about him. He should have told her the truth and made her believe him. He was a thoughtless rogue who only wanted to bed her and then leave her before she formed an attachment.

Or worse, before he did.

Finally deciding which way to go, he turned on his heel and was about to leave Whitehall through the west gate when a dulcet voice called his name.

He turned and saw Lady Pricilla Hollingsworth, a dark-haired beauty who had caught his eye when he first arrived at the palace.

"I missed you in the Banqueting House," she said, hurrying toward him. "Are you alone?"

His eyes roved over her parted lips and then lower, to the swell of her powdery white bosoms tightly confined in her low-cut gown.

"Fortunately, no' anymore." Slowly, he raised his gaze to hers and smiled.

"Lovely." Her mouth curled with the same decadence that shone in his. "Let's go for a walk, shall we?" Without waiting for his reply, she looped her arm through his. "Lady Hartley told me that you are a Highlander. I've heard many titillating tales about Highland men."

"No' more titillatin' than the tales I've heard aboot English ladies, I'm certain."

She giggled, exaggerating the shiver he apparently sent down her spine. "Oh, I do adore that lilt to your speech. It is both savage and graceful together. Much like your appearance."

Damn, she was eager. This one needed no pretty words

but desired something a wee bit more feral in nature. As he
had claimed earlier, aiding lasses was what he did best.

"Dinna' let my ruffled attire fool ye, lady. What lies
beneath is purely animal."

"Why, Mister MacGregor!" She threw her hand to her
chest in feigned offense. "I am a lady!"

It occurred to him when her hand sprang away from
her milky cleavage that she might go a step further in her
game of cat and mouse and actually slap his face. Instead,
she pressed her delicate palms to his chest and pushed
him deeper into the shadows.

"But please"—she purred hot breath up the column of
his throat—"do not let that stop you."

Closing his arms around her middle, he hauled her
hips against his and whispered over her lips before he
kissed her. "I wouldna' think of it."

"Pricilla!" A man's shout cut through the air like an
arrow.

"Hell," Tristan swore, letting her go.

"It is my husband!"

He cut her an irritated scowl as he went to meet justice. "Ye didna' tell me ye were married."

"You did not ask me."

True. He hadn't.

"My good Lord Hollingsworth. I—"

He ducked when the beefy statesman pulled a sword
from its sheath with surprising dexterity and slashed it
across Tristan's throat.

"There is nae need fer that," he said, avoiding another
jab to his guts. "Put doun yer sword and let's discuss this
like—"

Hell, that one was close. Speaking his brand of sense
into the enraged fellow's head clearly wasn't going to

work. He would have accepted a punch to the jaw as his penance for kissing the man's wife, but he sure as hell wasn't going to die for it.

The fourth swipe whistled over Tristan's head an instant before his fist landed on Hollingsworth's fleshy cheek. An uppercut to the chin next wobbled the nobleman's knees and gave Tristan an instant to snatch his weapon from his loosened grip.

He tossed the sword over the gate and into the street beyond, then turned angrily to Lady Hollingsworth's husband. "If ye ever raise a sword to me again, I will kill ye with it. Look to yerself fer the cause of yer wife's indiscretion and no' to me or the next man ye find her with."

He stormed back toward the gate entrance, swung open its heavy door, and disappeared down King's Street, leaving Hollingsworth's sword where he'd thrown it. He passed a dozen women hanging about the shadows, offering him pleasures beyond his expectations. He stopped for none of them. He wanted no company, no needy fingers clutching at his clothes, no pleas to return when he knew he wouldn't. Tonight, he didn't want to be reminded of what he had become.

Tristan glanced up at the afternoon sky, then gave the stone sundial a curious look. How the hell did anyone tell the time of day by looking at an arrow on a slab of rock? An even better question was what in blazes was he doing here waiting for a lass with a freckled nose and the sound of music in her laughter? He'd thought about her all night, and by the time he fell into his bed he was quite perturbed with her for not leaving him alone. But this morning, he had wanted to see her again.

Unfortunately, one of the disadvantages to a palace

with fifteen hundred rooms was that people were difficult to find. He was glad they had planned where to meet the night before.

"Greetings, Sir Tristan."

He didn't hear her come up behind him and smiled despite himself at what she called him. He turned to her and gathered her hand in his. He was surprised and a bit moved to find calluses there. "Lady Iseult." He dipped his head and swept a kiss across her knuckles. "Were yer brothers worried aboot ye yesterday as ye feared?"

She shook her head, and he watched the way the sun played over the rich reds and deep golds of her hair. "Their attentions were otherwise engaged by two French ladies who spent the evening giggling at words I'm sure they did not understand."

"They say love needs no words." Tristan crooked his arm and was surprised by the catch of his breath when the warmth of her hand touched him. "I say the right words are true love's adornment."

"Ye know much about true love then?" she asked him, with humor dancing across the vivid green of her eyes.

"I know nothin' of it," he admitted, leading her away from the crowded lawns. He thought of Lord and Lady Hollingsworth. "But it doesna' take a supremely intelligent man to know that the lady he loves enjoys it when he tells her that all he has is hers. His body, his mind, his heart. That she is the master of it all."

"Yes," she agreed, moving a little closer to him. "I would think that would be verra nice to hear. But how do ye know the secret of what women want when so many others do not?"

"Sir Gawain," he replied, happy that he had remembered the tale last night. "He gave his word to marry the old crone, Dame Ragnell, after she provided King Arthur with the answer to that eternal question and saved his life."

"Did he keep his word?"

"Of course he did," Tristan told her. "He was…" He paused, feeling oddly shaken by what he was about to say and the old sentiments it dragged to the surface. "He was a man of honor." Quickly, he changed the path of their conversation.

"D'ye have a man waitin' fer ye at home, fair Iseult? A husband, mayhap?" This time, he would ask first.

"No." She laughed softly. "There is no one who would grant me mastery over his heart."

"Fools then."

They looked at each other and smiled. She, seeming to see beyond his flippant resolve and touching a place he'd guarded for ten years. He, seeing a woman, mayhap the only woman capable of tearing away his defenses. He looked away, needing them to survive happily in the world he was born to.

"I saw him last eve in the Banqueting House."

"Who?" he asked, turning to her once again. He wanted to kiss her—to prove to himself that he could and still remain untouched.

"The devil who killed my father. I have never forgotten his face. When I saw him, I could not stand to look at him overlong."

"Ye saw him commit the deed then?" Tristan asked, his heart breaking a little for her. He had seen the man he loved lying dead on the ground. It was not a thing one was likely to ever forget.

"I watched from my window as he stabbed my father through the heart with his blade."

Hell. He stopped walking and reached his fingers to her cheek as if to wipe away the tears he imagined she had shed that terrible day. "Ye didna' tell me why this beast murdered yer father."

Her eyes closed for an instant at his tender touch. "He believed my father killed the Earl of Argyll during a raid."

Tristan's hand froze, along with his heart.

"The earl was their kin," she went on mercilessly. "The Devil MacGregor's brother-in-law, I was told. If he was anything like his barbaric relatives, he deserved his death."

Nae! Tristan's mind fought to reject what he was hearing. This lovely, spirited lass who had made him think on things he had forced himself to forget could not be Archibald Fergusson's daughter! She had not just told him that his uncle deserved his death! Dropping his hand to his side, he backed away from her. He wanted to damn her kin to Hades, but how could he when his uncle's death was his fault? She was wrong about Robert Campbell, but he was too angry about her accusation to tell her, too stunned to do anything but stare at her.

"I must go."

"What?" She looked surprised and reached out for him. He moved away from her hand. "What is the matter?"

He should tell her who he was, that everything terrible in her life was his doing. But he didn't have the heart, or the courage, to do so. "I just recalled that I promised my sister I would show her the king's theater. Good day to ye." He left without another word and without looking back. She was a Fergusson, and for her own safety, he would forget he had ever met her.

Chapter Three

"And to the right just a bit, you will see the Apotheosis of Charles I."

Tristan glanced up at the Banqueting House's painted ceiling where Henry de Vere, son of the Earl of Oxford, directed Mairi's view. Tristan felt a wee bit sorry for his sister, forced by seating arrangement to give the English nobleman her attention throughout eight courses. Tristan didn't care a whit about the aggrandizement of dead kings—or live ones, for that matter. But listening to the man's mindless drivel took his mind off Archie Fergusson's daughter.

He'd intended to put her out of his mind forever, but for the past six hours since he had left her, she had remained constantly present in his thoughts. Why? Why her? He had never had any trouble in the past forgetting a lass the moment he left her. Even the ones he'd bedded never plagued him the way Miss Fergusson did. Her delicate smiles, the calluses on her hands, all her damned talk about gallantry and her difficult home life that made him want to charge into it and rescue her from it all.

What the hell had he been thinking?

He was no knight plucked from the books his mother and uncle used to read to him. He'd given up ever trying to be one, and even if he hadn't, how could he save Iseult from the hatred of his own kin? For while he did not blame her father for what had happened, the rest of the MacGregors did.

"And that is the Union of England and Scotland," Oxford droned on, pointing upward and to the left.

Tristan downed his wine and motioned for a server to bring more. It was going to be a long night with this dullard sitting between him and his sister. Briefly, he thought of escaping to Lady Eleanor Hartley's table. He could delight for a bit in her lovely breasts, but she was about as sharp as the edge of a bedsheet. Before he could stop it, his gaze swept the crowded Hall seeking another face. One without powder and without guile.

"That is most interesting, m'lord."

Fortunately, his sister's voice dragged his thoughts away from his kin's worst enemy.

"I am astounded by yer vast knowledge of Whitehall's history," she practically sang. "I would love to hear more."

Tristan looked heavenward and shifted restlessly in his seat, readying himself for another hour-long discourse on the history of Whitehall. Just when he thought he might have to leave before he insulted Oxford and every other Englishman present, the tedious nobleman rose from his chair.

"And hear more you shall, dear lady," Oxford crooned. "But first, I must have a word with Lord Huntington, whom I see has just arrived for supper."

He excused himself. Tristan barely looked up. "Tell me

the truth, Mairi," he said, turning to his sister. "Ye dinna' find his lecture on the history of this place as uninspiring as the scar running from his eye to his jaw?"

"I find his scar rather intriguing." Mairi crooked her mouth into an elusive smile as she brought her cup to her lips. "And if ye had any sense in that pretty head of yers, ye would know that one can learn much from a man with a flapping tongue."

"Sister," Tristan sighed, knowing full well what she meant, "yer bloodlust to find Covenanters is beginnin' to worry me. No' to mention the gray hairs ye've added to our faither's head over the past year. He's still no' convinced ye had nothin' to do with the rebel militia that killed those four known Cameronians beyond the shores of Skye last spring."

"Ye know I cannot abide traitors to Scotland," she told him as softly as a purring kitten. "But I would never wield a sword against a man."

Tristan cast her a look as sly as her own, knowing that somewhere hidden within the folds of her kirtle were at least five daggers she could wield almost as well as the one in her mouth.

He was about to tell her to be cautious in her endeavors to save Scotland from its political and religious enemies when he saw Miss Fergusson standing at the entrance with a man on either side of her, waiting to be announced. She looked nervous and out of place among the statelier, more proper ladies of the court. Hell, he was a fool to think her not as beautiful as the rest. She was as fine as any. Finer, in fact, than most, with her long ginger curls falling loose about her shoulders, her eyes taking in the finery before her. She wore no adornment around her fingers or throat. She didn't need any. The flawless alabaster of her cleavage above the emerald green of her gown would draw more glances than any pricey bauble.

"Who is she?" Mairi inquired, following his steady gaze.

The lad on her right had to be Alex Fergusson. In the ten years that had passed, Tristan had not forgotten those piercing blue eyes filled with menace.

"I dinna' know who she is. She is no one," he added and looked away from the entrance. They were enemies. Let the lass think what she would about his uncle. He would think of her no more.

"She's lovely," Mairi commented, sizing her up.

Aye, she was. Tristan glanced at her again, only to find her looking straight at him. She smiled at him as her name was called out. Isobel Fergusson and her brothers Alex and Cameron. Isobel. Her name was Isobel.

"Fergussons!" Mairi's appreciative gaze sharpened into an icy glare. "What the hell are they doin' here?"

Tristan could have given her a dozen logical answers, but Miss Fergusson and her brothers were heading for his table and he could think of nothing but why the hell he hadn't told her who he was this afternoon.

"Do my eyes deceive me or are they truly approachin' our table?"

"Mairi"—Tristan finally broke his gaze away from Isobel—"dinna' risk more bloodshed. They have been through enough. Say nothin' and let them be on their way."

Mairi cocked a wary brow at him. "D'ye know her, Tristan?"

"Good evening, m'lord, m'lady," Miss Fergusson greeted them with the respect due to a noble family. Damn him, he should have told her and saved her from the mortification that was about to come. "I do hope ye will fergive this intrusion, m'lord, but I wanted ye to meet the brothers I spoke of." Her smile grew a tad bit animated as she motioned with bright, wide eyes to the older of the two men standing with her.

If he didn't think any one of their siblings would draw a weapon, Tristan would have smiled at her less-than-subtle plea for his aid, and then he would have granted it to her. After what his kin had done to hers, he would likely have granted her anything.

But as it was, Alex eyed him narrowly from beneath his dark, brooding brows. "Isobel, ye know this bastard?"

"Ye spoke to her this morn?" Mairi demanded at the same time, then whirled on Alex. "Watch who ye call a bastard, or I'll—"

Tristan set his hand on Mairi's arm, stopping her before she said something they would all regret. "Miss Fergusson," he said softly, turning to her, "why dinna' ye—"

"Stand away from my kin's table," Mairi finished for him, rising to her feet.

Tristan rose with her, but she missed the warning in his eyes not to continue when Lord Oxford returned to the table and stood between them.

"You heard the lady," Oxford sneered while his haughty gaze skimmed over Alex Fergusson's threadbare plaid. "Step away before I have you removed by the king's guard."

Tristan turned to stare at him. He might not believe in killing a man in cold blood, but that didn't stop him from wanting to smash out every tooth in Oxford's self-important snarl. It was unfortunate that he would only prove to Miss Fergusson that he was, indeed, a barbarian if he did so.

"My apologies for running off." The Englishman turned, feeling Tristan's eyes on him. "I returned as quickly as I could."

"How fortunate fer us all." A cool smile skittered across Tristan's lips and then hardened into something far less amicable. "Why dinna' ye take yer seat now."

Oxford blinked at him, and Tristan waited patiently for whatever response the nobleman could piece together in his dull head. When none came, Oxford bent to his seat.

Tristan timed it perfectly. Turning back to Isobel, he hooked his foot gingerly around the leg of Oxford's chair and swept it back two inches. His smile was more genuine when his gaze met hers and Oxford's stately arse hit the floor.

"Brother, are ye mad?" Mairi demanded while her champion floundered at her feet. "These are our enemies!"

The soft blush across Isobel's pert nose faded, leaving her flesh colorless and her eyes shimmering with alarm as she stared at him. "Yer..." she gasped for a breath and then continued. "Yer true name, please, m'lord?"

He knew why he hadn't told her earlier. It was the same reason he didn't want to tell her now. Hell, his father killed hers, and right before her eyes. What could he possibly say to change her opinion of him after that? And why in damnation did he care what she thought of him? "Fergive me fer no' introducin' myself to ye sooner. I am..." He paused, looking to the left at his father walking toward their table, his great belted plaid draping shoulders as broad as they'd been over twenty years ago when the Devil rode out of the mists to seek revenge on the Campbells...and later, on the Fergussons. Damnation, this just couldn't get any worse. "...I am Tristan MacGregor."

He watched the dreadful truth dawn on Isobel's face as his father stopped behind the chair closest to his and sized up Alex with a look that blended sheer terror into her hateful stare. She moved, as if on instinct, in front of her brother and then aimed the sting of her most scathing contempt at Tristan.

"My apologies," she said, clutching her chest with one hand and pushing Alex backward and out of sword's reach with the other. "I was gravely mistaken."

Hell.

Tristan watched her leave, pulling at both her brothers' sleeves to hasten their departure. She would never speak to him now. He could not fault her for that, but the way she had looked at him, as if he were the most vile mound of filth she'd ever come across, made him want to tell her that she was wrong—just as she was wrong about his uncle.

"What were Archibald Fergusson's bairns doin' at our table?"

"The gel thought she knew Tristan," Mairi answered their father's query.

"I met her in the garden yesterday," Tristan corrected woodenly. "I didna' know who she was, nor did she know me."

"Is that why you made a fool of me for her sake?"

Callum peered over Tristan's shoulder at the shaky nobleman adjusting the powdered wig on his head. "Who is this man?" he asked, sizing him up and his place near Mairi, and looking none too pleased about it.

"Lord Oxford, the earl's son," Tristan answered blandly, barely turning to look at him. "Someone who needs no help from me at being a fool."

His father gave Oxford a look that told him to close

his mouth and leave while he was still able to do so on his own. "I dinna' trust the English," Callum said, watching the nobleman scramble off. He turned his powerful gaze back to Tristan and frowned knowingly. "I like Fergussons even less. Ye know who she is now. There are enough women here to hold yer interest, son. Ye'll no' speak to that one again."

The hell he wouldn't. Tristan did what he wanted without concern about repercussions. It was what had earned him, thanks to half the fathers in Skye, the well-deserved title of Satan's Rogue. He didn't care what opinion he left in his wake. They were mostly all correct. He was the Devil's son, after all...and in a fortress filled with warriors, it was easier to be a careless scoundrel than...His gaze settled on Isobel's table across the grand room...a gallant knight. But damn it, he was no barbarian and he intended to tell her so.

"D'ye know what disagrees with me the most aboot yer ways of thinkin'?" he said to his father first, and then to Mairi. "The man ye avenged with such bloodlust would never have condoned it. Robert Campbell didna' go around skewerin' everyone who challenged him."

"'Tis no' just him that I avenged, Tristan," his father said, setting his eyes on his wife, who had returned with him and taken her seat opposite him at the table.

Aye, Tristan knew what the Fergussons had taken from his kin. Losing her brother had cost his mother, Kate MacGregor, her laughter for so long Tristan feared he might never hear it again. The Earl of Argyll's wife, Lady Anne, had near gone mad with grief and finally found her solace from God in a convent in France. They hadn't seen her since then. And he, the nephew who had lost so much more than an uncle. He had lost his thirst for being what his teacher had taught him to be, a man of integrity. A man of honor. For where does a man find honor in the presence of those he has hurt the most? He could not. In a moment he had changed his destiny, and instead of becoming what he'd dreamed of being, Tristan had become what it was easy to be. A thoughtless, reckless rogue.

Aye, he understood the fury and the pain, but Archibald Fergusson was dead. Should his children pay for their father's crime?

"Ye made them orphans."

His father did not look at him as he took his seat. "I didna' know it at the time."

"Would it have made a difference?"

"Enough, Tristan!" his mother snapped at him. "I understand your ways of thinking, perhaps better than anyone at this table. But even your uncle did not judge your father's decisions. You will not do so either."

"Verra well," Tristan said quietly as the shimmer of Isobel's auburn tresses captured and held his attention. "Then neither shall mine be judged."

"Whatever has passed between ye," Callum said, following his son's gaze, " 'twould be prudent fer ye to ferget her."

Aye, it would be. But Tristan, as anyone who knew him would agree, never did what was prudent.

Chapter Four

Isobel clenched a fine silver spoon in her fist and stared at her plate. She felt her chest growing tighter, constricting her breath until she began to feel light-headed. Damnation, she hadn't had a spasm in three years and she wouldn't have one now! Her hands shook. Her eyes grew misty with tears of humiliation and anger that she absolutely refused to shed. She wanted to scream. She wanted to leave her chair, storm back over to the MacGregor table, and shove her spoon into Tristan MacGregor's eye. She wished he were dead. No, she wished he were dying so she could watch. Dear God, she had called him gallant! She'd laughed with him, spoken of love with him! She'd shared her fears about Alex. Oh, he was a crafty, cruel snake. He probably knew who she was all along. He'd made a fool of her, letting her go on and on about her family, her life, her father! Bastard! Oh, what a chuckle he must have had hearing her speak of her dead father. How much longer would he have let her ramble on? What else had he been waiting for her to say? Did the Devil MacGregor suspect what she and her brothers knew about the earl's death?

"Ye claim that I am the thoughtless one, Isobel"—Alex leaned in to speak quietly against her ear—"yet it was ye who consorted with our enemies. What did ye tell him?"

"Nothing!" Isobel swore. She coughed and cursed her body as she drew in a tight gasp of air. Closing her eyes, she relaxed before she continued. "I did not know who he was. I thought him a noble gentleman."

"Tristan MacGregor, a gentleman?" Her brother laughed. "He's been here but a few days, and already whispers of his prowess with the ladies can be heard in every hall. Really, sister, ye must keep yer ears alert if ye mean to protect us from every evil."

"I could use a bit of aid from ye in that area," she pointed out, turning to him. "Alex, now more than ever I must insist we leave Whitehall the moment James is made king."

"Would ye have us refuse an invitation from the king?"

"Aye!" she said without haste. "Did ye not see the Devil MacGregor, or the hatred in his eyes when he looked upon ye? He still blames ye fer starting the feud."

Alex shrugged his shoulders and brought his spoon to his mouth. "It was not I who killed the earl."

Dear God, she was going to pass out. "Alex"—her whisper was fraught with panic and pleading—"I beg ye, do not speak of it."

"We cannot pretend it did not happen, Bel."

Isobel closed her eyes at the sound of Cameron's soft reproach. Dearest Cam. Of her six brothers, he was the quiet one, a ghost of who he once was, unseen and unheard. He'd been just eight summers old when their father was murdered, and he had never fully healed from the loss.

"We cannot pretend." Isobel smiled, feigning courage for his sake. "But we can try to ferget. We need to go home, Cameron. I just need to bring ye both home safely."

Shadows moved across his handsome features, dulling his somber green gaze behind a spray of deep auburn hair. He nodded and said nothing more.

Satisfied that at least one of her brothers had some sense in his head, Isobel scooped her spoon into her soup and brought it to her lips. Somehow, she would convince Alex to return home with her, but she would do so later, after she— Her gaze found Tristan over the span of tables separating them. Firelight shimmered across his features, softening the hard angles of his jaw, defining the naturally sensuous dip of his upper lip. After his swift departure from her this afternoon, she had expected to find him delighting in the company of a dozen giggling ladies all vying for his favor. What she found instead was a MacGregor with a dark temper and a sorcerer's smile, both equally dangerous. Dear God, for a single instant, just after the Englishman who had insulted her brothers crashed to his arse, she almost hadn't cared who her chivalrous stranger from the garden was. She looked away now, hating him even more than the rest of them.

She would think on him no more. She would enjoy the king's feast and all the different spices that graced her palate. She tried to name each of them and remember which to add to her garden, but it was not an easy task to ignore a wolf in the midst of a flock of sheep. She'd known he was rogue an instant after she met him. How could she have let his vibrant smiles and witty words deceive her? How could she have thought him noble, thoughtful, and more exciting than any man she had ever known?

More times than she could stop them, her eyes drifted back to his table. She watched, torn between incredulity and disgust, while, over the course of supper, four different ladies found the empty chair between Tristan and his sister and sat themselves in it to share a word with him. He gave them that and much more—his full attention and that lightning-quick grin riddled with frivolity, which, oddly, made it even more alluring. The ladies all left giggling like overeager milkmaids.

Well, Isobel thought, tearing at her bread, she was no damned sheep. She knew exactly what kind of man he was behind those wide, winsome grins. Her gaze moved to Tristan's father sitting at his right. They were MacGregors and they were all the same: loathsome, merciless, murdering bastards. She wished them all the same death.

Later, when the tables had been cleared away and the musicians took up their instruments, Isobel stood at the far end of the Banqueting House watching the dancers take the floor. She had no intention of joining the king's elegant guests. She didn't know how to dance, and even if she had, she'd much rather have looked on than participated. She'd never seen such magnificent gowns and wondered if she would be able to sew anything like them if she had the necessary materials. The colors swirling against the enormous hearth fire mesmerized her as beautiful ladies wove through rows of elegant men to music that made her forget the very different life she led.

Her heart warmed when Lady FitzSimmons, a striking young Frenchwoman, blushed—or mayhap it was just the red rouge painted against her ivory complexion—at Cameron's ardent grin as he looped his arm through hers.

Isobel took delight in her brother's pleasure, for he found so little of it at home. Truly, she hated cutting short his time here. She would have even agreed to let him remain with Alex if the MacGregors weren't in attendance. Cameron was the one brother who would not reach for his sword simply because of an askew look flung his way. Still, she didn't trust their enemies to not run any of her brothers through just to satisfy their thirst for revenge. And if they ever discovered the truth...Dear God, she couldn't think of it. And she wouldn't. Not now with the sounds of lute and harp filling the air.

She smiled at Cameron stepping around his partner and then cursed the night when she spotted Tristan weaving his way through the crowd. Her belly flipped when she realized that the fool was walking straight toward her, unconcerned with the danger in which he was about to put them both. Her eyes darted in Alex's direction, praying to God that her brother would not rush to her side, his sword ready to protect her. Relieved to find him otherwise engaged with one of the king's female guests, she slanted her nervous gaze back to Tristan. There was no mistaking his destination. He cut through the dancers with a predatory deliberateness, ignoring the come-hither glances of the ladies he passed. His eyes were fixed solely on her, as if she were the only other being in the house besides him. A wolf amidst the sheep. What did he want from her? Isobel exhaled, drawing her fingers to the tightening in her chest. Despite who he was, she could not deny his stark male beauty or the tender way he had touched his fingers to her cheek when she told him of watching her father die. He had seemed so sincerely sorry for her. But everything was a lie. She would not be so foolish again.

Just as he was about to reach her, she turned her back.

"I wish to have a word with ye, Miss Fergusson," he whispered against her hair as he came to stand behind her.

Her shoulders stiffened, along with her spine. "So ye can 'adorn' me with pretty words again? I think not!"

The sound of his easy laughter had a maddening effect on her nerves and she closed her eyes, willing herself not to whirl around and claw out his eyes.

"Go straight to hell, MacGregor," she said before she could stop herself. The last thing she wanted to do was to give any of the savages a reason to seek retaliation, even over an insult, but he deserved it for being so bold.

"Come with me to the garden, Isobel."

Was he mad, mayhap a halfwit? Or did he have other, more nefarious schemes in mind? "Are ye determined to start yet another feud?"

"Nae." Behind her, his breath fell softly to her ear, as warm as the lilting caress of his voice. "'Tis why I suggest we leave. If we dance in here, knives will fly."

Dance? Isobel balled her fingers into fists and glared at him over her shoulder. "D'ye truly think I would ever let any part of ye touch me again?"

She was tempted to touch him with the palm of her hand across his face when his dimple flashed, but thinking of her brothers, she held her temper. "I assure ye, MacGregor," she said, softening the edge in her voice and presenting him with a glib smile of her own, "I would rather be beheaded in the courtyard than dance with ye. Now please, be gone from my sight." She turned away, returning her attention to the dancers.

"Fergive me, then," he went on, ignoring her request.

"I thought ye might want to thank me fer speakin' to my faither on yer brother's behalf—"

Thank him? Thank him for telling his father everything she had innocently shared with him about Alex? Oh, she wanted to kill him and to hell with the consequences! She spun on her heel with such force that he snapped his mouth shut and took a step back. "Stay away from my brothers, Tristan MacGregor, or I vow I will cut out yer heart and display it on my front door as a warning to the rest of yer devil-spawned kin."

Her reluctance to spill his blood was sorely tested when a brighter, more vibrant smile than the ones before it curled his lips.

"Ye speak boldly fer one who claims to be afraid of my kin."

"I never claimed to be afraid," she assured him, staring him straight in the eye to prove her point. "I said I hated them."

"Well, that is unacceptable to me," he told her, completely unfazed by her scathing retort. "Both our families are guilty of the same crime. I wish to—"

"Our crimes are not equal!" She nearly shouted, then looked around, praying that she had not just drawn every eye in the house in her direction. Satisfied that she hadn't, she returned her glare to the man facing her. "Yer kin took our father from us."

"I know, and yer faither took my uncle," he replied without pause. "But neither of us will gain anythin' back by hatin' each other."

Damn him, Isobel thought, looking up at the thick, sooty lashes wreathing his topaz eyes. He was more beautiful than any law should allow. What a waste on such a cold, flippant MacGregor heart. "Ye must not have loved yer uncle verra much if ye can put aside his death so easily."

"I loved him more than anyone will ever know, save now, fer ye. He was…like a faither to me."

Isobel blinked away from his steady gaze. His uncle—the one who had told him his knightly tales. So, they had both suffered because of pride. It did not make them alike. It would never make them anything but enemies. If he truly did love his uncle, then she was sorry Tristan had lost him. But he would get no more than that.

And how much more did he want? Why was he standing here, determined to speak to someone he hated and risking another five or six years of raids when he could be sharing a more pleasant evening with a dozen ladies more beautiful than she? What had his purpose been in seducing her into liking him?

"What do ye want from me?" she asked him, drawing in a deep, silent sigh, afraid that he was after a truth she would die before giving up.

"A walk." His long lashes swept downward as he leaned toward her. "A smile, a chance to win yer favor again."

Isobel shook her head, already stepping away from him. "Ye must think me as mad as ye then."

"Give me but a wee bit of yer time and I'll tell ye what I think of ye."

She would not let her breath falter at the lush depth of his voice, or the way his gaze warmed on her, letting her know already what he thought. She had admired his honesty, but now she doubted there was any truth to his words. He was intelligent and well versed in the art of seduction. But truly, did he think she would give her favor to a MacGregor? If he did, then he was the most arrogant man she'd ever known. It made the satisfaction of refusing him even more pleasurable. "There is nothing ye have to say to me that I want to hear."

He looked about to say something more, but then his smile changed into one more practiced and courteous. Offering her a slight bow, he said, "Verra well then, Miss Fergusson. Farewell."

Isobel did not reply but watched him leave the Banqueting House alone. "Farewell, Mister MacGregor, and good riddance to ye." When she returned her gaze to Cameron finishing his dance with Lady FitzSimmons, she forced herself to smile. She hadn't felt this miserable in a very long time.

Chapter Five

"How do you feel about the coronation tomorrow?" Lady Margaret Ashley asked Tristan as they strolled through Whitehall's Stone Gallery overlooking the Thames. "Tristan?" She tugged his sleeve.

He looked into her lovely, if a bit lackluster, blue eyes and then at her mouth. "Aye?"

"The coronation? We will have a Catholic king on the morrow."

"Aye, we will."

"And what do you think of that?"

He didn't give a rat's arse. The only thing on Tristan's mind was Lady Ashley's lips. It was difficult enough, without her rambling on about politics, to keep his focus on wanting to kiss her and not on another lass with a freckled nose and a rapier-sharp tongue. He'd known last eve that trying to speak with Isobel would be a challenge. She hated him, and he didn't blame her for it. But finding himself still so completely beguiled by her was unexpected. He'd never had to try to win a lass who hated him.

Hell, he didn't know any lasses who hated him. He found himself looking forward to the challenge.

"You are not even listening to me." Lady Ashley pouted her ruby red lips and gave his arm a playful slap.

How would Isobel Fergusson's curses taste against his mouth?

"My father says that what Highlanders lack for in brains, they make up for in ruthlessness. What do you think of that?"

Tristan cocked his brow and his smile at her. Mayhap this English feather possessed a bit of a spark after all. "My guess is that would be true of any man who lacked brains. Highlander or Englishman."

"Hmmm." She made a sweet little sound and smiled up at him, giving in before they'd even engaged. "Are you ruthless, Tristan?"

Ruthless enough to send her back to her father unable to walk…or sit properly for at least a day. He wondered what she would think of that? She'd likely fall into his arms, a willing participant in his infamous inheritance. He'd been in England only a few days but already he knew how little it took to get these fine, powdery ladies into his bed—endeavors that left him feeling emptier than all the heads in Whitehall put together. He could take Lady Ashley right here, up against the enormous painting of Oliver Cromwell leading his New Model Army into Scotland. A month ago he might even have tossed Cromwell a mocking grin while he drove his body into one of England's daughters, but since Isobel's stinging rejection, he felt the way a lion might if gazelles began to fall dead in front of him instead of giving chase.

"Tristan." Lady Ashley paused her steps and tilted her mouth up to his. "You may kiss me now if you like."

He'd rather not. But how to tell her so without insult?

"I know I should exercise more prudence," she cooed, looping her arms around his neck, "but rumors of your prowess in the bedchamber intrigue me."

Tristan freed his neck from the arms that bound him. "Alas, fair Margaret." He brought her hands to his lips and kissed each one to soften his rejection. "But I fear my reputation fer bein' a ruthless rogue would wither at yer silken fingertips." When she blushed and smiled at him beneath her pale golden lashes, he sighed inwardly, not with relief, for she hadn't the mind to consider any deeper meaning to his words, but with regret—for the very same reason.

Releasing her hands, he caught a flash of fire out of the corner of his eye. Instinctively, he turned to let his gaze pursue the fair Miss Fergusson as she passed him on her way to the Shield Gallery.

"Pardon me." He stepped away from Lady Ashley, his eyes intent on his prey. "There is a matter I must see to."

But even as he steadied his pace to keep a short distance behind her, Tristan knew that his desire to speak to Isobel again had less to do with defending himself or his kin than was wise to admit aloud. He already missed the ease with which they spoke, the spark of intelligence in her emerald eyes, her ability to see the best in him when no one else had ever bothered looking.

Silently, he watched her make her way down the long corridor, passing the gallery without pause. He surveyed her form and cocked his head a little at the soft sway of her hips. The hem of her kirtle was somewhat tattered, but she passed a half dozen statelier-dressed ladies with her chin tilted upward. The pride she possessed made him breathless.

He was deciding how best to approach her when she suddenly turned, stilling him with a fiery glare.

"Do ye intend to follow me around the entire duration of my stay, MacGregor?"

Lifting his gaze from the roundness of her backside, he couldn't help smiling at her caustic tone and large, wary eyes. She was like an unbridled rush of fresh air to his lungs, and he wanted more. "Now that I've enjoyed the view from such a vantage point, Miss Fergusson"—he moved quietly toward her—"I confess the likelihood is quite high."

He didn't miss the high flush spreading across her cheeks, or the way she practically trembled with the effort it took her not to tear one of the old swords off the wall and strike him with it.

"Is this where I am supposed to swoon like all yer other little sheep?" she asked him, relying on her sharp tongue instead. She wielded it with zest. "They might think ye are a ram, but I know now what ye truly are."

No one knew that, not even him, Tristan thought as his wee game of seeking to bask in her temper came to an abrupt end. Outwardly, he could be many things, change with his surroundings like a chameleon. But nowhere in him was there a cold-blooded killer.

"Tristan?"

Someone called out from down the corridor. It was Mairi's voice. Hell. The rest of his kin might disregard his interest in Isobel, trusting that it would not last long and knowing there was nothing they could do about it short of locking him away somewhere, but Mairi had a tendency toward violence.

"Meet me in the Privy Garden at midnight," he said quickly, counting the moments until his sister saw them together, "and let me prove that ye're wrong."

Isobel looked about to laugh, and for an instant Tristan considered giving up all to watch her do it.

"My answer," she told him tightly, "is the same as the last time ye invited me fer a walk. Ye are deranged if ye think I will agree to a clandestine meeting with my worst enemy, Mister MacGregor. Utterly and completely deranged."

He had to agree with her. A casual interest was one thing. Trying to win the favor of Archibald Fergusson's daughter was another. He could likely be tossed out of Camlochlin for such betrayal. He didn't know why his father hadn't done it already with all the trouble he'd caused his kin over the years. "Please, fer yer brothers' sake then." He added a smile to his mad request and left her looking after him.

Four hours later, Isobel drew her cloak around her shoulders and cursed under her breath while she stepped out into the Privy Garden. What was she doing meeting Tristan alone in the darkness? She had to be as deranged as he, but for her brother's sake she would do anything. Oh, the scoundrel! Were his words a threat of danger, or a promise of protection? No, not protection. He was not the man she had first believed him to be. Why would any MacGregor promise a Fergusson safety? None of Tristan's kin had cared what had happened to her and her brothers after they killed her father. And why should they? The MacGregors had no understanding of what they had truly taken from Archibald Fergusson's bairns. They believed they had been merciful in leaving the children alive, a belief that for many years Isobel doubted was correct.

A brisk breeze snapped her hair across the bridge of her nose. She swept the lock away with her pinkie and looked around. Beneath the milky glow of the low moon, the statues appeared like ghostly sentinels, sent to watch over Whitehall's private Eden. As her vision adjusted to the dim light, she studied each sculpture, waiting for Tristan to step out from behind one of them.

She should not have come. Tristan MacGregor was too dangerous, not only to her brothers, but to her. She could not deny the dangerously charismatic appeal that drew women to him like insects to a flame—including her, before she had known his true identity.

She almost breathed a sigh of relief when she realized that he wasn't coming. It seemed he had more sense than she did. She would go back to the palace, back home to her kin, and put Tristan MacGregor out of her mind for good.

"Isobel."

His deep voice behind her played over her nerve endings as if on a drum. Or mayhap it was her heart she heard thudding furiously in her ears. She hated him for speaking her name with such tenderness, such intimacy that it felt as if he were touching her even when he wasn't. It reminded her of how at ease she'd felt with him the day she met him. Of the way his gaze lingered over her features, as if her plain face delighted him. She had gone to bed that night wanting to know him better, wanting to lose herself forever in the sound of his laughter.

"Ye're even bonnier in the moonlight."

Aye, it was her heartbeat. Her palms felt moist and her breath labored. Unbidden memories of the tender smiles they had shared, the sweet, musical lilt of his voice when he told her the story of Arthur and his brave knights, came rushing back to her, softening her kneecaps, melting her bones to the core. Scoundrel bastard. He practiced the charm and mannerisms of the most eloquent nobleman, but his urbane grins were meant to ignite passionate responses, like a cat playing with its prey. The mystery was why had he chosen to continue to play with her.

"Why do ye waste yer flowery words on me, when there are at least a hundred ladies in the palace"—finally, she turned to face him fully—"and mayhap some men, as well, who would enjoy hearing them?"

Genuine humor curled his mouth as his eyes washed over her like a sunrise, heating everywhere they settled. "Because 'tis no' their enjoyment that concerns me, but my own. That is why I'd rather be here with ye than with anyone else."

She gave him a doubtful look. He was eloquent, all right—his words sprinkled with a thick Highland burr to make him all the more peculiar. Her family was responsible for his uncle's death. He had to hate her. He was after something. She was sure of it now, and she was almost sure of what it was. What if the revenge his kin had taken on her father was not enough? What if, after ten years, their demand for justice had returned and they wanted proof that the lethal arrow came from her father's quiver? She was there when the MacGregor Chief killed her father. She'd heard what her father's closest friend, Kevin Kennedy, had shouted out moments before her father was murdered. She was sure the Devil MacGregor had heard it, too. Had he sent his son to her to discover the truth? Why else would Tristan MacGregor pursue her throughout the palace? She should not have come. Dear God, he could swerve any woman from her most stubbornly held convictions. And she had to hold tight to hers.

Straightening her shoulders, Isobel called up her strength of will. MacGregor's attempts to find the truth, no matter how determined they were, would fail.

"Walk with me." He stepped closer to her. So close, in fact, that her breasts grazed his chest. She moved back, doing her best to ignore the clean scent of heather that clung to him.

"No, I must return to my brothers."

"Then I will walk ye back to them." He hooked his arm at her and waited for her to accept.

She stared at him with scathing anger coloring her cheeks. "That is what ye want, is it not?" Her breath nearly stopped when his eyes dipped to the heavy rise and fall of her bosoms. "Ye want to give one of my brothers a reason to fight with ye."

Flicking his keen gaze back to hers, he said, "By yer own admission, 'tis Alex who is foolish enough to try to open old wounds. I simply want to walk with ye, and if I have to escort ye back inside to do it, I will."

"So, what ye are saying," she accused, folding her arms across her chest, "is that I have no choice."

"Aye, ye have two," he corrected. Oddly, there was no trace of victory in his tone. "Ye can choose to be with me alone or in the sight of many. As fer myself, I'd prefer yer first option. I risk as much as ye if any of my kin see us together."

"I doubt that." Isobel looked toward the palace and then back at him, trying to decide what to do. Would he truly follow her back to her chamber? She didn't have to ponder it an extra instant. Of course he would. This was the man who had kicked an English nobleman's chair from under his arse in the presence of all. "I think yer father is well enough aware of yer follies by now to expect the worst of ye."

The change in his expression was so quick and so complete that Isobel played her words over in her mind three times after she had spoken them, trying to discover what it was that made him go cold.

"Ye're probably correct," he admitted after a moment that looked as if he was through wanting to walk with her. His smile returned, artful and insincere. "But tonight I'd like to be unpredictable."

He turned away from the palace and offered her his arm a second time. Isobel did not accept it, but she did follow him when he began to walk to garden path. What choice did she have?

"It will be worse if we are discovered out here alone," she pointed out, picking up her pace to match his leisurely gait.

"Aye, but the wee hint of danger makes yer blood run quicker, does it no'?" He angled his face just enough for her to catch the glint of his playful dimple.

"Is that what this is about fer ye then?" She flicked her finger back and forth between them. "Danger?"

Turning to her fully, his grin widened, along with his eyes, in sheer amusement. "Why d'ye insist on believin' that 'tis some meaningless reason like revenge or danger that compels me to want to be with ye?"

"Because most MacGregors do not think revenge is meaningless."

"I am no' like most MacGregors."

She doubted that as well. "Then why?" She had to know why a man who had his choice of any of the beautiful ladies in the palace chose her. "What compels ye to take interest in me, Tristan MacGregor? Ye claimed to be honest, so tell me the truth."

"In truth, 'twas ye who pointed oot my honesty."

"I see," she bristled, but she refused to get caught up in his articulate trap. "Why did ye mention my brothers' sake when ye asked me to meet with ye? Our clans are sworn enemies. My name is spat with contempt from yer kin's lips, as yers is from mine. My father is the man who killed yer uncle, and yer clan has had their revenge. There is nothing more. So, tell me why?"

Judging by the way he stared at her, as if he was finally at a loss for words, Isobel guessed that no woman had ever questioned his motives before. But then his gaze skimmed across her hair, over the bridge of her nose, softening on her lips.

"Ye're a flame, Isobel," he said, lifting his eyes to meet hers. "And a flame is more allurin' than a pile of embers."

Oh, he did not have to go in search of danger, Isobel told herself, willing her breath to slow. He was the epitome of it. Dear Father Almighty, keep her from sighing like a besotted fool. Poor, poor Lady Ashley, and every other lady this man set his sights on. His words were as enchanting as the hint of vulnerability beneath his rakish grin. If he wasn't a MacGregor, she might be tempted to give in to his clever seduction all over again. It was that powerful. But he *was* a MacGregor, and she was not a besotted fool, so instead, she propped her hand on her hip and gave him a pointed look. "Ye are well-practiced at this."

His smile broadened with something akin to astonishment—most likely at the fact that she was not swooning all over him. "In truth, I am," he admitted, then shot out his hand to stop her when she turned to walk away. "But I dinna' usually care if anyone believes the things I tell them."

Why did he care if she believed him? And why did she still find his candor so disarming...so damned likable? God help her. She needed to hasten this walk along so she could get back to her room and away from him.

"What of my brothers? Why did ye ask to speak to me fer their sakes?"

"I wanted to give ye my word that I did not betray yer trust with the things ye told me of Alex. When I explained to my faither that yer brother had gone simple-minded after falling from his horse a few years ago, he agreed no' to take anything Alex says directly while he's here. So ye have nae more to fret over if Alex stays behind."

Isobel did her best to squelch the smile he was quite obviously after. To call Alex simple-minded was rude indeed, but if it would keep her brother safe, let the MacGregors think what they would. "Ye have my gratitude fer that."

His smile softened on her. "Ye're verra much welcome."

Mastering control over her breathing, she pulled free of his hold. What part of him was more perilous? His innate magnetism, his seemingly genuine sincerity, or the levity with which he treated just about everything? She didn't want to find out. "Well." She motioned him along the path. "Ye requested a walk. Let us get it over with."

"If ye'll recall," he answered, unaffected by her obvious rejection, "I requested a smile as well."

Isobel would have laughed in his face if she trusted herself to look at him and not give in to one of his requests. "Ye will be getting neither."

He shrugged, unconvinced as they walked. "'Tis a big garden."

She knew she should leave right then, when she felt the smile creeping over her mouth. She should run back to her brothers, but she couldn't seem to move her feet. Somewhere deep inside her, she wasn't sure she wanted to.

"Now ye have *my* gratitude."

"Fer what?" Isobel granted him only half her attention and the rest to the lanterns lighting their path. "It was simply exasperation ye saw on my face. The way one might grimace while beseeching God to grant one patience. I am afraid ye mistook what ye saw fer something it was not."

She could feel his eyes on her like brands, willing her to look at him. "Ye are so refreshin' to me, Isobel. Ye are like no one I have ever met before, and I—"

She heard the footsteps to her left, but she hardly had time to register that they were no longer alone. She should have run. One moment, he was speaking to her as smoothly as the serpent spoke to Eve, and the next, she was in his arms, bent slightly backward over the crook of his elbow and gaping up at his face—his extremely close face. She drew back and opened her mouth to demand he release her, but her words were swallowed up by his lips covering hers. Horrified at first, Isobel tried to pummel his chest with her fists, but her attempts to break free of him only seemed to ignite his ardor. Pulling her closer, he crushed her to him, devouring her with a kiss that drew the breath from her trembling body. His lips molded and teased. His tongue stroked and tasted every inch of her until she felt her will to resist him abandon her. When he finally pulled back, Isobel's breath came hard and heavy.

He smiled, looking quite pleased with himself despite his own labored breath and the smoky remnants of desire burning his eyes.

"That was clo—"

The remainder of his words were cut off by her swift slap across his face. But Isobel wasn't satisfied and slapped him a second time. She stared at him while he lifted his fingers to the sting in his cheek. She didn't trust herself to speak. She wasn't even sure if her tingling lips could form the curses he deserved to hear.

She finally did run then, and she didn't stop until she reached her chamber and bolted the door behind her.

Oh, dear God, he had kissed her. Tristan MacGregor had kissed her, and it was wonderful.

✢

Chapter Six

$\mathcal{T}$ristan left Lady Elizabeth Sutherland with a curse
on his lips and headed across the court to the
lawns. He was angry with himself, but he had Isobel to
blame for his sudden—and a bit frightening—lack of
interest in the fairer sex. It didn't matter that she had
avoided him like the plague since their kiss in the garden,
completely ignoring him at the coronation yesterday. She
haunted his every waking moment, and his dreams, as
well. Why? Was it the refreshing resistance she offered
to his most practiced advances that piqued his interest?
Or the succulent flame of her tongue that left him aching
for more?

When he'd heard the footsteps in the garden that night
and had seen who it was, he'd pulled her into his arms
and kissed her to keep her hidden from her brother's
eyes. He would have told her so if she hadn't slapped
him. His face pained him for two days, but tasting her
was worth it.

Mayhap it was the long-forgotten path he saw in
her eyes, tempting him toward it once again. She had

pointed out virtues he hadn't realized he possessed until now—wee remnants of his once-longed-for destination that were so ingrained in him, they came as second nature. It was why he didn't pick up his blade unless he was forced to, why he always spoke the truth, unless it was cruel to do so, and why he always found himself offering his aid to a lass, in whatever capacity she required.

His bonnie Iseult had shown him a path that led to honor. But did he still want it? Could he still attain it? He tried not to think on it too much.

Instead, he found himself smiling often during the day, recalling the trouble Isobel had in fathoming why he had sought her out above all the lasses in attendance for a walk in the garden. Hell, she'd accused him of every reason but the correct one. It was as if she wasn't aware of how delightful she was—which only made him want to tell her, show her, all the more.

"Tristan!"

His thoughts of Isobel shattered at the high-pitched voice rushing his way.

"Lady FitzSimmons." Tristan smiled, his boots clicking past her as he hurried onward.

"Where are ye off to?" she cooed, capturing him by the arm, her batting black lashes offering more than just her company.

"To the tilting yard," he said, trying to disengage himself from her and wondering what the hell was wrong with him. "My kin await me there."

"Oh?" She looked up at him with renewed interest. "Are you competing then? I've never seen a Highlander fight before."

"Nae, just observin'."

"I am heading that way myself. You may escort me, if you wish."

"Of course." He offered her a bland smile, wishing to be rid of her sooner, rather than later.

The walk across Whitehall's vast grounds proved to be every bit as tedious in Lady FitzSimmons's company as Tristan had feared. She was familiar with most of the people strolling about and shared with him their names and every bit of gossip she'd heard of them. Which, disturbingly, was a lot. He was glad when he finally found his kin watching the competition from just beyond the short fence. He broke away from his admirer's talons with a hasty farewell.

"Lady Hollingsworth was lookin' fer ye," Mairi said, making room for him between her and her father. "That is her husband on the field." She pointed over the fence to the man Tristan already knew, leaning against a post and sharpening his blade.

Tristan threw his sister a dry scowl. "Yer concern fer me is touchin', Mairi. But I have nae interest in Lady Hollingsworth or in who her husband is."

"Tristan, why don't you compete?" His mother smiled at him across the span of her husband's chest. "Graham already gave his mark."

"And ye, faither?" Tristan asked, glancing at him. "Ye're no' takin' this opportunity to smash a few English skulls?"

"If the right head presents itself, I might."

"You absolutely will not!" Kate MacGregor pinched her husband's arm. "This is a friendly competition and you, my dearest beloved, do not know how to fight cordially."

Tristan turned back to the field and the two challengers readying to fight. Without the rage of finding his wife in the arms of another man, Lord Hollingsworth was a bit clumsy with his sword. Eventually though, the force behind his blows wore down his opponent.

Dull.

Tristan's eyes scanned the many faces encircling the field; more than half of them smiled back. He could have almost any woman in attendance with the right amount of charm, the carefully chosen words that came to him on pure instinct alone. But since he met Isobel, every coy smile cast his way by the ladies he had previously found so appealing blended into the same powdery, lifeless face. Saints help him, but how could he find pleasure in the bland when he'd had a sample of such alluring spice? Worse, how could wanting one lass keep him from wanting any others?

The next competitors were announced, and when he heard his sister mutter an oath, he returned his attention to the field.

Alex Fergusson stared at him from the large enclosure, his sleeves rolled up to his elbows and murder in his eyes. "I have a request!" he shouted, holding up his hands to silence the crowd. "I wish to call to the field someone other than my opponent."

Immediately, Tristan closed his eyes, knowing what was coming next.

"Tristan MacGregor! Let us finish here, on a fair stage, what ye once began."

Was he drunk? Tristan smiled coolly and shook his head. "We already finished it, Alex. Ye won. Ye broke my nose." From the corner of his eye, he saw Isobel shoving her way to the perimeter of the fence. Hell.

"And I will break it again if you have the courage to step inside."

"Alex!" she shouted at him. His only acknowledgment was a swift, dark warning for her to remain silent.

"Come on, ye coward. Or should I call your murdering father to fight me? Let us see how skilled he is without his claymore."

Tristan stepped forward before his father did. "I have it," he said, turning to him and thinking how quickly Alex would find himself down and possibly dead if Tristan let them fight.

He stepped into the enclosure and met Isobel's terrified gaze. Damn Alex for putting her through this. "No swords," he called out to the officials, then looked across the field at his opponent. "We will end it the same way we started it."

Alex nodded and came at him, fists flying. Tristan blocked three punches with relative ease and ducked to avoid a fourth. They separated for a moment and then Alex rushed forward again. Tristan could fight with any weapon, thanks to his father's careful training, but it was his uncle who had taught him to fight with his hands— and his elbows. He brought one into Alex's nose now with cracking authority and watched, mildly satisfied, as blood shot forth in every direction.

His father cheered. Isobel covered her face in her hands. It was over. "Ye have my thanks fer lettin' me even the score, Alex," Tristan told him and began to turn away.

"Not just yet," Alex called out, catching a sword from a Lowland onlooker.

"Dinna' be a fool," Tristan warned. "Choose to quit while ye can still hold up yer head."

Alex swung the blade around in front of him, looking quite awkward and out of practice. Tristan looked heavenward and shook his head.

Isobel's brother did not come at him with fury the way Lord Hollingsworth had. His swings were slower, but the weapon gave him the boldness to advance. Callum tossed him his sword, and when Tristan scooped it off the ground he heard Isobel cry out his name. He had no intention of killing the fool. She would *never* forgive him for that. He only meant to stop Alex before he was injured.

Unlike his competitor's, Tristan's blade danced in his hands and flashed beneath the sun. They both swung at the same time, and Alex lost his balance at the force of Tristan's strike. Patiently, Tristan waited for him to straighten and ready himself again. The moment he did, Tristan brought his claymore down in a chopping, grinding blow that sent sparks through the air. Over and over, Alex found no defense against him. A dozen times, Tristan could have easily cut him, but not once did he do so. Instead, he sent Alex to his knees before him, metal tangled in metal, until with one swift twist of his wrist, Tristan disengaged the hilt from Alex's fingers and the sword fell harmlessly to the grass.

The crowd cheered, while some called out to him to finish the deed with blood. Tristan found Isobel's gaze and bowed slightly, letting her know his mercy was for her sake.

He left the enclosure and handed his father back his sword.

"Well done," the Chief said, smacking him on the back. Tristan was pleased and a bit surprised that his father was not among those calling for blood.

His eyes found Isobel across the perimeter, standing with her bloody-nosed brother. He couldn't hear what it was she was telling him, but she looked angry enough to set his nose and then break it again herself. She sent him off with her brother Cameron and then turned to meet Tristan's gaze. She tipped her head to him as if offering him thanks for not hurting Alex, then left the fence.

"There is Lady Hartley," Tristan told his kin and hurried off before anyone had a chance to look.

He kept his pace steady until Isobel reached the line of trees in the garden. He caught up with her quickly once they were out of sight of either of their families.

Her steps were quick and light, her cool green gaze fixed straight ahead, with no intention of sparing him the briefest glance.

He wasn't about to have that. "Greetings, Miss Fergusson." He stepped into her path, blocking her from moving forward. "I was afraid ye had left this morn withoot biddin' me farewell."

When she looked around at him, his gaze dipped to the heavy rise and fall of her bosom beneath her kirtle, her creamy flesh pulsing with the rhythm of his checked breath. He wanted to taste her there.

"My brothers are expecting me. Let me by, please."

He looked up unrepentantly and moved aside. "Are ye still angry aboot me kissin' ye, then?" he asked, picking up the pace beside her. "I only did it to—"

"Ye have my gratitude for not killing my foolish brother, but never speak of kissing me again or it will be *my* fist in yer face."

"Hell, I didna' think 'twas *that* vile." He held back the smile trying to creep over his lips when she stopped and turned to him, green eyes blazing.

"Exactly how vile did ye think it was?"

Ah, there was the fire he was after. A lesser, more cowardly man would have politely bowed out of the battle he'd foolishly entered. But Tristan forged ahead, driven toward her like a parched traveler who'd discovered a garden in the arid dunes. "I'm thinkin' 'twas yer first time, so 'twas understandable that it might be lackin' just a wee bit."

She tilted her chin up at him, her plump, shapely lips drawing in a shallow breath that flared her nostrils and stiffened her shoulders. She reminded Tristan of an untamed mare that would never tire, and he drenched his vision in the glorious sight of her. "I'd find it a pleasure, quite possibly beyond what I could endure, to help ye become better at it."

She was about to slap his face, mayhap keep her word and punch it if the crimson of her cheeks was any indication. "I would rather be hurled into a vat of hot tar than ever have yer mouth on mine again. I hated it, just as I hate ye, MacGregor."

"My name is Tristan," he said, wanting her to see the man she had seen in the garden when they first met. "And if we had no' been interrupted the other night, I would have told ye that I dinna' approve of what our kin have done."

She laughed, but the sound of it left only anger drifting across the damp courtyard. "Ye are the son of the Devil."

"But I was reared by another man."

She did not hear him, or mayhap she did and she didn't care. Her lips hooked into a knowing sneer. "Whatever dark purpose ye have in trying to win my favor, let us be clear here and now; ye will never succeed."

Tristan guessed she was correct. It would take more time than they had at Whitehall to woo her to his bed. He understood now why he wanted her there so badly. He wanted to feel her passion beneath him, hostile and hot atop him, purring with delight while she rode him.

His dark purpose? Indeed, it was always his ultimate goal when he saw a desirable lass. Isobel was no different.

But she was. She hated him for who he was, not for who he was whispered to be. For the first time he wasn't certain he could change someone's opinion of him, but he was determined to try.

"Isobel"—he closed his fingers around her wrist, stopping her when she turned to go—"is wantin' to convince ye that I'm no' the savage ye think I am a dark purpose?"

"It is when I ask myself why ye would want to convince me of anything at all," she shot back. "We are enemies. Nothing ye say or do will ever change that truth."

"Mayhap it will," he argued, the words spilling from his mouth before he had time to consider them; "mayhap you and I are the ones who can finally bring an end to all the hatred and pain."

She eyed him with a quizzical quirk of her brow and one corner of her mouth. "Ye offer yer aid, yet again."

"Aye," he vowed.

"Ye would have me believe that ye truly care about such a thing?"

He did care, and for more reasons than he could ever tell her. "Ye *will* believe it if ye give me a chance to prove it to ye."

She laughed and tugged her wrist loose. "By becoming lovers?"

This time, he let her pass him. "By becoming friends."

She stopped, and as she turned, Tristan didn't know what reaction to expect from her. Mentally, he prepared himself for whatever was coming.

In the golden light filtering through the trees, she stood draped in waves of burnished fire and flushed cheeks. But this living flame had a core carved of ice. "That would require trust, and ye will never gain mine. In fact"—she took a step toward him, her hands fisted at her sides—"I find the idea that ye think ye can offensive. It proves to me that ye have no understanding of what yer kin have taken from mine." When he opened his mouth to speak, she cut him off. "Ye speak of hatred and pain, but ye did not have to watch yer brother dig a hole big enough to lay yer father in. Yer sister never had to worry over what her siblings would eat from meal to meal, or lie awake at night afraid fer their safety because yer clan abandoned them after they were left with a boy as their Chieftain. How many times do rival clans who know ye have no defense attack yer home and destroy what yer hands have bled over? Yer kin did not take my father's life alone. They robbed me of mine and of my brothers', as well. How much more do ye want?"

His reply was immediate and spoken with a sincerity he had offered to only a few before her. "Fergive me. My intentions are no' to trivialize the loss ye suffered, but to prove to ye that there's a MacGregor who thinks another way."

She stepped back as he moved toward her, the smolder of her eyes fading into cool disregard. "If ye speak the truth, than ye betray yer clan in a far deeper way than by speaking to me. Why would I want a 'friend' who holds no allegiance to his own kin?"

She didn't wait for his answer but turned and left him alone and staring after her as she hiked up her skirts and stormed all the way back to the stairs of the upper gallery.

For the first time in Tristan's life, words escaped him; right ones, wrong ones, any words at all. How the hell had he just become the scum on the soles of her shoes? Not that he wasn't already. He wanted to go after her, to tell her she was wrong about him. He was not betraying his clan. If anyone, he was betraying himself by always trying to deny who he had been born to become.

He wanted to strip her of this image she had of him slashing away at the helpless, laughing as his victims' lifeblood soaked the ground. He was not that man. His kin were not those men. He could convince her if he had a few more weeks with her, mayhap a month. It would be difficult, Tristan knew, and he smiled up at the gallery. What quest for honor was ever easy?

Chapter Seven

$\mathcal{I}$nstead of going directly to her brother's chamber, Isobel entered the Banqueting House. Let Alex tend to himself. This time, he had gone too far. Was he trying to get more of their small family killed? Oh, wait until she told Patrick what he had done. Should she even tell Patrick? He had enough to do at home without worrying over their rash, reckless brother. She was busy cursing Alex when she walked straight into a thick muscular arm.

"Ye're Patrick Fergusson's sister, aye?"

Isobel looked up into a pair of bloodshot eyes and a red bushy beard speckled with bits of food. His thick chest blocked her view of a third of the king's guests.

"I am John Douglas," he said, looping his beefy forearm around her shoulder and herding her to a less crowded area. "I've seen ye with Patrick at the market in Dumfries. Is he here?"

"I regret, he is not." Isobel smiled politely and slipped away from his grasp. "But my other—"

"Duncan!" the husky Lowlander called out, capturing

her elbow in his palm to stop her. "Have a look at who just dropped into my arms." As his friend approached, his grin as wide as the gaping holes in his mouth, John Douglas tossed his arm around her again and dipped his face to hers. "Best tell Duncan yer name, lass. He'll be wantin' to recall it tomorrow, I'm certain."

Isobel coughed at the stench of ale saturating Mister Douglas's breath as it fell over her. The hair along her nape rose as his arm snaked tighter around her, keeping her close. A sense of danger swept over her. Instinctively, she looked around for help. None of the king's other guests looked overly interested in her predicament, and even if they were, Isobel didn't think any one of them would risk a fight with these two. Douglas and his companion might be too soused to wield a sword with any precision, but they were big, and a swinging fist could likely break a jaw.

"Speak up now, little one." Duncan inched toward her. "We won't bite."

Isobel glared at his toothless leer. Truly, she didn't want to start something her brothers might have to finish, but she wasn't about to let these two ill-bred swine see her squirm. "I've nae doubt about that." Plucking Douglas's arm from her shoulder, she stepped away. "If ye will pardon me..."

Fingers closed around her wrist, stopping her yet again. This time, though, she was yanked rather forcefully back into John Douglas's chest. "Nae, I don't think I will. How about ye, Duncan?" he asked, turning to his companion. "Will ye pardon the bonnie Miss Fergusson?"

Duncan shook his head, his hungry gaze spilling over the swell of her breasts. "Mayhap we can persuade her to come back to our chambers."

"John Douglas!"

Isobel's captor swung around, bringing her with him to meet Tristan's amiable smile.

Isobel wasn't sure if she was happy to see him. She didn't want to be. She wanted to continue hating him, but it was proving more difficult each time he came to her rescue. She'd lost too much because of his family, and it angered her that he believed that if they became friends, all crimes could be forgiven. His kiss that night in the garden had nearly swayed her opinion of him. But she'd put away all memories of his mouth on hers. Or at least, she had tried to. Tristan MacGregor's mouth was not an easy thing to forget. The supple fullness of his lips as they fell against hers, the hunger of his tongue, dashing her resolve to pieces with the barest lick.

Never again. She would never again give in to his manly wiles. He was used to getting what he wanted from women, and as she'd suspected, he wanted more from her than a kiss. He wanted her "friendship," even her trust. Mayhap he wanted her secrets, but he would never learn them.

"Last I heard," Tristan said jauntily, moving closer to her captor, "auld Martin MacRae shot ye dead when he caught ye sneakin' oot of his daughter's bedroom window."

Douglas eyed him narrowly. "Gossip travels far, MacGregor."

Tristan's dimple deepened. "Aye, it does."

"He got me in the arse," Douglas finally admitted, obviously not feeling at all threatened by Tristan's jovial demeanor. "But ye know us Douglases; we don't stay down fer long."

Isobel cursed him when Tristan laughed and gave

the brute's shoulder a hearty whack. She should have guessed these savages were friends. MacGregor wasn't here to offer his aid, but likely to join in whatever they had planned for her.

"My kin will be pleased to hear it." Tristan's gaze skimmed over her without a trace of recognition. "A drink." He flashed Duncan a wide, white grin. "To celebrate our hardy Scottish constitutions."

Before Duncan had a chance to reply—which Isobel was certain would have been a resounding aye—Tristan raised his arm to a nearby server and plucked two cups from the tray. He handed one to Duncan, the other to John Douglas, whose tight grip on Isobel loosened just a bit. The last cup he took for himself.

"And to the king's fine wine." Tristan lifted his cup in salute. The other two agreed and merrily followed suit when Tristan tossed back his head and swigged the full contents of his cup.

He was fascinating to watch, really, Isobel had to admit to herself as he swiped his sleeve across another of his dashing smiles. There had been a moment, just as Tristan's cup reached his lips, when his heavy-lidded gaze met hers. Beyond the shadows of his long lashes, his eyes twinkled with purpose and the confidence to carry it out. Was his purpose to get soused with these two fools and drag her off to a place where no one would hear her screams? No. Considering him while he quaffed his drink, she didn't think so. He'd done nothing but offer her his aid from the moment they met. She didn't want to believe that he was truly the most gallant man she had ever met. She much preferred thinking of him as the serpent-tongued rogue that all the other ladies at court knew him to be. But she would be a fool to refuse his aid at the present moment. She would not thank him again, though.

"Perfection."

The husky cadence of his voice settled over her nerve endings like an intimate touch, making her cheeks flush as if he'd spoken the word to and about her.

"Another round, brothers!" His robust tone returned, Tristan snatched up three more cups and handed them out. "This time we drink to the king's fine guests."

Isobel's face burned hotter. She could feel his eyes on her singeing through her shift and kirtle.

The men drained their cups again and John Douglas swayed on his feet as he turned his glossy gaze on her. "Ye'll be sorely disappointed that ye wasted yer toast on this one, MacGregor. She's Patrick *Fergusson's* sister."

Tristan's smile finally faded and Isobel swore that if he said something crass about her brother she would kick him in the kneecaps and to hell with the consequences.

"Patrick Fergusson, ye say?" Tristan cast the two brutes a worried look and took a step back from her. "Och, Douglas, ye have more courage than I handling that bastard's sister the way ye are."

Douglas laughed, but when he spoke his voice was hushed with alarm. "Why d'ye say that?"

"Did ye no' hear aboot what he did to Jamie Mackenzie after the poor lad tried to kiss her?"

Who in blazes was Jamie Mackenzie?

"Ye know we MacGregors dinna' fear anyone," Tristan went on, looking around as if he expected Patrick to materialize out of the crowd, "but after Fergusson took his axe to ten Mackenzies while they slept..."

"While they slept?" Duncan's voice rose, his gaze taking on a hollow look.

"Hacked them to pieces in their beds fer takin' liberties with the lass when he wasna' with her. Is that no' correct, Miss Fergusson?"

Isobel gave him her most scathing glare—which he ignored.

"I'll wager a dozen sheep that she didna' tell either of ye poor fools aboot the trail of blood and guts that followed Patrick all the way back to his homestead that unholy night. Did she tell ye that he cut the lips off Jamie's face and keeps them in a pouch around his neck?"

Duncan, looking a bit green around his jowls, shook his head and stepped back, closer to Tristan. "Ye'd best let go of her, John."

John Douglas began to sweat. A warm droplet spilled onto Isobel's wrist, still clutched in his fingers. She looked at it, feeling a bit ill herself. If the brute didn't release her in the next instant, she was going to snatch his dagger from his belt and plunge it into his arm.

"I admit," Douglas said shakily, "I did manhandle the lass a wee bit." Fresh beads glistened at his pale temples. "Think ye he'll come after me fer that?"

Taking pity on him, Tristan rested his hand on John's shoulder. "No' if ye do as I say."

"I'd be in yer debt, MacGregor."

"Of course. What kind of friend would I be to allow yer faither and mother, and most likely yer sisters as well, to be hacked to shreds by a madman?" While Douglas pondered the horrific thought, Tristan snaked his arm around John's shoulder, drawing him closer. At the same time, he reached out his free hand, plucked Isobel from her captor's grip, and moved her behind him. He did it all quickly and with the fluid grace of a dancer exchanging partners on the floor.

"Here is what ye shall do." While he spoke, he gathered Duncan under his other arm. "Leave the palace tonight. Both of ye, before she tells her two other brothers what ye've done, aye? Good!" He grinned when they nodded nervously and gave them each a heavy whack between their shoulder blades, almost sweeping their unsteady feet from under them and making their chests collide. "Have a merry journey, lads!"

Cupping Isobel's elbow in his palm, he led her away into the crowd, looking quite pleased with himself.

Briefly, Isobel pondered snatching up another cup from a passing server and smashing it over her rescuer's head.

Chapter Eight

$\mathcal{A}$s much as I would enjoy hearing yer clever tongue fail ye at my brothers' reproach"—Isobel tried to yank her elbow free of Tristan's hold—"I do not want to suffer the same if they return to the hall and see us together."

"Then let's go somewhere they willna' see us." He spun right, toward the entryway of the Banqueting House, pulling her with him. He paused momentarily and swayed on his feet, then shook his head as if to clear it.

"Ye are as bad as Douglas and his friend," Isobel said through clenched teeth when he tugged her along.

"Probably worse, but I think ye already suspect that."

She gave the back of his head a black look and a nod as he led her out of the house. His steps were quick and light across the gallery, and twice she glanced over her shoulder to see if either of her brothers was following.

"Let me go! Ye are going to get us all killed!"

"Nonsense, I—" He paused again and gripped the heavy banister.

Isobel peered down the long staircase and thought

about kicking him the rest of the way down. "Ye are drunk."

"A sacrifice I was willin' to make fer ye." He tossed her a wink over his shoulder and continued down.

"I did not need yer aid."

He remained quiet this time, having the decency, at least, not to refute her claim or laugh in her face. The blatant intent in John Douglas's eyes churned her stomach. At some point, before the brute dragged her into some dark corner of the palace, with his drooling companion close behind, she would have had to call out for aid. God only knew what would have happened then. Still, being hauled to the outer courtyard with Tristan MacGregor was no better. Why, then, didn't she feel afraid? At least, not for her physical safety. He was after something from her and, as he'd proven moments earlier, he did not need to use force or threats to get what he wanted. It was his sorcerer's tongue she had to guard against, the dash of playfulness and the hint of humility in his wicked smile that tempted her to like him despite who he was.

"There now," he spoke softly as they stepped into the cool afternoon. His hand was warm and much bigger than hers when it slipped down her forearm and closed around her fingers. His touch was intimate and bold at the same time, heating Isobel's blood and her temper. "Is this no' better than bein' bunched within four walls with a dozen faces ye dinna' know?"

"Ye seem to enjoy a crowd," she said rigidly, pulling her hand away and keeping carefully hidden the effect that being alone with him was having on her nerves.

"No' always."

Oh, aye, and that trace of vulnerability that sometimes

rose to the surface of his voice as unexpectedly as a summer downpour...was it all part of his spell?

Isobel forbade herself to look at him. "If ye dare try to kiss me again, I shall set ye on yer knees."

"I've nae doubt about that." His deep laughter fanned a swarm of dragonflies in her belly. "The taste of yer mouth nearly dropped me to the ground the first time. But ye have my word that I only wish to speak with ye."

A proposal already proven to be just as perilous.

"I am not as easily swayed as yer last two adversaries, MacGregor."

"Thank God fer that," he murmured under his breath and picked up his steps. When she didn't immediately follow, he stopped and turned to her, his smile soft and mesmerizing in the sunlight. "Come on with ye now, lass. Sit with me by the gate, fer if I dinna' take a seat soon, I may break my nose again when I fall to my face in a drunken stupor."

When she still didn't move either toward him or back to the stairs, he headed for the bench without her, calling out as he went, "I know ye're afraid of my kin, but ye have nothin' to fear from me."

She hiked up her skirts and as she marched past him, muttered, "I do not fear any MacGregor." When she reached the bench, she spun on her heel and dropped her rump down hard on the stone. She stared at his less passionate approach and then looked away when he slid down beside her.

"And to clarify," she told him stiffly and a bit short of breath, "my brother Patrick would never hack families to pieces in their sleep. That was a terrible thing to say."

"Fer men like John Douglas and his friend," he said,

resting his head against the gate behind them, "fear earns respect."

"Well, Patrick is nothing like ye portrayed him." She glanced at him out of the corner of her eye. "He is kind and serious, and deeply devoted to our family. He works our land day and night and has kept us alive fer ten years."

"He sounds much like my brother Rob." He looked about to say more but went a little green. "The clouds are spinnin'."

"Mayhap it would help if ye were not staring up at them."

He dipped his head forward and offered her a thankful smile.

Isobel shifted her gaze. "What kind of Highlander cannot hold his drink?"

"The kind who prefers to keep his wits sharp."

"And yet," she turned to cast him her own rapier smile, just to remind him that he sat with no swooning halfwit, "here ye sit as dull as a wilted petal."

"That should count fer something, aye?" He closed his eyes and leaned his head back once again. "Fer ye alone would I sacrifice my good senses."

Looking at him, Isobel shook her head with disbelief. How did he manage to shrug off every insult she threw at him as if his skin was made of stone? And she was wrong about him. He was no wilted petal. Even muddleheaded, he brandished his tongue with finesse.

"Do ye speak these kinds of pretty words to all the ladies ye meet, or do ye spare them fer me alone, as well?"

"I speak the truth—most of the time," he claimed without opening his eyes. "Unless 'tis more merciful no' to."

"How benevolent of ye."

He laughed softly at her dry tone but said nothing more.

Given the opportunity to look at him when he wouldn't notice her staring, Isobel's eyes grazed over a profile such as Michelangelo probably dreamed about when he sculpted David. Her gaze slipped slowly over the rest of him sprawled across the bench like a languid prince waiting to be served. By God, there was so much to examine…and admire. His chest rose and fell slowly beneath a gauzy white shirt, cut to fit his firm physique to perfection. Spread over his flat belly, his fingers were broad and lean and fashioned for dexterity. His covered legs stretched out before him, extending far beyond her own.

"Why do ye not wear yer plaid like the others?" she asked him before she could stop herself. "Are ye not proud of yer heritage—even though ye are a MacGregor?" She said the last letting him hear the distaste in her mouth.

"I'm happy to be who I am, a MacGregor and a Campbell combined."

Aye, he was the late Earl of Argyll's nephew. She had almost let herself forget that. Not wanting the conversation to head in that direction, she veered off into another. "And what kind of name is Tristan fer a Highlander anyway? According to your story of King Arthur, it is an English name."

He opened his eyes and quirked his mouth at her. "'Tis a knightly name."

She quirked her mouth right back at him. "Why ever then did yer mother give it to ye?"

His smile widened into a grin. It was quite irritating.

"My name was taken from the *Prose Tristan,* the true

tale of Malory's Tristan and Iseult in *Le Morte d'Arthur*. 'Twas my mother's favorite tale when she was a child. She and my uncle read it to me often. Would ye like me to tell it to ye?"

"I would not," she told him, looking away. Heavens, but he was peculiar. What kind of rascal, who by his own admission cared little about the consequences of his deeds, held knightly deeds in such esteem? "I am not at all interested," she lied.

"'Tis the story of a legendary knight and the lady he loved and how he betrayed his beloved king." He sat up straighter, seeming a bit more clearheaded. "I havena' thought of that tale fer many years, though my name reminds me of it each day." He smiled to himself and then, as if remembering she was there, blinked at her. "Now that I remember it," he said softly, his smile fading, "'tis a story I dinna' think ye'd enjoy after all. The endin' is tragic."

Isobel turned away from the seductive warmth heating his eyes, its source some inner flame that always burned—to draw insects to their deaths.

"'Twould be a cruel twist of fate if we ever came to care aboot each other as my namesake and his lady did."

Lord, but he was arrogant, as well as curious. "I can assure ye," she replied, "that is not something ye need to fret over."

"I will if ye continue to enchant me with yer sassy mouth."

She gave him a pointed look. She had to admit the rogue's tongue was very likely the best weapon in his arsenal. Why, he didn't even bother to wear a sword at his side or behind his back.

"Are ye going to try to beguile me fer the remainder of

our short visit, Mister MacGregor? Because if so, then ye are only wasting my time and yers. I would much prefer yer frankness, no matter how crude it might be. If there is something ye wish to ask me, then simply do so and let us get this pretense over with."

He stared at her for a moment, looking a bit bewildered. Then his eyes darkened, falling to her mouth. Isobel was prepared for him to ask her about his uncle's death. She suspected that was what he had been doing with her from the beginning—hoping to seduce her into talking. She was not prepared for him to ask her for another kiss.

She closed her eyes, turning away from him again. She couldn't let him do it and still hate him.

But Tristan MacGregor did not ask for a kiss. What he asked for was far more dangerous.

"Isobel." He set his hand atop hers, setting her heart racing. "Will ye accept my sincerest condolences fer the death of yer faither?"

She didn't move. She couldn't breathe. Did he speak in earnest? A small part of her wanted to believe he did. Hadn't he already told her this very day, just a few dozen yards from where they sat now, that he did not think like his kin and that he did not approve of what they had done? But he was clever. He would do anything, say anything to seduce her into liking him, trusting him. Was he so determined in his task that he would abandon his charm and feign contrition in order to win her favor?

"Bel?"

She vaulted to her feet at the sound of her brother's voice just a few feet away. It was Cameron, and he'd seen them together, their enemy's hand locked over hers.

"We began to worry when ye did not return to our

chamber." His eyes darted to Tristan, then sank to the ground.

Isobel straightened her spine, forcing her lungs to expand, trying to think clearly. But how could she explain what she was doing here alone with a MacGregor? Especially to Cam? She wished it had been Alex who found them. She would have preferred his sharp tongue and cruel temper to the disbelief and fear she saw in Cam's eyes.

"Fergive me fer making ye fret, Cameron. I was…I was…"

"She was on her way to ye when I stopped her." Tristan rose to his feet, a full head above Cam. "The fault is mine, so 'tis I who should ask yer—"

"No," Isobel warned him on a scathing breath. She would *not* let him weave his artful spell over Cam. "Come, Cameron," she said, taking her brother's arm, wanting to get him away from Tristan without anything else said between them. "We must pack fer our morning's journey."

"Wait," Tristan said, stopping her. "Ye're leavin' Whitehall?"

The disappointment in his voice urged her to turn around and look at him one last time. "Aye, we are going home."

He broke his gaze away from hers, carefully shielding what she'd heard in his voice. His purpose had failed, at least with her.

"Mister MacGregor." She took a step toward him. "I would ask ye to grant me one thing before I go."

"What is it?"

"I cannot persuade Alex to return with us. I ask ye to stay away from him. Please, do not speak to him at all and do not cause him any harm, no matter how troublesome he may become. Will ye grant me this?"

He didn't ask her why he should grant her anything at all. She didn't think he would agree to her request and almost smiled at him when he looked at her again and nodded.

"Of course, Miss Fergusson. Have I no' already proven that to ye?"

"Ye have." She nodded. "But if ye should desire to speak to him..."

"He is in nae danger from me. Ye have my solemn vow."

She left, feeling a bit better. She believed him. She didn't know why, or if she was the biggest fool in England. But she believed him.

Chapter Nine

"By the time we arrived," Colin MacGregor told his kin in the privacy of the clan Chief's guest bedchamber, "St. Christopher's Abbey was engulfed in flames."

Tristan's youngest brother had arrived at Whitehall an hour ago with Captain Connor Grant and his band of English soldiers. His appearance had, at first, brought joy to his parents' faces, but when they realized that neither Rob nor any of the others in his party traveled with him, they grew concerned and fearful.

Colin's usual sedate tone did not change when he assured them that their brother Rob and the rest were safe and on their way back to Camlochlin, and then requested an urgent audience with the king a moment later.

His request was denied, at least until his father heard first what had happened since Angus left them.

"We rode on to Ayrshire to deliver Lady Montgomery to the sisters of Courlochcraig, but..."

Watching Colin across the firelight, Tristan tried to discern what it was about his brother that had changed since the last time he'd seen him. Other than his generally scruffy appearance, Colin was the same unflappable, cocksure lad who had parted from his father's company a fortnight ago. But now, an undercurrent of softness marked the unflinching timbre of his voice when—

"...It turned out that Davina...that is, Lady Montgomery was not safe in Ayr either."

—he spoke of the lass Rob had rescued.

Tristan smiled and reminded himself to tease Colin about his obvious infatuation later. Right now, though, he yawned at the whole tedious tale. His thoughts wandered, as they did more times during the day than he would ever admit, to Isobel. He tried to push her from his memory, since she'd left Whitehall a sennight ago, but she returned, plaguing him like an irksome nettle wedged in his boot, always there, always just beyond his reach, impossible to pluck out. Truly, he didn't know why his days seemed less vibrant without her in them. He hardly knew her, but strangely he felt as if he'd been waiting for her all his life. She most certainly did not like him and he should not like her. But, hell, he did. He liked the feeling it gave him when he helped her, and she seemed to need a lot of aid—mostly with her brother, and with drunken Lowlanders. But there was more to be done if what she had told him about her life was true. And it wasn't just his dusty sense of chivalry that drew him to her. He liked the fire in her temper and the pride in her step and the fact that she would not be easily seduced. He wanted to pursue her, catch her, and enjoy her. But even if winning her was somehow possible—he looked to where his mother sat—succeeding might cost him his kin.

Kate Campbell didn't give a rat's arse if anyone approved of her son and the way he lived his life. She had told him once, after his aunt Maggie compared him to his older brother, that his passion sprang from a different source, and therefore led him on a separate path in search of it. But he hadn't searched at all. It seemed, instead, that his path had found him.

What would his mother think of him if he told her that the path to regaining his honor began with Isobel Fergusson? That mayhap, while he could not bring back the dead, he could heal the living and restore what he had helped to destroy.

Aye, it was a quest his uncle would have been proud of. Tristan had started the feud between the MacGregors and the Fergussons. He wanted to be the one to end it.

"Who is she?" Callum asked, jarring Tristan from his vexation. "What do the king of England's enemies care aboot a novice of the order that they would burn doun her abbey and pursue her across the braes?"

Ah, now they were getting somewhere. His interest piqued, Tristan caught the anxious glance his best friend, Connor, tossed at Colin. A moment or two passed in silence with all ears perked.

"I gave Rob my word to tell no one here who she is, including the king," Captain Grant finally said. "But ye are his kin and ye should know the danger he is in. The danger I fear he may be bringing on Camlochlin."

Callum moved forward in his chair, as did Tristan. Rob putting Camlochlin in danger? It was difficult to believe.

A short time later, while everyone else remained stunned in his or her seat after learning Lady Montgomery's true identity, Callum bolted from his. "Pack yer things. We're goin' home."

· · ·

Isobel pushed a shrub out of her way after her careful inspection revealed it to be useless. She swiped her forearm across her brow and continued along the rocky riverbed. How long had he been searching for the vital addition to her garden? Four hours? Five? Every year her precious butterbur became harder to find. She had to keep looking, else it would be too late to replant. She needed it for her tea in the winter months when it became harder to breathe.

What made her lonely quest more difficult was that Tristan MacGregor was with her almost every step of the way. He invaded her thoughts in the day and in the night, no matter what she was doing, no matter how hard she chased him away. She'd been afraid of him at Whitehall—afraid of what he wanted. Afraid of how he looked at her, as if he meant to possess her at any cost. Why would he want her? And why could she not put his kiss out of her thoughts?

She hated him for haunting her, and in her mind she told him so, often. But he only smiled.

It was a peculiar thing about his smile. At the palace, it always seemed to be lurking somewhere about his face, ready to shine forth and ravish the heart of anyone looking at it. Ah, the first two days spent with him, before she knew who he was, had been blissful indeed. His laughter made her forget everything else. He seemed to take such joy in simply living—though at times she was certain she saw a hint of melancholy carefully shielded behind the crook of his decadent mouth. What was his inner turmoil? Did he hate himself for being a rogue instead of being one of the men from his tales of chivalry? She almost laughed at the thought of him hating himself. Indeed, the man knew he was mesmerizing and wonderful. For a MacGregor, that is.

Being away from him this last sennight had done nothing to lessen his effect on her. In fact, during Patrick's tirade when she'd returned home without Alex, she had found the memory of his smile rather calming. It was careless and unshakable, as if nothing was bad enough to spoil his day—no matter how gloomy. She wished she possessed that kind of resolve.

She pushed through four more shrubs and stabbed her finger on a prickly leaf. What did he have to be so happy about? Cursing, she brought her bloody finger to her lips and kicked Tristan from her thoughts for the thousandth time.

She had to find the plant soon. Patrick needed her. Damn Alex anyway. He was a grown man, and she refused to worry over him. If he chose to leave his family for risk and adventure, there was nothing they could do. They would all split up his chores and make do without him.

Would Tristan stop his savage family from cutting Alex down? Was Alex with Tristan right now, sharing ale and secrets with him in one of the king's grand rooms? Dear God, she prayed that Tristan kept his word and did not try to befriend her brother.

Ye're a flame, Isobel. And a flame is more allurin' than a pile of embers.

She patted her cheeks with her palm and muttered an oath about Tristan's wily tongue. "Go away from me now, ye bastard." Hiking her skirts above her ankles, she trampled through the next line of bushes, determined to forget him.

She spotted a dense patch of foliage in the distance and picked up her pace. Even if she could search tomorrow, she'd have to start from this point, hours away from her home. As she grew closer, one of the shrubs brought a thankful smile to her face. There it was, her miracle plant. Her mother had been giving her butterbur tea since she was a babe. Not too much and never dry, for it could harm the liver. Isobel never asked how her mother knew these things. Mothers just did. Oh, how Isobel missed her. But the plant was becoming scarce, and it frightened Isobel to think of her life without it. Ox-eye daisies could be used as well, but butterbur worked faster.

She reached out to graze her fingers over one of its heart-shaped leaves, bigger than her entire hand. She'd need to dig up the—

Her thoughts ended abruptly at the click of the pistol somewhere behind her head.

"What are ye doing on m' land, lady?"

Isobel closed her eyes and willed herself not to scream. Who the hell would hear her? "I...I was just going to..."

"Speak up!"

She nearly leaped from her skin and instinctively turned around to face him. When she saw the man's barrel aimed at her face, she caught a breath that felt like the last one in her body.

"I need yer butterbur," she said, trying to regain control over her breathing. "Please, lower yer pistol, sir."

He was old, likely in his fiftieth year. His skin was tanned and weathered with wrinkles. His hair was long, scarce, and oily. He squinted at her and then turned his head and spat something out of his mouth.

"I have a...condition"—(her mother had taught her to never use the word *sickness*, lest others think her contagious)—"and the butterbur heals me. I have searched long fer it and have only found it here. I only need a small part to plant in my garden."

For a moment, he looked about to refuse and shoot her between the eyes. "Take it. Then be gone and dinna' come back. I know ye are the sister of those three red-haired, demon-spawned Fergusson lads. If I see them near my horses again, I'll shoot them dead."

Later, after Isobel returned home, she lingered over the small patch of freshly turned soil in her garden and admired her prize. Her feet were blistered, her hands lacerated, and she'd looked down the barrel of a pistol. But she had found it, and she would nurture it until it grew strong. Just as she had done with her brothers.

As dusk settled over the glen she wiped her hands and spread her gaze over the violet-hued hills. She spotted her brothers bringing in the last of their sheep and raised her arm over her head. They all did the same and she smiled. They were all she had in the world. All she needed to be happy.

That is, as long as no man ever kissed her again the way Tristan MacGregor had in the king's Privy Garden.

Chapter Ten

*I*t is not like you to be so dismal." Kate MacGregor reined her horse in beside Tristan's as they traveled home. "Why, you look as if your closest friend just fell to the sword."

Tristan glanced sideways at his mother. He could not tell her the truth about what was plaguing his thoughts. Alex Fergusson was not his closest friend. In fact, Tristan didn't care for him at all, but that hadn't stopped him from fearing for the fool's life ever since they left Whitehall. "I was thinkin' of Mairi and Colin," he told her instead. It wasn't really an untruth. "D'ye think 'twas wise to let them remain in England?"

"Aye, your father believes they will be safer there for now with Connor and the rest of the king's army. If, heaven forbid, Camlochlin is attacked by the king's enemies, your brother and sister would be the first to join in the battle."

Tristan nodded, knowing she was correct. His younger siblings loved the sword as much as Rob loved the land. Neither of them would think twice about skewering Alex Fergusson to one of Whitehall's painted walls if he insulted the MacGregors in their presence. Hell, Isobel would never forgive him.

"I should have remained in England with them." When Tristan realized he had spoken aloud, he flashed his mother a quick grin. "Alone, Connor doesna' stand a chance against Mairi."

Kate rolled her eyes heavenward and laughed, lightening Tristan's mood. "I think the captain can take care of himself without your help."

"Aye, but Mairi is his weakness."

"True," his mother conceded. "But it is Colin who concerns me more. He seemed to take a liking to the king. I fear he might find himself more suited to a life in the English army, as Connor did."

"The captain had little choice; he has Stuart blood."

Tristan looked up to find that his father had slowed his mount until they caught up with him.

"Colin is a MacGregor," Callum continued when they reached him. His formidable gaze settled on Tristan first, then softened on his wife. "He'll never leave Camlochlin to stand with the English."

Tristan's graceful smile was tinged with shadows of his boyhood, when both he and his father first began to understand that Tristan was not at all like the rest of his rough-and-ready clan, but rather sought to emulate ancient ideals he had learned from books.

"I've nae intention of standin' with the English when I leave Camlochlin, faither," Tristan reminded him for the hundredth time. "I simply want to live my own life."

"In Glen Orchy," Callum pointed out as if Tristan didn't know.

Tristan shrugged. "Mother's home is mine by my birthright. 'Tis the only thing that may ever be mine."

"Our clan is yers."

Hell, Tristan thought, looking away. Why did his father fight so hard to keep him at home? His indiscriminate attraction to the fairer sex had brought as much trouble to Camlochlin in the past several years as Callum's had in his outlaw days. His father should be glad to be rid of him.

"Ye belong at home, Tristan."

Did he? "Campbell Keep is my home, as well. The men who help me restore the keep may bring their families and stay with me."

Callum turned his gaze north and remained silent long enough for Tristan to shift beneath the weight of things he wanted to say, but couldn't.

"I dinna' understand why ye want to leave," his father finally said. "I confess I understand *ye* even less."

Aye, Tristan was aware that the loneliness of no one's truly knowing him was his own fault. He'd always found it easier to misdirect and confound his father, rather than tell him the truth—that as a boy, he'd often wished Robert Campbell had fathered him. It wasn't because he didn't love the man riding beside him, or that his father didn't love him. They were blood, and nothing could destroy that, but that was all they had in common.

"I love Camlochlin," Tristan said, wanting from someplace deep within to prove to his father that they were not so different after all. "But I belong in Glen Orchy." It was the truth and the only one he could give for now.

From atop a windswept crest, Tristan fixed his gaze on the castle carved from the black mountains behind it, its jagged turrets piercing the mist. Camlochlin. An impenetrable fortress built by a clever warrior determined to keep his kin safe from their enemies. Would it be enough to hold off the Dutch should they come looking for Lady Montgomery?

Watching his father flick his reins and thunder into the vale, Tristan pitied any army that came here. He pitied his brother, as well. Hell, he might have kissed a Fergusson, but Rob had brought Davina Montgomery to Camlochlin, and mayhap an enemy army with her.

Meeting her a short while later helped Tristan understand Rob's reckless decision to bring her here. She was enchantingly beautiful, with pale, damp locks draping her slender shoulders and enormous silvery blue eyes that grew even wider when she nearly careened into him on her way to meet his parents. He guessed almost instantly that Rob loved her. It would be easy for any man to lose his heart, mayhap even his mind, to such a guileless smile. It had happened countless times in history, according to the tales in his books, tales he had found himself recalling more over the past several weeks, of faithful knights swaying from their duties, even betraying their kings, all for the love of a lass. Tristan had never thought the tales untrue, but he'd been with countless women and never fallen in love with any of them. And he never would. He would never open his heart to such a powerful emotion again. He had already lost the most important person in his life, and it had destroyed him. For ten years he had kept himself apart from everyone else, never allowing anyone to get too close to him. Why would he be so foolish as to risk losing someone he loved again?

He certainly would never allow himself to love a lass his kin hated. He was fond of Isobel Fergusson, but that was all. She was a greater challenge to win than any lass before her. Everything she had lost in her life—everything his kin had lost—was his fault, and he wanted to make it right. Aye, the more he thought about it, the more he needed to do it.

There was a choice to be made. One that could change his destiny yet again. The path was set before him, and it was about damned time that he followed it. If he failed, he would be no worse off. He would lose nothing he hadn't already given up. But if he succeeded...

"You have the blood of knights in you and will grow to be a man of honor."

He would not fail, for he had his uncle urging him on.

Tristan knew Rob would again find favor in their father's eyes. Colin, too, even after the latter returned to Camlochlin with the king of England and a small army at his back. There would be no such hope for Tristan if anyone discovered where he was going the morning he left Camlochlin. Not that anyone would search for him during his absence. He was the restless son, the reckless one, who did what he wanted and damn the consequences. It was not unlike him to go off alone seeking to wreak havoc on another poor lass.

It was simply...Tristan.

Passing the cliffs of Elgol, he didn't turn back. He never did when he left on one of his journeys. It was always easier to leave than to try to fit in.

Mayhap, with Isobel's help, he could change that too.

Chapter Eleven

"Take back what ye said!"

John Fergusson swung his bow to his shoulder and drew back his arrow. "Why should I when it is true?" He aimed at the skin nailed to the tree fifty meters away, shot, and turned to grin at his brothers. He never saw the small rock coming straight at his head. Only the vast sky filled his vision when he opened his eyes a moment later—that, and young Tamas's crown of red hair and unrepentant scowl.

"Next time," said Tamas, "I'll use a bigger stone."

"What the hell did I tell ye about hitting us with that thing?" Lachlan, the oldest of the three brothers, smacked his palm into the back of Tamas's head. Without waiting for a reply, he leaned down and snatched the well-worn sling from his brother's fist. "Ye will not be getting it back this time."

Tamas balled up his fists and tossed back his head. "Isobel! Lachlan will not give me back my sling!"

"That's because," Lachlan shouted toward the barn where their sister was milking the goats, "he struck John in the head and made him bleed."

Inside the barn, Isobel pressed her forehead to Glenny's flanks. "God, give me strength." Honestly, could she not enjoy a day's peace without the threat of the three of them killing something…usually one another? "I am coming!" Leaving her stool, she hiked up her skirts and shooed a chicken from her path as she exited the barn.

When she saw John sitting in the grass looking a wee bit dazed but, fortunately, unbloodied, she gave Tamas a stern look. "Why did ye strike him?"

"He called me a babe!"

"And by not controlling yer own temper," Isobel replied while she knelt to give John a thorough looking over, "ye convinced him that he is wrong?"

Tamas shook his head. "I convinced him never to call me a babe again."

Isobel glanced up from her inspection. "Then I will," she said with enough snap in her voice to wipe the challenging smirk off his round, freckled face. "Ye are eleven summers old, Tamas, and still young enough to have yer hide beaten." She eyed the other two, who were doing their best to look innocent and failing miserably. They were constantly terrorizing someone or something. What was she to do with them? Just yesterday they had declared war on the huge hornets' nest behind the house—and lost. The horses didn't like them, the goats were afraid of them, and four farmers from neighboring villages had already threatened to shoot them dead if they set foot on their land one more time. "In truth, ye all could use a good beating. I honestly do not know why I have not asked Patrick to simply do it."

"Patrick would never beat us." John smiled up at her, making her heart twist with the thought of what might become of her brothers if she ever left them. Their mother had died shortly after Tamas was born, leaving Isobel to nurture and nourish her family. When their father was killed a year later, the other half of the parental duties fell to Patrick—and he fulfilled them all well, save for one. He'd never once taken the stick to any of them.

"Mayhap there lies the dilemma, aye?" She winked at John and gave his knee a playful pat.

"May I have my sling back now?" Tamas asked after an impatient sigh.

"Ye may have it tomorrow." Isobel helped John to his feet and wiped the trickle of blood from his forehead with her apron. "After ye have finished John's chores."

Tamas's steely blue eyes widened with disbelief and then anger. He looked about to protest, then thought better of it, knowing it would do him no good. He cut his tumultuous glare to John and then pounded away. Isobel tossed John as reassuring a look as she could muster.

"What's fer supper?" Lachlan asked, scratching one of the welts left on his upper arm by a hornet.

"Turnip and rosemary soup," Isobel told them as they headed back toward the house. "And whatever Patrick and Cameron bring back with them."

"I wanted to go hunting with them, Bel."

"I know, John, but ye…Tamas, stop chasing the dogs!"

"He will stop," Lachlan offered, shaking his head at his youngest brother, "when one of them takes a bite out of his scrawny arse."

Coming up behind him, a string of limp hares flung over one broad shoulder and a quiver of arrows behind the other, Patrick Fergusson clipped Lachlan in the back of the head. "Mind yer mouth."

Isobel smiled at Patrick as he passed them, and then at the hares. There were enough to feed her brothers for a sennight at least. "Where's Cam?" she asked, looking behind her.

"He will be along," Patrick answered without turning to look back at her. "We met Andrew Kennedy and his sister Annie on the road. He is walking back with them."

Isobel's steps came to a slow halt as his words reached her ears. When they did, she hiked up her skirts and took off after him. "The Kennedys are coming here?"

"Aye," he affirmed, shielding his pale blue eyes behind a damp mop of dark curls.

"This night?"

When he merely nodded, Isobel's temper flared. "Why would ye invite Andrew here, knowing what he wants?"

"He wants ye."

Damn him, if he didn't care about her feelings, he was going to look at her when he told her. She tugged his elbow, demanding he stop and give her his attention. "But I do not want him, and I have told ye so a dozen times."

Patrick shoved his fingers through his hair, clearing it from his face, and met her baleful gaze with an imposing one of his own. "He is a good man, Bel."

She folded her arms across her chest and dug her heels into the ground. "And that means I have to have feelings for him?"

He looked away again, from her and from his younger brothers, who'd stopped to listen. "Feelings or not, he has asked me fer yer hand and I have agreed."

"What?" Isobel shrieked at him, following him toward the house when he picked up his steps again. "Patrick, ye could not have—"

"Ye should be married by now, Bel, starting a life of yer own and—"

"I have a life of my own," she cut him off.

"Taking care of us?" He stopped again and turned to face her fully. "What kind of life is that?"

"What will be so different about taking care of *him*?" she argued, doing her best not to cry…or give him a slap he would not soon forget. "How different will my life be caring for a husband—one that I do not even love—and his family?"

"Andrew will be Chieftain to the Kennedys. His land is vast and his kin are numerous. There will be safety with him."

"I am safe here!"

"Aye." He laughed dryly. "With the Cunninghams raiding whenever the mood strikes them because they know we are so few and have no protection."

"I will not do it, Patrick!"

"Ye will. I will not be moved on this, Isobel. Not on this. I love ye more than anything in this world and I will see to yer safety and to yer happiness."

"I am happy here," she pleaded as he turned to go. "Please, Patrick, do not do this."

"It is already done."

It wasn't easy, but Isobel managed to avoid Andrew Kennedy's eager gaze during the first half of their visit. At supper, though, tasting the rich blend of fresh herbs and spices flavoring her thick hare stew, she had to ask herself who in blazes wouldn't want to marry a woman who could cook like this.

"I confess, Patrick," Andrew said, holding his heart at the other end of the long table. "I could live happily fer the next thirty years on yer sister's cooking."

A curse. She should have used more salt and last month's mushrooms.

"Tell me, Isobel"—Andrew swung his eyes to her and smiled beneath his coarse ginger beard—"d'ye cook all yer meals with such craft and care?"

"Nae," Isobel told him with exaggerated remorse, "I confess, I do not. Sometimes, I do not cook at all. Patrick does."

Beside her, Lachlan snickered, while Patrick merely sipped his mead, refusing to let her goad him.

"It does not matter," Andrew cooed from his seat. "I'm certain ye look bonnie at whatever task ye perform. Ye will make me a verra happy man when ye are my wife."

Good God, she was tempted to give Tamas back his sling and beg him to crack her in the skull with the biggest rock he could find. She had no doubt that Andrew would be happy. It was her misery she was worried about. She already knew what kind of life was in store for her as his wife. His wife! Damn him to Hades for not even having the decency to ask her himself.

She shot Patrick one more unforgiving stare before she turned her attention to Andrew's sister. Annie Kennedy was pretty enough, with long vermilion braids and a downy complexion that turned claret every time Cameron addressed her. It was sweet to watch, really, and it gave Isobel something more pleasant to think on than being forced to marry Annie's brother.

It wasn't that her newly betrothed was a homely man. Andrew was near Patrick's age, with a sturdy physique and good teeth. His father was the clan Kennedy Chieftain, with lands that spread across the coastline. Most women would be glad to take him.

"Isobel," his voice grated across her ears, "might I ask ye to share a walk with me after supper? Mayhap a stroll through yer garden where I can pick a fragrant bloom fer ye?"

Memories of a kiss in another garden flooded her thoughts and she blushed against the candlelight illuminating the small dining room. She doubted Andrew would try to kiss her—even if he had laid claim to her behind her back. He was not as bold or as silver-tongued as Tristan MacGregor.

His tongue, so curious and hungry for the taste of her.

"There are no flowers in my garden, Andrew," she practically snapped, gaining control over her thoughts. "And it is not the kind of garden I would let anyone walk through." If he was so eager to prove his devotion to her, he would have already known that.

Fortunately, he was bright enough to know when to quit—another virtue he did not share with a certain Highlander she refused to think about. Hell and damnation, when *would* the image of Tristan's jaunty grin leave her alone? His words were as insincere as Andrew's, but he spoke them with a flair that made her want to believe.

"How did ye enjoy England?"

Isobel blinked to Annie and then was relieved when she found the lass addressing Cameron. Her brother had never asked her about Tristan after that night when he found them together in the courtyard. He never brought up the MacGregors at all. Isobel loved him for not bringing them up now.

The conversation wore on long into the night. The men talked of her wedding, deciding that next spring would be best (Isobel decided to run off to the old man who had held his pistol to her face), and of the raiding Cunninghams, who had twice in two years attacked their holding and burned their crops. Andrew promised to send some of his best men to guard their harvest after he and Isobel were wed. Why hadn't he done it already, if he cared so much for her? With only herself and six brothers living here, Andrew knew her family was defenseless, as did the bastard Cunninghams. Why hadn't he offered his aid before? Tristan would have.

Isobel knew that by the time Patrick and Andrew finished off what was left of the whisky, it would be too late to send their guests home on foot. Still, when Patrick offered them lodgings for the night, with an offer to cart them home in the morn, she wanted to kill him.

❖ ❖

Chapter Twelve

Tristan reached the northern Lowlands with a scowl on his face and a curse on his lips. What the hell had possessed him to travel so far to see a lass? He'd bloody lost his mind. No lass, no purpose, was worth the sorry state his arse was in. He was tired and hungry and likely to come down with some deadly illness from bathing in the freezing waters of Loch Katrine. A half dozen times during his mad quest he'd almost turned around and gone back home. It wasn't so much the pain of being in the saddle for so many days, and just after he'd returned from England, that gave him pause. It was his state of mind to have begun such a journey in the first place. Was he mad to think he could end a ten-year-long feud that had cost both clans so much? This was Isobel Fergusson his body was aching over. This went beyond anything his kin would forgive if they discovered where he'd gone and his quest failed. What if what he wanted—what he needed—could not be found in the direction he had taken? The more his arse ached, the more he began to doubt his purpose. Still, he continued, driven by a memory of delicate ankles and the fragrant fan of auburn hair.

"Ye're daft," he told himself out loud as he trotted his tired mount along the River Nith. "She doesna' need ye in her life, and ye sure as hell dinna' need her in yers."

But he didn't listen. Indeed, with each league that brought him closer to her, he grew more eager to see her again.

He began to fear that his journey had been for naught when the first four travelers he met on the road did not know of any Fergussons living in the vicinity. Fortunately, a quarter of an hour later a fifth man, driving a cart that creaked as loudly as his bones, pointed him in the right direction, with a warning to take care.

The Fergusson holding was eerily quiet, save for the bleating of a goat somewhere in the distance. Slowing his horse, Tristan dismounted behind a stand of trees and watched, hidden from sight, for any signs of life. He did not want to startle Isobel by appearing at her door. He sure as hell didn't want Patrick Fergusson to shoot him in the chest for appearing on his land without invitation— not that Patrick would not shoot him anyway when he discovered who Tristan was. Damn it, he hadn't even considered what excuse he might give Isobel's brothers for being here. How many did she say she had? He looked around but saw no one. Odd. Was this the right place? Save for the smoke rising from the chimney of a small manor house, it appeared deserted. There were half a dozen bothies scattered about the lush green hills, but none looked to be occupied, and all were in a sad state of disrepair.

A large barn stood not far from the house. Its heavy

wooden door, slightly ajar and creaking against the afternoon breeze, drew his attention. The bleating goat was inside, but where the hell was everyone else? He remembered Isobel telling him that her clan had abandoned them after their Chieftain died. Who tilled the land? Surely there were too many acres for one man, even with the aid of a few brothers, to manage alone. He surveyed the territory more closely. Bales of hay were stacked neatly against the barn's eastern wall. Rows of freshly plowed soil lined one-half of an enormous sunlit field, while the other half was in full harvest, boasting an impressive display of pumpkins, turnips, cabbage, corn, and an array of barley, oats, and other grains.

The tinkling music of feminine laughter beyond the barn door caught Tristan's attention and drew him out from his hiding place. Was it Isobel? Was she alone? He had scrambled to another tree, closer to the holding, when the door swung open. A man stepped outside toting a bucket in each hand. He looked around, as if searching for the same people Tristan had been looking for a moment ago. When he didn't find them, he shook his head and continued on his way toward the manor house.

From his position, Tristan recognized Cameron Fergusson. Where were the rest of Isobel's brothers? His gaze settled back on the barn. She was inside. For a moment or two he fought with himself about whether he should go to her. He'd imagined their meeting a thousand times on the road, but now that he was here, his feet felt rooted to the ground.

The barn door opened again, and when he saw the fiery glimmer of her hair against the sun, he took a step forward with no difficulty at all. He watched her as he moved forward, glancing while he went at the manor house. Light of foot, he made no sound as he wove around trunks and bushes, just out of her sight. Instead of going directly to the house, she plucked a large fork off the barn wall and jabbed it into a nearby haystack. She had made two trips back into the barn carrying a small bundle of hay at the end of her spear by the time Tristan left the cover of trees. When she disappeared for a third time, he moved fifty more paces ahead, then stopped. Rather than creep up behind her, he would wait here for her return and let her see him.

Stinging, hot pain flared through his left calf, up to his thigh. His leg gave out and he fell to one knee, already turning to see whose arrow was jutting from his boot. He had reached for his sword (he was not fool enough to travel alone without one) when another arrow tore through his shoulder.

"I vow," he proclaimed, albeit rather weakly, looking at the three ruddy faces staring back at him, "ye wee buggers will pay fer—" He didn't finish. The eyeball-sized stone hitting him between the eyes knocked him out cold.

Isobel left the barn just in time to see Tamas fire a rock from his swinging sling. She let out a choked squeal as it struck a man, already on his knees, and felled him dead.

"Oh, merciful God." She dropped her fork and took off running. "What have ye three done?"

"He's a Highlander," Lachlan pointed out hastily, as if it gave him leave to shoot the poor man.

"He was after ye, Bel," Tamas defended. "We watched him stalking ye from the trees. May I have his horse?"

But his sister was no longer listening, no longer breathing. Tristan. For an instant, the shock of seeing him again stilled Isobel's blood. What was he doing here alone? Why had he come? She'd made it clear to him that they could never be friends. Had she been correct about him all along and friendship was the farthest thing from his mind? She remembered the man who made her think about knights while they strolled and smiled in the king's garden. Her breath quickened as she crouched beside him. Was he the devil's most clever deceiver, or did his arrival have a nobler purpose?

"John!" she wheezed, with relief that her brothers' victim still lived. "Get Cameron! Hurry! Tamas, we need a blanket to get him into the house."

"The house?" Tamas recoiled as if she'd slapped him. "He's a stranger. Patrick is going to—"

"Tamas!" Isobel quieted him with a frosty glare. "Fetch a blanket this instant, or I will tell Patrick about the two dozen eggs ye pilfered from the Wallaces' farm beyond the river."

Her brother's face went white a breath before he dashed for the house.

When they were alone, Lachlan bent to her side and said, with the same alarm in his voice that was coursing through her, "We thought he came to do ye harm."

Her gaze settled on the decadent shape of Tristan's mouth and lingered there. "He may have."

"How d'ye know, Bel?" Lachlan asked. "Who is he?"

Dear God, she could barely breathe, and her butterbur...he'd landed in her butterbur and ripped it away from its roots. Useless. "He is called Tristan. Tristan MacGregor," she told him as Cameron and John reached her. "I met him in England."

She looked up at Cam, and then wished she hadn't. No one knew she had spent time alone with Tristan at

Whitehall. No one but Cameron. He hadn't questioned her about what she was doing with their enemy or what they had been speaking of when he found them. His eyes questioned her now, though. What had she told this MacGregor that made him seek out their home and dare to set foot on their land?

"Cam, he's alive," she told him. She would worry about what he thought of her later. "Fer all our sakes, we must keep him that way. If he dies on our land, his family will…"

"I know." Her brother nodded and questioned her no further.

Chapter Thirteen

He was heavier than he appeared, and Isobel cursed him a little as she and her brothers heaved his limp body onto the blanket and dragged him into the house.

"We have to remove the arrows," she gasped out as they climbed the oak stairs to the upper floor. "We will put him in Alex's bed."

"Alex will not be liking that when he finds out. Ye know how he hates the MacGregors."

Isobel was tempted to let go of her end of the blanket and slap Tamas in the back of the head.

"Patrick will not be liking it either when he returns from bringing the Kennedys home," Lachlan added.

Isobel tossed them both an exasperated look. "Would ye have me tend to him in the barn?"

"Alex's bed is fine," Cam said quietly, tugging his end. "Quit quibbling with Isobel and do as she says fer a bloody change."

"I never quibble with her," John disputed while they carried Tristan into Alex's room and transferred him carefully to the bed. "It is those two who cause all the trouble." He motioned with his chin to Lachlan and Tamas, who immediately took offense.

Exhausted, frustrated, and terrified, Isobel sank into the closest chair and covered her face with her hands. What was she doing bringing a MacGregor into her home, into her brother's bed? She needed a little time to think without the lads constantly quarreling in her ears.

"What is the matter, Bel?" John bent to her and asked tenderly. "Are ye squeamish about pulling out the arrows?"

"Why would she be?" Lachlan shoved him out of the way. "She did just fine last spring when Tamas missed his target and shot me in the arm."

"We could do it fer ye, Bel," Tamas volunteered with a hint of malevolence in his eager smile. "We do not mind the blood."

Aye, she knew that well enough. "No, Tamas, I will do it." She rose from the chair, rubbed her forehead, then pulled herself together for her brothers' sake. "I will need fresh, boiled water and clean cloths. Tear strips from my bedsheets. I washed them this morn, so they should be safe." She stepped closer to the bed to examine Tristan's wounds. God have mercy, she was going to have to remove his clothes. "John, go to my garden—what is left of it—and bring me four leaves from my ribwort plantain. I will need ye to boil them fer me and crush them into a poultice. Lachlan, bring my needles and thread. He will need stitching." How was she going to do it when her hands were already shaking? She pressed her head to his chest. His heart was still beating, but slower, a little weaker. "Make haste!" she ordered, and leaned closer still to have a better look at the knot above the bridge of his nose. His breath warmed her cheek, and she dipped her gaze to his long, lush lashes.

"What am I to do with ye, MacGregor?" she whispered, cursing her own heart for pounding so feverishly at his return, his nearness, the raw beauty of his countenance.

He opened his eyes and looked directly into hers, filling her, for a terrifying instant, with the promise of retribution. She vaulted away from him, but his fingers closed tightly around her wrist and she nearly dragged him off the bed.

She didn't see Lachlan reaching for the clay potted plant she'd given to Alex last Christmastide. Dirt and leaves peppered her face as her brother brought the pot down onto Tristan's head with a loud crack, knocking him out for the second time that day.

"What in bloody hell did ye do that fer?" She slapped Lachlan's arm, ordered him out of the room, and then shut the door behind him.

Turning back to Cameron, she found him at the side of the bed, already removing the sword at Tristan's side, along with his plaid.

"I wonder," he said quietly, without looking at her, "why he wore either of these to come here and not while he was in England."

"Aye," Isobel replied, noting her brother's careful observation. One could easily forget to notice Cameron amidst the chaos her other brothers seemed to enjoy. But it was foolish to believe that anything escaped *his* notice. "I wondered the same thing."

When he moved away from the bed, saying nothing more, she went to him, desperate for him to know the truth and for him to believe her. "I remember what they did to Father, Cam. I have not befriended him. I do not know why he came here."

His smile was genuine. But then, Cam's smiles always were. "I know that, Bel," he said, putting an end to the topic. "Now quit talking and get to saving him."

Isobel had always believed, after her mother died and she was forced, without even time to grieve, to begin caring for her brothers, that was the most difficult task she would ever have to perform. But she was wrong. Peeling off Tristan's clothes was worse. Even cutting away his boot made her blush with the heat of a hundred summers. Untying the laces of his shirt nearly brought on an attack. She forced herself to breathe and steadied her hands when she spread open his shirt. Her fingers skimmed across his bare nipples, and breathless, despite her best efforts, her gaze slipped down his taut belly. Truly, he was sculpted from some great artist's dreams. "I...I do not think it proper fer me to relieve him of his breeches, Cam. Ye do it, and when ye are done, cover him with his plaid, and then I will begin."

Only Cameron and John remained with her while she tended to Tristan's wounds. They were the only two she trusted, though it was John's arrow that had done the most damage.

"I could have shot him in the heart instead of his leg, but I was not aiming to kill him."

"That is good." Cameron gave John's shoulder a gentle squeeze while Isobel carefully applied her poultice to Tristan's calf. "Ye spared his life and saved ours in the bargain."

Isobel was about to agree when the door burst open and Tamas plunged into the room. "Patrick is back!"

She looked up and shared an anxious glance with Cameron, then went back to her work.

What in blazes was she going to tell Patrick? How was

she going to stop him if he decided that their most hated enemy should die for coming here?

"He said to tell ye," Tamas continued, "that when ye finish, ye are to bind him to the bed."

Isobel shook her head. "I cannot do that."

"He also said not to quarrel with him over it." Tamas grinned, obviously enjoying the turning of the tables.

Setting down her dressings, she gave her youngest brother a level stare. "Did he?" When he nodded gleefully, she stood up from her chair. "And where is he now?"

"Outdoors, tending to the chickens."

She went to the window and, peering down at the barn, called out to Patrick. She listened for his reply, and when it came she leaned out further. "If I tie his wounded arm to the bed, his shoulder will not heal properly and we will send the Devil MacGregor's son home lame. D'ye think that is wise?" She waited, breath held, for his answer. She knew Patrick would give his life to keep them safe, but would he spare a MacGregor life for the same reason? Best to know now so she could be better prepared to argue with him later if she needed to.

"Verra well," he finally shouted back; "bind only one wrist then."

Isobel turned to offer Tamas a triumphant smile, but he was busy pointing at Tristan.

"He awakens!"

She tried to stop him, almost tumbling over her chair in her effort to snatch the bowl of bloody water from Tamas's hands. But it came down hard on Tristan's head, and she finally had to accept the fact that a MacGregor might not make it out of her home alive.

• • •

Isobel remained with Tristan while he slept, mainly to keep him safe from any more objects being smashed over his head. She watched his steady breathing beneath his plaid and wondered again what he was doing here.

It had taken her over a pair of fortnights to get him and the feel of his mouth on hers out of her head completely. How carefully he had seduced her, and in only a few days! He frightened her with his ability to sweep her so effortlessly off her feet. She had thought, had hoped, that she was rid of him. Now here he was, back to haunt her dreams all over again, this time with the vision of his bare male physique sprawled across her brother's bed like a captive angel. He was taller than Alex, his ankles hovering over the edge of the bed. She let her eyes drift over him slowly, her gaze lingering on his shapely legs—one of which she'd had to shave in order to clean his wound properly. Her fingers tingled at the memory of his warm skin beneath her palm, the length of hard sinew running up his calf to his darkly dusted thigh. Growing more breathless, her gaze rose to the plaid draped low across his hips. He was naked beneath. She felt her cheeks go all hot. How many women had smiled at him while he stripped out of his garments, hard and ready to take them? She swiped the back of her palm across her brow and cursed under her breath. Andrew Kennedy had never had this effect on her. No man had! Then again, she'd never met any with such raw animal appeal in the mere slant of his mouth, or the...

No, they were sworn enemies, with no place for attraction between them. Besides, she was betrothed! At least until she found a way to get out of it. She had to stay focused on the truth. There were only two possibilities for why Tristan had come here. Either he wanted information from her about his uncle's death, or he had been sent here by his father to murder her family. She should have left him to die in her garden. He'd already killed her butterbur, after all. But his life wasn't worth the lives of her brothers. She had no choice but to save him, to tend to him despite their hatred for each other.

The door opened and she looked up at Patrick, entering the room for the first time that day. He stood at the entrance, silently taking in the sight of the unconscious man in his brother's bed. When his gaze settled on the bandages she'd wrapped around Tristan's forehead, he hooked his mouth into a slight smile that made Isobel look away.

"Where is his sword?"

She shrugged her weary shoulders. "Cam took it."

"I assume he knows how to use it?"

Isobel remembered how expertly he had wielded it against Alex and nodded. "Quite well."

Patrick crossed the room and stood at her side, staring down at the bed. "I understand from the lads that ye first met him at Whitehall?"

"Aye." She nodded. She should have told him. She did now. She told him everything, only leaving out Alex's foolishness and her and Tristan's kiss. There was no reason Patrick should know about that. It meant nothing.

"So, he protected Alex from his father," Patrick mulled thoughtfully, "and ye from John Douglas."

"Aye, he told John Douglas that ye hacked the lips off the last man who handled me without liberty to do so."

Patrick's smile was wider this time, but faded all too quickly. "And why did he do those things?"

"I do not know," she answered quietly, staring at Tristan, as well. "Fer a name, mayhap."

Her brother knew what she meant and drew out a long exhalation of breath. "Fetch me when he awakens," he said, turning to leave the room. "And remember, he is a Highlander. Keep him tied up and his sword carefully hidden. If yer suspicions are correct about why he came here, it will be easier to end this if I do not have to fight him."

Isobel stared at the door after he left. Well, at least Patrick had more sense in his head than Alex. In truth, he had more sense than all of them did—save when it came to her marrying Andrew. But what could Patrick possibly do against all the MacGregors in Skye if he harmed Tristan? Oh, why had she gone to England? It would have been better for her family to have the king angry with them than to spark the MacGregors' blood-lust once again.

Tristan moaned her name in his sleep, startling her from her thoughts. She leaned over him, some basic, nurturing instinct taking over. "Ssh," she whispered, "the worst is over...fer now." He tossed his head back and forth, as if fighting something in his dreams. Alarmed that he might cause more damage to his already wounded skull, she pressed her hand to his crown and stilled him with a gentle touch. "Sleep, and then be gone from here, Tristan MacGregor—if ye know what is good fer ye." She smiled to herself, thinking of her unruly siblings. Despite what they had done to him, they meant well. "We may not be an army, but as ye have no doubt discovered, we can protect ourselves."

She didn't realize right away that she was stroking her fingers over his silky waves, and when she did, she did not stop. She could not deny that a part of her was painfully attracted to him. He was so perfectly crafted he seemed unreal, and she touched him to convince herself that he was merely a man.

"Oh, why have ye come here? Why d'ye haunt my dreams and call my name in yers? What is it ye want from me?"

He slept, giving her no answers. She knew somehow that getting them from him, even when he awoke, would be impossible.

Chapter Fourteen

Tristan was dreaming about the day that Brigid MacPherson's father caught them together and shot him in the thigh, when an aroma, finer than anything he had ever smelled before, pulled him toward consciousness. He did not drift blissfully into his final state of awareness, but was catapulted into the white-hot wakening of excruciating pain—the worst, from his head.

Panic engulfed him when he couldn't recall what had happened to him. He tried to sit up but was immediately hurled back by the blistering agony in his skull, and the ties that bound his wrist to the bedpost behind him.

Isobel. His quest.

He'd been shot with an arrow. Twice. So far, things were not going according to plan. Then again, he didn't have a plan. He usually didn't, and he saw the foolishness of this now more than ever. He looked at his other arm, bandaged and secured to his bare chest. Someone had removed the arrows and dressed his wounds. But what the hell had happened to his head? He tugged at the leather laces that held him captive and then quit when pain lanced through his shoulder.

Helpless, he tried to keep his wits about him and consider his situation. It was troublesome indeed. His sword, along with his breeches, was nowhere in sight. He had two holes in him, had an agonizing headache, and was tied to a bed in the house of his kinsmen's worst enemy. To make matters worse, he was hungry, and whatever was cooking beyond the door made his mouth water and his stomach rumble. Would the Fergussons feed him before they killed him? Then again, if they were going to kill him, wouldn't they have done so already?

He heard voices behind the door and closed his eyes as it opened and the ambrosial fragrance of cooked rabbit wafted through his nostrils.

"He still sleeps."

"Good. Come, before Isobel discovers us." The floor creaked and Tristan's pulse accelerated as the two boys crossed the room. "She will skin our hides if she finds out what we are up to, Lachlan. The way she has been looking after him, ye would think she fancies him."

"He is a MacGregor, Tamas. Ye know how she feels about them."

"Aye," the other agreed. "Besides, it is not like we are trying to kill him. We were stung by hornets and we are no worse fer it."

"Aye, but it hurt like bloody hell."

Tristan opened one eye and watched the lads hovering by the open window. He remembered the taller of the two pulling back his bowstring and shooting him in the shoulder. The other wee scoundrel had fired something else at him, and with deadly accuracy. A stone? Aye, he remembered now.

"Spread the honey around, Lachlan," the smaller one ordered cheerfully. "And when we are done, we will put a bit in his bed. It will draw the hornets directly to him."

Och, so it was to be like that, was it? Tristan opened his eyes and hooked his mouth into a rueful smirk.

"'Tis a clever scheme against me, lads," he said, startling the poor runts nearly out of their boots. "But I should warn ye, ye'll pay fer it tenfold."

His threat sparked a challenging glint in the younger one's eyes. "Is that so?" the lad mused, reaching for the leather sling at his side. "Where should I hit him this time, Lachlan? He seems to have a rather thick skull."

Tristan pulled on his bonds while the boy plucked a stone from his pocket. "Dinna' do it," he warned, cursing his hasty threat, impotent as he was at present. "I swear," he began, nervously watching the lad drop the stone into the pouch, "If ye—" The bratling twirled the sling over his head. Son of a . . . !

"Isobel!" Tristan roared, unable to do anything else.

Immediately, the boy dropped his sling and fixed him with a vengeful stare. Tristan matched it with a dangerous glare of his own. He would take care of the runt later.

The door burst open a moment later and a pale-faced Isobel Fergusson rushed into the room. Behind her, filling the doorframe, stood a man whose size and scowl rivaled that of any of Camlochlin's fiercest warriors. Tristan knew that caution, mayhap more than at any other time until now, must be liberally exercised. But he could not keep his eyes from slipping to the red-haired goddess coming toward him. Or from meeting the fire in her gaze when she reached him. Hell, he'd missed her.

"If ye are still in possession of yer wits," she muttered,

bending to examine the bandage around his head, "ye'd best call upon them now."

"First," he whispered close enough to her ear to keep the others from hearing, "let us be clear on this one thing."

She looked down at him, their breath mixing together while his eyes fell to the swell of her bosoms.

"I dinna' like bein' tied down." His dimple flashed as his gaze found hers again. "Unless 'tis by my own suggestion."

"MacGregor." The giant at the door halted any further words between them. Tristan looked at him, his smile cooling. "I am Patrick Fergusson, but then, guessing by the name ye called out, ye already know where ye are."

"Aye." Tristan attempted a nod, then closed his eyes as pain lanced through his head. "I know where I am."

"Is this where ye meant to find yerself?" Isobel's brother continued without mercy. "Or did ye take a wrong turn?"

Tristan opened his eyes slowly. "In truth," he admitted, knowing the sharp, contemplative eyes staring back at him would see through any meager deception. "I am no' lost."

Patrick's gaze cut to Isobel for an instant while he took a step forward, finally entering the room. "Ye seem well enough to answer a few of my questions, MacGregor. So let us begin. Why did ye take a liberty not granted to ye and use my sister's Christian name?"

Without the slightest alteration in his breath, Tristan slanted a look to the lads still standing by the window. "Because 'tisn't *yer* name they're afraid of."

The dark stare Patrick gave the boys convinced Tristan that they were either too slow-witted to fear their older brother or Isobel's temper was far worse than he'd imagined.

"What did ye two do?" Isobel demanded, commanding the boys' attention. "And why are ye even in here?"

"It was all Tamas's doing," the larger boy responded, giving up the younger without a fight.

"Well?" Isobel fisted her hands on her hips. Everyone in the room, including Tristan, looked at Tamas, waiting for his answer.

"Fine." The boy gave in with a defiant tilt of his chin. "I smeared honey on the windowpane to draw the hornets."

Isobel squeaked out a tight little gasp and marched toward the window. When she saw that he had told the truth, she whirled around and slapped her apron against her thigh. "Ye will be cleaning that…after ye clean the barn tonight!"

Tamas nodded and flung Tristan his foulest look.

"What else did ye do?" she continued, still glaring at the boy.

"Nothing else," he replied, dipping his gaze to the floor.

Watching him, Tristan noted Tamas's fingers tucking away his sling beneath his belt.

"Mister MacGregor?" Isobel's voice was just as stern when she snapped Tristan's attention back to her. "What else did he do that made ye call out?"

"Nothing else," Tristan repeated mildly, meeting Tamas's gaze across the room. He would repay the boy for his pounding head when he was out of this blasted bed. For now, it was between them. He would not turn him in as easily as his brother had.

"So then, MacGregor," Patrick said, doing little to mask his humor. "Ye sought the aid of a lass because ye are afraid of insects?"

"Hornets, aye." Tristan managed a smile back at him while Isobel ushered the boys to the door. "They dinna' sting just once, ye know."

Before he left, Tamas turned and set his curious gaze on him one last time. Tristan winked, but the lad's expression remained unreadable as the door closed in front of him.

When they were alone, Patrick folded his arms across his broad chest and studied Tristan long enough to make another man squirm. Tristan was careful to move as little as possible, as everything from his toes to the top of his head ached.

"My next question."

Like his sister, this man wasted little time on the false formality of the day. He was direct and to the point— attributes Tristan favored, despite Patrick's resemblance to his younger brother Alex.

"What purpose d'ye have in coming here?"

From the door, Isobel shielded a nervous look Tristan's way.

He didn't like the way she worried every time he spoke to one of her brothers. What did she think he would tell them? That they had shared a kiss and some forbidden smiles? Knowing what it would cost her, he would not admit that while their kin were still enemies.

"I came here to bring word to Miss Fergusson about her brother Alex." His gaze followed her when she moved around Patrick to return to the end of the bed. "When my kin left England, he was well."

He thought he saw relief softening her features— mayhap even the trace of a smile. He saw no reason to tell her that he had no idea how Alex fared with Colin and Mairi alone at Whitehall to do as they pleased.

"MacGregor," Patrick said, raising a doubtful eyebrow. "Ye expect me to believe that ye traveled all the way from England just to tell my sister that?"

"From Skye, actually," Tristan corrected. "She was quite distressed about leaving him at Whitehall with my kin. I gave her my word that while I was there, no harm would come to him."

It wasn't a complete falsehood. He simply saw no reason to speak of his quest and ignite a Fergusson's wrath against him by thinking him a liar while he was helpless to fight back.

Patrick's smile was rapier thin as he sized Tristan up from foot to crown. "I see. So I am to believe ye are a man of honor, then?"

Tristan did not take offense at Patrick's jeering tone, for he already knew he was anything but honorable. Instead, he found himself wondering if the qualities Isobel had seen in him when they first met, she had learned from this man. His mood lightened considerably. Mayhap Patrick would understand why he had come here. Although being here and settling his gaze on his bonnie Iseult again made Tristan question his true motives.

"In truth," he admitted, "I am not what ye suggest. But I am workin' on it. In the meantime, ye may believe what ye like. But I would ask ye to keep such an assumption to yerself, lest my reputation suffer an enormous blow."

Isobel rolled her eyes heavenward and went back to the window. Patrick stared at him for a moment, as if coming to some conclusion in his mind, and as Tristan's smile widened, so did his.

In the hour that followed, Tristan discovered that Patrick was not half as arrogant as Alex. His questions, and he asked many, seemingly without concern for Tristan's throbbing head and stinging limbs, all centered on one thing, the safety of his family. He warned, without any boastful clamor, that if Tristan had come to his home to bring harm to his kin in any way, Patrick would kill him and bury his body behind the barn.

"My intentions," Tristan finally confessed, "are to bring an end to the hatred between our kin."

Patrick looked across the room at his sister. "Why?" But when Tristan began to answer, he cut him off, turning to him once again. "We do not need yer aid, MacGregor. We simply want to be left alone."

He turned to leave and motioned for Isobel to come with him. Tristan cursed under his breath. Patrick didn't believe him. Why would he? Why would a MacGregor want to end a feud and not ask for something in return— like his sister? Hell, any man with a brain in his head would suspect a more treacherous secret motive. Now, Patrick would keep them apart.

"Miss Fergusson."

She stopped and turned slowly to look at him.

"D'ye no' have a concoction fer the pain? Mayhap just have one of yer brothers hit me in the head with something to put me oot?"

She went to him, deep concern marring her brow. "Is it that bad?"

"Aye." He hushed his voice when she came nearer to feel him for fever. "If I canna' see ye again until I am well enough to leave, I would rather sleep through my recovery."

"Oh, Lord," she drawled, pulling away from him. "D'ye never cease?"

He smiled and awakened a thousand butterflies in her belly.

"I will make him something to drink," Isobel told her brother at the door as she stepped past him.

"Cam will feed it to him," Patrick called out, letting her know.

"*I* will feed it to him," Isobel called back, ending the argument.

Tristan took a moment to enjoy the sway of her hips as she strode down the hall and turned for the stairs. "Fergusson," he called out when Patrick began to pull the door closed. "Might we have a word aboot releasin' my arm?"

The door slammed shut.

Hell.

Chapter Fifteen

"What d'ye think of him?"

Isobel paused on her way back to the kitchen and looked down at what was left of Tristan's elixir. She hadn't expected Patrick to ask her such a question about their guest. She figured he knew perfectly well what she thought of him.

"He is a MacGregor." She looked across the hall to where her brother stood taking a rest from his work of cleaning the hearth. "What I think of him would soil the walls around us, should I utter it."

Patrick leaned on the hilt of his shovel, his features relaxed and unreadable in the dim light. "How d'ye manage to remember who he is, when fer even a hairsbreadth of time, he made me ferget?"

Isobel felt her spine stiffen. Always the logical brother, Patrick sorted things out in his mind with the precision of a battle-hardened warrior. She'd always had to be on her toes to keep up with him.

"Ye would do best not to ferget. Now leave yer work

and wash up fer supper." She turned to leave, but he stopped her yet again.

"It is a simple enough query, Bel. Will ye not answer it?"

She had no choice now, lest he think she was hiding something. Which she most certainly was not. "Mayhap," she told him with a paltry shrug and continued toward the kitchen, "I am stronger than ye."

"In this instance," he countered meaningfully, "let's pray that ye are."

She did pray. Oh, how she prayed. Still, every time she was near Tristan, she feared she might grant him the smile he was after. She wasn't certain which of his many weapons he wielded the best. The rakish twinkle of his dimple that made her belly flip, or the symphony of words that played across his lips that could make any foolish woman's heart dance.

Her breath shortened at the memory of what he'd asked her while she fed him his elixir.

"Are ye glad to see me, Isobel?"

"Glad to see ye alive. Ye are a fool fer coming here just to tell me about Alex. Though I suspect it was another reason entirely that led ye here."

"Then ye're no' just ravishin', but clever, as well."

His slow, sexy smile kindled a fire below her belly, heating her body all the way to her cheeks. If she hadn't spent the last ten years hating his kin, or if she believed that he simply meant to make her one more of his conquests, she might be tempted to play along with his game of cat and mouse. She would take much enjoyment in watching him flounder at her rejection. But she knew the true motive behind his flowery words. He was arrogant enough in his prowess to admit that one existed. He was too dangerous. There was too much at stake to regard him as anything but her worst enemy. She would stay away from his room and let her brothers tend to him. She smiled. Aye, he deserved that much.

"Lachlan!" she called out, bending to the trivet and stirring the thick rabbit stew simmering in the pot above the fire. "Bring MacGregor his supper."

Pushing back his chair where he sat waiting to eat, Lachlan lumbered into the kitchen and watched her dip her ladle into the pot. "But how will he eat? Should I untie his wrist?"

"No, ye will have to feed him."

Following behind his older brother, bowl in hand, Tamas chuckled at Lachlan's feeble protests.

"And ye can go with him," Isobel said, pointing her ladle at Tamas. "Clean that window before he is attacked by hornets."

For a moment, Tamas stared at her as if she'd lost her mind. "But my supper will be cold by the time I get to eat it! I will close the shutters fer now. Nothing will— Patrick!" He swung around when Patrick entered the kitchen. "Why should that MacGregor enjoy a hot meal while my belly goes empty? So what if he gets stung a few times? It will make a man of him!"

"Did it make a man of ye when ye were stung, then?" Patrick asked while Isobel filled his bowl.

"I am not the one who screamed out fer a maid before they even attacked me."

Patrick smiled but didn't give in. "Do as ye're told before ye—"

Tristan's pleasant but somewhat apprehensive voice rang out from behind the door of his room, interrupting them.

"If any one of ye can hear me oot there, there's an urgent matter concernin' my bladder that needs attention."

Tamas's wide eyes went all the rounder and the color drained from his freckled face as he looked up to find both Isobel and Patrick staring at him. "I will do anything but that. Untie him, I beg ye."

To this, Patrick agreed, and headed off first to see to the task. Isobel handed Lachlan a bowl filled with steaming stew and watched him reluctantly follow behind.

"Why d'ye like him?" Tamas asked her, accepting the rags she offered him.

She would have laughed right in her little brother's face if she hadn't asked herself the same question a dozen times since she met the Highland rogue. "Why d'ye ask me such a ridiculous question?" She gave him a slap with her apron. "Ye are getting more like Patrick each day." She gave him a gentle shove and sent him on his way.

She finished filling her brothers' bowls and carried each one to the dining table. During each trip she noticed her hands shaking more. Damn him. She looked up the stairs, wringing her hands through her apron. She'd thought she was rid of Tristan MacGregor. She was learning to live with his face always appearing in her thoughts, but living with him... *living with him*... one floor above her, lying in a bed half naked and at her mercy—well, it was just too much. His presence filled the house and saturated her senses with a crackling bolt of awareness that made her reel. What had he already done to her that showed itself so blatantly that two of her own brothers would question her feelings for him?

There was only one thing to do about it, and she would do it loud and clear. She forced a smile when Cam and John entered the house toting bundles of firewood under their arms. She didn't ask Patrick how everything had gone when he returned to the hall and took his seat at the head of the table. She didn't care, and she was going to let all her brothers know it.

She couldn't have planned it any better herself when Lachlan pounded down the stairs and announced that MacGregor refused to eat anything from anyone's hand but Miss Fergusson's. He sent his apologies, but hers was the only hand he trusted not to poison him.

"Let him go hungry then," Patrick muttered, shoving his spoon into his mouth.

"No," Isobel said, rising from her chair. "If he wants me to feed him, then by all means, I shall."

She took the bowl from Lachlan's hand and tugged on Patrick's sleeve. "Ye are not going to drink that unholy whisky ye and Andrew Kennedy brewed behind the barn last winter, aye?"

"Not unless I want to be abed fer the next sennight, sick as a dog."

She smiled, looking a bit like Tamas. "Lachlan, fetch it fer me, will ye?"

"Ye are not going to make MacGregor drink that, are ye, Bel?"

"No, Cam," she replied, turning to him. "I am going to feed it to him."

Patrick grimaced into his cup but voiced no objection. John asked if he could watch. Isobel refused and emptied some of Tristan's stew into her bowl to make room. When Lachlan returned, she took the bottle from him, popped the cork with her teeth, and poured a goodly amount of the foul-smelling liquid into his supper.

"Ye will not get him to agree to a second spoonful, sister," Patrick said, laughing, as she reached the stairs.

"Aye," she answered in a low voice her brothers could not hear. "I will get him to eat every drop."

She didn't look at Tristan as she entered the room. She thought it best not to. Tamas turned from scrubbing the window and tossed her a scowl such as could have been found on the face of the most miserable battle-scarred warrior. She ignored that, as well.

"Yer brother Lachlan boasted that ye cook better than any lass in Scotland." Tristan's voice seeped through her bones like sun-warmed honey.

"He embellishes," she said, refusing to allow his husky tone to sway her from her task. "Has my elixir relieved yer pain?" She sat down in the chair beside the bed and finally spared him a glance.

He nodded, fixing those wolf-colored eyes on her while she stirred his stew. Her hand trembled just a little and she cursed silently that he should see his effect on her. His arm was still bound to the bedpost. The rest of his body certainly posed no threat to her, and yet she had the uncomfortable sensation that he was in complete control and she was the prey here. "I do not expect ye to trust any of us, Mister MacGregor, but I would have ye know that none of my brothers would poison ye." She scooped some stew onto his spoon.

"Nae, they would only shoot me with arrows and fire stones at my head." He smiled at her when she finally met his gaze. Hell, he wasn't even angry . . . or mayhap he was and masked it extremely well.

"We were not trying to kill ye," came Tamas's hard voice from the window. "If we were, ye would be dead."

"He speaks the truth," Isobel assured. "We wish to send ye home alive and escape yer kin's bloodlust fer further revenge. Now, open yer mouth, please."

Tristan followed the spoon as she brought it to his lips and then lifted his eyes to hers again. "It smells foul; I thought—"

Deftly, she dipped the spoon's contents into his mouth. A look of horror came over him as the flavor settled over his taste buds. He looked about to spit it out, so Isobel did what she promised herself she would not do. She smiled at him. "Good? I prepared it myself as I do all our meals. I would not claim to be the best cook in Scotland"—she scooped up another heaping—"but I admit that I do take pride in my dishes."

He swallowed, rather forcefully, and retreated deeper into his pillow when the spoon came near a second time. "Why, just a few nights ago Andrew Kennedy claimed that he could live happily fer the next thirty years on my cooking."

He opened his mouth, accepting more. "Who is this…" He shivered from his toes to his shoulders, chewing quickly and swallowing even faster. "Andrew Kennedy?"

"One of Patrick's friends." She fed him a third helping.

"And what is he to ye?"

"An admirer…of my cooking," she added, smiling as brightly as the sun.

He seemed to melt before her eyes. Ah, good, the brew was taking affect. She remembered how drunk he had been in England after only two cups of the king's finest wine. She forced back a nervous giggle at the potency of the whisky he was ingesting now. He was going to feel like hell for the next few days, but it would prove to her brothers that she felt nothing for their sworn enemy.

"Ye know," he said, his eyes and his voice going all soft on her. "Ye grow more bonnie to me each day."

She almost dropped the spoon on his chest, unprepared, not for his craftily spun words, but for the way in which he spoke them. Tenderly, meaningfully, as if nothing in the world meant more to him than having her believe him. She glanced at Tamas, wishing now that she hadn't made him clean up the honey.

She shoved more stew into Tristan's smiling mouth and leaned in closer to him. "Ye must not speak so in front of my brothers."

"Ye smell pleasant too." He chewed more slowly now and even licked a drop off his lips.

The sight of his tongue so close nearly made her spring from her chair and run from the room.

"Clean and fresh like dewdrops on the grass—"

Such pretty words. A little more stew and she would not have to listen to them again for a few days.

"—and like some lost memory of Eden, ye have haunted me."

Isobel swallowed, the spoon poised in midair. She haunted him? No, he was lying, trying to seduce her.

"What is that he is saying?" Tamas moved away from the window and took a step toward the bed.

Quickly, Isobel pressed her finger to Tristan's lips. "Cease yer talk, MacGregor!" she whispered on a swift breath. "I will not have them think there is anything between—"

He kissed her finger.

Isobel pulled back with a shriek and Tamas rushed the rest of the way to her side.

"What is it? What did he do?"

"Nothing." She tried to sound calm, but Tristan's unbidden, intimate kiss stole her breath. "Here." She shoved the bowl into Tamas's hands and stood up. "Finish feeding him. I...I cannot stand the sight of him anymore."

She had never lied to her brothers before, and she felt terribly guilty as she fled the room, heart pounding through her kirtle. He kissed her again! The bastard! The bold, reckless, profoundly charming—even on his way to becoming completely soused—son of a dog kissed her again!

Tamas studied their groggy captive thoughtfully, lifted the bowl of stew to his nose, and then pulled it away with a snarl. Patrick's failed brew. They all remembered the smell of it permeating the house like an attack of angry skunks.

"My sister wants me to make certain ye finish eating it all, and I always do as she says. But first"—he carried the bowl to the window, plucked up the rag he'd used to soak up the honey, and practically skipped back to the bed—"ye will be needing this in case I spill some on ye." He grinned while he spread the cloth over his victim's bare chest. He felt only a tad bit guilty when MacGregor grinned back at him.

❖
Chapter Sixteen

*T*ristan woke from his delirium two days later. Or rather, he was revived from it. One does not wake from death, after all. He opened his eyes and a cannonball smashed across his skull. Good God, he'd never felt anything like it. Tamas's well-aimed stone hadn't made him hurt this much. It pained him to breathe. What had they done to him this time? What had *Isobel* done to him? Hell, she had poisoned him, and she did it with a smile on her face. They were all mad! Somehow, he had to move. He finally had to admit defeat. It had been a mistake to come here. Clearly, they did not want peace. He had to escape their demented clutches, but he couldn't even think without a wave of nausea threatening to overtake him. He tried to calm himself, slow his heartbeat in the hope that his wits would return to him.

Isobel had claimed that none of her brothers meant to kill him, but she had deceived him. They were taking turns trying to end his life slowly, torturously.

Two hours later, he still could not believe she had hand-fed him poison. He tried opening his eyes again and realized for the first time that no one had entered his room all day. Likely, they believed him dead, so why bother?

Lunatics.

The pain in his head had subsided a bit, but the wrapping above his brows was driving him mad. He rotated his wounded shoulder, pleased and relieved that it, too, felt better. Slipping his arm from its sling, he pulled the wrapping away from his head and set about working on the thick knot securing his other wrist to the bed. He was getting the hell out of here while he still had breath. His healing arm was stiff, so he used his teeth to tear the rest of the knot away. The moment he was free he became aware of another kind of pain stabbing through him. Nae, not through him, but *on* him. His flesh felt as if it was on fire. Stinging, itchy, burning a little . . . He pushed himself up on his good elbow and looked down at the angry welts covering his chest and belly. He knew there were more beneath the rag affixed to his chest. That rotten runt of a Fergusson's work. Och, Tristan didn't give a rat's arse how young the boy was, Tamas was going to regret this.

He sat up fully and then leaned over the side of the bed and threw up what was left in his stomach, which was practically nothing after two days without food.

Pushing himself up, he tore the rag from his chest and tightened his jaw against the agony of his hair being ripped out. What manner of devils were they? He swiped his mouth with the cloth, then threw it at the wall.

Hell, he was hungry. He would hunt just as soon as he was a safe distance away. He had to find his breeches and his horse. He looked around the room. Where was his sword? Could he even walk to it once he found it?

He swung his good leg over the edge first and then

carefully eased the other over the side. He was about to attempt to stand when the door opened.

Ah, it was the fair Isobel come to check the corpse. He almost smiled at the stunned look on her face when she saw him sitting up.

"Sorry to disappoint ye, ye heartless wench," he snarled.

"How did ye...?" Her wide gaze swung to the bed-post where the rope that had bound him lay wilted on the mattress.

A small head, the one Tristan remembered as belonging to the lad who had shot him in the leg, appeared around Isobel's left arm. Damnation, how many of them were there?

"John"—Isobel pushed him away from the door—"go fetch Patrick."

"Aye," Tristan shouted after him. "Fetch Tamas, too, so I can hurl him oot the window!"

Isobel gasped and when he looked at her, her eyes narrowed into thin slits. "How can ye even jest about doing such a thing?"

"I am no' jestin', Miss Fergusson," he snapped back. "And ye'll be next."

"Quit threatening her, MacGregor." This time Tristan knew the face appearing at her side. Cameron. And the bastard had Tristan's sword.

"Ye're a bunch of thieves as well, I see."

"Do not move!" Cameron warned, waving the blade at him when Tristan tried to push himself off the bed.

"So then," Tristan jeered at him, "ye mean to kill me with my own sword?"

Almost instantly, Cameron lowered the weapon, and his gaze along with it. "I do not mean to kill anyone."

"Aye." Tristan laughed hollowly. "None of ye do."

"D'ye scoff at my words?" Isobel charged, now looking as angry as he felt.

"Aye, I scoff at them! D'ye stand there and deny poisonin' me, Miss Fergusson?" He cut her off with the force of his fury when she opened her mouth. "D'ye deny that 'twas yer own brother who mopped the honey off the window and placed the sweet rag on my chest while I was fightin' death?"

"Fighting death?" Isobel looked about to laugh at him and Tristan felt his blood boil.

"Look!" He pointed to the welts searing his skin. "And I should believe ye mean me nae harm?"

Patrick appeared at the door with John. Tamas was nowhere in sight. "Who untied him?"

"I did!" Tristan shot at him. "I'm gettin' the hell oot of here. Is my horse still alive?" He turned to scorch Isobel with his blackest look. "Or was that him ye fed to me when ye tried to kill me?"

"What are ye talking about, MacGregor?" Patrick demanded from the door. Tristan was quick to note Cameron passing him the blade.

"I'll be happy to tell ye, Fergusson." He wrapped his plaid around his waist and pulled himself to his feet, clinging to the bottom post for support. "I was a fool to come here. A fool to think I could change anything. I'm goin' home."

"Ye cannot!" Isobel took a step into the room. Patrick stopped her. "Ye cannot leave with yer wounds still raw. The moment yer father sees them he will come after us."

Hell, he'd had enough of listening to how terrible his father was. "Ye call my kin barbaric, Miss Fergusson, but so far, 'tis I who have been shot, not once but twice, knocked out cold by a flying rock and God knows what else, poisoned, and attacked by an army of hornets led by an unholy hellion who makes my faither look tame! 'Tis ye who willna' let go of the past."

"We have put it aside," Patrick argued. "No one tried to poison ye. I can assure ye of that."

"He speaks of the brew," Isobel drawled, casting Tristan a look that said he was the biggest dimwit in Scotland. "It was nothing more harmful than whisky in yer stew, MacGregor."

Tristan stared at her for a moment, then blinked. "Ye expect me to believe that whisky did this to me?"

"Aye, it was Patrick's own concoction, but it was a wee bit too potent to sell. It likely had an even stronger effect on ye since ye do not partake often."

Tristan saw the shadow of a smile pulling at the corners of her mouth. He wanted to strangle her. She knew perfectly well the effect drinking such a potent brew would have on him. He had thought he could trust her. He was wrong. Pity. She possessed a streak in her as wicked as her brothers'. She had no idea whom she was dealing with. None of them did.

"Now, Mister MacGregor," she said, that mocking lilt still lacing her voice, "if ye would be so kind as to sit back down and let me tend to yer wounds—"

He laughed, draping the loose end of his plaid over his shoulder. "Ye'll no' be touchin' me again, but ye can saddle my horse and bring me the rest of my clothes." He realized his belt was also missing and leaned backward over the bed to reach for the rope. His injured leg gave out beneath him and he went down like a felled tree.

Much to the horror of the others, all huddled in the doorway, John broke free and rushed to his aid.

"John, ye fool, get back here!" Patrick commanded, lifting Tristan's sword over his shoulder, ready to strike—or to bat something unseen out of his way.

"Och, fer hell's sake." From the floor, Tristan flung him an exasperated look. "Put doun my damned sword, will ye? I'm no' goin' to hurt the lad."

Cameron went to him next and tucked his hands under Tristan's arms to aid him back to the bed. The moment they sat him down, he stood up again, leaning this time, on John's shoulder. "I've been abed long enough," he said, answering the worry in Isobel's eyes. "To appease ye, I'll wait a few more days before returnin' home. But unless ye intend to attempt tying me doun again, I prefer to be on my feet."

"But yer leg—"

"My leg is healin' nicely. 'Tis just a wee bit stiff. If ye'll hand me back my sword, I can use it to aid my walkin'."

"No," Patrick said immediately. "Ye will not be getting it back. I will not have an armed MacGregor traipsing through my home."

Tristan's eyes darkened on him. "Verra well, a walkin' stick then. Ye have my word no' to bash in anyone's skull while I recover."

"John, get him a stick," Isobel said, then turned to Patrick. "It is his tongue that requires our vigilance."

Tristan flicked his gaze to hers and smiled coolly. She responded by fisting her hands at her sides and looking away.

"I do not wish to tend to him any longer," she ground out, a bit shakily, to Tristan's satisfaction. "If he can tend to himself, then let him." She wheeled on her heel, slapping her long braid against Patrick's chest, and left the doorway.

"Is she always so irritable?" Tristan asked, turning to Cameron.

Without giving him an answer, Cam left his side and followed his sister out of the room. Left alone with Patrick, Tristan sighed. "Yer kin have nothin' to fear from me. Ye have my word. My anger has subsided."

"I want to believe ye, but since I do not know ye, yer word means little to me."

Feeling a little more like himself than he had in a sennight, Tristan's mouth broke into a pleasant grin. "Ye'll just have to get to know me then."

Patrick looked him over, his expression tentative. He said nothing but motioned for Tristan to follow him after John returned with a long branch to help him walk.

"Fergusson," Tristan said as they left the room, "what in blazes did ye put in that brew? I thought fer certain I was dyin'. But after the effect wears off..." He rolled his injured shoulder and smiled to himself. "...I must admit I feel stronger than I have in months."

Patrick didn't look too happy to hear that as he paused at the top of the stairs. "Where would ye like to go first? I have much work to do."

"Will ye be followin' me, then?"

"Aye," Patrick told him with a look in his eyes that said he would not be swayed. "I will."

Tristan's mouth quirked at the corners. "All right, then. To the privy."

Chapter Seventeen

*I*n comparison to Camlochlin's grand halls and forti-fied walls, the Fergussons' manor house was just large enough to fit the seven of them in comfort. But to Tristan, it seemed larger on the inside. He wasn't certain if it was the many clear-glassed windows spilling sunshine into every nook or something else entirely that infused the house with a feeling of warmth and intimacy. Something as small as linens on the tables and potted flowers decorating the windowsills. Such personal details were not found in a castle.

Patrick escorted him to the kitchen after he insisted on watching his meal being prepared. "Poison or brew," he told Isobel's brother, "I never want to feel the torment I felt upon waking from my death sleep again."

And it was partially true. The other part was that the heavenly aroma of roasting fowl and freshly baked bread filling the house tempted him to risk it.

Isobel looked up from chopping a clump of herbs and blew a bronze tendril away from her cheek. "Yer meals will be ready shortly. Patrick, why do ye not show Mister

MacGregor to the stable so he can see that his horse was not part of what he left on the floor above stairs."

Tristan felt the barb pierce his flesh along with the other dozen inflicted by hornets. He smiled, remembering one of the reasons he came here.

"I'll no' be leavin', Miss Fergusson; I want to watch ye."

Her chopping knife missed her fingertips by a hair. Her eyes darted to Patrick.

"Fergive me if I dinna' trust ye alone with my food."

She breathed an almost audible sigh of relief and shrugged her shoulders at him. "As I told ye at Whitehall, ye will never gain mine."

"Aye, I remember," Tristan replied, doing his part to convince Patrick that she had not betrayed her kin's cause in his absence. "And now I understand the hatred between us better."

She stopped chopping and looked at him while he picked a small jar off one of the many shelves lining the kitchen walls and uncorked it.

"So, ye admit ye hate me then? Ye hate us?" she added, remembering that they were not alone.

Tristan looked up from sniffing the contents of the jar and offered her a polite smile. "'Tis as ye told me in England, we are enemies. I wish 'twas no' so, but ye have helped me to accept it."

"Good. I am happy to have helped." She didn't look happy about it. In fact, she looked like she wanted to fling her knife at him.

They both turned to Patrick when he began to pace in front of the doorway. "Where is Cam? I do not have the time to sit idly while ye both haggle over a dead cause. I must finish curing the grass for hay. Lachlan!" he called into the next room when the front door opened. "Bring Cam in here to guard our guest." He glanced at Tristan with a rueful quirk of his mouth. "Forgive me if I do not trust ye alone and unbound with my sister."

"Of course." Tristan accepted the check with a slight bow and a swift glance at the alluring curve of Isobel's backside as she moved toward the trivet. Patrick would be a fool if he trusted any man alone with her—and flicking his gaze back to Isobel's eldest brother, Tristan already knew Patrick was no fool. As for the rest of them, so far the odds were not stacked in their favor.

"Ye keep many herbs."

"Say again?" Patrick turned to him briefly, then realized to whom Tristan was speaking and went back to waiting for Cameron.

"Ye're a healer," Tristan continued, keeping his eyes on Isobel as she finally turned from her work.

"I thought that was quite obvious already." She gave him a good looking over while she wiped her hands in her apron. "Ye are up and about, are ye not?"

"I am," he agreed, stretching out his arms and grinning down at himself. When he lifted his gaze to her, she lifted hers from the same view. "Ye have my thanks fer puttin' me back together so well."

She looked as if she might blush, but the flash of fire in her eyes proved that it was her temper coloring her cheeks and not some coy trick to enchant him. "I had no choice. I was not about to let one of ye die on our land."

Tristan knew he should feel spurned by her resolve to reject him, but he couldn't help wondering if she, too, felt the crackle in the air around them. It made his skin feel raw, his blood, hot.

He had to win her.

Cameron appeared at the door and switched places with Patrick. He acknowledged Isobel beneath a cascade of cinnamon lashes but turned away from Tristan's greeting.

Resolved once again to his original cause, Tristan knew he had to win them all.

Well, mayhap not all, he corrected a short time later when supper was ready and Tamas sauntered into the kitchen to have his plate filled.

After exchanging their darkest glances, the runt looked to where Tristan was pointing to the welts on his chest and shrugged. "Ye are fortunate to have been on the top landing, else ye might have found a boar in yer bed when ye awoke."

"And ye're fortunate that I've a merciful heart," Tristan countered, a bit taken aback by the boy's blunt boldness. "Else ye might find poison oak in yers."

Tamas narrowed his eyes on him as if he were trying to decide if Tristan was jesting or not.

Someone snickered beside him, and Tristan turned to look down at the lad who had fetched his walking stick. John, he was called. Upon closer inspection, Tristan noticed the shadow of a knot on his forehead about the same size as the one he himself sported.

Tristan winked at him. "There are a number of ways to make a younger brother pay fer his foolishness."

John's smile was less hesitant than that of any of his siblings. "D'ye have one of yer own then?"

"I do," Tristan told him. "He gave me this in practice." He held out his forearm for John to see the thin scar that began at his elbow and ended halfway to his wrist.

"What did ye do to him fer it?"

"Mister MacGregor!" Isobel scolded before Tristan

could reply. "Retaliation might be a part of yer upbringing, but we do not encourage it in this house."

Tristan looked up from John's wide eyes and set his gaze directly on hers. As much as he delighted in her determination to hate him, it was time she admitted to a basic truth. "Then ye might consider settin' a better example yerself, Miss Fergusson."

Her eyes blazed, her lips went taut, and her hands twisted at her apron until Tristan was certain he heard it tear. He couldn't help smiling, watching her struggle to form a rebuttal. It was difficult to deny that they were not so different.

"Here." She shoved a plate under his nose and nearly lost his interest when the heavenly aroma of his supper filled his lungs. "Ye can eat outdoors," she told him as he opened his eyes. "I kept ye alive. I do not have to tolerate yer company."

Tamas sneered up at him, and for a fleeting instant Tristan considered extending his walking stick as the boy walked past him. He caught the warning in Isobel's eyes and let the bratling pass without incident.

"Cam," she said, filling her brother's plate and handing it to him, "show Mister MacGregor to the door."

With nothing more than a shadow of disquiet marring his features, Cameron obeyed without argument and led Tristan out of the kitchen.

Of all Isobel's brothers, Tristan knew this one might be the most difficult with which to find favor. The others, at least, gave him something to fight—and when one drew a weapon against Tristan MacGregor, one quickly found oneself put out of combat. But Cameron gave him nothing. Not a word of anger, nor a sign of intellect. Not even a glance to prove he knew Tristan was there. It made

Tristan feel utterly defenseless, and he didn't care for that feeling at all.

"I think I will check on my horse after I eat. If that is all right with ye."

Cameron didn't answer, but continued toward the door like a soldier heading off to war.

"Good, ye're the quiet type," Tristan tried, offering him a genial smile. "After meetin' the rest of ye, 'tis a welcome virtue ye possess."

"The door." Cameron stood aside and held out his empty hand, showing Tristan the way out.

With nothing more he could do about any of them, Tristan stepped outside and looked down at his plate as the door closed behind him.

At least his supper was hot, and undeniably the most delicious food he'd ever put into his mouth. The meat was so tender and tasteful he sighed out loud twice. Hell, her cooking alone made Isobel a prize worth dying over.

He paused in his chewing, remembering that he wasn't the only man who thought so.

The door opened behind him and he turned to find John standing at the entrance with his bowl of supper cupped in his hands. Tristan smiled at him. John smiled back just as brightly.

"May I eat with ye?" the boy asked, already coming toward him.

"If yer sister doesna' mind."

John shrugged his narrow shoulders. "She was not all that happy about it, but I do not think it fair that ye have to sit out here all alone."

Tristan nodded and offered him the empty space beside him. "So ye do what's right despite what others think, eh?"

"Sometimes it is hard," John said with a sigh, folding his legs beneath him.

"It sure as hell is," Tristan agreed and went back to eating. "That's what makes it such an admirable quality." He cut his gaze to the lad and winked. "Compassion, too, is admirable. Ye helped me when I lost my balance above stairs. I thank ye fer that."

John beamed. "Cam helped, too."

"Aye, he did."

They ate together in silence for a while longer, and then, setting his gaze over the landscape to the vast fields beyond the hillside, Tristan turned to John once more. "Let me see yer hands."

As he suspected, the boy had calluses from his fingers to his palms. This small family tended to everything themselves. No one was spared. "I will help ye do yer chores as soon as I can walk on my own. Consider it repayment fer aidin' me."

"Thank ye." The boy grinned and continued eating.

"I understand Andrew Kennedy thinks yer sister is a fine cook. Does he fancy her as well?"

"He must. They are betrothed."

Tristan dropped his spoon into his bowl and turned to stare at him. "Isobel is betrothed? She didna' tell me."

John looked up at him with wide eyes. "Was she supposed to?"

Och, hell. Aye, she was supposed to! Why was it expected of him to seek out if the woman he wanted to caress and touch and kiss was married—or practically married? And damn it, he *had* asked her! She had lied to him. Why?

"What's he like, this Andrew Kennedy?"

"He is nice enough." John spooned more food into his

mouth, oblivious to Tristan's rising temper. "He is a bit long-winded, and he drinks a lot of whisky."

Why the hell would she want to marry someone like that? Had she kissed him? How many times? Why did the thought of it make him want to smash someone's skull? Setting down his bowl, Tristan stood up and looked around. He felt trapped suddenly, as if a cage door had just slammed shut somewhere inside him. He scratched the welts on his chest, which were beginning to itch like hell. Nae, she wasn't like the others, ready to cast aside their husbands, their reputations, for a night of passion. Isobel was rigidly loyal to her family. Besides, she wasn't after some lewd tryst with him. Hell, she'd made his jaw ache for two days just for kissing her.

"I need to take a walk," he said, bending to snatch up his stick.

"Do not get lost," John called out to him as he made his way toward the spot before the tree line where he'd been shot.

She couldn't be betrothed. He raked his hand through his hair while he trampled the grass underfoot. Why couldn't she be? She didn't belong to him. She hated him. Why should she have told him that she loved another? As she had told him countless times, they were enemies. She owed him nothing.

"Get yer feet out of my garden!"

He turned toward Isobel's shriek, already glaring at her.

"Did ye hear me?" She stood with her hands fisted on her hips, her ginger braid snapping in the breeze and her eyes on his feet. "Do not take another step!"

He looked down at the thyme, mint, and agrimony plants swaying around his toes. Her garden.

"Just step to the left and get out."

He scratched his chest again and then moved carefully, which was a bit more difficult with the addition of his stick.

"Are ye trying to kill what ye did not fall on the first time?"

"Ye're betrothed."

Her hands dropped to her sides. Well, at least she had the decency to look surprised that he'd found out.

"Yes, I am."

He nodded but turned away, not knowing what to say to her next. Why the hell did he care? He didn't. "Why were ye no' honest with me when I asked ye in England? D'ye know how many lasses I know like ye?"

Her expression went from soft to glacial in an instant. "I do not even want to think about how many lasses ye know, ye underhanded bastard!"

"What?" He laughed. "Me? Ye're the one—"

"I was informed about my betrothal a few days before ye arrived here. I did not lie to ye. I am nothing like the trollops ye know, Tristan MacGregor, except in one thing. *You* have lied to *me!*"

Did she say she had only known for several days? Hell. What had he done? Why had he done it? "Isobel, wait." He reached for her hand and stopped her when she turned to storm away. "Hell, I…Fergive me, I dinna' know why I…" His words could not abandon him now. He could talk his way out of almost anything. Why couldn't he think of a single thing to say to her?

"Let go of me."

"D'ye love him?"

"Isobel?" They both heard Patrick coming up behind them. "What are ye doing there?"

"Let me go," she said, with panic rising in her voice this time.

Tristan released her hand and watched her turn to her brother.

"I am speaking to Mister MacGregor about the plants he killed."

Patrick looked around at his three youngest brothers, who had followed him from the house. "D'ye lads have no work to do?" he said, pointing to the fields. He passed a glance between Isobel and Tristan, his expression unreadable. "Ye can go back inside now," he told Tristan. "There's a fire in the sitting room to warm ye up, or ye can go back to yer room and rest. We will return later. Come, Bel."

"I will be along in a moment."

When Patrick hesitated, she folded her arms across her chest, indicating she would have her way. "Look at him." They both did and found Tristan clawing at his plaid. "He is in no condition to cause me harm."

When her brothers finally left, she looked up at Tristan with the residue of his insult still fresh in her eyes. He decided in that moment that every lass who had ever called him a thoughtless bastard was correct.

"When ye said I lied to ye, ye were right, Isobel. Ye are nothin' like anyone I know or have ever known. I reacted the way I did because I fear I will never know anyone like ye again."

Her gaze softened on him for a moment, but then she flicked her long braid over her shoulder and straightened her spine. "How long will ye keep this up?" she asked him. "When will ye finally admit what ye are doing here? We both know it has nothing to do with Alex."

"I told ye why. I want to end the feud... and I wanted to see ye again."

"Why?"

He pulled at his plaid to lift the wool off his burning flesh. Unholy little bast—

"Is it getting worse?"

He looked at her, liking the concern he saw in her eyes better than the suspicion it replaced. "Aye, it itches like hell."

Without another word, she pushed past him and strode toward a tall shrub at the edge of her garden. She snapped off three leaves, put one into her mouth, and began to chew it. She motioned for him to come forward, making certain that he watched his step. When he reached her, she tugged his plaid away, baring his reddened chest. Tristan had no idea what she meant to do, so when she plucked the chewed leaf from between her lips and reached for him with it, he backed away.

She moved forward and said with a sigh, "I am not trying to poison ye, MacGregor. This will draw out the irritant that is making ye itch and prevent infection." She didn't wait for his consent, but spread her fingers over his skin and rubbed the mashed leaf over the welts. She seemed completely unaffected by touching him, but every nerve ending in Tristan's body came alive. Her touch was gentle, warm, and sensuous to the point of muddling his senses. She deposited another leaf in her mouth and he watched, mesmerized, while she chewed, then parted her lips to expel the next treatment.

"Does it feel better?"

"Aye," he answered in a husky whisper as her fingertips flittered down his belly. His muscles twitched with the urge to take her in his arms and kiss that luscious mouth senseless.

"One more." She popped the last leaf into her mouth,

but when she moved to touch him, he grasped her wrist to stop her.

"Isobel, unless ye're tryin' to drive me mad with desire fer ye, 'tis best if ye stop now."

Her face went pale in the fading light. Her mouth opened to form some sort of protest Tristan ached to snatch from her lips with his own. He wanted to haul her closer and pull her hand down over the rest of his hardening body and let the healing begin! He wanted to. Ah, God, he wanted to so badly. But he had things to prove to her, to himself, and couldn't prove them with a lass who was betrothed. So he let her go.

Chapter Eighteen

Isobel watched Tristan turn and limp back to the house. She stood alone for a long time, her feet rooted to the soil beside her garden, her emotions roiling within. Dear God, what was he doing to her? She had to keep her wits about her. His silken words and alluring mannerisms had been practiced on countless women before her. She'd heard what they called him in England and had felt the effect of his charm more than enough to know the names they gave him were correct. How could she allow herself for a moment to believe his words were sincere? Though, God's mercy, when he spoke of becoming mad with desire for her, his heavy voice quaked in evidence. She still felt the sting of his fingers around her wrist.

When she'd first come upon him, he had looked like he wanted to throttle her. She had never seen him angry before. Goodness, but his dark scowls were just as alluring as his grins. She couldn't tell if it was the fact that she was betrothed or that he thought she had lied to him that had him so riled up, even going so far as to insult her. He had been quick enough to repent, but why would he care about either?

She turned away before he entered the house. She was made of stronger stuff than the women Tristan MacGregor was used to. She'd already proven it to herself by touching him and not going weak in the knees. Of course, making herself think of Andrew Kennedy while she stroked Tristan's chest helped. She would not fall victim to his wiles, or to his chiseled body. Whether he was mad with desire for her or not, he still hadn't told her the truth about why he had come here. She simply could not believe he had traveled so far, to his enemy's holding, just to see her... or even to bed her. He said he wanted to end the hatred and pain of the feud, but why? What purpose would it serve for him?

She met her brothers in the field and began her work, determined not to spare Tristan another thought. After an hour of digging holes that made her think of graves she might as well be digging for herself if she continued to let the warmth of his rigid belly invade her thoughts and influence her opinion of him, she felt miserable. Why in blazes could she not be anywhere near the man without finding something attractive about him? She wished he would recover fully and be quick about it and be on his way.

"Why did ye offer him the comfort of our fire?" she asked Patrick when he came up beside her and took the shovel from her hands. It was her brothers she had to look out for the most. They weren't familiar with Tristan's persuasive abilities. Trusting him could cost them their lives.

"His body is recovering and susceptible to chill," Patrick told her. "Would ye have him grow sick and remain here longer?"

Isobel couldn't argue with that bit of logic. "Still, we must remember who he is and what has most likely brought him here."

"He will not get what he seeks from me, Bel," Patrick assured her.

"Nor from me," she promised back.

He smiled and gently hauled her around. "Go back to the house. Take John with ye and—"

"No." She turned back to him. "I will not have ye do this alone."

"There is not much more to be done," Patrick insisted. "Ye look a bit pale, and without yer butterbur I will not have ye overworked. Now go. The rest of us will join ye shortly."

Isobel left the field with John at her side and another of her brothers on her mind. Curse Alex for staying in England when he was needed here. Then again, had Alex been the one to find Tristan hurt and helpless on their land, he would have gladly killed him.

Tristan. She looked toward the manor. He was alive and vibrant and, she hoped, asleep in his bed. The house was quiet and the halls empty when she entered, but she could feel his presence, sense it all around her, like a lioness picking up the scent of a male. She peered toward the stairs as John broke away from her and headed to the kitchen.

Slowly, she walked down the softly lit hall, toward the sitting room and the crackling fire growing louder as she came closer. She wasn't sure what she was doing or why she didn't rush up the stairs to her room. She had no intention of speaking to Tristan if he was awake. She was too damned tired to engage in a battle of wits with him. She reached the door and found it ajar, spilling golden light and heat into the hall. She looked inside. He was there, before the fire, partially hidden from her view by the door and by Patrick's high-backed chair, in which he sat.

Part of Isobel wanted to storm inside and order him out of the Chieftain's seat. Another part of her refused to move, to blink, to breathe. Damn it all to hell, but his profile was handsome against the firelight. She wondered what he was thinking, staring into the flames as if the answer to all life's secrets could be found there.

Her secrets.

"What are ye doing, Isobel?"

She whirled around and aimed the full force of her scowl at John.

"What did I do?" he asked, then looked around her into the sitting room. When he saw Tristan inside, he pulled back, glanced up at her, and then back at the door. "Well," he said, coming to some conclusion in his mind that Isobel was certain was the incorrect one, "we should probably go inside now."

She couldn't. She didn't want to go in there and see Tristan smirking at her mortification. But she didn't want to send John in alone for fear of what questions Tristan might put to him. With no choice now but to follow her brother, she smoothed her skirts and squared her shoulders. "We will only stay fer a moment."

John nodded and stepped around her. He disappeared inside before Isobel had time to finish composing herself.

Damn it. She put one foot in front of the other and forced herself onward. She glanced up long enough to see Tristan rise from the chair when she entered. He had to have known she'd been standing outside the door spying on him before John exposed her, but he didn't offer her a smug greeting. In fact, he looked a bit unsettled, as if their arrival had disturbed some great quandary he'd been contemplating.

"We came to check on ye," John informed him, saving Isobel from having to speak. "Are ye faring all right?"

"Aye," Tristan replied, his magnetic smile returning to its full glory and aimed straight at Isobel. "I was just thinkin' how much I like this room. It reminds me of another. Quiet and peaceful."

"Oh?" her brother asked, slipping into one of the other chairs as Tristan regained his seat. "A room in yer castle?"

"Nae, somewhere else I havena' been to in a long time."

"Are there many people where ye live then?"

"Aye, more than I can sometimes stand." His gaze rose to Isobel, still standing close to the door. "Miss Fergusson, am I sittin' in yer chair?"

She blinked, trying to scatter from her mind the images of his heated, far less courteous gaze when they were alone in her garden. "Ye are in Patrick's chair," she blurted out coolly.

"Patrick will not care," John announced, sparing her a brief glance before turning back to Tristan. "What is yer castle like, Mister MacGregor?"

Oh, she could have slapped him! She sank into the nearest chair instead and listened while Tristan spoke of his hated clan. It was all too intimate, too comfortable. A MacGregor, sitting here in her favorite room, beside her hearth fire, talking softly to her brother as if they were friends. They weren't. They could never be. John was too young to remember what had happened, and they barely spoke about it, save for when Alex had too much to drink. Tomorrow she would warn John to stay away from Tristan. Right now though, she had to fight sleep and stay alert.

"...And my faither's sister, Maggie, does no' eat meat, though I believe Isobel's cookin' could convert her." Tristan smiled at her across the room and she closed her eyes, concentrating on her brother's sweet voice instead of Tristan's husky one.

"Who is seeing to yer chores while ye are away?"

A pause, and then, "My brother Rob sees to most of them with my faither."

"So then, what do ye do all day?"

Isobel opened her eyes and waited for Tristan's answer.

"I am...no' needed as much as ye all are here. There are many strong men at Camlochlin who see to the daily chores."

"Will ye not be missed then?"

Looking at him closely for the first time since she came into the room, Isobel noted the forced smile Tristan wore when he shook his head. "I willna' be gone long enough to be missed. Besides, my kin know that I plan on leavin' fer good next spring."

"Why will ye leave?" Isobel was drawn to ask him by that same innate instinct she had to take care of her family.

He shrugged his shoulders. "Because I dinna' belong there."

She wanted to ask him why, but Patrick stepped into the room with Cameron and stopped when he saw Tristan sitting in his chair. Tristan was about to rise, but Patrick motioned for him to stay where he was.

"John, off to bed with ye now," he ordered gently, then turned to Isobel as he sat. "Some warm mead, please, sister."

"Of course." She got up and left the room without another word.

She returned a short while later carrying a tray with four cups of mead. After Patrick and Cam took theirs, she held the tray to Tristan. He eyed the cup suspiciously until Isobel snatched Patrick's from his fingers and gave him Tristan's cup instead.

Patrick hid his smile behind his drink while Isobel marched back to her chair with a string of muttered oaths spilling from her lips.

"My sister would tell me to go to Hades if I asked her to serve me," Tristan told her brother and sipped his drink.

"Mayhap," Isobel said, hating that her anger only seemed to fuel Tristan's delight, "that is because yer father and brother do all the work." She didn't look at him to see if her words had the desired effect. She looked at Cam instead, and then wished she hadn't when he cast her a disapproving glance.

Damnation, she was tired and in no mood to be pleasant to a man who was afraid to put anything she served him into his mouth. She snuggled deep into her chair, happy that she had used all that extra sheeps' wool when she restuffed it last winter, and angry with her brothers for being so patient with a MacGregor. She closed her eyes, half-aware, as she drifted off to sleep, of Patrick's voice asking Tristan if he cared for a game of chess. She should stop them. Tristan was a snake with a forked tongue. The Devil's son, with eyes the color of sunset and strong, quick hands that could hold her still while he whispered of his forbidden desire.

"Does she snore every night?" Tristan asked Patrick, and moved his rook two spaces to the right. He'd played chess hundreds of times at home and almost always won, but tonight he found himself losing. He couldn't concentrate with Isobel's limp body draped over her chair, her braid spilling into her lap, her plump lips relaxed and softly parted. Every muscle in his body ached to go to her, lift her gently in his arms, and carry her to her bed.

"Is it distracting ye?" her brother asked, capturing his knight.

"Nae, 'tis…" What the hell did he almost just say? 'Twas what? Endearing? A sweet respite from her sharp tongue? "I…what I mean to say is…" Damn, being at a loss for words whenever Isobel was involved in them was beginning to worry him.

"Do not fret that I will be offended, MacGregor. I want to beat ye fairly." Without another word, Patrick rose from his seat and went to his sister.

"Come, love, to bed with ye," Tristan heard him mutter as he pulled his sister gently to her feet. He motioned for Cameron, who had been watching the game in silence, to help her to her room.

Isobel swayed a moment, her sleepy gaze settling on Tristan first and then moving back to Patrick. "Do not trust him," she said, falling against his broad chest. Patrick whispered something to her that Tristan couldn't hear and then handed her over to Cameron. She smiled. "And do not let him kiss ye."

Both brothers went still. Both turned slowly to graze Tristan with very different looks, one blacker than the night sky, the other fearful and wary.

Tristan stood to his feet, leaning on his walking stick

as Patrick waited for Cam to lead her out of the sitting room. When they were alone, the hulking Chieftain took a step forward around the chess table.

"Is this how ye intend to end the hatred between our clans? By kissing my sister?"

Tristan had never run from anything in his life. Well, almost nothing—but never from a man. Still, Patrick Fergusson's arms were cut with slabs of muscle from his long hours of labor, and Tristan did not fancy a fight with him. He could deny the charge easily enough, but deceit would not earn him this man's favor or respect, and he needed it to see his task through.

"She didna' enjoy it," he admitted, and closed his eyes as Patrick's fist sailed through the air and smashed into his jaw.

Tristan didn't go completely unconscious. He fell back into his chair with a hard thump and was aware of three things. A tooth in the back of his mouth had come loose, his indiscretions had finally caught up with him, and last, Patrick growled deeply as he sat back down and said, "Yer move, ye bastard."

Chapter Nineteen

Tristan opened his eyes and groaned. Would there ever come a day when he woke up in this blasted small bed without pain searing through his body? He touched his palm to his jaw, then pulled it away with a muffled curse. He guessed he deserved Patrick's blow, and losing to him at chess, but if he had to get hit by one of Isobel's brothers, he would have preferred John. Still, it said much about the young Fergusson Chieftain's even temper that he had hit Tristan only once.

Tossing his feet over the side of the bed, he stretched, rolled his shoulder, and looked around for his walking stick. He spotted it by the open window and scratched his head. He didn't remember leaving it there, but then, Patrick's heavy fist had jumbled most of his senses. He was fortunate to have made it to the bed without falling back down the stairs.

He stood up and felt his plaid slip off his waist and crumple to his ankles. Where the hell was his belt? For a moment, he felt completely disoriented, as if he hadn't yet fully awakened and might still be dreaming. Had all the blows to his head finally taken their toll? He bent to his plaid, snatched it up, and lumbered over to the window to retrieve his stick. He looked out over the landscape, carefully shielding his groin with his bunched-up plaid. He saw Patrick at work in the fields with Cam and Lachlan, but Isobel was nowhere in sight. He remembered her snoring last eve and smiled, thinking about what it might be like to wake up with her in his bed. He remembered Andrew Kennedy and cursed under his breath. Did Isobel love him? If she did, how could Tristan continue to try to win her when she belonged to another? In the past, a lady's betrothal might not have stopped him. But wasn't he trying to be someone different? Wasn't that why he had come here?

Turning on his heel, he set his weight on the walking stick for support. He heard the slight crack of wood an instant before he lurched forward and toppled over. He lay sprawled on the floor, his plaid landing a few feet away, his leg, arm, head, and jaw throbbing from the impact. He stayed there for a moment, thinking about what the hell had just happened and how close he had come to careening out the window. His temper rising like molten lava, he slanted his gaze to the broken walking stick, already knowing what he would find. The break was neat and clean. Someone had purposely cut the wood almost in half, leaving a bit intact so that it wouldn't crack completely in two until he leaned on it.

Tamas.

Tristan barely felt any pain at all as he gained his feet. It was time for the hellion to pay.

Busy thinking up ways to make the runt's life a living hell, Tristan seized the two sticks from the floor, wrapped his plaid loosely around his waist, and stormed out of the room. On his way down the stairs, he told himself that helping Isobel wasn't worth the injuries to his body. To hell with the feud! If the MacGregors ever came here again he would direct them straight to Tamas Fergusson.

He was still muttering to himself when he entered the kitchen, hungry for something to eat before he set hell loose on the deadly rascal. He looked up from tying the ends of his plaid into a knot below his belly and saw Isobel returning a pot to one of the shelves above her head.

Tristan's eyes fell immediately to her rump, round and shapely beneath her woolen skirts. Her thick auburn hair fell like liquid fire down her back to her slender waistline. He wanted to run his hands through it, bury his face in it and breathe her into his lungs.

Hearing him enter, she turned to look over her shoulder. For an instant, he forgot everything else and smiled at the beguiling curve of her jaw, and the light spray of scarlet across the bridge of her nose, and her eyes, lighting on him like verdant pastures beneath the summer sun. Hell, she *was* worth it.

"I did not hear yer approach." Her eyes widened, skimming across his torso.

"Fergive me." He fumbled for the drape of his plaid to cover his bare belly, but he'd tied it too tightly at his hips. He gave up and dropped his hands to his sides. "Mayhap ye'll return my clothes to me? I dinna' want ye to think me too barbaric to look at."

"I would not think that." Her voice held a pleasant note that Tristan decided he liked. "I…" She blinked her gaze to his and blushed an even darker shade of crimson. "I was just noticing how nicely yer welts are healing."

He couldn't help the smile creeping up his lips. "My clothes?"

"Of course, I will bring them— What happened to ye?" she gasped suddenly, bringing her hands to her mouth.

Unfortunately, he remembered again all too quickly. "Yer brother is what happened to me, Isobel. I vow the wee bastard is bent on killin' me. I will no'—"

"Tamas did that to ye?" she interrupted, pointing a finger at his jaw. "What in blazes did he strike ye with?"

"He didna' strike me; Patrick did." Her eyes opened even wider, but Tristan didn't give her a chance to question him further. He held up his broken walking stick instead. "D'ye see this? 'Twas cut! Tamas did it and left it beside the window!"

When she gave him a befuddled look, he clenched his jaw and then cursed inwardly at the pain.

"He left it, seemingly in one piece, beside the window, hoping that when it broke, I would fall to my death! And I nearly did!" His voice rose along with his temper. "Och, and he didna' stop there. Nae! He took my belt so that when I fell, I would do so naked! He's a clever, evil work of the devil and— D'ye find this humorous?"

She shook her head, but Tristan was certain he heard her giggle behind her hand.

"He needs to be punished, Isobel."

She nodded and moved toward him. "I will speak to Patrick about it."

When she stopped directly in front of him, her earthy scent filled his lungs and muddled his wits. He shook his head to clear it.

"I will have John fetch ye a new walking stick."

"I dinna' need it," he told her, his voice low and thick above her auburn crown. "My leg is better." Good enough to lift her off the floor, hike her legs around his waist, and take her on the way to the wall.

"Will ye be returning home soon then?"

Was that disappointment he heard at the edge of her voice? Hell, it was nice to think so. "I suspect I should." But he couldn't. Not yet. There was too much to do. She still didn't like him. Her brothers still didn't trust him. Thanks to his wounds he hadn't yet done anything to restore his honor.

"Your jaw is purple." She lifted her fingers to it for a closer examination. "Why did Patrick strike ye?"

When his gaze dropped to the billowy mounds of her bosom beneath his nose, she moved away, leaving him cold. "He was angry that I kissed ye."

She reeled back, horrified. "Ye told him?"

"Nae, ye did, and Cameron along with him." He looked around the kitchen for food. It seemed that everyone had already eaten.

"Ye are mad! I never told them any such—"

"Ye were half asleep and ye warned Cameron no' to let me kiss him. They figured oot the rest."

Her face went pale as she looked toward the window and twisted her apron into a wrinkled mess. "Why has Patrick said nothing to me about it this morn?"

"I told him ye didna' enjoy it. He is angry with me, no' with ye."

Her color returned a bit and she inhaled a deep breath. "Ye have my thanks fer telling him that," she said, softly enough that he almost didn't hear her.

"'Twas the truth, aye?" he asked her, speaking over the rumble of his belly.

Miracle of miracles, she smiled! "Ye may sit at the table. I will bring ye some food."

Now this was better! Tristan gave her a cheerful thanks and turned to leave the kitchen while she plucked a plate from another shelf.

The clay shattering to the floor an instant later stopped him. He turned and found Isobel gaping at his backside. He looked down over his shoulder. His bare backside. He hooked his mouth into a repentant smile and released the bundled hem of his plaid behind him.

"Apologies fer that," he said, leaving her floundering for her composure.

Isobel lived in a house with six males. She'd seen men's backsides before, but seeing Tristan's tilted her world on its axis. It wasn't just the tight, decadent shape that made her mouth go dry and her palms grow hot, though Heaven help her, that would have been enough. The full vision of his fine buttocks and thick, muscular thighs sparked a lurid desire in her to see the rest of him. And that wicked grin! Dear God, he knew how ruthlessly beautiful he was, and he enjoyed knowing she knew it, too.

She slammed a new plate down on the table before him and turned to walk away. She wasn't angry with him for being so damned appealing, but it was her only defense against him, and every day she needed it more than the day before. His potent gaze melted her insides. His artful, easy smile snatched the breath from her lungs, and when he spoke, she had to call upon every shred of control she possessed to withstand the passion in his words. He was, quite honestly, the most vibrant, the most irritatingly irresistible man she had ever met. Why, oh why did he have to be a MacGregor?

"Will ye sit with me fer a moment or two?" He looked up at her before she stepped away. "I dinna' like eatin' alone."

God help them all, that sweet trace of humility softening his smile was more lethal than a thousand wicked grins. "I should not."

"Why?"

"I have much to do."

"I'll help ye do whatever 'tis. I ask fer but a few moments with ye."

She guessed she owed him a moment or two, since he'd told Patrick that she didn't enjoy their kiss. It was the truth—as he understood it—but he didn't have to tell it to her brother. He'd protected her yet again, and still she didn't know why. He'd also taken a beating from the rest of her brothers since arriving and he hadn't really complained all that much. Could he possibly be the man he claimed to be?

"May I ask ye a question?" She pulled out a chair and sat beside him.

"Only one?"

"It is a good one." She couldn't help returning his smile when he glanced at her from his plate. The moment was much like the one they had shared the first day they met. They both remembered it. "Why did ye stop at only breaking Alex's nose when he provoked ye to fight him?"

"Should I have drawn blood from him because he is prideful?"

"Another man would have."

"I am no' another man."

No, he wasn't. He was two men; one elegant and the other untamed. One wickedly irresponsible and the other charmingly irresistible. He was a rogue, self-admittedly "less concerned with every consequence," and yet he had gone out of his way to aid her with dilemmas that had nothing to do with him.

"Who are ye then?" she asked him quietly, needing to know. Wanting to believe that it was the gallant man who had come to her and not the seducer of women's secrets.

"I canna' tell ye that yet."

He could not or he would not? Damnation, it was not the answer she was looking for. "Verra well, then," she said, leaving her chair. If he refused to tell her the truth, then she would not sit here with him another minute. "I will get ye something fer yer jaw. It looks like it is pain-ing ye—and then I have work to do."

He caught her hand and looked up at her from beneath his lusciously long lashes. "Stay. 'Tis no' too bad, and ye've already done enough fer me. I'll be in yer debt until I'm an old man."

Two men.

She watched him, her body going rigid while he drew her hand tenderly toward his mouth. "Yer hands are as rough as my brother Rob's. Ye do too much."

"I do what is needed of me."

Her inhalation of breath was cut short when he dipped his head and pressed his lips to her knuckles. "Let me help ye, lass."

"Please, do not…" She pulled away, her voice trem-bling from the aftermath of his intimate touch.

"Help ye?"

"Kiss me again."

His smile faded as he let her go. "Fergive me, ye are betrothed."

Since when did that matter to a rogue? She backed away when he rose from his seat only inches from her. "Ye have my thanks fer the food. I promised to help John with his chores, so I'd best get to it." His smile flashed and was gone an instant before he was.

✢

Chapter Twenty

*T*ristan jabbed his pitchfork into the mound of hay and carried it inside the barn. His arm and leg were still sore, but the hay wasn't heavy, and John and Lachlan's endless questions took his mind off the dull pain—and off Isobel.

"D'ye know how to wield that sword Patrick carries around fer ye?"

Tristan nodded at Lachlan when he came back outside.

"Have ye killed many men, then?" John asked him, scratching his nose.

"I havena' killed any."

"Why not?"

"Because 'tis no' always the right thing to kill every man who comes against ye."

Lachlan cut him a skeptical glance, then shrugged his shoulders. "I can fire an arrow and hit my target at a hundred paces."

"So then," Tristan said dryly, stabbing the mound again. "Ye were no' aimin' fer my heart when ye shot me?"

"We had no intention of killing ye," John promised.

Tristan smiled at him. He liked this little one. John reminded him of himself at about the same age. "Then ye're on the right path."

"We cannot speak fer Tamas, though," John admitted with a dash of sympathy shading his smile. "He is a menace."

Tristan knew that all too well. "Aye," he said, carrying his hay back to the barn. "I've already figured that oot."

"Isobel was mad as hell when he shot ye and ye dropped into her garden," Lachlan called out, following him with his own bale.

Was she angry with her brothers for shooting him, Tristan wondered, or with him for destroying half her crop? Angry or not, she had tended to him and nursed him back to good health—so that a MacGregor would not die on her land.

"She was angry only because ye killed her butterbur," John offered in Isobel's defense a moment later when Tristan rejoined him.

"And why is her butterbur more precious than any of the others?"

"It helps her breathe in the winter."

Lachlan elbowed his brother in the ribs, which Tristan deemed unfair, since Lachlan was twice John's size, with shoulders as wide as those of any Highlander bred at Camlochlin. He was about to tell him so when he looked past the boys and saw Isobel and her youngest hellion of a brother exit the house and begin walking in his direction.

In her arms, she carried the clothes she'd promised earlier. Briefly, Tristan eyed the boots swinging from Tamas's fingers, then returned his gaze to her. He studied her mouth, the healthy flush about her cheeks that made her eyes appear larger, greener. It could not be true that this gloriously strong-willed lass had a breathing condition. Was it serious? Why the hell was she doing so much labor if it was? *No one else is here to do it for her,* he answered his own question, and vowed to do something about it.

When she reached him, Tristan was very pleasantly surprised to see the same smile she had worn the day he'd offered to help her with Alex.

"Truly, Mister MacGregor, ye do not have to tend to our work. We are used to—"

"Call me Tristan, please," he said, sticking the fork into the ground and leaning on it. "And I want to help."

"Thank ye then," she conceded, dropping her gaze when she saw Lachlan staring at her to Tristan's right. "Here are yer clothes." She pushed them at him. "I replaced yer torn boots with Alex's. They might be a bit snug, since ye are taller than he is." She lifted her gaze to glance at her brothers and then whirled on her heel and marched toward the fields where Patrick and Cameron were working.

Tristan watched her go for a moment, then accepted the boots Tamas shoved at him. He stepped in front of him when Tamas turned to follow his sister.

"Will ye hold these fer me?" Without giving Tamas a chance to decline, Tristan handed him his shirt and breeches. He smiled at the miscreant while he turned each boot upside down and shook the rocks from them.

"I expected worse. This was disappointin'."

Tamas smiled right back at him, dropped Tristan's clothes on the ground, and popped his tongue out at him as he stepped on them.

In his arrogance, he didn't see the thrust of Tristan's foot in front of his ankles and went reeling over Tristan's breeches to the hard ground beyond.

"D'ye wish to call a truce?" Tristan asked, coming to stand over him. "Or d'ye wish to find oot how an experienced hellion does it?"

Tamas rolled over on his back and stared up at him. "Ask me that after I put worms in yer food."

"Verra well," Tristan sighed, and bent to retrieve his clothes. "'Tis yer choice."

Tristan made no sound as he crept along the dark wall toward Tamas's door. He didn't intend to hurt the boy. Not seriously, at least. Tamas was coming into manhood without the careful guidance he needed to grow with a wee bit of honor and humility.

What he was about to do to wee Tamas was for the boy's own good, and the peace of his family in the future. Patrick seemed to possess the values his youngest brother needed to learn, but he had no time to teach the boy how to be a man. Alex had already proven that he was certainly no example of any shining traits. Cameron was too quiet, too passive to stop Tamas from becoming a menace and causing his sister misery. Tamas needed to be taught by someone who would not cease until he learned his lessons well. The lad was devious and would be tough to win; Tristan would give him that. He smiled, looking forward to the challenge.

"Where have ye been?" a voice said from the shadows. "I thought ye were not coming."

"I always keep my word, John." Tristan shone his grin down at his accomplice and held out his hands. "Did ye get enough?"

"Two bags," John said, handing one to him.

Tristan had required his aid, and when he had put his plan to the lad, John leaped. John needed to do this as much as Tamas needed it done to him.

"Good. Let's go."

Like thieves in the shadows they stole into Tamas's room while he slept and spread dozens of thistles that John had collected along the floor, in Tamas's boots, his pockets, and in his bed where he slept. On his way out the door, Tristan spotted what he was looking for set lovingly on a bench atop Tamas's trews. He snatched it up and shoved it into the pocket of his breeches.

"What do we need the twine fer?" John whispered, handing over his next donation to this worthy cause.

"I'll show ye." Tristan knelt at the entrance and tacked both ends of the twine to the opposite doorframe, about ankle high. He took up the bags and scattered what remained of the prickly plants outside the door and then carefully shut it.

John was quick to figure out what the twine was meant to do and yanked on Tristan's sleeve before they parted ways.

Before he spoke, Tristan leaned down and patted his shoulder. "Dinna' fret, he wears a nightdress. The stings will be minor."

John nodded, smiled, and then dashed away.

Tristan did not go directly to his room but swept down the stairs and into the kitchen, hungry for something to eat. He found an apple, rubbed it against his shirt, and looked out the window. Curiously, a light was coming from the barn. Who was awake at this late hour but him and John? He bit into his apple and left the kitchen. Did Patrick work in the middle of the night? he wondered as he stepped out of the manor house. He was likely the last person Patrick wanted to see, but Tristan would offer to help him, and mayhap they could begin to sort some things out between them.

He pulled opened the barn door and entered with a resounding crunch, taking another bite of his apple. It wasn't Patrick he startled, though, but Isobel, and seeing her stopped Tristan in his tracks. "What are ye doin' in here?"

She turned away from him and went back to her work. Her profile against the soft glow of the lantern at her side went pensive and anxious at the same time. "It is not obvious to ye then that I am milking a goat?"

He moved closer to her. "At this hour?"

"I was not able to get to this today, and Glenny was full." She didn't look at him but gave the goat a gentle pat on the flank. "She does not like being full. "What are ye doing awake so late?" She spared him a brief glance while he dragged over another stool and sat down next to her.

He smiled and held up his apple, then pulled it away when Glenny swung her head around and tried to chomp it out of his fingers. "We can share it, lass. There's nae need to be uncivilized." He took another bite, then handed over the rest.

"Ye should not have done that." Isobel told him, her hands busy beneath the goat's belly. "She is going to expect food each time she sees ye now."

"Then I will bring her some," Tristan promised, and patted Glenny's head.

"Then ye will have to bring it from yer own plate," Isobel pointed out. "If ye had not noticed, we harvest most of our food here. There's not always enough to go around, so I am sure ye will not be seeing her often."

Until that moment, Tristan had not fully comprehended the weight of Patrick and Isobel's responsibilities to this family. At Camlochlin there were many people to help with the daily chores, and with his brother Rob always willing to do most of them, Tristan didn't feel all that needed. But here there was no one else to turn to, no one else to rely on to help them out of danger. If their brothers were to live, it was up to them to see it done. More than before, he was sorry his father had taken theirs.

"Then I'll milk her and tell her exciting tales that will make her ferget aboot fruit altogether."

Isobel blinked at him in the clandestine light and then, much to his soaring heart's delight, smiled.

"Is there nothing or no one who can resist yer consummate charm?"

He shook his head, serious though she mocked him. "There is but one."

Her smile went cool in an instant. "Ye think ye can win my brothers then?"

"I hope to in time," he told her honestly. "'Tis the only way to gain peace between our two families." Why would she not want him to do what he could to lessen the hatred between their kin? He didn't know if such a feat was even possible, but he wanted to try, for her good.

"So, ye would defy yer father?"

He shrugged. "'Twouldna' be the first time I did."

She studied him for a moment, searching his eyes for something. He wished he knew what it was. "Ye told me once that ye are not like most MacGregors. Am I to believe then that ye do not seek revenge upon my family fer yer uncle's death?"

"The man who killed my uncle died with him, Isobel."

"And if he was still alive?"

He blinked back to Glenny, severing his darkened gaze from her. "Then mayhap, things would be different."

Things would be different. Isobel's lungs seared her chest. What would he do then?

"Ye should leave," she ordered, turning back to her work. "Patrick will be angry if he finds ye here."

Tristan's gaze dipped to her fingers closing around the goat's dangling teats, squeezing up and down, up and down until his own body grew tight with the desire to feel her hands on him the same way. "I am willing to risk it."

She sighed and threw back her head. "I am not! I do not know what ye want or what ye are doing here. What has happened between our families can never be repaired, Tristan."

"Ye're wrong," he told her. "My parents are a MacGregor and a Campbell. Their love ended a feud between their clans that had lasted three hundred years. I dinna' think—"

"Love?" she cut him off with a chuckle. "Are ye trying to make me fall in love with ye then?"

"Nae," he said, feeling slightly insulted by her humor. "I—"

"With ye? A notorious rogue known to break the heart of every woman he toys with? How many of them have ye loved?"

"None, but I am no' tryin'—"

"Precisely. I know what ye are and I—"

"—to make ye fall in love with me. The last thing—"

"—will not succumb to yer skilled seduction, only to—"

"—I want is a lass tryin' to make me her husband."

"—want ye more when ye leave."

They both stopped talking over each other at the same time, leaving the air between them sizzling. This time, Tristan knew she felt it. Her eyes gleamed from the challenge of going head to head with him. The creamy roundness of her bosom swelled at the quick, short breaths she drew in and out from between her parted lips. Hell, he wanted to kiss her, to take her right here, right now in the hay.

"I think ye should lea—"

Curling his ankle around the leg of her stool, he dragged her, still sitting on it, between his knees. He took no mercy at her startled gasp, but cushioned her face in his palms and bent to kiss her. Her lips were as soft as he remembered, her breath, warm and mingled with fear. He held her gently and took her mouth with a slow, seductive urgency that made him groan against her teeth. He didn't think it odd that she didn't pull away. He intended to make her too weak to stand with the tender, hungry glide of his tongue. Curling his fingers around her nape, he deepened their kiss, molding his mouth to hers to taste her intoxicating sweetness more fully, breathe her in more completely. He knew by the tightness of his breeches and the pounding of his heart that he needed to stop before it became any harder to do so.

He withdrew slowly, gazing deep into her eyes and hoping she wouldn't slap his loose tooth out of his mouth. "Fergive me," he whispered along her jaw. "Ye are difficult to resist."

She stared at him through heavy, hooded lids, the residue of their passionate kiss fading from her eyes as she blinked. She said nothing to him, though it was clear by the way her fingers began to twist her skirts that she wanted to say or do something. Finally, she did. She stood up, offered him a charitable smile, and then kicked his stool out from beneath his arse.

"Fortunately, Mister MacGregor," she huffed, bending to retrieve her bucket of milk, "resisting *ye* is not difficult at all." She stormed away, sloshing milk this way and that.

Tristan listened to her leave the barn and rose up off his elbows. "So I'm back to bein' Mister MacGregor, am I?" He righted the fallen stool first and when he was back on his feet, gave Glenny a rueful look. "Restraint, I'm sorry to say, isna' one of my best virtues, but I'm workin' on it."

Isobel closed the barn door behind her and leaned against it, one hand clutched to her chest. She needed a moment to breathe, to regain her strength and clear her head. Panic engulfed her momentarily when she discovered the last would be impossible. Heaven help her, but the man knew how to kiss! He knew how to make her burn in places she'd rarely had time to think about in the past. She closed her eyes, remembering the longing in his smoldering gaze when he dipped his mouth to hers, and that gaze had grown hotter still when he released her, his passion insatiable and barely restrained. His kisses were not enough. He wanted to bed her. She had tasted it on his tongue, fevered male desire that made her skin hot and her nerve endings tingle. How could she clear her head when it was filled with lurid images of Tristan MacGregor's hard, naked body poised above her, ready to take her, resolved to pursue his victory? How could she continue to push him away when every smile, every heated look he cast her way brought her closer to defeat?

Hearing him move about inside the barn, talking to

Glenny, as he'd promised he would, Isobel was tempted to peek through one of the cracks in the wall and look at him. He made her smile when she tried her best to hate him. He claimed to want peace between their families. Could she believe him? Did she dare?

And what, oh, what, would he do if he ever discovered the truth?

"Things would be different."

Chapter Twenty-one

It wasn't at all odd to hear one or more of her brothers shouting for her aid before Isobel even rose from her bed. Usually it was John or Lachlan calling to report some trouble Tamas had instigated, but this morn, things were different. It was Tamas's pitiful wails that brought Isobel to her feet and out the door. When she stepped into the hall, doors were opening on every side as her brothers, and even Tristan, rushed from their rooms to answer the call for help.

Seeing her youngest brother lying prone on the floor outside his room nearly stopped Isobel's heart, and her breath.

Patrick reached him first, swearing an oath when his bare foot stepped on one of the many thistles spreading outward beneath Tamas's fallen body.

"What in blazes...?" Patrick swore again, kicking the thorny blossoms out of his way.

Isobel followed, and when the path was made clear, she bent to Tamas and tried to help him stand.

"Nae!" he bellowed. "They're in my feet! Get them out, Bel! Get them out!"

Horrified, she scanned Tamas's small nightdress. From front to back, he was covered in thistles. Some were still intact, while others had fallen apart, their tiny needles sticking out of the thin wool that covered him.

"They are in my bed," Tamas cried. "And on the floor. When I put on my boots so as not to step on them, they were in there, too! And then..." He sniffed. "...And then I tripped over that and fell into the rest!" He pointed to a limp length of twine hanging from one end of his doorframe.

Isobel regarded the disassembled trap with fury coloring her cheeks. She looked directly at Tristan and found him standing by his door, a slight smile curling one end of his mouth. "How could ye?"

To her surprise and dismay, John stepped forward. "He—"

"He had it comin'," Tristan cut him off. "He'll be fine, though his feet might be sore fer a few days."

"MacGregor," Patrick growled at him, "the sitting room. Now." He continued to bark out orders as he followed Tristan to the stairs. "Cam, carry Tamas to Isobel's room—and Lachlan, get that grin off yer face and get to work feeding the horses. John, ye come with us."

John cast Isobel a worried look but did as he was told and marched, along with Tristan, down the stairs.

"Patrick will make him pay," Tamas whined while his brother carefully lifted him off the floor.

Behind them, Isobel clenched her hands and glared down the stairs. Was this Tristan's idea of making peace? Oh, she was a fool! He was nothing but a vengeful savage, just like his father.

"Cam," she said after he helped lay Tamas in her bed. "Go to the sitting room and tell me everything that is said. Make certain Patrick does not strike Mister MacGregor again. More bruises will only keep him here longer."

When he left, Isobel set about tending to her brother's hands and feet first. She removed as many spikelets as she could, but some were too small to take out with her fingers. She would need to apply a draw-out balm. The rest weren't so deeply embedded, caught up in his night-clothes rather than in his skin.

When she was done, she kissed Tamas's tear-stained face and promised to return with her healing ointment and something warm for his belly. She was about to leave the room when Lachlan's calls from outside stopped her dead in her tracks.

The Cunninghams were coming.

"Who?" Tristan bounded from his chair in the sitting room and raced Patrick to the door.

"Cunninghams," Patrick told him, drawing a dagger from his belt. "They have come to burn our crops. Cam, get John above stairs!"

Lachlan's shouts reverberated through the house as Patrick swung open the front door. The clatter of horses chilled the morning air and Tristan's heart along with it. In an instant, he was transported back in time, back to that same fear he had felt when his father opened the door to Campbell Keep. Only this time, Tristan wasn't about to let anyone die.

"Stay here!" he ordered Isobel when he saw her at the top of the stairs. He didn't wait to see if she obeyed, but ran to Patrick's side.

Six riders circled Lachlan in the field, laughing at the pitchfork he swiped at them. One of the men carried a lit torch that he poked at the boy like a sword, taunting him while Lachlan tried to protect himself from the flames.

Patrick charged with a roar that shook the ground beneath. He reached one of the riders closest to his brother and hauled him off his mount with one hand. He was quickly surrounded and whirled around for the next rider. The boot to his face stopped him momentarily.

Tristan didn't wait to see who hit Patrick next but sprinted toward the melee and leaped for the rider about to toss his torch into the harvest. Both men fell to the ground with a heavy thud, Tristan taking less of the blow on top. He didn't let his opponent catch his breath but rendered him unconscious with a swift, bone-crunching fist to the jaw. Springing back to his feet, he found Cameron beside him stomping out the torch and another Cunningham bearing down on him, his mount only inches away. With lightning-quick reflexes, Tristan pulled Cam away seconds before the rider would have trampled him where he stood. The bastard wheeled around for a second assault but fell from his mount with an arrow in his shoulder. Tristan turned to John and smiled as the boy nocked another arrow, ready to shoot again.

Lachlan shouted a warning to Patrick, and Tristan and John both swung around to see the remaining riders surrounding the Fergusson Chieftain with swords drawn.

So, they came for blood, did they? Tristan's heart went cold as one of them swung and nicked Patrick across the arm. His dagger fell from his hand. Cameron sprinted to his brother's side and deflected a second blow with the pitchfork Lachlan had wielded earlier.

John's arrow flew and caught Patrick's assailant in the thigh. The man didn't fall but bellowed an oath that spewed spit from his mouth. He set his black gaze on John and charged.

Tristan's heart thrashed in his chest, quickening his blood and tuning his senses like a fine violin. They had come for a fight, and Tristan was more than happy to oblige. Drawing in a deep inhalation of breath, he let himself revel in the thrill of besting this bastard who aimed to kill a boy. It didn't matter that he had no sword of his own. Tristan would take his opponent's. Unarmed, there would only be one moment in which to do it. He had to let the rider strike first.

With the horse almost upon them, he stepped into his path. The rider swung his massive blade. Tristan ducked in time to hear the sword sing above his head and around to the other side. Springing for the arrow jutting from the man's thigh, he yanked with all his strength and dragged his victim from his horse, snatching up his sword as he fell and bringing the hilt down with a smashing crunch to the nose. Lachlan made a quick end of him with a heavy rock to the head.

Tristan didn't look back but took off with his purloined sword toward Patrick and Cam, still fending off the two remaining intruders. A third, the man Patrick had first felled from his horse, crept up behind them, his blade flashing under the morning sun.

One of the boys behind Tristan screamed out to his brother, and Patrick spun around as the sword came down over his head. But only sparks rained down upon Patrick's shoulders as Tristan's blade parried the blow, inches from his face.

With a grunt that hauled the assailant away, Tristan

turned on him with a warning smile. "Are ye certain ye want to continue? I give ye the choice."

The man rushed at him, and the clash of their swords rang throughout the glen. With two swordsmen still threatening Patrick and Cam, there was no time to teach the bastard a lesson in losing gracefully. He'd have to go down quickly.

Smacking his blade against the other, Tristan advanced, feigned a swipe to the shoulder, reversed his direction, and swept the flat of his blade across the back of his opponent's knees. The man went down on his back and found Tristan's sword against his throat when he opened his eyes.

"Call off yer kin," Tristan warned him, close to his face. "Now!" he demanded, digging the sharp edge in deeper. "Or I vow I will sever yer head fer the others to bring back to yer Chief."

The man did not hesitate, but did as he was ordered, and the two remaining riders backed away.

"Get up." Tristan yanked him to his feet. He kept his sword pointed at the Cunningham's chest while he plucked the man's sword from his fingers and tossed it to Patrick. "Why are ye attackin' this family and destroyin' their land?"

"Who the hell is asking?" the man demanded, and quite boldly, too. Tristan poked him with the tip of his blade to remind him who was in charge.

"Tristan MacGregor is askin'. Do I need to ask again?"

"I am John Cunningham, son of—"

Tristan gave him another jab. "I didna' ask fer yer name. Did I, Cameron?" He flicked his gaze to Cam, then back to Cunningham when the lad nodded. "Ye see? But yer time fer answerin' is over." He raked his gaze over the other two Cunninghams on their horses. "All ye need to know now is that if ye come back here, ye willna' return to yer kin alive."

"Since when do the MacGregors stand with the Fergussons?" the one with the sword tip against his chest asked.

"Why, as of today." Tristan's smile was as cold as the metal he wielded. "I thought that was quite obvious. Ye may return in a few days to ask the rest of my kin when they arrive. I'm sure they will be eager to prove my words true."

All three Cunninghams shook their heads. "We will not return."

"Good!" Tristan's smile warmed on the man facing him down the end of his blade. "Is that yer word, John Cunningham?" When the man nodded, Tristan released him and swung his blade over his shoulder. "There is one more thing I want from ye before ye're free to gather yer fallen and go. When next ye see the lady of this manor, ye'll ask her fergiveness fer frightenin' her."

"They can ask her fer it now," Cameron muttered, looking past Tristan's shoulder.

Tristan turned and saw Isobel standing close by with John clutched under her arm and the wind fanning her long, loose hair. Her smile, when she met his gaze, began slowly and ended like an arrow shot into his guts at close range.

She didn't have to thank him. It was all there in her face, her eyes. As if he were some kind of hero who had stepped from the pages of a book, a champion come to win the day, and his lady with it.

She waited, never taking her eyes from his while John

Cunningham repented. When the Cunninghams were gone, she gave Patrick's wound a quick going over. "It is not serious. Come." She let her brother pass her and turned to look over her shoulder at Tristan again. "Let us go home."

✤

Chapter Twenty-two

*I*sobel hadn't forgotten what Tristan had done to Tamas, but what he did for the rest of them more than balanced his offense. He did not have to put his life at risk by fighting the Cunninghams. Why should he care if they set fire to Fergusson land, or if her brothers were threatened with the sword? She looked at him sitting across the table with her brothers, breaking fast with them, smiling with them. Despite all his artful charm, there was something utterly genuine about him. Could it be that he was what he claimed, a MacGregor who thought another way?

"Why did ye tell them yer kin were coming here?" Lachlan asked him while she bandaged Patrick's wounded arm.

"Because they are cowards," Tristan answered, pouring more honey into his bowl of oats. He licked his fingers, and as Isobel watched him, a thread of heat coursed down her spine. "When John Cunningham skirted my query about why his kin attacked yers, I suspected 'twas because the Cunninghams know there isna' much of a defense here. Making them believe that the MacGregors stand with ye will keep them away."

Clever, Isobel thought, finishing up with Patrick's wound. He had done the same for her at Whitehall with John Douglas and his drunken friend. "Why do all men need to be afraid in order to behave civilly?"

Tristan looked up at her, his topaz eyes gleaming with warmth. "No' all men are the same."

"Are ye afraid of nothing then?" Cameron asked, glancing up from his oats.

Tristan nodded. "Younger brothers."

Even Patrick couldn't help but smile at him. All her brothers at the table did. He drew others in with an innate knack for making them feel as if they had something in common with him. With her, they shared the loss of someone they both loved. With John Douglas, it was an appreciation for fine wine and women, and with her brothers, a fear of the smallest.

He was approachable and inviting, yet somehow he managed to remain remarkably aloof toward the people in his life. How many women had he slain with his beguiling smile and sorcerer's tongue before he left them with nothing more than his memory? He even planned on leaving his kin in the spring. Nothing touched him. He was a master of many, but no one would ever be master of him. Isobel believed it.

"I do not know how to thank ye fer standing by us today," Patrick said.

Isobel took her seat at the other end of the table, closing her eyes and praying as she went that they were not all being deceived by a skilled assassin disguised in a suit of armor.

"'Twas an unfair fight," Tristan replied, making light of what he'd done.

"Aye." John laughed, digging into his bowl. "After ye joined it, it was." He turned to Isobel, his eyes wide with admiration. "Ye did not see how he took the sword from Edward Cunningham's hand, Bel. Why, he..."

But she had seen. From a safe distance she had watched Tristan step directly in front of John, shielding him from a charging horse and a deadly blade. She saw him save Patrick and then fell Edward's brother, John, with a few quick clips of his sword and a flick of his wrist. She wondered if it was the cause for which he fought or his fluid grace and lightning-quick precision that had made him so breathtaking to watch...and his violent threat to sever John's head so terrifying to hear.

She blinked at John and then smiled, realizing that he was waiting for her to do so. "He is skilled, indeed. We owe him much."

John beamed. "Can he stay here with us?"

Her spoon paused at her lips. Oh, damnation, he did not just ask her that. She cut her gaze to Tristan, hoping he would say something witty and clever to swerve John from his question. When nothing came, she looked to Patrick, sincerely stunned when no immediate help came from that end either. "I do not think that would be wise, John," she told her brother, not knowing what else to say without insulting the man who'd just risked his life for them.

"Just because of his name?" John pressed, too young to remember what they had lost when their father was killed.

She was thankful when Patrick interceded. "Mister MacGregor has kin who await his return, John. They are likely alarmed by his absence, even now."

"In truth"—Tristan cleared his throat and set down his spoon—"they are no' likely alarmed at all. I travel often."

He did? Isobel listened with ears perked. Where did he go? Whom did he visit? Women, no doubt.

"If ye stay," Lachlan chimed in, as eager now, and as lost to Tristan's charms, as John. "Would ye teach me to use the sword?"

Tristan looked around the table at her brothers, stopping when he came to Patrick. "I was curious why none of ye had a sword with ye today. Do any of ye know how to wield one?"

"I do, a wee bit," Patrick told him. "My father preferred..." His voice trailed off as he realized what he was about to say. His eyes met Isobel's for a brief moment before veering away. "...the bow. I have always wanted to learn, but we have just enough to trade fer food. A sword is a luxury we cannot afford."

If Tristan gave any thought to their father's weapon of choice and the way the Earl of Argyll had died, it was not revealed in his wide grin. "Well, we have three now. Mine and the Cunninghams'." He turned to Isobel with a twinkle in his gold-brown eyes. "It shouldna' take me too long. A month at most, and then I shall be gone from yer sight."

Just as he was with everyone else. What did she care? She wanted him to leave, and the sooner the better. "Do what ye like, Mister MacGregor. I am certain ye will anyway."

With nothing more to say between them, she stood to her feet, picked up her bowl, and left the table.

Tristan made his way down the hall to Isobel's bedroom door, which was slightly ajar. From outside, he could hear her brothers beginning their day of work. He would join them soon, but first, he wanted to check on Tamas.

When he reached the door, he stopped, hearing Isobel's voice inside. She was talking softly about what had happened earlier with the Cunninghams. Tristan listened for a bit, enjoying the slightly breathless way she described him when he saved John. If he lived to be fifty, he would never forget the way she had smiled at him when it was over. But all too soon the shadows of doubt and mistrust returned to her eyes, and by the time they finished breaking fast, she was back to hating him.

He pushed open the door and smiled when both Isobel and Tamas went startled at his appearance.

"Good day, Tamas," he said, stepping inside. "How d'ye fare?"

The boy glared at him and raised his bandaged feet off the bed to show him. "First chance I get, I am going to show ye."

"Tamas!" Isobel scolded.

"Then I look forward to the day when ye're well and we can pick up where we left off." The devilish quirk of Tristan's mouth produced a troubled look on the boy's face. "Miss Fergusson," he said, turning to her, "might I have a word with ye alone?"

The same look passed over Isobel's features, but she nodded and followed him to the door. "As soon as he's done with the morning's work," she said to Tamas on her way out, "Patrick will carry ye back to yer clean bed." She shut the door behind her and turned her iciest look on Tristan.

"I will not have ye threatening to do him harm."

"I intend to speak with ye and Patrick aboot that later. This is aboot us."

"Us?" She blinked and lifted her hand to her chest as if to hold up her resolve against the force coming at her.

"Aye." He moved closer to her. She took a step back, deeper into the afternoon shadows. "Tell me what I must do to gain yer favor."

"What would ye do with it if I gave it to ye?"

"I would show ye who I am. The man I've been hidin' from everyone else."

Her breath stalled against his chin as he bent his face closer to hers. He knew she was betrothed. How could he find what he'd lost by dishonoring the only woman who saw in him a spark of who he had once wanted to be? But he didn't want to think of that now. He couldn't, not when her lips were so close to his, driving him mad with the need to kiss her. "Ye thrill me with yer saucy mouth and swingin' hips, but 'tis yer will to hate me that I admire, fer it proves that yer heart is loyal to yer kin."

"What of yer heart?" she asked softly, turning her face away. "Is it loyal to yer kin, as well?"

How should he answer? Would it damn him in her eyes either way? He told her the truth. "It should be, I know, but my loyalty to my beliefs comes first."

"And what are yer beliefs?"

He touched his fingers to her jaw and gently urged her gaze back to him, her mouth close to his. "Tell me that ye want me to stay fer a while longer..." His breath mixed with hers as his fingers swept over the throbbing pulse beat at her throat and then curled around her nape. "...and I promise to tell them to ye."

He took her mouth with excruciating tenderness, a commendable feat when what he really wanted to do was hold her against the wall with the strength of his kiss while he untied his breeches. Closing his other arm around her waist, he hauled her against him, teasing her lips apart with shorter, hungrier kisses. As his tongue plunged into her, she looped her arms around his neck and answered his fervor with the same. He went hard at the feel of her soft body yielding to his and was glad that more than a flimsy yard of plaid contained him. He wanted more than a victory with her. Still, her mouth was so hot, her kisses so sweetly wanton that before he could stop himself he pressed his hips to hers and surged his full, thick length against her warmth.

She gasped into his mouth and his control nearly snapped. But he wouldn't take her as if this were some casual tryst. She was more than that. So much more.

With more strength than he'd ever been called to summon before, he broke their kiss and withdrew.

"Fergive me."

She fell against the wall, out of breath and sapped of strength. "That is," she said, bringing the backs of her fingers to her flushed cheeks, "the third time ye have kissed me and apologized afterward."

The languid veil over her eyes tempted him to carry her to his bed, make slow, ravenous love to her, and then watch her fall asleep in his arms.

He smiled at her, willing himself to do the right thing, and stepped away. "I was correct aboot ye, Isobel. Ye're already makin' me a better man."

Chapter Twenty-three

The midday sun robbed what was left of the spring chill and warmed Isobel's skin as she knelt in her garden. She surveyed the contents of the basket at her side, trying to decide what else she would need for her salad. Celery herb, crowberry, parsley, sweet violet...stolen kisses. She mopped her forehead with the back of her palm and tried to think of anything else but the feel of Tristan's arms around her, the salacious strokes of his tongue marauding her mouth, the rigid measure of his arousal against her...She coughed into her hand and looked around, mortified by her thoughts. Her eyes found him instantly. He stood beside Patrick, his blade outstretched before him while he gave her brothers their first lesson in sword fighting. How could she have let him kiss her so passionately yet again? Unable to look away, she let her gaze absorb the powerful play of muscle beneath his snug breeches as he lunged forward at an unseen opponent, the vigor of his thrust as he jabbed the air with his blade. She marveled at his speed and at his patience when John dropped his heavy sword twice. How easily he could turn his weapon on them all, cut them to bits because of the uncle they'd taken from him—the uncle who had taught him tales of another age when men of honor were not so rare. But instead he chose to teach them how to defend themselves. Oh, how could she have resisted him? How could any woman resist him? God help her, she was doomed.

Just when she thought she couldn't get any more pitiful, he looked up from his instruction and winked at her, coaxing a fresh flush from her cheeks. She looked away, cursing her foolish heart. Did she truly believe that someone like him would take interest in her? She lifted a self-conscious hand to her hair. She barely had time to plait it properly in the mornings—and the color didn't please her either. What man would not prefer the gentle radiance of flaxen or the rich gloss of ebony to the hues of autumn pumpkins? She rubbed two fingers down her nose. Why could she not have Patrick or Alex's clear complexion, free of freckles? She looked down at her dirt-stained hands, realizing, even as her blasted eyes searched him out again, that she had smudged soil over her already dotted face.

He was there, tossing back his mane of sun-streaked hair, laughing with Lachlan as if he'd been here all their lives. Isobel did not blink while she watched him. Oh, why did he have to be a MacGregor? If she could truly win his fickle heart, she would be content to bask in his kisses until the end of her days. But even if he meant what he told her, even if there was a part of him that no one else knew, a part he wanted to show only her, Patrick and the MacGregors would never allow anything between them.

Still, she could not help but wonder, while he rubbed

his sore shoulder, who was the man he claimed to hide from others. It didn't matter, she thought, rising to her feet. There was hay to bale, and a secret that needed to remain hidden.

After supper, Isobel and her brothers retired to the sitting room and invited Tristan to come with them. They needed to discuss what he had done to Tamas and make certain that nothing like it occurred again while he remained here.

Isobel could tell, by the way Patrick avoided the issue for a solid hour, that he did not want to scold Tristan after what he had done for them. After all, Tamas was not seriously hurt. Still, something had to be said. Tristan had to understand that Tamas was just a babe.

When she told him so, her patience with Patrick at an end, she was stunned to find her brother on the opposite side of the camp.

"Tamas is not a babe anymore, Bel."

"Patrick!" She gaped at him. "He is one and ten!"

"Old enough to know right from wrong." Cameron captured Lachlan's knight and met her gaze from across the room.

"I think he deserved thistles in his bed." John smiled up at Tristan from the floor, where he lounged comfortably before the fire.

Isobel caught the covert wink Tristan threw him before her little brother turned to her. So then, they *were* in on this trick together. She never knew John to possess a vengeful streak. He had never fought back against Tamas. Though John was two years older, Tamas could outrun him, outwit him, and outfight him.

"And not just fer what he has done to Tristan," he told

her now, speaking up against Tamas for the first time. "But fer what he has done to Lachlan and me."

"John, darling, ye know yer brother loves ye." She looked up at Tristan. "He is a bit wild, that is all. I am verra firm with him, but I will not take a stick to him as if he were a stubborn horse."

"I would be quite disappointed if ye did," Tristan agreed with her, then turned to Patrick. "May I speak openly?" When her brother nodded, he continued. "Tamas is young, but he's headed toward a dangerous path. If he's to grow into a fair and honorable man, he needs to learn humility. A wee taste of what he inflicts on others will teach him compassion."

"Tamas is compassionate," Isobel defended, but when she actually thought about it, she couldn't remember a time when he had been.

"How many times have I had to stop the neighboring farmers from shooting him, Isobel?" Patrick asked her. "MacGregor is correct. Will we wait to discipline him until after he has caused permanent injury to John or Lachlan?"

"Of course not, but—"

"D'ye want to see him hanged someday fer killin' someone?" Tristan's voice overrode hers. "Mayhap be killed himself when he picks a fight with the wrong person?"

She stopped and closed her eyes at his words. Oh, just the thought of it… "No," she said quietly. "But I…"

"Ye love him," he finished for her, and smiled when she looked at him. "I know."

Oh, it was a lethal weapon he possessed. That smile, always hovering about his mouth and brightening his eyes with confidence and optimism, as if he knew things would always work in his favor. Was it mad that she found it so soothing despite who he was? Despite what he might do if he ever discovered who had truly killed his uncle? She had no guard against him. No matter how furious he made her or how much she feared him, his quicksilver grin relaxed her defenses. "What are ye proposing?"

"That ye trust me."

Ah, here it was. His victory. Is this not what he had wanted from the beginning? Her friendship, so that he could win her trust?

"I've noe malice in my heart fer the lad," he continued earnestly, the warm ocher hues of his eyes deepening to rich, smoky brown. "No' even when he set hornets loose upon me did I want to cause him serious injury. He's a boy in need of a firmer hand than yer good brother Patrick has time to provide at present."

Isobel didn't find it odd that her brother did not voice any objection. How could he, when Tristan had only spoken what they already knew was true, but found difficult to admit? Sweetening the truth with just a dash of honey to help it go down was all a part of his winning appeal. Isobel didn't want to be won. She did not want to trust him and then fall victim to a cruel heart hidden by an enticing smile. *That* error would cost too much.

"Ye ask too much of me, Tristan. Of us," she corrected, looking around at her brothers. "How can we trust a man we do not know?"

"We know he is resilient," Lachlan interjected, smiling at Tristan and losing his bishop. "He proved that after two arrows, a rock, and a clay pot."

"Clay pot?" Tristan asked, bringing his hand to the top of his head, as if he were just remembering.

"He is more patient than I would be if someone else's

brother did half the things to me that Tamas has done to him," Cam joined in, in a quiet tone, and then explained to Lachlan where his move had gone wrong.

"And lest we forget," Tristan told them all, as if they could ever forget such a thing, "I was raised high in the mountains with the Devil MacGregor fer my father. It has made my mettle sturdy enough to manage whatever Tamas throws at me."

"Speaking of whatever Tamas throws at ye"—once again, it was Cameron who spoke, looking up briefly from beneath his shield of dark lashes—"one of us should collect his sling."

Tristan grinned and then reached into a pocket in his breeches and held up Tamas's prized weapon. "I already have it."

Her brothers laughed, even Cam, and watching them made Isobel smile, too, despite the growing fear that Tristan MacGregor had done what he said he would do.

He had won her brothers. All except one.

.

The next few days proved to be as taxing for Isobel as they were for poor Tamas. Aye, her youngest brother was confined to a bed that had mysteriously become home to a family of field mice. It was true that his small feet were still too sore to run from the menagerie of terrors Tristan had rained down upon him. It tore her heart to shreds knowing the helpless babe suffered under their eldest brother's approval, but the screaming and crashing of furniture above her head was seriously beginning to rile her.

At night, when Tristan dined with them after a day of torturing Tamas and training the rest of her brothers to fight, she slammed his food down in front of him and ate,

sharing with him neither a look nor a word. She didn't
like Tristan's Highland tactics, whether they were good
for Tamas or not. Tamas was her responsibility. All her
brothers were, and she wasn't ready to give that up, especially not to a MacGregor. She barely listened to him during the family's nightly chats in the sitting room—with
Tristan usually doing most of the talking.

Besides the Kennedys, they had few visitors from
whom to hear tales they hadn't already heard at least a
dozen times before. It was only natural for the boys to be
beguiled by this rogue's adventures. He'd led a...frolic-
some life. Aye, that was the best way to describe it. Finding himself in dangerous circumstances more times than
Isobel cared to count while she sewed—and mostly due
to women—he'd always escaped unscathed. That did not
mean he hadn't been shot with an arrow, stabbed with a
dagger, and hit with a fist a time or two, but as the carefree timbre of Tristan's voice attested while he captivated
his audience, his good humor recovered quickly, at least
until the next time he found himself staring down the end
of someone's sword.

"What did ye do as a boy?" John asked him one night
while he warmed his feet beside the crackling hearth
fire.

Isobel looked up from her cup of mead when soon the
crackle was all she heard. They all waited for Tristan to
answer, but he said nothing, his gaze fixed on a place they
could not see.

"Did ye get into much trouble then, too?" John
pressed, forcing Tristan back to them, his smile restored.

"Hardly any. I was more like ye than like Tamas.
Besides, my mother wouldna' tolerate us swingin'
punches the way many of my cousins do."

"What did ye do then?" Patrick asked, putting more wood on the fire.

"I read books and practiced my—"

"Ye can read then?" John asked, wide-eyed. When Tristan nodded, he inched closer to him. "What kinds of books did ye read?"

Isobel watched Tristan shift in his chair, looking uncomfortable for the first time since he had taken his usual place by the fire. "Mostly books written by Monmouth, Chaucer, Sir Thomas Malory."

John cast him a befuddled look. "What did they write about?"

"Knights," Tristan said quietly. He lifted his glance to Isobel and let it linger long enough for her to miss his attention when he returned his warm smile to John. "They wrote about chivalric behavior, courtly love, quests fer honor."

"Tell us one," John pleaded, then yawned, sprawled out in his chair.

With only a hint of reluctance, he told them a story called "The Knight's Tale," as he remembered it— a tale of two champions who were the embodiment of the chivalric principles of their time. John laughed at the pretty words Tristan recited about the fair maiden Emelye, whose favor the two knights sought to win. Isobel listened, captivated by the passion in his voice, the gleam in his eyes when he spoke of honor. She wondered how he could hold such values so close to his heart as a child and still have grown to manhood breaking the hearts of so many women. What part of him was real?

"Off to bed with ye now, lads," Patrick ordered gently an hour later, when Tristan's tale was over. "'Tis late."

"But just—"

"John," Patrick said without looking up from his chess game with Cameron.

Immediately John and Lachlan picked up their boots and marched off to bed, kissing Isobel on their way out.

The sitting room grew as quiet as a town plagued by the death fever. Isobel could feel Tristan's eyes on her. He was going to say something to her, and she would have to answer. She was still angry with him about Tamas, and she wanted to stay that way. It was safer for her heart. She couldn't let herself fall for him when she'd hated his name for so long, when she didn't know which of the two men he really was. The rogue or the hero.

"Iso—"

She vaulted to her feet, pricking her finger on her sewing needle. "I am going to bed also. Good night."

"Allow me to escort ye to yer room, then," Tristan had the boldness to say.

Isobel stopped, her back to him, her shoulders stiffening when he passed her and reached for the door. Oh, but he was a dauntless, determined fool. After a shocking moment passed without a single utterance from either of her brothers, she fisted her hands and stormed for the door.

"Ye know I do not wish to speak to ye," she paused to fire at him the instant they were alone in the hall.

"Aye, ye've made that clear."

"Not clear enough, it seems." She hiked her skirts up over her ankles to stay ahead of him on her way to the stairs.

"Ye're angry with me because of Tamas," he said, keeping pace beside her.

"Why ever would I be? Oh, wait, mayhap it was the ants ye put in his bed, or the mice, or the spiders. Or I could want to take out yer eye because of the whitewash ye smeared on yer face late at night so ye could frighten him witless when he opened his eyes, believing the angel of death stood at his bedside."

"He thinks he is fearless."

Isobel stopped to glare at him while he smiled at the recollection. "And ye are determined to prove to him that he is not. Ye said ye were different from yer kin, but all I see is a man taking revenge on a child."

She hoped to see some guilt in his eyes, perhaps a glimmer of doubt about his tactics, but he remained untouched and coolly replied, "Then close yer eyes and allow me to save his life before ye have another Alex on yer hands."

She spun on her heel, not wanting to hear his logic, and reached for the banister. His arm curling around her waist stopped her. His warm breath against her nape sapped her of her anger and sent titillating fissures to the pit of her belly. He had told her that he admired her will to hate him, but she did not hate him. When had she stopped? She wasn't even truly angry with him about his treatment of Tamas. She knew now, locked in his arms, that she had stayed away from him because she was afraid of what he had the power to make her do...if she allowed it.

"When will ye begin to trust me, Isobel?"

"Never."

He turned her in his arms, keeping her body pressed close to his. She arched her back, afraid of his closeness and how it made her want to cast her caution to the four winds. He followed, bending over her, his eyes searching hers with a desperation that tore her defenses to shreds and made her blood burn.

"Verra well then, but shun me nae more. I would rather hear ye revile me all day long than pretend I dinna' exist."

Dear God, was it her own heart or his thrashing against her chest? How could a savage speak so eloquently and with such humility? How could he mean her harm when he'd protected her from every threat beginning with Alex at Whitehall? He wasn't like his kin. He couldn't be.

When he lowered his face to hers, Isobel closed her eyes, giving in to the exhilarating memory of his kisses.

He traced his lips over the hollow of her throat, inhaling her as intimately as any lover had the right to do. She trembled in his arms as her defenses fell away and her mouth sought his with a desperate need of her own. With one hand splayed across the small of her back and the other cradling her nape, he licked his way up her throat. Was this her writhing in a MacGregor's arms? She didn't care. She cupped his face in her hands, tunneled her fingers through his hair, tugging him closer. Their lips collided with a mutual moan of delight. Isobel opened to his plunging tongue and surprised him with a lick of her own. She might doubt many things about him, but his skill at kissing was not one of them.

Just when she decided to allow herself to fully enjoy this moment, the door to the sitting room opened. She leaped away from Tristan's embrace, but he snatched her hand and pulled her into the dark kitchen.

They listened, their hearts beating hard against each other's chest, while Patrick and Cameron spoke softly to each other on their way up the stairs.

"Walk with me ootside." Tristan's breath fell over her cheek in the shadows even before her brothers disappeared.

She shook her head, too aware of the thrill he presented every time they were together not to be wary of it.

"I . . . I am betrothed." Oh, she hated speaking it aloud. "We should not be alone."

"We're alone right now." The laughter in his voice as he pulled her toward the front door tempted her to follow wherever he led her. "Ye have my vow to be a perfect gentleman."

Did she dare trust him, even in this small thing? She smiled and followed him out of the house.

Chapter Twenty-four

They walked together beneath the gentle radiance of the full moon. Neither of them spoke for a little while, stilled by the beauty of the earth and the heavens bathed in silver, and the awkward comfort of their entwined fingers.

Tristan's gaze slid to Isobel beside him. He missed arguing with her, smiling at her and seeing her smile back. She had put him through hell these last few days, and he understood why, but that hadn't made her disregard any easier to bear. She wasn't angry with him anymore though, about Tamas, or about his kissing her again. Hell, she'd kissed him back this time, and he would be damned if her mouth wasn't just as hungry for him as his was for her. Looking at her, he wondered if he would be damned anyway for touching her, for pulling those delightful little groans from her mouth that gave him hope of finally winning her favor. He didn't intend to remain here with her. He was fond of her, more so than any lass before her. He wanted to prove to her that he was not the barbarian she had called him and his kin in

England. He wanted to repair the damage he'd caused in her life and mayhap regain some honor in his. He didn't want to love her. He didn't know if he even could. What purpose would it serve to love a lass who belonged to another? If he loved her, losing her would tear away what remained of his heart.

But how was he going to keep his word and not touch her when the sight of her, the taste of her drove him mad with desire for more?

"Ye never told me if the uncle who taught ye his favored tales was Robert Campbell."

Tristan blinked his gaze away from her when she looked at him, unprepared for the topic she presented. "Aye, 'twas him."

"I ask ye," she went on softly, "because ye said ye would show me who ye are and I want to know. I need to know. Was it his stories ye loved so much, or him?"

He'd asked her to trust him. First, he knew he must trust her.

"He was the men in his stories, Isobel. He lived his life the way every man should."

She closed her eyes, shielding him from the pain and regret he saw there. "Then I am sorry he is gone from this world."

He smiled at her moonlit face. "As am I."

"I do not wish to bring him up and cause ye sorrow."

He stopped and, turning to her, he lifted his fingers to a bronze tendril sweeping across her cheek in the cool night air. She opened her eyes again and looked into his.

"His memory doesna' cause me sorrow. I have hardly spoken of him to anyone in many years, and that has caused me greater pain."

Her gaze on him softened and suspended his breath. "I

would like to hear of him, then," she told him, covering his hand with hers.

"Verra well," he replied, turning his hand around hers and bringing it to his lips. "I shall tell ye." Curling his fingers through hers, he let their hands drop between them as they began walking again. "I dinna' know why he favored me. My brother Rob carries his name, not I. Mayhap 'twas because he wanted me to live up to the name I had been given." He smiled softly to himself, surprised at how easily the words spilled off his tongue. "He invited me to spend my summer months with him and his wife at Campbell Keep, and there he trained me to be like him. That became my home."

"He became a father to ye," she said, recalling the words he'd first used to describe the earl to her. "Was yer true father so terrible, then?"

Tristan knew she probably didn't want to hear anything good about the man who had killed her father, but he wanted her to understand that he was not spawned from some bloodthirsty monster who killed without provocation. "My faither was no' terrible at all. He never treated any of his bairns poorly. He is simply cut from another mold. He, along with the rest of my kin, had to fight in order to protect what was rightfully theirs. My faither became what was necessary to keep his name alive."

She was quiet for a time while they walked together toward the hills and the tree line beyond, and then, as if she knew exactly who he was, she turned to him and asked, "How did a gallant little boy fit in with men who knew only battle and bloodshed?"

"I never belonged in Camlochlin," Tristan admitted quietly. "And after my uncle died it felt like there was nae more place fer me in the world. After he died, I stopped carin' if I ever found my place again."

"But why?"

"Because I loved him and what he taught me more than anything I have ever loved in my life..."

...There are many moments in a man's life when the choices he makes will decide his destiny.

"...And in a moment of anger, an instant of allowin' my prideful MacGregor blood to rule me, I destroyed it all. So I turned my back on my uncle's code and on my faither's."

When they came to the trees, she stopped and turned to him. "How did ye destroy it?"

He studied the shape of her, lithe and very feminine against a backdrop of stars. His body trembled for an instant, racked with desire to sweep her into his arms, tell her everything she wanted to know, and then kiss her until she believed him. He didn't want to fall in love with her, but any man who didn't was a fool.

"I fought with Alex."

Tears spilled down her face, and through the haze of milky moonlight her eyes shone like twin seas. He wanted to plunge deep inside them, cleanse himself in the cool spring of renewal only she could offer. "Ye blame yerself fer his death then? Tristan, tell me please if ye have come here to avenge it. I understand now what he meant to ye..."

His heart wrenched at the fear in her voice. He lifted his hand to cleanse her of her tears. When she pulled away, he moved toward her, unable to keep away another instant.

"Isobel, 'tis because of what he meant to me that I didna' avenge him."

"I am sorry my father took him from ye. He...he had been drinking that night. I did not know what he meant to do. I was a child. We all were."

She didn't want him to blame himself, and for now, he would do as she asked. "Aye, we were innocent children." He cupped her face in his hands and dipped his mouth to hers.

"Yes," she breathed across his lips.

She closed her eyes and parted her lips, smashing to bits his resolve to remain gallant. Slipping one hand behind her thick tresses and the other down her back, he gathered her in and captured her sweet breath with a kiss.

They met at the tree line, beneath the stars and the slow-waning moon, every night for a full week. They spoke about their pasts and the dreams that had pushed them to go on during their most difficult days. Isobel told him her worst fears and her deepest hopes for her brothers' futures—things she had never shared with a single soul before him, not even Patrick. Of course, she did not tell him everything, but during their nightly visits she began to trust that his coming to her home had nothing to do with his uncle. At least not in the way she had feared.

After their first walk together had ended in Tamas's room, she had even completely forgiven Tristan for his treatment of the youngest Fergusson.

He'd taken her to the edge of Tamas's bed, where they sat together waiting for the dawn. She listened in silence while he admitted to her brother that he had taken Tamas's missing sling, and that in order for Tamas to regain it, he would have to earn it. She remained as still as Tristan when her brother began to wail at her, and then when he flung his small feet over the side of the bed. Tristan had reached him first when he stumbled on his weakened legs, and she watched, her wary heart softening, while he took his time helping Tamas walk around the room.

She was certain that at least some of her brothers were aware of her and Tristan's secret meetings, but none of them objected, despite her being betrothed. Like her, they seemed to have forgotten all about Andrew Kennedy.

Until, as unexpectedly as a summer rain, he and Annie arrived at their door.

Isobel could have smashed her heaviest pot over Patrick's head when she saw them stepping into her dining room. The moment Andrew's eyes met hers, she knew she could never marry him. He smiled at her, glad enough to see her there in the kitchen doorway, but his eyes lacked the luster and the spark that Tristan's possessed when he entered a room and saw her in it.

"I hope we are not imposing," Andrew said, more to Patrick than to her.

"Do not fret, Andrew," Isobel said, wiping her hands on her apron. "We will all simply eat less so that ye can dine with us."

"Ye see?" Annie slapped her brother's shoulder. "I told ye it was poor manners to arrive uninvited and unannounced."

"The reason we did," Andrew hastily explained, "is that auld Edward the Tanner came by our land two days ago and told us that he met a man on the road a while back who asked him where to find the Fergussons. I grew concerned. Tanner said he was a Highlander."

"Yes, he"—Patrick began, but then stopped again when Tristan appeared in the doorway—"is most certainly a

Highlander. Tristan, this is Andrew Kennedy, Isobel's betrothed, and his sister, Annie."

"Isobel's betrothed!" The resounding crunch of Tristan's teeth biting into his apple behind her made Isobel cringe. "How fortunate fer ye."

Andrew nodded and reached out his hand as if she were in some terrible danger from which he meant to deliver her. Annie said nothing. She simply gaped at Tristan until Isobel wanted to slap her.

"Andrew." Isobel narrowed her eyes on him. "Ye were concerned fer our safety, so ye brought yer sister along?"

"Och, but she's a clever, intuitive wee wife to be, is she no', Kennedy?" Tristan said proudly and then stepped around her when he spotted Tamas making his slow way down the stairs from his room. "God smiles doun upon ye."

Annie's large, dreamy eyes followed him, dipping to his clingy breeches as he passed her. "He does not look like a Highlander," she said with a little sigh. Isobel cursed his plaid and the fact that he rarely wore it, preferring to don his more English attire.

Andrew's cool gaze lingered on him as well. "Should I have brought a troop of my kinsmen for one man?"

"If he meant to harm us," John pointed out, already seated in the chair at the table. "It would not have been enough."

"Oh?" Andrew arched a doubtful brow while he studied Tristan helping Tamas down the last step. "And exactly what kind of threat would he pose without a sword at his belt?"

Oh, Lord. Isobel shook her head at the ceiling and smacked her thigh. It was going to be a difficult evening. Andrew was clearly riled by Tristan's presence. Then again, what man wouldn't feel inferior in the same room with him? And while Tristan's amicable smile never wavered, she knew him enough to know that it was not genuine. Before another challenge was offered that Tristan might be tempted to answer, she shooed Andrew to the table.

"Now that ye are here, why do ye not have a seat and share a word with Patrick." Isobel turned to Annie next. "Annie, would ye go outside and see if Cameron and Lachlan have returned from hunting?"

"Who?" Annie smiled at Tristan when he lifted Tamas over his seat and set him down gently.

"What happened to him?" Andrew asked, pointing to Tamas.

"Nothing," Isobel snapped, glaring at Annie. "He is perfectly capable of gaining his own chair."

"My feet are still sore, Bel." Her youngest brother scowled at her, then turned to their guests. "Tristan put thistles in my boots."

Andrew's eyes opened wide on Patrick and then grew dark on Tristan.

"Ye had it coming," John defended.

"And ye have a rock coming to yer—" Tamas's threat came to an abrupt halt when Tristan leaned down and whispered something into his ear.

Isobel inhaled a deep breath and prayed for patience when Annie smiled at Tristan's backside. They just had to get through this night and Andrew would be gone. She spared Patrick one last scathing look for putting her in this predicament by promising her to Andrew. She still didn't know how she was going to get out of it, but she would try not to think of it tonight. "John, come help me serve supper."

"Let me." Tristan offered her a bright grin and, before she or anyone else could object, sauntered past her into the kitchen.

"Tell me, Isobel, I beg ye," he said, reaching for the bowls on the shelf above his head, "ye're not honestly considerin' marryin' that hairy simpleton."

"Lower yer voice," she warned, taking a bowl from his hand. "He already does not like ye."

"Pity." Tristan's smile was rapier thin. "I was so lookin' forward to a long, lastin' friendship with him. Mayhap I could wed his sister and we could raise our bairns together."

Isobel paused at the trivet and offered him a murderous glare.

"Dinna' look at me like that," he said brusquely. "The prospect of me weddin' her is as ridiculous as ye marryin' her brother."

"What would ye have me do, Tristan?" She filled the bowl with rabbit stew, handed it back to him, and snatched another from his fingers. "Patrick is Chieftain. He is trying to do what is best fer me."

"Andrew Kennedy is no' best fer ye," he argued, watching her fill the next bowl.

"Who is, then?" When he remained silent, she had the urge to dump someone's supper over his head. "At least I will know that Andrew's heart will be true to me."

She marched out of the kitchen and back into the dining room with Tristan hot on her heels. They both slammed the bowls they carried onto the table, too busy glaring at each other to notice Patrick and Andrew glaring at them.

"Are ye sayin' my heart would no' be true to ye?" Tristan demanded the moment they returned to the kitchen.

"Yer heart is not meant to love, but to conquer." She sashayed past him on her way to the rest of the bowls. "I am certain any lady in Whitehall Palace or in Skye would agree with me."

His fingers closing tightly around her wrist stopped her. When he pulled her around to face him, his eyes on her were hard and a bit hurt.

"Do ye deny it?" She prayed that he would. She prayed for some of his pretty words to adorn his proclamation of love for her. When none came, she blinked back the sting of tears behind her eyes. She was a fool for allowing herself to believe he could come to care for her. "Let me go."

He released her with a pained smile and turned on his heel to leave. He came face to face with Patrick standing at the doorway.

"Tristan," her brother said quietly, looking from her glistening eyes to Tristan's dark ones. "She belongs to Andrew. I should not have allowed this thing between ye."

"There is nothing between us," Isobel interjected.

Patrick held up his palm to quiet her and returned his gaze to Tristan. "I gave him my word, which he reminds me of even now. Would ye have me go back on it?"

"Nae." Tristan shook his head, stepping around him. "I wouldna' ask that of ye."

❊

Chapter Twenty-five

Isobel murmured an oath under her breath as she toted two buckets of goat milk from the barn to the house. She squinted against the glare of the afternoon sun and swore silently again at Andrew leaning against the front of the house, polishing his sword. Her pounding head didn't improve her sour mood, nor did the memory of Andrew's insisting, after he arrived two nights ago, that he and Annie should remain at the manor house for a few more days.

Of course, Tristan had everything to do with Andrew's wanting to stay. For two days she'd had to put up with Andrew following her everywhere she went, clinging to her arm the moment Tristan entered the same room. Andrew had always been kind to her, but lately he was sickeningly sweet, doting on her every word, complimenting her cooking before he even shoved his spoon into his mouth.

Isobel truly didn't understand why her unwanted betrothed was behaving so possessively. Tristan had barely spoken to her since his little talk with Patrick in the kitchen. She hardly saw him at all. He spent every daylight hour with her brothers, practicing with them behind the house, or going out of his way to find some chore to do that would keep him away from her. He'd even given up his nightly talks in the sitting room, much to her younger brothers' disappointment. His voluntary absence was driving her mad. Did he truly not care one whit about her? She had begun to believe he did, that she meant a little more to him than his need to pay for a tragedy that was not his fault, but he showed no signs of jealousy or anger. He simply stopped paying any attention to her. It was worse for her than finding out he was a MacGregor.

"Do ye need help with those buckets, m'dear?"

Isobel scowled at Andrew. Did she need help? Did the milk sloshing all over her shoes not give him a clue? "No, but ye could open the door, if it is not too much of a bother."

Why the hell was he polishing his sword anyway? Tristan hadn't threatened him. He did smile at him, though, but that was only after Andrew had insulted him upon learning who their Highlander was. She had to marvel at Tristan's ability to remain unfazed—untouched.

From the kitchen where she poured the milk into jugs, she heard the front door slam shut.

"I could help ye plant," Annie's breathless voice pleaded. "I have seen Isobel do it. I know how."

"I dinna' need help, but ye have my thanks fer yer offer."

Isobel turned in time to see Tristan heading straight for her. He met her gaze and then looked away.

"Ye see, lass? I told ye she was carryin' the milk in by herself. If ye want to lend yer aid, lend it to Isobel." Without another word or a glance in her direction, he turned and left the kitchen.

Isobel watched his departure. He'd come to her rescue again. Or at least, had tried to. But how had he seen her working from the fields? She didn't care how. She wanted to go after him. She wanted to talk to him, walk with him, see him smile at her again, feel his mouth on hers.

"He is positively glorious," Annie sighed.

Isobel really couldn't blame the girl for following him around like a puppy begging for the bone in her master's fingers. With a cloth tied around his head to hold back his shoulder-length hair, his damp shirt clinging to his corded torso, and snug breeches that boasted more than just muscular thighs, Tristan could make the most pious nun feel lewd and lusty.

"Really, Annie, ye know that Cameron fancies ye," Isobel snapped at her. "It is cruel of ye to flaunt yer attraction to Tristan so openly."

"In truth, I do not know what Cameron thinks of me," Annie pouted. "He is so quiet all the time."

"Well, now I have told ye, so please stop hounding Tristan."

Annie's mouth curled into a smile as impish as Tamas's. "Why, Isobel, if I did not know any better I would think ye fancied Tristan fer yerself."

"Do not be absurd." Isobel laughed, and then quickly turned back to her milk.

"I thought mayhap he fancied ye as well," Annie went on mercilessly. "Whenever ye are about, he stops what he is doing and looks after ye. I asked him if he meant to steal ye from Andrew."

"And his reply?" Isobel asked and silently cursed her hands for trembling.

"He assured me that he is not a thief."

So that was it? Isobel wiped her hands on her apron

and closed her eyes. Why did his reply make her feel as if she'd just been stabbed in the heart with his sword? Because she cared for him, God help her. She had let him seduce her just as he'd done with all the other women he played with and then left. He would leave her the same way. In the beginning she had wanted him to go, but not anymore. Now, she couldn't imagine her days not filled with his vibrant smiles, or her nights robbed of his passionate kisses. But he didn't love her. He was willing to hand her over to Andrew without so much as a raised eyebrow. She wanted to hate him for it.

Tristan did not go to the sitting room after supper that night, and neither did Isobel. She went to bed, promising herself, as she laid her head on her pillow, that she would never let herself fall in love with a man who did not love her in return.

She didn't think Andrew loved her, but at least he was willing to fight for her.

Chapter Twenty-six

*T*ristan had never met a man he wanted to kill until he met Andrew Kennedy.

After what had happened with Alex when they were lads, Tristan had prided himself on his mild temper. He'd learned how to strengthen his hide against the emotions that raged within the hearts of other men. He'd refused to let envy corrode his soul when his brothers succeeded at drawing praise from their father's lips where he had failed. He never succumbed outwardly to the wrath at losing his uncle or to the pain and loneliness that came soon after and never truly left. He did not hide his emotions; he simply mastered them.

But his resolve to honor Patrick's promise to let Isobel wed Kennedy was quickly deteriorating.

If it weren't for young Annie constantly under his feet, he would have dragged Isobel to the hills, the barn, anywhere they could have a few moments alone. He tried, ah, hell, how he tried to do the right thing and respect Patrick's wishes, but after three days of biting his tongue and keeping his hands at his sides rather than around

Kennedy's throat, he feared he might never find the honor he sought.

The worst part of it all was that he didn't care. He could not let Isobel marry Andrew. The thought of losing her sparked a fear and a rage in him he never wanted to let loose. He had to speak to her alone and tell her that Andrew was not good enough for her. No mortal man was, but Tristan wanted to try.

He knew he should have thought out his course of action more thoroughly, but it was not in his nature to be cautious. He waited until after supper, when they all headed for the sitting room with warm mead in hand, and snatching Isobel's arm, drew her back into the hall.

"Come with me to the hills. I wish to speak to ye."

She looked so surprised and relieved, he was tempted to kiss her right there in the hall.

"Ye dinna' love him, aye, Isobel?"

"Not him, no." She shook her head and smiled with him.

Hell, she was bonnie. He missed her face and the way she looked at him. He did not want to wait until they were outside to tell her. "I have been miserable these last few days without ye."

"Why have ye stayed away?" she asked him softly, bringing her hand to his jaw.

"I thought 'twas right." He covered her hand with his and brought her fingers to his lips. "But I canna' let ye wed him without—"

"MacGregor!" Andrew's voice boomed through the hall. Get yer hands off her!"

Facing her, Tristan closed his eyes and drew in a frustrated sigh.

"Patrick, ye allow this?"

Splendid. Tristan ground his jaw as he turned his dark gaze on his accuser. Patrick was involved now as well, and being put to the test of his friendship. "What is it that ye're implyin' he allows, Mister Kennedy? Think well on yer answer," he said, a silken thread of warning in his voice. "Fer I willna' allow a slight on her honor to go unpunished."

Behind him, Isobel clutched his arm, pulling him back from the place where he was his father's son, where for an instant, he saw his sword cutting through Andrew's flesh.

"Ye speak of honor like ye know what it means," Kennedy spat. "Ye are a MacGregor. The scourge of Scotland. A name that should have been exterminated—"

"Andrew!" Patrick cut him off. "This *MacGregor* stopped the Cunninghams from burning our crops. He saved John's life, and my own. Ye will not insult him again in my house."

"Call him friend if ye like, Patrick. But what is he still doing here? Ye told me he was injured, but he is fit enough now to be on his way."

"He is helping us," Lachlan said, stepping around Patrick to smile at Tristan.

"Aye, we do not want him to go," John interjected. "Do we, Isobel?"

"No, John, we do not."

Beside her, Tristan exhaled a breath he felt as if he'd been waiting ten years to release.

"That is verra touching." Andrew made the error of mocking them. "But she is to be my wife, and I do not want his soiled hands on her."

"She will be yer wife only if I am dead," Tristan said in a mild, thoroughly controlled voice. He was done being gracious. He didn't want to lose Isobel, and he sure as hell wasn't about to let this bastard have her.

"Easily arranged," Andrew snarled. "I have no difficulty with killing a man whose father murdered theirs."

"Both our families are guilty, Andrew," Isobel said, stepping around Tristan. "He lost his uncle, a sorrow that has taken as much from him as ours has taken from us."

"The way I heard it, it was no tremendous loss on the Campbell side."

"Kennedy," Tristan growled from deep in his chest. "Apologize fer that or lose yer tongue."

"Tristan." Isobel turned to him, her soft voice anxious to calm him. "Do not—"

"He turned his back on the kingdom his kin served fer generations."

"Andrew, that is enough!" Isobel turned to shout at him, and blocked his view of Tristan's hands.

"He sided with outlaws." Andrew moved forward and pushed her out of his way. "Because he was afraid of them."

Tristan caught Isobel in his hands, pushed her behind him, and snatched Andrew's dagger from his belt all in the space of a breath. In the next, he held the bastard by the hair in one hand and pushed the edge of the blade to his throat with the other.

"Ye dare use force with her?" He didn't recognize his own deadly whisper or Annie's terrified scream. "Ye scorn a man fer bein' good?" The blade cut through Kennedy's flesh and a trickle of blood flowed.

"Tristan!" Patrick stepped closer to them and reached out for the blade.

"Let him have it, Tristan, please," Isobel cried.

Tristan's eyes burned into Kennedy's as he stepped

away. He flipped the dagger over in his hand, shoved it back into Andrew's belt, and walked away from him.

"Patrick," Kennedy whined the moment he was free. "Throw him out before he tries to kill one of ye!"

"I think it is ye who should go, Andrew," Patrick told him, standing at Isobel's side. "It is late, so Annie can stay. Cam will bring her home in the morning."

"He is the dangerous one," Andrew argued, wiping the blood from his neck with his palm and showing it to them. "A murderer just like his father. I saw it in his eyes! How do ye know that he will not kill Cameron?"

Tristan didn't know why he might kill Cameron, but he was already sorry he hadn't knocked out some of Andrew's teeth. He noticed Patrick's face drain of all color first, and then, beside him, Isobel grasping at her chest.

"Isobel?" Tristan moved toward her. She sucked in a short, shallow breath and then clutched Patrick's chest.

She couldn't breathe. "Isobel!" he reached her and touched his fingers to her cool cheek, watching her gasp for another elusive breath.

"She is having an attack!" Patrick snatched her up in his arms and carried her into the dining room, calling out orders as he went to Cam and Lachlan to get to her garden.

"But she has no butterbur." John wrung his fingers together as he followed his brothers to the door.

"Ox-eye daisies, John. Go!"

Butterbur was better. John and Lachlan had told him of the plant that helped her breathe the day he learned that he'd destroyed it. Hell, she didn't have any because of him.

Bending at her chair as Patrick set her in it, Tristan

took her cold hand in his. She was awake, her eyes wide, glassy, and frightened. Her nostrils were flared, her colorless lips drawn, dragging in rapid, shallow gulps of air.

"What can we do?" Tristan looked up at Patrick. "How can we help her?"

The boys barreled back into the house and ran straight for the kitchen with Cameron.

"We'll make her tea. It will help, aye, Bel?" Patrick somehow managed to brave a smile for his sister, and Tristan admired him even more than he had before.

She nodded and squeezed Tristan's hand. He kissed it in return and didn't glance up at Patrick or anyone else who might have seen.

The tea seemed to take an eternity to boil, but Tristan used the time to sit with her, to soothe her with his steady voice and promises to take care of her. She smiled at him twice, claiming sole ownership of his heart.

Andrew stood off to the side looking frightened, and a bit overwhelmed. He hadn't counted on taking a sickly wife. He disgusted Tristan.

Cameron fed her the medicinal tea when it was ready and steaming hot. It took two cups and an hour before she began breathing normally again. Tristan remained with Cam by her bed while she slept. Long into the night they remained quiet, keeping careful vigil over her. Tristan didn't feel uncomfortable in the silence. He'd come to expect it from shy Cameron. All the more surprising when Cam looked up at him sometime just before dawn and cleared his throat.

"Do ye love her?"

"I...I dinna' want to love her," Tristan answered, lifting his gaze from her face to her brother's. "But I do."

Cam's smile was so slight, Tristan thought he might

have imagined it. "Why do ye not want to love her? Because she is a Fergusson?"

Tristan shook his head. "Because I am afraid."

"Ye?" Cam's smile was gentle, not mocking. "I do not believe it."

"The last person I loved was taken from me. I dinna' know if I can survive it a second time."

They were quiet for a time, listening to the sound of Isobel's breath. "Do ye always speak the truth so openly, Tristan?"

"How do ye know that everything I tell ye is the truth?"

Cam shrugged and looked at his sleeping sister. "Sometimes when ye watch a person, ye can hear more."

Tristan grinned at him. "In that case then, aye, I usually find myself bein' truthful."

"Honesty is an honorable virtue to possess."

"Ye've been listenin' to my tales about the knights of the Round Table, then, aye?" Tristan laughed.

"Aye, but I fear I do not remember their names as well as John does."

"'Tis their virtues that should be remembered, no' their names."

Cam nodded and was quiet for another moment or two. "Tristan?"

"Aye?"

"I love Annie Kennedy."

Tristan went silent, playing over in his mind how many times the lass had giggled at him like a lovesick kitten these last few days.

"I know she is a bit smitten with ye at present." He held up his hand to stop Tristan when he tried to interject.

"If ye could win Isobel, I know ye could help me win Annie. Will ye?"

Tristan sat forward in his chair and beckoned Cam to come closer. "I'm goin' away fer a few days."

"Why?" Cam asked him quietly. "I did not mean to—"

"I will return," Tristan assured him. "But while I'm gone, here is what ye must do with Annie."

In the sitting room the next morning, Isobel paced before the hearth fire, wringing her apron into a tight knot. By the time she was well last night, it was too late to send Andrew off alone, so he sat with Patrick now quietly watching her while they waited for Cameron to finish his morning chores and join them.

"I do not understand why ye are so vexed by MacGregor's departure," Andrew said after another ten minutes of her marching back and forth.

Isobel flicked her scalding gaze to him and bit her lip. This was all his fault and she wondered, not for the first time since last eve, how such a foolhardy man would ever lead his clan.

"I do not know why he left so suddenly, Andrew," she practically barked at him. "He had no idea that my father did not kill his uncle until ye blurted out Cameron's name."

"How was I supposed to know what ye told MacGregor and what ye haven't told him?"

Now Isobel turned on him. Oh, how could Patrick think she would ever take this man for a husband? "Do ye think Tristan would have been so friendly and kind to Cameron if he knew? Do ye honestly think any one of us would have confessed to the Devil MacGregor's son that it was Cameron who killed the earl?" Just speaking it made her stomach clench and her breath falter. But truly, could the man be so dull-witted?

"I saw him before he left," Annie said quietly, sitting by the fire. "He did not say he was leaving, but he asked my fergiveness fer frightening me last night."

"He did not know what I meant, Isobel," Andrew defended.

"He is verra clever, unlike ye, Andrew," she told him. "Why would ye expect him to kill Cameron? Why Cameron and not Patrick or Lachlan? Ye said Cameron! He would have no reason to kill anyone else save fer if they killed his uncle!"

"He does not know it was me," Cameron said quietly as he entered the room, shutting the door behind him.

"Ye were just a babe." Isobel hurried to him. They never spoke of that terrible day. She did not want to speak of it now, but perhaps it was time. Cameron had lived with his guilt, his remorse that their father had died in his place for too long. "Ye were younger even than Tamas. Father should not have taken ye with him." Her hands shook as she placed them on her brother's arm. Dear God, it was a tragic accident that had cost her family so much—and Tristan's as well. She hadn't even known the earl had been killed until two days after when the MacGregor Chief had come to take his revenge. They were children, terrified and desperate to hide from the unholy fire that raged in Callum MacGregor's eyes as he slowed his mount at their front door and shouted her father's name. Isobel would never forget that day, or the look on her father's face as he left the manor house. She had watched by the window with Cameron while Alex fought with Patrick to keep him inside. She could not look away as Archibald Fergusson stepped up to that great, snorting warhorse. She thought her father would be trampled before her eyes, but she could not look away. She tried to block Cam's vision when MacGregor dismounted. He was so very big compared to her father, so fit and strong and silent as he drew his sword.

She turned her gaze now to Andrew. The MacGregors would have never suspected that the fatal arrow had not come from Archibald's quiver if it wasn't for Andrew's father. Kevin Kennedy had gone to Campbell Keep with her father. He had known it was Cam's arrow, and he shouted for Archie to save himself, to plead his innocence before the Devil. But her father had refused to give up his son.

Isobel had watched, horrified, while MacGregor's sword disappeared into her father's chest. She didn't remember screaming, though she must have done so, because those murderous eyes found her through the window. She thought he was going to come inside and kill the rest of them, but he let her father fall at his feet, and then he was gone.

Oh, how could she have let down her guard with Tristan? She didn't want to believe she had been correct about him all along, that he had come here because his father wanted the true killer's name. But why had he left the holding before dawn without so much as a farewell, taking his horse and a few days' worth of food? And why had he done so after Andrew had implicated Cam in something terrible?

"Ye were the last one to speak with him, Cameron," she said softly to her brother. "Did he not mention where he was going?"

Cameron shook his head. "He said he would return. That is all."

But with whom? His father? An army? Isobel closed her eyes to stop the panic rising in her like bile.

She'd almost made it to the kitchen when Cameron's voice stopped her. She turned, swiping at the tears she tried to hide from him.

"He will not bring harm to us."

"How do ye know that, Cam? His family has hated ours fer ten years."

"Because he is a good man."

"I know that, but he said things would be different."

Her brother gave her an addled look. "What things? How would they be different? Bel, ye are makin' no sense."

"I asked him if he would take vengeance on the man who killed his uncle if the man still lived, and that was his reply. Things would be different."

"It does not mean—"

"Cam, did ye not see how close he came to killing Andrew last night because Andrew spoke poorly of Robert Campbell? No matter what he has done fer us, or how much we have come to care fer him, he loved his uncle more than anyone in his life. He told me this. I fear he will avenge him."

"He is in love with ye, sister. He told me this as well. He remained at yer side all through the night."

Isobel wiped her tears. She wanted to believe he loved her. She had almost believed it last night when he spoke of making her his wife. But if she had truly won his heart he would not have left her the morning after she had an attack—the morning after he might have deduced the truth. "Whatever he told ye, Cam—whatever he told any of us—where is he now?"

Her brother looked away, unable to give her any answers.

Chapter Twenty-seven

$\mathcal{H}$ours stretched on into days filled with growing terror for Isobel. She tried not to think about hordes of MacGregors hurdling over the hills, ready to hack them all to pieces, ensuring that this time, they killed the right man. But where the hell had Tristan gone but home? Oh, if he had betrayed them she would kill him. She would poison the drink she offered him before they cut her down. She prayed it would not come to that, and for the first time, she prayed it for more than just Cam's sake. She'd fallen victim to Tristan's wondrous charms. She'd discarded every warning going off in her head for the thrill of being in his arms, the delight of his warm, hungry mouth on hers. The sight of him, whether he was working in the fields or teaching her brothers how to wield a sword, heated her blood, and her cheeks along with it. She loved his easy laughter and effortless smiles, and had hated him all week for continuing to exhibit those smiles in Andrew's presence.

She looked up from her garden and squinted toward the hills. *Please,* she beseeched God, *let him come back, and let him be alone.*

Cameron walked past her, shirtless, on his way to the field. Isobel was worried about him. He'd been acting strangely since the morn that Tristan left. He seemed not to care at all about his fate, only about impressing Annie Kennedy. At night, he brought her mead to the sitting room and boldly sat near her. He wasn't as quiet as usual, but he spoke just enough to heighten the mysterious air he already possessed. The biggest change in him, though, besides his traipsing around bare-chested, was the way he let his eyes linger over Annie, even letting her catch him looking, rather than always shielding his beautiful eyes behind his lashes.

Isobel wanted to be happy for him, especially since his new approach seemed to be working wonders on Annie—who'd asked to stay another week. But she couldn't relax. Not with his possible demise so close at hand.

"If they wed," Isobel told Patrick later that night while Cam and Annie laughed together beside the fire, "and Andrew comes here to visit every other day, I still will never marry him."

Patrick checked her bishop. "Who do ye wish to marry, then?"

"What?" Isobel looked up at him from the board. "No argument?"

"I would not let ye marry Andrew after he proved to me that he is as foolhardy as Alex. And I also do not want ye to marry a man just because he is the only one available at the moment."

"I am glad ye changed yer mind."

Her brother shrugged and said quietly, "I had already changed it before he provoked Tristan to nearly kill him in our hallway."

"Oh?" She glanced at him curiously.

"After a conversation I had with Tristan about it a few days ago. He told me that ye would wither away and die wed to a man who did not love ye passionately and with purpose."

Isobel sank back into her chair. Passionately and with purpose. It was how Tristan lived, how he would love the woman who captured his heart. She wanted to weep. She had never cared about having another man in her life. She already had six, and that was enough, until Tristan stepped into her life and swept all her carefully laid plans aside with the flash of a frivolous dimple and kisses that set her heart to ruin. He fired passions in her she hadn't even known she possessed. He excited her, angered her, and made her feel like a woman instead of a caretaker. "He was correct to tell ye that. I would wither and die."

"I know," Patrick told her. "And I am sorry it took him to help me realize it. It seems he knows my sister better than I do."

It seemed he did, indeed. Tristan had crawled under her skin and into her veins . . . and stolen her heart.

"Why do ye suppose he left?" she asked Patrick, forgetting the game.

"I do not know. But I cannot believe that after saving Alex from his family, Tamas from himself, and the rest of us from the Cunninghams, he would put us in danger. Have faith in him, Bel. I do."

"I want to," she admitted. "More than anything, I want to."

Two days later, Tristan still had not returned. Isobel had begun to miss him more than she feared him. The days were duller without him in them. Her brothers felt the impact of his absence, too. Without the extra pair of hands to help with the daily chores, Patrick could barely keep awake at night long enough to finish a game of chess. John spoke of him constantly, reminding the rest of them what Tristan would say about this thing or that. It near drove Isobel mad. Tamas was the only one glad to see him gone, except that the Highlander had stolen his sling.

By the end of the seventh day of his absence, they had all begun to suspect that he was never coming back, so when John plunged into the kitchen shouting that a rider was approaching over the hills, Isobel nearly dropped her bowl of rabbit stew.

"Is it Tristan? Is he alone?" She didn't wait for John to answer but raced him back to the door and pulled it open. She stopped in her tracks at the sight of him dismounting a few yards away. He was alone, save for Patrick and the others surrounding him and welcoming him back with warm smiles and eager questions.

Dear God, she had tried to forget how beautiful he was, but it all came back to her like a cannonball to her chest. With a flick of his head that swept his hair from his face and sent it tumbling over his shoulders, he turned toward her as if he could hear her heart beating against her ribs. Their gazes met and he seemed to forget everyone else around him as his smile deepened. No man had ever looked at her before with such replete joy, as if his life had just been returned to him. Isobel wanted to run to him, but John beat her to it. She could only watch, her breath stalled at the tenderness of their reunion. Did Tristan truly care for her—for all of them?

She moved toward him slowly, not wishing to steal his attention from John's cheerful questions.

"We thought ye were not coming back." Her brother

laughed when Tristan mussed his fiery hair. "Where did ye go?"

Tristan lifted his gaze to hers, stopping her advance. "Did ye miss me, then?"

She did not answer him. She couldn't. She feared if she opened her mouth, her heart might drop out of it and fall at his feet. She was angry with him for leaving, frightened of where he had gone, and so happy to see him again, and alone, that her legs nearly gave out beneath her.

"Aye, we missed ye," John assured him hastily, saving her from speaking. "Isobel feared ye went home."

She opened her mouth to deny the charge, but Tristan cast her a repentant grin. He moved to retrieve a long parcel from his mount and then another large bag tied to his saddle.

"I went to Glasgow, to a marketplace I had seen when I traveled with my kin to England."

"To Glasgow?" Isobel asked on a tenuous whisper when he turned back to her. "Whatever fer?"

"Fer this," he said, reaching into the bag and pulling out another sack secured in twine.

"What is it?"

"Butterbur."

He held it out to her, but she did not accept the gift right away. Oh, how she had doubted him. He hadn't gone to his father but all the way to Glasgow. For her. For butterbur. It was almost too much for her to take in, and Isobel stared at his offering through misty eyes.

"I spoke to a merchant and he told me that mullein also works fer what ails ye, so I purchased some of that as well, and—"

Her arms around Tristan's neck halted the remainder

of his words, and his breath, for he did not breathe in her tight embrace.

"Thank ye," she whispered, clinging to him, delighting more than she ever could have imagined in the feel of his arms closing around her. He hadn't betrayed them.

"Tristan?"

Isobel broke away from their embrace at the sound of John's voice. She blushed and then smiled at the clear effect she had on Tristan's normally unruffled composure.

"Did ye purchase anything fer me in Glasgow?"

"John!" Isobel scolded, but Tristan only smiled, gaining back what he'd lost a moment ago locked in her arms.

"Of course I did, John. I'd no' ferget ye."

Isobel blinked back the tears stinging her eyes. She didn't know why Tristan's declaration would make her weep like a fool, except that he cared for them and, finally, she trusted him.

"Come now," he prodded John tenderly. "I'll show ye what I brought fer ye inside the house."

When Cam drew close to help him with his offerings, Tristan tossed his free arm around him. "And how goes it with ye, Cameron? Did ye do as I said?"

"I did." Cam grinned at him, a bit shyly still, but changed, with a dash of confidence he had not possessed before.

"And?"

"And she has agreed to let me court her."

Isobel looked at the two of them laughing together. She should have suspected that Tristan had something to do with Cam's bold behavior. Her brother must have asked him for help with Annie, and Tristan had given it. Clearly, Tristan did not suspect what Andrew had implied. Or mayhap he did and he didn't care. Oh, it was almost too much to hope for.

"I love it when I am correct."

She looked up at Patrick and smiled, taking his hand as he led her back to the house behind Tristan and the others.

"He is not what any of us expected, aye, Bel?"

No, he wasn't. Although she had seen traces of his chivalrous character from the beginning, she had never allowed herself to believe that a MacGregor could be so kind, so thoughtful, so...honorable. But Tristan MacGregor was a man who thought a different way. He was not what she expected. He was infinitely better.

Chapter Twenty-eight

Tristan stepped inside the house and paused to inhale. Hell, he'd dreamed of her cooking while he was away. He'd dreamed of this house with its warm, intimate rooms and a bed that was too small to house him. And he'd dreamed of Isobel, a woman who had somehow looked beyond what everyone else saw and shown him a path toward home. Not toward Camlochlin, for though he loved the place of his birth, he had never truly fit in. He didn't want to. What he wanted was gone, and he had made himself an outcast, never belonging to anyone or anywhere again. Until he met Isobel. It scared the hell out of him to let himself feel again, but he had no defense against it when he looked into her eyes, her smile, and saw home.

He smiled as she passed him, entering the house. He wanted to come home to her every night. He wanted to know she was his and at the end of the night he wanted to take her to his bed. Only her for the rest of his days.

He refused to think about his kin or what they would say or think of him for courting a Fergusson. He had lost as much as they had, even more, because he had lost his purpose when Robert Campbell died. He had found it again, here, with Isobel and her family, and he would not allow his kin to carry the blame to her or her brothers. They were innocent, and it was time for his family to let old hatreds go. He would see to it.

"Sit in the dining room," Isobel said, heading for the kitchen. "I will bring ye some supper."

Was she truly afraid he'd gone home? Did she want him to stay, then?

"Open that long parcel, John," he said, taking a seat at the table. Someday he wanted a table just like this one to sit at with Isobel and their bairns. His eyes settled on her instantly when she returned carrying a bowl in one hand and a cup in the other.

"Och, hell, woman, but ye can cook," he sighed with a mouthful of food, and then smiled at John and Lachlan's excitement over their gifts.

"Our verra own swords!"

"Aye, we canna' keep practicin' with only three and ye're both ready to have yer own."

"There's one fer Tamas, too." Lachlan gave his youngest brother a skeptical look.

"That's fer Cam," Tristan told them, then shoveled another spoonful of stew into his mouth and winked at Isobel. "This is fer Tamas." He pulled a brand-new leather sling from his pocket and tossed it to the boy. "Ye earned it before I left. I'm trustin' ye no' to use it on me."

"What else is in the sack?" John asked, hefting it to the table and barely pulling Tristan's attention from Isobel.

Still gazing at her, he dipped his hand inside the leather bag and produced another, smaller satchel and slid it to Patrick. "New chess pieces, carved, I was promised, in oak by a master carpenter." Patrick thanked him and Tristan smiled at him briefly before turning back to Isobel. He pulled out a jar of ointment and offered it to her. "To protect yer fine hands from calluses, and this"—he gave her a skein of yellow silk next—"is fer a bonnie dress ye'll wear on a special day."

When the flush of her cheeks deepened, he had the urge to leap from his chair and snatch her up into his arms and tell her, oh, tell her that she was bonnier to him than a thousand sunsets. More glorious—he feasted his eyes on her long, burnished hair—than the sun itself. He'd been certain nothing could make him want her more than when she was rejecting him. But he was wrong. Winning her was much better. She had fought hard, and with good reason, and had made him want to be the man he used to dream of being. He wanted her to be his wife and would let nothing come in the way of that. If he never returned to Camlochlin, so be it. For her, he would give up anything. He wanted to tell her.

But it would have to wait. For now, her brothers demanded his attention, and he was happy to give it.

"We have missed yer stories," Lachlan said as they made their way to the sitting room after Tristan finished his supper. "Tell us one now."

"I shall do even better," Tristan announced, pulling one last item from his bag. "I will read to ye." He held up the book he'd searched four marketplaces to find and paid too much for. "The first and second book of Sir Tristan of Lyones."

"Is it a book about ye, then?" John asked, taking his place at Tristan's side.

"I've asked myself that same question recently," Tristan admitted, sitting down and opening the book. "It seems my mother knew the darker side of chivalry would be my path." He held his finger to his lips when John would have more answers, and began to read. He had forgotten most of the tale, and speaking it aloud in the Fergussons' sitting room with the hearth fire crackling against his voice brought him back to his youth and his uncle Robert reading the tale to him. Home. Ah, God, he was home.

"But if Sir Tristan had honor, why did he betray King Mark by taking his wife?" Cam asked an hour into the tale.

"Some authors would have us believe 'twas a love potion that made Tristan fall in love with the king's wife," Tristan explained, "but I think 'tis more likely that he truly lost his heart to the lady and was helpless against it." He glanced at Isobel sipping mead in her chair. "Sir Tristan," he said, returning his attention to the lads sitting around him, "was not faultless as were Percival and Galahad. 'Twas his shame and guilt over his love for Iseult that made his struggle for honor more believable. My uncle used to ask what lessons can be taught when there is no effort taken to learn them."

"He was wise," Cameron said, nodding in agreement.

The room was quiet while they all pondered their own separate thoughts on the matter, then Isobel stood up from her chair and informed them that it was time for bed. The boys went without argument, while Patrick and Cam set up the new chess pieces Tristan had brought back and started a new game.

Isobel excused herself and left the sitting room with a quiet glance over her shoulder at Tristan. He remained in his chair for a few more moments, tapping his boot on the floor, until Patrick looked up from the board and asked him politely to leave.

He nearly bolted from his chair.

He followed her up the stairs, watching her, his heart beating a mad litany in his chest as she ascended into the shadows of the second landing.

"I dreamed of yer face," he whispered in the darkness as he reached the top step, "and now ye would hide it from me."

Her fingers touched his and he held them before she moved off. She leaped the rest of the way into his arms, surprising him enough to make him sway backward on his feet with her attached. He laughed as his mouth descended on hers, then swept her up with more purpose, crushing her against him, pushing her deeper into the shadows. God in all His mercy, help him. No woman had ever made him feel like this. His thoughts, his body, his heart were no longer his own, but hers. He licked the inside of her mouth, feasting on the scent of her, the flavor of her. She answered his ardor with equal fervor, stringing his muscles as taut as bowstrings. Everything he wanted to tell her fled his thoughts, leaving room only for the passion boiling his insides. Slipping his fingers down the silk of her loose tresses, he cupped her buttocks and drew her hips hard against his rigid erection. She gasped and broke away from their kiss, but he hauled her back. This time, though, he did not try to kiss her again but simply held her close to him.

He thought he was content to breathe her in, to know that she accepted him, wanted his affection. That was enough for now. "I would hold ye in my arms and never want another thing." When she moved against him, he knew he was lying. He stroked her hair and smiled against her forehead when her soft voice reached his ears.

"Ye would not be happy here with this quiet life."

"I would be happy wherever I was if I could but look at yer face each day."

"Such pretty words, wolf." He felt her smile against his chin and then her giggle when he bit her earlobe.

He dipped his face and scraped his teeth down her neck. When she arched her back over the crook of his arm, he bent with her, kissing a slow, hot path over her collarbone. He wanted her more than anyone or anything he'd ever wanted before. Whatever control he thought he possessed shattered when she curled her calf around his.

That is, until he heard the hushed laughter of young male voices from the other end of the hall.

"Tamas! John!" Isobel scolded, still locked in his embrace. "To bed with ye now!"

Tristan rested his forehead against hers while they listened to the sound of the boys' footsteps running away. He smiled when she sighed. He wasn't angry at the interruption, for he had found his lady and he wouldn't take her in dishonor. But hell, it was difficult.

"Ye should go," she whispered, the desire in her voice belying her gentle command.

"Aye." He didn't want to. Never before had he been called to use so much restraint.

"Tristan," she called softly when he stepped away from her. "I am happy ye returned to us... to me."

He was almost glad she couldn't see the raw emotion in his gaze, for it frightened him to think what he would do to anyone who tried to separate him from her. His past was gone. He'd been reborn in a suit of polished armor that wasn't cumbersome at all.

He rushed back to her, scooped her in his arms, and kissed her good night.

Chapter Twenty-nine

Sunshine spilled into Tristan's room, barging in on his dreams of Isobel's bare, creamy breasts against his lips, her warm, wet niche throbbing around him. He awoke with an erection as hard as steel. He'd been with many lasses, but he'd never physically ached for one before. He wondered, lying there in Alex's small bed, if his body was reacting to the desire of his heart. For he'd never loved any of them either. He understood now why heroes died for the ladies they loved. Why men like Sir Tristan and his own brother defied kings. He would fight a war for her, defy a king—or his father—for her. He would do whatever it took just to look upon the smile she had kept from him for so long. He ached to touch her, craved the taste of her, and hungered like a ravenous beast for more of her.

Rising from the bed, he dressed quickly, leaving his plaid still neatly folded in his saddlebag. Today, he would tell her how he felt. If she laughed in his face, he would simply try again in a few days, after he had worked the fields without his damp shirt. He'd caught her admiring him a few times. That fire in her eyes—and in her cheeks—was difficult to miss. If he had to resort to using his sweating body to woo her, then so be it.

He hopped out of his room on one foot, fitting the other into his boot, and nearly collided with Isobel leaving her room at the same time.

"Good morn to ye, sunshine," he said, a bit out of breath, and straightened, setting both feet on the floor. His shirt was still unlaced, and catching the direction of her gaze along his tight belly, he smiled. Mayhap he should leave it open.

"Sleep well?" she asked, stepping around him.

"In truth"—he swung around and followed her—"my slumber was fraught with dreams of a frustratin' nature, so nae, I didna' sleep well."

She cut him a wry glance as they walked together down the stairs. "I could prepare ye a drink that will help ye sleep more soundly."

His smile widened when he realized she was deliberately keeping the question she knew he was fishing for from her lips.

He let her know anyway. "But then I'd only miss ye more after I've awoken."

Her smile was playful and ravishing, and Tristan almost lost his footing. "I see," she teased. "So ye dream of me and ye find that frustrating?"

He nodded, moving closer to her and leaning into her ear. "Aye, fer I canna' do to yer body here what I do to it in my dreams."

That sobered her quickly enough. Tristan cursed his own mouth. "'Tis nothin' ye didna' like havin' done," he said, trying to mend his tactless error. He didn't realize that she'd stopped until he had stepped down three more stairs. He looked up to find her staring at him. For a moment she looked afraid, as if she was standing at the edge of a cliff instead of on her staircase. He climbed a step closer, wanting to promise her that she never had any reason to fear him. Her smile stole softly across her features as he reached for her. Their hands clasped as they closed the distance between them in a rush of need.

Taking her in his arms, Tristan covered her mouth with a bold caress that left her limp and weak against him. "I want to speak with ye alone. Where can we go?" he asked, kissing her again before she could answer.

"To the barn?" She curled her fingers through his hair and drew him down for more.

He angled his mouth over hers and pulled tiny breaths from her lips with a series of short, insatiable kisses. Hell, he didn't want to tell her he loved her in a barn. Beneath the braes of a mountainside carpeted in heather would do nicely. "Ride with me later."

She nodded, smiling against his mouth. "Am I pitiful fer not refusing ye?"

"Nae, ye're sensible, fer I would never stop askin'."

She laughed, and his heart swelled until he felt as if his chest could no longer contain it. "Isobel, I—"

John came barreling down the stairs, almost knocking both of them down in a race for the door. "Did ye look out yer window, Bel?" He barely looked at either of them locked in each other's arms. "The cattle are here!"

"Cattle?" Tristan turned to watch John disappear outside.

"Aye, come see!" Isobel closed her fingers around his and pulled him down the rest of the stairs. "They arrive twice a year."

"What do ye mean, they arrive?" Tristan queried as

she hurried for the door, dragging him with her. "Who brings them in?"

"We do not know." She stepped outside, stopped, and pointed to the six woolly cattle grazing in the small enclosure by the barn. They were Highland Kyloe of the red variety, with long, wavy pelts and thick horns. Slung over each beast's back was a heavy bag bursting at the seams. "Someone brings them here at night," Isobel continued. "We do not know who, but Patrick thinks it is one of our father's tenants who left after he died. Perhaps our cousin James Fergusson. We heard he was doing well in Aberdeen."

"What's in the bags?" Tristan asked, walking toward them. John was already unpacking one, and looked up to wave Patrick and Cam over when his brothers stepped out of the manor house.

"Dried meats, grains, bolts of fabric, spices, books." Isobel smiled, happier than Tristan had ever seen her. "Things the merchants in Dumfries are all eager to purchase."

"Books?" Tristan stepped into the enclosure, smiled at John, then ran his hand over the thick pelt of one of the Kyloes. His father bred cattle like this at Camlochlin.

"Aye." John dug inside one of the sacks. "We sell almost everything, even the cattle, to buy seeds, farming equipment, pots fer Isobel, whatever we need." He found what he was looking for and handed it to Tristan. "We sell the books, too, since none of us can read. Mayhap ye can read them to us before Patrick brings them to the market."

Tristan looked down at the leather-bound book in his hand and blinked at its title. *Historia Regum Britanniae,* or *History of the Kings of Britain,* by Geoffrey of Monmouth. Monmouth's works contained some of the first stories written about King Arthur. He glanced up again at the cattle, his heart racing in his chest. Impossible. "Ye say these gifts have been left since yer father died?" He didn't wait for Isobel to answer when she entered the enclosure with Patrick, but cut another sack loose and began to rifle through it.

"Aye, they kept us alive and fed fer the first year after the crops failed." It was Isobel who spoke. Patrick remained silent, still staring at the book under Tristan's arm.

"What are ye looking fer?" he finally asked, while Tristan discarded an assortment of roots, two woolen earasaids hand-dyed in different shades of green and brown, a bundle of spun flax shirts, and three pewter lavers. Nothing that could not have come from any Highland home.

"Bel," John called out, holding up a small brooch that glimmered in the sun. "Have a look at this. I think it is silver!"

Isobel went to him and reached for the delicate clip, but Tristan seized it from John's fingers first. He stared at it, not believing the evidence of his own eyes.

"Ye have seen it before, then?" Patrick asked quietly.

Tristan nodded. "'Tis my aunt Maggie's." He looked up, setting his eyes on the cattle, the bags of goods all meant to help support the children his father had made into orphans. He couldn't help but smile. Never in his wildest imaginings would he have suspected his father of giving aid to the bairns of his most hated enemy. Could he have been wrong about Callum MacGregor all these years? This was not the work of a prideful warrior. This was mercy. This was compassion.

"What are ye saying?" Isobel asked faintly, drawing a step nearer to him. "That all this is from the MacGregors?"

"Aye," he told her, proud to be one for the first time.

"No." She shook her head at him and pulled away when he reached his hand out to her face. "I do not believe it."

"Dinna' be angry," he said gently, moving closer. "I know 'tis hard fer ye to accept these things from my kin. But it bodes well."

"Fer who?" she asked, looking up at him.

"Fer us." He swept forward, taking her hands in his and bringing them between both their chests. "Dinna' ye see, Isobel? These things prove that my kin are fergivin'. My faither and his sister spent long years in a Campbell dungeon to pay fer their faither's crimes. I feared his heart would be ferever turned against ye, but he knows yer faither's bairns are innocent."

Tears filled her eyes and broke his heart.

"Dinna' weep, fair Iseult, I will dash yer fears to pieces. I will change the things that sadden ye to things that give yer heart joy. I told ye," he said, hooking his mouth into a gallant grin, "'tis what I do best."

Satisfied with the soft smile he pulled from her, he turned to Patrick. "Let me bring the goods to Dumfries fer trade. I know their value and can get ye a fairer price." He released Isobel's hands and raised his to her brother when Patrick looked about to refuse. "Yer hands will be missed here, and the heaviest labor would fall to Cam. If I go, ye'll no' have to worry aboot the crops."

"Aye," Patrick said, tossing a knowing glance at Isobel. "I can worry about my sister with ye instead."

Tristan discarded his concern with a wave of his hand. "Cam can come with us, then," he said, not bothering to deny that he meant to bring Isobel with him. "We will no' stay a day longer than necessary. I give ye my word nae harm will come to either of them."

Patrick mulled it over for a few moments, then crooked his finger at Tristan, beckoning him to follow him a short distance away. Tristan followed, and when they were out of earshot of the others, Patrick turned to him. "Cameron has informed me that ye have given yer heart to my sister."

"I have," Tristan admitted quietly, feeling a bit like a heel before him. "Fergive me fer no' payin' the respect ye're due and comin' to ye first."

"It is quite all right." Patrick let him off easily with a pat on the back and his first smile of the day. "I was not surprised to hear it. In truth, I am more astonished that she does not know how deeply ye care fer her."

"I was no' aware of it myself until recently."

"Hell"—Patrick cocked a dubious brow—"even I was aware of it."

"And ye didna' toss me oot on my arse?"

"Ye are a good man, Tristan. Ye are fair and honest and merciful. In truth, I liked ye from the first day we met and ye did not betray Tamas to Isobel." They smiled together, remembering the lad's sling slipping secretively into his belt.

"But what of yer family?" Patrick sobered. "Sending us supplies is one thing. Giving yer heart to Archibald Fergusson's daughter is another."

"I dinna' know the answer to that. It is a road I will travel when I come to it. But this I do know. I want to protect her and make her happy. I want my kin to be yer kin, bound by our marriage never to cause ye harm again but to come to yer aid if ye ever need them."

"I would be grateful fer that." Patrick smiled again, and Tristan thought how much he would like his brother Rob, for their passion to look after their own was the same. "Are ye asking me fer her hand then, Tristan MacGregor?"

"I am."

"Ye have it with my blessing." Patrick looked over his shoulder at his sister. "She loves it here. She will not want to leave."

Turning to sweep his eyes over the small manor house in the center of nowhere, Tristan nodded. "I love it as well. We will visit here often."

"Verra well, then." Patrick took him by the shoulders and patted them. "Go to Dumfries, get me the fairest price on the goods, and keep my sister and brother safe."

"Ye have my word."

❊ ❊

Chapter Thirty

The royal burgh of Dumfries, Isobel told Tristan as they crossed the bridge over the River Nith, was well known for its bloody history. The English had plundered and occupied the town on more than seven different occasions. When political wars turned religious, one of the burgh's grand castles surrendered to the Presbyterian Covenanters after a thirteen-day siege that left the place in ruins to this very day, and Dumfries a haven for enemies of a Catholic king.

Tristan shook his head, turning his eyes to the road and away from Isobel. And they said the Scottish were barbaric.

"It is a fortunate thing that ye did not wear yer plaid here, Tristan," Cam called out from the back of the cart. "It trumpets that ye are Catholic."

"Blendin' in is better than fightin' a man simply because ye believe a different way," Tristan replied over his shoulder. As he turned back to the road, Isobel's smile caught his eye.

"Did yer uncle teach ye that?"

"Nae, lass," he said, helpless to do anything but smile back at her, despite the pain of his words. "I learned that lesson on my own."

Her smile faded and then returned softer, understanding all that he did not say. "Later, ye will tell me the tale?"

"Aye," he promised, wanting to tell her all; truths he'd kept hidden from everyone, even himself. "Later, when we are alone."

He couldn't wait. He wanted to kiss the blush off her freckled nose, feel her body in his arms surrendering her prejudices and her passions to him while he tasted the honey of her mouth and then every other inch of her. He had to find a priest—and fast, if he intended to do the honorable thing.

"What convinced ye no' to wed Andrew Kennedy?"

She glanced at him through the corner of her eye as he slowed the cart to a halt in front of the first inn they came upon. "Who says I am not going to wed him?"

He laughed at her teasing smile. "I do," he said, just missing her fingers as she slipped from his grasp and onto the ground.

"And who are ye that I should call off my wedding?"

Vaulting from the cart, he skirted the horse and stepped up behind her. "I'm the man who's tryin' his damnedest to be good enough fer ye."

She turned to him as he reached up to catch the first sack Cam tossed him. He looked at her over the bundle before he hauled it to the side. "The man who wants to give ye a better life than the one ye have now."

"I have a good life," she was quick to tell him.

"Ye work too damn hard. I've watched ye balin' hay and plowin' soil until ye can barely breathe."

She lifted her hands to the next sack, prepared to catch it. "The work needs to be done."

"The only work ye should be doin'," he caught the bag before it reached her, "is tending to yer babes and yer husband."

She actually laughed straight at him. Tristan didn't know whether to be offended or delighted.

"Beneath all that flair and finesse," she said, her green eyes twinkling beneath the sun, "yer ways of thinking are really quite antiquated—and irritating."

He stared at her, mute. Antiquated? Irritating? Him? He nearly careened to the ground when Cam flung another sack over the side and hit him in the shoulder.

Isobel retrieved the fallen bundle and tossed it into the pile with the rest. "Women are capable of doing more than just tending to babes and husbands. If my family is going to starve if the harvest fails, I will do whatever it takes to see that it does not. I will not stay in bed, lazy and useless but to my husband at night."

He nodded at her, smiling. How could he dispute her words when he found them so refreshing, so honest, so…Isobel? Mayhap his ways of thinking when it came to a wife were indeed antiquated. He knew enough women in Camlochlin who could wield a sword as well as any man. Isobel possessed the strength of those women he'd always loved and admired: his mother and sister, Lady Claire, his Aunt Maggie. They would approve of Isobel once they came to know her.

"I stand corrected." He gave her a slight bow and came back with a dimple flashing. He caught another load from the cart and swung it to her. "Now let us discuss what is irritatin' aboot me, aye?"

She looked a little stunned that he'd knocked the wind

out of her, and that he found her expression so vastly amusing. "What have I done now?" He chanced a grin when her eyes smoldered. "I have trust in yer strength."

"And I have trust in yers." She laughed, this time with genuine humor, as she hurled the bag back at him.

"Last one," Cam called out from the cart. When he hefted the bag in his arms, a muffled voice shouted at him from inside.

"That is my nose ye are squeezing!"

Cam dropped the bag and stared at it, eyes wide. Tristan leaped back up, hauled the sack to him, and tore it open. When Tamas's head popped out, Isobel let out a string of oaths that made the lad cringe in his spot.

"What the hell do ye think ye are doing, Tamas Fergusson?"

"I wanted to come along and—"

"Did ye tell Patrick?" she shouted up at him. "Ye did not tell him, did ye! He is going to be sick with worry! Oh, ye little—"

"Isobel." Tristan stopped her, giving her a subdued look. "He's here now. We'll trade the wares and return home as quickly as we can. Tonight, he will sleep on the floor beside yer bed." He helped Tamas out of the sack and gave him a soft clip on the back of the head.

After exchanging glares with the lad, Tristan paid two of the inn's stable hands handsomely to carry the bags inside, and then to their rooms.

"Would it not have been better to sell some of the goods *before* we stopped fer the night?" Isobel asked him when he caught up to her, about to enter without him.

Nae. He wanted time with her alone first. "'Tis better to bargain with a merchant when he has the prospect of a full day's customers ahead."

The inn was nothing Tristan hadn't seen a dozen times before. Dim lighting, the sickeningly sweet aroma of wine, whisky, and ale, a handful of tables and chairs scattered about. He scanned the patrons first. Mostly travelers with nothing on their minds more pressing than a hot meal and a warm bed.

They paid for two rooms and sat at an empty table as supper was being served.

"What'll it be then?" a buxom brunette serving girl asked, fisting her hand at her side and giving the fingernails of her other hand an uninterested glance. "We have rabbit sautéed in honey or roasted mutton served with mushroom and parsley soup…" Her short list came to a skidding halt when Tristan looked up and offered her a pleasant smile. Her powdery blue eyes darkened on him like a storm on a hot summer night. "…or if yer appetite craves something with a bit more flavor, I could have something sent up to yer room later."

Tristan was acutely aware of Isobel stiffening beside him in her chair and was vastly delighted to discover that she was jealous. "The mutton will do fine."

"I want the rabbit," Tamas brooded.

"Ye'll have the mutton." Tristan kicked him under the table, then turned back to the girl. "And some mead to go with it. And would ye happen to know if there is a priest in the vicinity?" he added as she stepped away, visibly discouraged.

"A priest?" Isobel tugged on Tristan's sleeve, but then turned, along with the rest of them, when someone called out Cameron's name.

"I thought it was ye!" Annie Kennedy rushed forward, breaking away from the two hulking lads at her side. "Isobel, Mister MacGregor." Annie offered them both a warm smile. "It is good to see ye again." For Cam's sake more than Isobel's, Tristan did not smile back. "Whatever are ye doing here at the Golden Hillock?"

"We are planning to do some trading in the morn," Cam told her, looking like a fresh-faced squire who'd just been addressed by the queen of England.

"So then yer night is free?" Annie asked him boldly, green eyes wide and gleaming. "I was just about to go out fer an evening stroll with my brothers—Andrew is not here," she interrupted herself to cast Isobel, and then Tristan, a darting glance before turning her attention back to Cam. "I would like it verra much if ye joined us."

Cameron nearly turned over the table to reach her side quickly, then slowed his pace when he caught Tristan's edifying gaze. "Nothing would give me more pleasure," he said smoothly, his mouth cocking to one side as he offered Annie his arm, "than spending the night with ye."

Tristan would have cheered his student's success if Isobel weren't staring at him with a look of heightened suspicion arching her brow.

"I want to go, too!" Tamas said, scrambling from his chair before anyone could stop him. "I do not like it in here. It smells. And I do not like mutton."

Tristan had heard good fortune was a lass. He guessed she loved him well, for she followed him always. Even on his longest days. Of course, when Cameron looked to him for aid, none came. Cam didn't want a chaperon, but better him than Tristan. He sent them all off with a smile.

"What did ye tell Cameron before ye left fer Glasgow?" she asked him as the others left the table to rejoin Annie's brothers. "He reminded me a bit of ye when he accepted her invitation."

"Och, 'twould no' interest ye," Tristan assured her with a playful wink. "'Tis a wee bit antiquated."

"I see." She grew quiet again when the serving girl returned with their supper, and then sent her on her way with a venomous glare. "Why did ye ask her about a priest?" she asked when they were alone again.

Tristan dipped his spoon into his soup and brought it to his mouth. "I hope to be needin' one." He frowned into his bowl and then at her. "Ye're no' goin' to like it."

"Why do ye hope to be needing one?" she pressed, ignoring her soup and his reaction to it.

"Well, I dinna' know what they do here, but in the north we usually call upon a priest when we wish to wed." He cast her the briefest smile before turning to the trencher before him. "I hope the mutton tastes better. I fear eatin' at yer table has spoiled me."

"Tristan." She tugged on his sleeve again, drawing back his full attention. "Are ye asking me...?"

He touched his hand to her face, longing to somehow ease the trepidation he saw in her eyes, could hear in her soft voice. Would she never give him her full trust?

"Aye, Isobel. If ye will have me."

Something in her expression changed. She almost smiled at him, and it would have been her most joyous, most radiant smile yet, for all her fears fell away for an instant. They returned a moment later. "There are things..."

"Aye?" He dragged her gaze back to his when she tried to look away.

"Things that still...concern me. I do not—"

"I love ye, Isobel," he said over her before she had the chance to refuse him. Hell, this wasn't how he wanted to tell her, not in some run-down inn with foul food beneath their noses and their arses sore from bouncing around like eggs in a saddlebag. "Ye are the delight of my heart. I would give up anything fer ye: my honor, my kin, my life. I want to take care of ye, provide fer ye, hear yer laughter, yer voice every day. I will no' give up until ye are mine, so ye might as well marry me now and save yerself the trouble."

She looked as if she were going to weep, but then her lips softened into the smile he'd been waiting for. He cupped her face and drew her in for a long, deep kiss that pulled the breath from both their bodies.

"We still have some of the food I packed fer our journey in the bags in one of our rooms," she whispered, breaking their kiss and looking up at him a bit shyly.

"Then let us go find it." Tristan pulled her to her feet and then followed her up the stairs.

Doing the honorable thing with her, for once, be damned.

Chapter Thirty-one

*I*sobel stepped into the small candlelit room. Her eyes fell to the small, threadbare bed in the corner and she let loose a tiny squeak. A few moments ago she had wanted to be alone with Tristan, crushed in his arms and smothered in his kisses. She'd even suggested it after he confessed to loving her, but being here, completely alone with him and a bed...She turned to him and stopped breathing for a moment while he bolted the door. He loved her. Oh, she had hoped for it more than she had been willing to admit to herself, and for many reasons. She peeked up at him as he moved silently toward her, forgetting the bed and everything else. The only reason that mattered in that moment was that he was hers. This magnificent man, physically crafted from some mad artist's dream, molded within by a most gallant knight. She had let Tristan MacGregor win her heart. She had never expected to win his as well.

"Ye're shakin', my love," his husky voice drummed across her ear when he reached her and bent his head to hers.

"Do ye truly love me, Tristan?"

She saw the truth in his eyes before he spoke, in the way they took her in almost in relief, as if he needed her, thirsted for her, and could not believe he'd finally found her.

"Aye, lass." He lifted his hands to her face and traced her cheekbones with the pads of his thumbs. "I love ye more with every moment that passes. My heart grows more and more alive every day that I spend with ye." He kneeled at her feet and took her hands in his. "Ferget my past, as I have, and know only that I have never loved a single lass before ye and I will never love anyone but ye."

She blinked away the moisture that blurred her vision of him and smiled. "Such a silver tongue ye have on ye, Mister MacGregor."

"A blessin' granted me fer the pleasure of yer ears."

"And fer my mouth?" She bent to him, aching for his kiss as she had since the night in the king's Privy Garden.

"Woman," he whispered against her parted lips as he rose, "how can I tell ye of yer beauty and what it does to me when ye entice me to show ye with my body?"

His body. How many times had she watched him labor beneath the sun, his bare arms glistening with lean muscle, his flat, moist belly tempting her vision downward? She knew that what lay hidden beneath his breeches was as vibrant as the rest of him. She'd felt it surge against her on a few different occasions when he'd kissed her, swollen hard and ready to take her where they stood. She darted her tongue into his mouth and then gasped into it when he rose up like a wave and eased her down on the bed.

She'd always thought that a man's body atop her might be a bit suffocating and unpleasant, but Tristan was neither. In fact, his tight muscles trembling over hers felt so sinfully good that she bit his lip, instinctively wanting more.

He smiled against her teeth, groaned, and bit her back. A surge of delight washed over her, sending bursts of heat to her crux and more vigor to her kiss. His tongue stroked the deepest recesses of her mouth like a flame setting her on fire. She answered with short, quick, hungry breaths, sucking gently on his tongue when he withdrew to taste her from a different angle. She had no idea what had come over her, only that it was a force she could not resist. She didn't want to. This...desire she felt for him was like nothing she had ever experienced before. Her body throbbed with need until it was almost painful, satisfied only by his passionate responses.

He spread her beneath him with his knees, knowing what she craved even if she didn't fully understand it yet. When he pressed his full arousal between her thighs, a deluge of pleasure drenched her.

"I am afraid," she whispered, clinging to him.

"I vow I willna' hurt ye," he promised, his voice thick with need of his own. "I aim to give ye pleasure." He smiled, gazing down at her. "Trust me."

He'd already given her more than she'd ever imagined. But what was expected of *her*? Oh, she knew where he wanted to put that rigid muscle between his legs. She'd seen bulls mating with cows before, but what if it was painful? As hard as he was, it certainly felt as if it might be. She'd never had another woman to ask. Should she stop him if she didn't like it, or let him do as he wished?

How could she push him away when she wanted him exactly where he was now, pressed to her, his heart beating madly atop hers, his mouth branding her as his and his alone? She stopped trying to think clearly and let herself surrender to his masterful touch.

He scored his mouth over the thrashing pulse-beat at her throat while his tender fingers unlaced her kirtle. With a flick of his wrist he slipped his hand under her shift and caressed her bare breast in his hand. His rough skin against her soft flesh made her breathless, lightheaded with wanton delight and reckless anticipation. Her heart pounded wildly as he tugged on her shift, exposing her to him fully. For a moment, he simply gazed at her beneath him, then he looked into her eyes and smiled.

"D'ye know how bonnie ye are to me, Isobel?"

She shook her head, sincerely not knowing.

"Lookin' at ye is like baskin' in the summer sun after a long, cold winter. 'Tis like seein' home after a battle that's left ye empty and alone." He kissed her mouth, her nose, her eyes. "I dinna' know how 'tis possible, but each time I see ye, ye grow more beautiful to me."

Oh, his tongue truly was a blessing for the pleasure of her ears. But these were not just pretty words, spoken to a hundred different women. She *was* beautiful to him. He had made her believe it more each time she'd caught him looking at her. It didn't matter if her hair was often hanging around her shoulders instead of pinned up with sparkling jewels, or if her face was smeared with dirt from her garden. His eyes always drank her in like the finest wine.

He dipped his tongue to her eager nipple and laved his warmth across her. "Ye taste even better than I dreamed." Closing his lips around her, he suckled until she writhed beneath him, needing more. He retreated just enough to lift himself off her while he pushed her skirts over her knees, his fingers treading beguilingly across her bare calves. Freeing her legs, he curled them around his waist and dragged her hips upward to meet his.

"I'm goin' to erupt in my breeches if I dinna' have ye soon," he said, bending to plant a kiss along her inner thigh.

His promise, along with his intimate kiss, frightened her and sent a scintillating spasm down her spine at the same time. Her clothes felt heavy, suffocating. She wanted to rip them from her body—and then start on his. Passion, like the swell of a rushing wave, washed over her. She tilted her hips, rubbing herself along the length of his full erection.

He groaned from someplace deep in his throat. His eyes gleamed, pinning her to the bed as he rose off her. "So then, ye wish my defeat to come quickly?" His lips hooked into a slow, sensuous smile as he shook his head. "Another woman who is the bane of her knight." He stood over her and pulled at the laces of his breeches, freeing himself.

Isobel's heart stalled at the sight and size of it springing upward like a lance ready to pierce the heavens. Oh, *that* was going to hurt.

"No' yet," he growled, closing his fingers around the thick shaft and squeezing.

A muscle between Isobel's thighs convulsed.

"First," he whispered, bending to her and slipping his other hand under her skirts, "tell me that ye'll be my wife…and then let me lick ye here." He rubbed his finger over her engorged bud. His smile deepened when her eyes widened in surprise.

"I will marry ye, Tristan MacGregor," she gasped while he stroked her.

"No, ye cannot," she protested weakly. "It is immoral. It must be." She closed her eyes as another tremor of pleasure coursed through her.

"Immoral it might be, but I promise ye're goin' to enjoy it." He kissed his way up the soft flesh of her trembling thigh. Her body jerked. She wound her fingers through his silky hair, torn between pulling him away and driving him closer. His mouth was so hot, so hungry as he kissed and nibbled his way upward to the damp mound at her center. When he flicked his tongue over her, spasms wracked her body, and she shuddered to her soul. She tried to squeeze her knees together, but he hooked her leg around his neck and buried his face deeper. His tongue darted inside her, then licked its way up over her scalding need. He kissed her there, pulling her sensitive flesh with his lips, then sucking her into his mouth with a tender pressure that made her cry out. He did not cease, but drank to his pleasure, spreading her wider with his fingers to taste her more fully.

Isobel felt dizzy, drunk with want. Her breath came hard. Her thoughts went dark as ripples of feral passion, sheer titillating delight, consumed her. She dug her fingernails into his shoulders, undulated her hips beneath the ravenous stroke of his tongue, his teeth. She tried to speak, to tell him how good he felt, but only tight, languorous gasps escaped her lips as he brought her to the pinnacle of ecstasy.

She grasped for him as he moved away, leaving her weak and panting for more. He smiled in the candlelight and tugged his breeches down over his thighs. His shirt and boots he flung away next. Isobel's languid gaze took

in the glory of his hard, naked body, the slight tics of his
trembling muscles as he moved toward her to slowly peel
away her kirtle and shift until she lay exposed to his dark
male desire. She wasn't afraid anymore. Whatever he
meant to do, she wanted it, needed it.

"Hurry," she whispered on a stilled breath.

He was there instantly, poised over her, kissing her
demands away with his mouth. Her nipples grew tighter,
pressed against his chest, tickled by his coarse hair. He
dipped his head and sucked each in turn with a maddening mixture of tenderness and wild desire.

"No' yet, my love," he whispered on an uneven breath
as he surged his length against her. "Och, hell." He rose
up on one splayed hand and with the other clasped his
thick, glistening shaft as his seed shot upward in three
long spurts. For an instant, he looked as astounded as
she did. Isobel was mortified for him, but happy at the
same time to know this had never happened to him
before. Then his dimple twinkled at her as he scooped
up a drop of his passion's nectar off her belly and spread
it over her red-hot core. "My body will wait fer ye nae
longer."

"Nor will mine." She felt indecent saying it, but she
didn't care. She reached for him, yearning for his mouth,
his kiss. Oh, it was the first thing she had come to love
about him.

Their lips met with equal fervor, open, tongues meeting with the same urgent desire. He slowed, guiding the
broad head of his cock to her opening. Stilled on a breath
of anticipation, they stared into each other's eyes, seeing
all they needed. He broke through her barrier with a slow,
salacious thrust that somehow managed to feel excruciat-
ingly good while threatening to tear her in half.

"No, no!" she cried out, clutching him to her, thrashing her head back and forth. "It pains me."

He stopped moving and stilled her with a gentle hand and soft, tender kisses. "There is nothin' to fear," he soothed, capturing her anxious gaze with his adoring one. "Relax yer breathin', my delight. I will go slowly. The pain will subside."

He kept his promise and moved slowly, thoughtfully, all the while looking deep into her eyes, tracing the contour of her mouth with his fingers, his lips. He whispered to her of how she felt and how desperately he wanted her—withdrawing and advancing with long, languid thrusts.

Ecstasy darkened his eyes, tightened his jaw, and the mere sight of him over her, aching to drive his body hard into hers and exercising enough control not to, made Isobel's nerve endings burn. She lifted her legs around his waist and dug her toes into his back. Even though it was painful, she liked it and what it was doing to him. She didn't want him to stop.

He smiled at her boldness just before he took her bottom lip between his teeth and impaled her to the hilt.

She didn't cry out in pain again after that, not when his hot flesh felt so exquisitely good.

Boldly, she outlined the muscles of his chest with her fingertips, her mouth. When she stroked her palms down his tight buttocks, he lifted his weight off her, withdrew slowly to his head, and then drove her deep into the bed. She cried out his name and he slowed again, this time dragging her hands up above her head. He dipped his mouth to her nipple and sucked it into his mouth, pulling in and out of her quivering body with slow, deliberately exquisite care.

He whispered her name on a ragged breath as he burst inside her. But he withdrew before he was done and stroked her nub with the damp brush of his stiff erection.

With his hot liquid spilling over her from the tip of his lance, she cried out one last time with the thrill of her release.

Chapter Thirty-two

Tristan watched her rummage through the bags in their room wearing nothing but his shirt. He grew hard almost immediately but talked himself out of making love to her again so soon. Still, it was difficult not to want to take her from behind when she bent over one the sacks and the alluring curves of her buttocks peeked back at him.

"Are ye certain ye dinna' want my aid?"

"No." She held up her palm. "Stay exactly where ye are."

He smiled and pulled the thin blanket covering the bed a little higher on his hips. His bonnie siren had reverted to blushing. He found it quite appealing to be the only man in the world who knew what a fiery temptress his bashful goddess truly was. Hell, she'd had him panting like an animal in season. He had been with many women, but none of them had ever roused such fevered responses from him as Isobel had. Always mindful of not creating a bairn in every burgh, he prided himself on his command over his body. He had never once lost himself completely to passion, prematurely expelling his seed only to ache all over again to release his full bounty inside her. Her eager, curious touches and unrestrained responses drove him wild with desire until he barely recognized himself. Hell, but the tales were true. Love did make a man surrender all.

"Thank goodness, I have found it." She spun around, smiling and holding up a small bundle in each hand.

Tristan wanted to leap from the bed and throw her on it beneath him. "Aye, thank goodness."

"It is the bread and cheese we ate outside Dumfries," she informed him merrily as she climbed back into bed.

He nodded, catching the flash of her smooth thigh.

"Are ye hungry?"

He smiled up at her from his pillow. "I'm always hungry fer yer delectable kitchen wonders. I fear I will grow fat livin' with ye."

"I will make certain ye do not."

His blood scorched a straight path to his groin when she smiled at him beneath the veil of her lashes.

"My brothers have been enjoying my cooking fer a decade, and they are not fat."

"Who taught ye how to cook?" he asked.

"My mother. I was almost the same age Tamas is now, so she had plenty of time to teach me. I used to love to watch her cook. She taught me every spice and the medicinal value of almost every plant."

"Ye miss her."

"Of course." She smiled, remembering her mother's gentle voice and radiant smile. "We never stop missing our parents after they leave us."

"That is true." He folded his hands behind his head and closed his eyes. "I would like to travel to France to see my aunt Anne."

"Robert's wife?"

"Aye." He opened his eyes. "She lives in a convent. I would like to see her again." He looked at Isobel and smiled. "Ye have the same color hair as she has."

"Was she like a mother to ye also?"

He shook his head. "My mother would never have allowed it. She would deny it, but she favors me. I think 'tis because I resemble her brother."

"She is going to hate me, Tristan."

The quaver in her voice pulled him to her. "She will no' hate ye. I will see to it." Hell, he didn't want to think on this now. "Come here, lass."

Patience was a virtue, he told himself as he turned her on her side and spooned his body close to hers. He had to repeat the phrase a dozen more times as he closed his arms around her and pressed his hips to the softness of her backside. "All will be well," he promised her and brushed his fingers over her breast. He kissed the waves of her hair and then scooped her lush tresses away and pressed his lips to her nape. When she moved her rump against him he went as hard as his sword. "Careful, lass," he groaned, moving away from the heat of her body. "I know ye're sore, but I can be a merciless bastard."

"I do not believe it." Her soft laughter emboldened him to show her. She did not stop him or move away when he regained his position close against her back and cupped her bottom in his hand. "I want to make love to ye again, Isobel."

If she couldn't, if she refused him, he would do as she asked, for nowhere in him was there a desire to ever hurt her. But she swung her arm over her shoulder and looped it around his neck, pulling his hungry mouth closer to hers. When her tongue darted over his swollen lip, his control snapped. He rubbed his hot shaft between her buttocks and groaned into her mouth, devouring its softness.

His hands sculpted her shape beneath the gossamer fabric of his shirt. The warmth of her skin drove him mad with desire to get closer, be inside her, and feel that heat encompass him. He spread his palms over her soft belly, her firm, round breasts, and outlined the tight tips with broad strokes that made her squirm against his hard curves.

His shaft throbbed and swelled harder. He could wait no longer. His fingers tarried at her knee until he felt her breath against his cheek, short and shallow. Her passion for him nearly caused him to burst, and his heart along with it. Lifting her leg, he spread her wide and guided his moist tip along her scalding opening. Her muffled cry against the pillow as he entered her coaxed him to patience. He moved slowly, pressing his hips to her, deepening his thrust with tender expertise.

"We fit nicely, aye, my betrothed?" his voice rasped against her ear. He licked her lobe and then clutched it gently between his teeth.

"Ye are too big."

"And ye are tight and hot." He groaned and slipped his hand between her legs to stroke her center while he moved against her from behind. She grew firmer, wetter in his fingers. Her breath came hard. Her body tightened even as her leg relaxed over his. He withdrew slowly, then sank deep inside her again, clutching her to him.

"Tristan, I—"

He halted her words with a kiss that bound them together as intimately as their bodies, all the while petting her, rubbing her until her sheath tightened with little spasms around him. He impaled her deeply, withdrew even more slowly, relishing every stroke, every warm, wet shudder of her body as they drenched each other in the rapture of their release.

Spent, they remained silent for a time, kissing and smiling at each other in the darkness.

"Will we always be happy, Tristan?" she asked a little while later, wrapped in his arms.

"Aye, always." He would make certain of it. She would grow to love him as much as she loved her brothers—even more.

"I want to believe it. But yer family..."

"Isobel, I canna' be the man I wish to be withoot ye in my life."

"But how can ye be that man without being loyal to yer family?"

He pulled her closer and inhaled the scent of her hair. He had indeed betrayed his kin by loving Isobel, just as Sir Tristan of old had betrayed his king by loving Iseult. Would their ending be as tragic? He wouldn't let it. There was hope. "I told ye, my love, my kin are fergivin'. Hell, it isna' like *ye* killed the earl."

She moaned as if her body pained her, and Tristan gathered her closer in his arms. He hadn't meant to take her again so soon.

"Tristan, I—"

A knock at the door stilled her words and drained the blood from her face.

"Tristan, it is Cameron. Is Isobel with ye?"

She practically clawed her way out of his arms and leaped from the bed. "Tell him ye have not seen me!" she ordered, scrambling for her kirtle.

"Aye, she is here," Tristan called back, leaving the bed

and winking at her scathing stare. "Give me a moment or two to unbolt the door."

Isobel's eyes opened almost as wide as her mouth.

"I canna' open the door like this." He stretched out his arms to point out his nakedness, then flashed her a grin when she went crimson. He reached for his breeches and boots and watched regretfully while she hurried into her kirtle.

"Come in, Cameron," he said, opening the door.

"Where is Tamas?" Isobel demanded when Cam entered the room alone.

Cam didn't answer right away, and Tristan followed his gaze as it settled on his sister, still wearing his shirt beneath her wrinkled gown. "He is below stairs with Annie," he finally said, blinking away from her and her scarlet face. "We...we have something to tell ye."

"Aye, so do we," Tristan said, trying to save Isobel from her mortification. "I've asked Isobel to be my wife and she has given her consent."

A shadow passed over Cam's expression before he turned and eyed his sister's rumpled clothes again. Hell, how could Tristan explain to him that he could not wait?

"We shall find a priest as soon as we can."

Finally, Cam smiled and drew Tristan in for a quick embrace. "This news pleases me."

Leaving him with a pat on the back, Cam went to Isobel and hauled her in next. She was still a bit stiff and glassy-eyed when he released her with a blessing on their union.

"I have some good news of my own," he told them, grinning wider than Tristan had ever seen him. "I have asked Annie to be my wife as well, and she has agreed."

Instantly, Isobel's alarm vanished into delight. After a

dozen questions, she sat her brother on the bed and began to go over the plans for his wedding feast.

"Let us celebrate this night with the inn's finest wine," Cam suggested, leaving the bed.

Tristan had to laugh at that. "The only way ye'll be findin' fine wine here is if ye make it yerself."

"Come." Cam motioned them both toward the door. "Annie and Tamas await us. We will drink to our happy futures."

Finding his plaid folded in one of the bags, Tristan draped it over his bare shoulder, tied it haphazardly around his waist, and left the room behind them.

Annie Kennedy was a bonnie lass with bright green eyes and a bow-shaped mouth designed for asking an endless array of questions. The more wine she drank, the more she spoke. Twice Tristan and Cam shared a smile at her tireless chatter.

Isobel seemed to be enjoying herself, despite shifting her weight constantly in her chair. She blushed three different shades of scarlet when Annie asked her if something pained her. Tristan merely smiled into his cup, then scowled into it when its sour contents touched his lips.

"Ye do not like spirits, Mister MacGregor?" Annie asked, catching his displeasure.

"No' particularly. I've seen them make men do foolish things."

"Oh, do tell!" Annie pressed eagerly. "What kinds of things?"

"Alas, I would no' trouble yer delicate ears with such distasteful tales."

She giggled without a trace of a blush. "Speaking of

distasteful tales, what do ye think Andrew will say about yer betrothal to Isobel?"

"Mayhap he will challenge Tristan to a duel," Tamas answered, a flash of enthusiasm brightening his eyes for the first time that evening.

"I never pledged my love to yer brother," Isobel told Annie.

Tristan slipped his gaze to her. It occurred to him in that moment that she had never pledged it to him either. He scowled again and downed his wine.

"Well," said Annie with a sly grin aimed in Tristan's direction. "I can certainly see why not when ye had this one waiting in the wings."

"Careful, darling," Cameron warned playfully. "He is soon to be wed, and ye are soon to belong to me."

Turning to face him, Annie went all weak in her seat. "And ye know how happy that makes me, my dearest. He is pretty, but my heart is yers." She leaned into him for a kiss, whispering when she withdrew that she loved him.

Tristan called for more wine. Of course Isobel loved him. Why would she agree to marry him if she didn't?

"I know Andrew will be pleased with *our* news," Annie sang happily, holding up her cup for a refill when the server returned to their table. "He is quite fond of Cameron. Henry and Roger were delighted when I told them. Do ye have many siblings, Mister MacGregor? What will they think of ye wedding a Fergusson?"

Isobel stopped the server and let her pour more wine into her cup as well.

"They will come to love her as I do," Tristan said, swigging his drink and refusing to think about Mairi and her hidden daggers.

"Do they look like ye?" Annie asked. When Cameron rolled his eyes heavenward, she hastened to explain that she only wanted to know for the benefit of her sister, Alice. "Remember, she is twenty and two and still unwed. It is difficult to find a husband these days."

Tristan refused to look at Isobel to see her reaction. Of course that wasn't why she had said aye to his proposal. She could have had a husband in Andrew Kennedy if that was all she wanted.

"Rob and Mairi resemble my faither."

"And ye? D'ye take after yer mother, then?"

"My uncle, actually. I could have been his son." Tristan didn't realize his tone had taken on a hollow sound until Isobel reached for his hand beneath the table. He turned to smile at her, but a stinging poke to his shoulder stopped him. He turned and looked up at a tall, bearded stranger clutching a tankard in his beefy fist.

"What have we here?" The stranger grinned, exposing a missing tooth in the front of his mouth—a sure sign of a man who liked to fight.

Damnation, Tristan was not in the right frame of mind for this. When he noted the four—or were there five—men of equal height and build snaking around the table, he mumbled an oath through his clenched jaw.

"A Highlander in the Golden Hillocks!" The ruffian eyed Tristan's plaid and shook his head with pity. "Ye have a pair of bollocks sitting here drinking our wine."

"I must warn ye," Tristan said, trying to clear his head of the wine's effect and failing, "if ye claim ownership to this piss, it only proves that Covenanters lack good taste as well as good judgment."

Annie giggled behind her hand and then gasped when the stranger hauled Tristan to his feet.

"Ye're a brave, if not foolish, bastard to insult me in my own town, *Catholic*."

The inn spun in a circle from his brisk ascent upward, but Tristan hooked his mouth into a grin that warned the others to back off. "I'm pleased ye think so. Ye'll be doubly impressed when I set ye on yer back in the rushes if ye dinna' release me."

The stranger swung. Tristan ducked, swayed on his feet for a moment, and then drove the heel of his palm into the man's chin in an upward, bone-crunching motion. The ruffian went down as Tristan had promised he would, crushing a chair beneath him. The inn came alive with shouts and chairs being pushed aside. Tristan turned to see one of the brute's friends rushing for his table. He shoved Isobel and Annie out of the way and shouted to Cameron, "Behind ye!"

Cameron blocked a punch to his jaw with his left arm and sent the man reeling into the table behind them with his right fist. Tristan took a moment to smile. The lad had learned his lessons well. His satisfaction was halted by a blow to his chin.

"Ye knocked Willy out cold, ye son of a pig!" Unconscious Willy's third companion readied himself for another strike while Tristan regained his balance.

"I dinna' have to do the same to ye," Tristan offered, wiping a trickle of blood from his mouth. "There is still time fer ye to withdraw."

The man's eyes went red. His furious fist whipped past Tristan's nose, missing by inches when Tristan took a step back. He came forward just as quickly and delivered a tight, crisp punch into his opponent's belly, followed by a hard cuff to the jaw.

That wasn't so bad, Tristan thought, straightening

his plaid and watching Willy's friend crumple to the floor beside him. Cameron had finished off his opponent neatly and efficiently, and Tamas...What the hell was the lad doing standing on the table with the leg of a chair clutched in his fists?

Someone tapped him on the shoulder. Tristan turned and looked up—and further up still. Och, hell, he thought, as a fist, big enough to block out everything behind it, flew toward his face—there were five.

The last he saw before he slumped to the ground was Tamas swinging the chair leg around like a sword. He remembered nothing else as splinters of wood flew, and the brute who'd struck fell like a tree on top of him.

✤

Chapter Thirty-three

Tristan opened his eyes and smiled at Isobel's face hovering over his. "Good morn, my sunshine."

She smiled back and dabbed a cloth to his lip. He flinched. "It is evening," she told him softly. "Ye have been out fer a quarter of an hour. Cam carried ye to the bed. He is returning Annie to her room and will come back shortly. He is worried sick over ye."

Ah, the brawl below stairs. It came back to Tristan slowly. Why the hell had he drunk wine? It slowed his reflexes and his wits. "Are ye worried fer me, as well?"

She shook her head and brought her cloth to his brow. "Ye have been hit before—many times, if those tales ye told were true."

"They were," Tristan assured her, growing a bit agitated over the fact that she wasn't even worried about him. "But that doesna' mean I canna' be seriously injured by a giant's hammerin' fist."

"Tristan, ye are sulking." She leaned back to dip her rag into a bowl of water and cast him an infuriatingly mocking pout. "Did that terrible man injure ye more than ye wish to say?"

Tristan grinned at her, but it wasn't a happy look. "Even if he took a blade to my throat, it wouldna' slice as sharply as yer tongue."

He was certain he heard the tinkle of her laughter, but Cam's voice from the door distracted him.

"Ye are awake!" He cut a hasty path to the bed with Tamas hot on his heels. "I was growing alarmed when ye did not come to straightaway."

"Did ye no' see the size of the oaf who struck me, then?" Tristan answered incredulously.

"He was not so hard to put down." They all looked at Tamas with a mixture of fresh admiration and worry.

"Come." Isobel left her place beside him and shooed her brothers toward the door. "Let him rest. He will need his wits about him tomorrow when we meet with the merchants." She bent to kiss him good night, and then hovered over him a moment longer. "I would have beaten the brute over the head with Tamas's chair if he had dared aim anything at ye but his fist."

Tristan grinned at her as she stepped away, ignoring the pain of his split lip.

"I will be along in a moment," Cam told her. "I wish to have a word with Tristan."

Isobel nodded and took Tamas by the hand to leave.

"Tamas"—Tristan stopped them—"I am grateful ye fought on *my* side tonight."

Miracle of miracles, Tamas smiled at him and then looked up at his sister. "I am thirsty," he complained as she closed the door.

When they were alone, Cameron remained quiet and

pensive while Tristan sat up and swung his legs over the side of the bed. "Hell, I hate drinkin'."

"Tristan? Will ye keep yer word and wed her?"

"Of course. I always keep my word."

When Cameron began to pace in front of him, Tristan looked away to stop the room from moving. "If 'tis my kin ye worry over, rest assured I will deal with them," he said. "My father is no' so merciless as ye all believe. Ye would be astonished to learn who my brother Rob brought home to Camlochlin recently and made his wife. Dinna' fret over things, I shall work them all oot."

Tristan was thankful when Cam stopped moving—and taking the room with him. Now, he stood as still as a rod and looked at Tristan with something akin to dread in his eyes.

"There is something I need to tell ye. Before ye marry my sister, ye should know the truth."

Tristan rose to his feet and moved toward him. "What is it?"

"I cannot keep it in me any longer. Whenever ye speak of him, the weight becomes heavier fer me to bear, and now it is not just fer my father, but for him as well."

"Fer who?"

"The earl. Yer uncle. It was I who killed him. My father took the sword fer what I did."

Tristan stopped moving. He stopped breathing. In an instant, images of his uncle's limp body in the rushes of Campbell Keep flooded his thoughts, his mother and his aunt wailing in anguish, his father promising to kill every last Fergusson. He shook his head. Nae, Cam could not have been responsible for that. "The life I knew ended that day."

Cameron closed his eyes, unable to face him. "As did mine."

Tristan's blood went cold. He didn't want to hear this terrible confession from a lad whom he had come to love as a brother. He didn't want to think of the guilt Cameron had carried for a decade over the death of his father. He only felt his own pain bubbling to the surface from the place he'd kept it since that fateful night. He'd lost so much, and the man who had taken it from him stood before him now.

He snatched Cameron's collar in both hands and dragged him closer. "I..." Isobel's brother did not try to escape the rage he saw in Tristan's eyes. He looked away from them instead, ready to take his punishment.

It did not come. Already Tristan was calculating Cam's tender age at the time of the shooting. He had been a babe! Too young to even know... "Och, hell, Cam." Tristan released his shirt and hauled him in for a tight embrace instead. "Fergive me."

"No, brother, it is I who needs forgiveness. It is I who robbed ye... yer family of such a good man."

Releasing him, Tristan slumped back onto the bed. Dear God, if his father ever learned of this... "How did it happen?"

"It was dark." Cameron's voice quaked with torment as he spat the awful truth from his lips and finally from his heart as well. "My father was shouting. I was afraid that the men who came out of the keep were going to kill him. I fired my arrow hoping to frighten them away. I—I did not mean to kill him. I did not want to kill anyone."

Tristan knew in that moment that the noble ideals his uncle had taught him were the right ones. He'd been correct about the feud, correct in his opinions against revenge. "Ye were a babe," he said quietly. "'Twas no' yer fault."

"I will understand if ye must tell yer father. But Isobel...she is afraid."

Tristan looked toward the door. She was afraid of his finding out and rushing back to tell his father. Her caution with him, her mistrust...they made sense now. She had thought this truth was what he was after. She was right to keep it from him. He would have tried harder to keep himself from loving her if he'd known his father's wrath against her kin could be rekindled by this secret. Callum MacGregor had killed seven of the Fergusson men he'd seen at Campbell Keep that night. He had killed them just for being there. What would he do if he discovered the one whose arrow had pierced his brother-in-law's heart and his wife's along with it was still alive? Did Tristan's mother have the right to know who had killed her brother?

He'd begun this quest to find honor, to end the pain both families had suffered. He had found much more. He would never again lose anyone he loved over this tragic accident. The journey was not yet over, but it had just become more difficult.

If true honor was easy to attain, Tristan, his uncle's patient voice whispered in his thoughts, *most men would have already attained it.*

He turned back to Cameron just as the door to his room burst open. Tamas stood on the other side, his sling dangling from his fingers, his eyes wide with a mixture of fear and excitement.

"Ye better come quick. Yer father has just arrived."

Chapter Thirty-four

"I will ask ye again, Miss Fergusson. Where is my son?"

Isobel looked up, past a broad chest cloaked in Highland plaid, beyond a jaw chiseled from granite and just as unyielding, to hard, blue-gold eyes that scalded her soul. Eyes that had filled her childhood dreams with nightmares.

"Does he..." The mighty MacGregor Chief paused to tighten his jaw around words he clearly found difficult to utter. "Does he still live?"

Isobel nearly tripped over her feet trying to back away from him. The drink she still carried for Tamas spilled onto her kirtle. A large hand from somewhere to her right steadied her before she landed on her rump.

"Careful, lass."

Her rescuer sounded like Tristan. He spoke the same first words Tristan had ever spoken to her, but this man was bigger, broader, and less delighted to see her than Tristan had been when he discovered her and not his sister in the king's garden that first morning.

"We didna' mean to come upon ye so suddenly." Though his words were kind enough, his deep blue eyes, as hard as the Devil MacGregor's, glinted at her from behind a raven forelock. "We didna' expect to find ye here. Is my brother with ye?"

His brother. This had to be Rob MacGregor, the eldest of the Devil's sons. But who were the other two Highlanders rising from their chairs? Where were the other patrons? Likely, Isobel answered herself, they had all run for their lives at the sight of the murderous Chief.

"Miss Fergusson"—his thick burr dragged across her ears like rolling thunder—"I have never in my lifetime harmed a lass. I want an answer from ye."

Isobel wasn't going to give him one. She couldn't. Clear, logical reasoning had abandoned her and left her with cold, raw panic. She tried to tug free of her captor's hold, but his fingers did not budge.

"Faither," Tristan called out from the stairs. "What the hell are ye doin' here?" Without waiting for a response, he stepped around his father and glared at his brother. "Let her go."

Only after Rob complied did Tristan turn to the Chief. "How did ye find me?"

"We stopped to quench our thirst on our way to the Fergusson holdin'." His father raised a cup in his hand as if to prove his words true. "Rob's wife told us where ye might be when yer mother began to fear that ye were dead."

Tristan cut a sharp scowl to his brother—who merely shrugged, his expression unchanged.

"So ye hunted me doun like a babe?"

"Ye left fer our enemies' holdin' almost a month ago, Tristan," his father argued. "Did ye think I would no' try to discover what happened to my son?"

Tristan looked only mildly remorseful. "As ye can see, I am fine."

"What the hell happened to yer lip?" One of the other Highlanders left his chair and narrowed his cool gray eyes at Tristan's face.

"A fight," Tristan told him.

His curiosity piqued, the Highlander raised a dark brow. "Any broken bones?"

"Nae, Will, just the lip."

"Ye call that a fight?" Will sneered and walked away, no longer interested.

"Son," his father said, regaining Tristan and Isobel's attention, "why have ye come here?"

Tristan turned to her. "To see her. And ye should know—" His words were halted when Will suddenly sprang for the stairs. Isobel whirled around in time to see him snatch Tamas's sling from his hand and haul him up by the back of his shift.

"One of yers?" he asked Isobel, while her brother dangled two inches off the ground.

"Damn it, Will"—Tristan came to Tamas's defense— "put him doun."

"He was aboot to fire this thing at yer faither!"

"Put him doun," Tristan repeated more forcefully. When the tall brute released him, Tamas pulled back his foot and kicked him in the shin, then ran to his sister's side.

"Lucky fer him," Will said, limping back to his chair, "I dinna' hurt children."

Isobel breathed a deep sigh of relief and pulled Tamas's ear hard enough to make him squeal.

"Rob," the Chief growled, eyeing the stairs, "there is another one to yer left. Relieve him of his sword."

Cameron held up his palms as Rob reached him. "I do not carry one."

"Ye should," Rob told him, and yanked him forward.

Isobel had had enough. Who did these MacGregors think they were anyway? She didn't care if every man in Dumfries was afraid of them. She had been afraid all her life, and she was damned good and tired of it.

Lifting her skirts over her ankles, she marched straight up to Rob and gave his arm a stinging pinch. "Get yer hands off my brother, thug. I warn ye, I will not tell ye twice."

Tristan probably would have grinned at her had she been so bold with him, but this one did not flinch when she pinched him, nor did he let go of her brother.

"Are ye deaf or just terribly thick-skulled?" She fisted her hands on her hips and did all she could to control the growing tightness in her lungs.

"Thick-skulled." Will laughed from his chair. "Now there's an understatement if ever I heard one."

When Rob still did not release Cam, Isobel turned to the Chief and tilted her chin at him, then wished she hadn't. His gaze was so intense and powerful it coiled her nerves and quickened her breath. She understood why armies fled from him, why Cromwell himself had never pursued him.

It took every ounce of courage she possessed to speak to him, but she was determined to stand her ground—the way she couldn't for her father. "Tell him to take his hands off my brother this instant." She knew Tristan had come up behind her when his father's gaze lifted there. She didn't want his protection. Not in this.

"I am not afraid of ye anymore."

The MacGregor looked down at her again. "I am glad to hear it. Rob, let the lad go."

Was it her imagination, or did his eyes soften on her when he spoke? If they did, it lasted only a moment. "Tristan, why are ye still standin' there? Get whatever ye came here with and let us go home."

"I'm no' leavin' her." Tristan pulled her to him and closed his fingers around hers.

His father noted the gesture with alarm cooling his fiery gaze. "Ye canna'—"

"Aye, I can. She's to be my wife."

Isobel's knees nearly gave out at Tristan's unexpected confession. She would have preferred it if he had taken time to prepare his kin for what he'd done, but Tristan was not one for caution. Slowly, she turned to glare at him for setting this entire debacle in motion. He smiled at her, somehow soothing her roiling emotions instead.

His father was not so easily persuaded. The Chief's mouth hung open, the remainder of his words caught between disbelief and anger. His eyes raked over her, both of her brothers, and then back to Tristan. "Of all the women..." He rolled his jaw around the words he wanted to say, but didn't. "D'ye wake in the morn thinkin' of ways to defy me?"

Tristan's empty laughter cooled the air and pulled at Isobel's heart. "Of course no', faither. There are many more interestin' things to do in a day than fall short of yer expectations."

The inn was quiet save for the fourth, younger Highlander, who until now remained silent, whispering in disbelief that Tristan was finally going to take a wife.

"Ye fall short of yer own expectations, son, no' of mine."

"Ye are correct in that, faither," Tristan told him, again

unexpectedly. "But I have changed, and she is the reason fer it. I'm no' leavin' her."

His father looked as if he wanted to say more, but he shook his head and looked up at the heavens. "Were the years yer brother took off my life when he chose *his* wife no' enough?"

Astoundingly, Tristan's humor returned. "At least ye dinna' have to worry about a Dutch army attackin' Camlochlin again."

His father did not smile back. "I would rather face an army than yer mother."

Tristan's smile faded. "I know."

"Good, because I willna' be the one to tell her that ye have given yer heart to a Fergusson. Ye will. Both of ye get yer things so we can leave this den of Presbyterian cutthroats."

"No, Tristan!" Isobel protested immediately. He simply could not mean for her to go to Camlochlin with him. Oh, she thought she could marry him. She told herself they could find happiness together even if he learned the truth. She knew in her heart that he would never hurt Cam. But seeing his father before her, just as huge, just as menacing as when she was a girl of ten, convinced her that there would never be anything between their families but hatred. Sending provisions every year was a kind gesture, but it was not the same as forgiveness. "I cannot go with ye!"

"Isobel, my love..." Still holding her hand, he brought it to his heart.

"Fergive me," she pleaded. She couldn't bear the thought of going and looking into his mother's eyes. What would she see? Accusation, more bitter hatred. His kin, all unhappy at her presence. She hadn't considered it all before. If she had, she might have fooled herself yet again into thinking she could actually face them all, for Tristan's sake. Now, though, after hearing in the Chief's voice the amount of control it took for him to even speak to her, let alone be somewhat courteous about it, she knew she could not do it.

"I will not go there to be spat upon," she told him, covering their entwined fingers with her other hand. "I realize that what they lost was great, but none of us came out of this unscathed."

"Ye're right," he told her. "And that is why ye must come with me. So that they can know it as well. 'Tis the only way to begin anew, Isobel. Fer all of us."

She shook her head, but she knew she had just lost the battle. For she understood in that moment who he was and why he needed to make things right. She wanted it for him. He deserved it. She almost loved his uncle Robert for the man he had taught Tristan to be, antiquated and all. She would go with him and do whatever she could to help him in his quest, but she could never marry him. Their union would bring their families together as it did now, many more times, mayhap enough for them to discover the truth on their own—and she could never risk that.

She nodded her consent and watched his beautiful smile wash over him, knowing that what they thought they had could never truly be. Not with her family's secret always threatening to destroy all that Tristan had accomplished.

"I am coming also."

Isobel wiped the moisture from her eyes and glared at Cameron. "Ye are not coming. Go home with—"

"With the laird's permission, of course."

Callum MacGregor blinked at her brother's slight bow and then nodded, tightening his jaw as if he already regretted his reply but could not take it back.

"Cameron, I forbid it!" Isobel pushed Tristan out of her way, but Cam was already halfway up the stairs.

"I must tell Annie not to fret. All will be well."

The MacGregor watched him go and then exchanged a knowing look with his eldest son. Together, they eyed Tristan, recognizing his work.

"Tamas"—Isobel pushed him forward—"go with him and tell the Kennedys to bring ye home to Pat—"

"And miss seeing a castle?" Tamas snorted. "I am coming with ye." When she opened her mouth to set him straight, he stopped her. "I was not going to tell ye this, but Roger Kennedy cuffed me hard on the head last eve. Twice. I do not think he likes me very—"

"Mister Fergusson!" The Chief's voice boomed through the inn calling for Cameron and startling her and Tamas both. "We are leavin'! Now!"

Chapter Thirty-five

"What is the matter with her?"

Tristan glanced at Isobel slumped against the tree a few feet away from the fire, then at his father standing over her.

"She has a breathin' condition." He turned back to the butterbur tea boiling over the flames and was glad she had remembered to pack it for their journey to Dumfries. This attack wasn't too bad—not like the one she'd had at home the night Andrew had upset her—but Tristan wanted to give her some tea before her breaths became any more shallow.

"It is almost ready," Cam said, squatting beside him.

"She is sickly, then," his father murmured, shaking his head at her. Isobel glared at him in return.

"Nae." Tristan gave him a hard look as well. "It only comes upon her at times. I think being on a horse all day has irritated her lungs." And seeing his kin towering over her at the inn likely hadn't helped either. "She will be better soon."

His father made a small grunting sound, as if tugging

with his own conscience. "We will make camp here fer the night, then."

Tristan watched him saunter back to where Rob sat on the stump of a tree. The two of them shared a few words before Rob rose to unpack the horses.

"I am glad we are resting." Cameron looked at Tristan and smiled. "My thighs and arse feel like someone took a mallet to them."

Aye, Tristan knew the Fergussons were not used to being in the saddle for so long. Poor Isobel had to be in pain from riding with him all the way to Dumbarton, but she hadn't complained. In fact, she hadn't said much of anything at all the entire way.

"My apologies fer this, Cam. The cart would never have made it to Camlochlin. I'm grateful to the Kennedys fer lettin' us use their horses."

Cam shrugged it off. "It is better this way. Henry and Roger will return our wares to Patrick, and Annie will assure him that we are safe. Although I do not fancy the thought of traveling so far with Tamas in my lap."

"I do not like it either, Cam," Tamas complained from across the fire. "I want my own horse."

"This one," Will drawled, pointing at Tamas before he sat beside him, "is goin' to set Camlochlin on its bluidy arse. Ye should have left him at the inn."

"And I should have aimed my rock at yer head instead of yer Chief's."

Will only smiled at Tristan, his point proved.

Ignoring the lot of them, Tristan poured Isobel's tea into a piece of hollowed bark, blew on it, and then fed it to her.

"Do not let him hurt him," Isobel said between sips.

"Ye need no' worry aboot Will. He is a good-natured fellow fer all his bluster."

Isobel looked up from her tea and sighed. "I was speaking of Tamas causing Will injury, not the other way around."

Tristan laughed softly and stroked her cheek while she drank. "All will be well, my love. Trust me, aye?"

"I do," she said, making his heart clatter in his chest.

He bent to kiss her forehead, then turned to look directly into another set of bright green eyes.

"I never would have believed it if I did not see it fer myself."

"Go away, Finn." Tristan gave him a playful push that set the crouching young Highlander flat on his rump. "Yer duty is to follow Rob, no' me."

Finn set himself right and aimed his wide grin at Isobel. "'Tis not my duty yet," he explained, though she hadn't asked. "But I do hope to someday be the new laird's bard. I am Finlay Grant, son of Commander Graham Grant, brother of Captain Connor—"

Tristan shoved him off his haunches a second time and then smiled when Isobel giggled. She was feeling better.

Finn thought so, too, and graced her with his sweetest smile. "Ye may call me Finn."

"Finn, the lady is—why the hell are ye starin' at me like that?"

"'Tis hard to believe that ye lost yer heart to one lass, Tristan. 'Tis going to leave many at Camlochlin heartsick. I would wager..." His voice trailed off as Tristan aimed his darkest glare on him.

"Aye, then. I am going." Rising to his feet, Finn dusted off his plaid and offered Isobel one last breathtaking smile. "He is not usually so sour. We can speak later when we get home."

"Dinna' believe a word he tells ye aboot me," Tristan told her as Finn joined the others around the fire.

"I already know what a rogue ye are, Tristan MacGregor," she said softly, touching her finger to his dimple.

"Nae, no' anymore," he promised her, turning his head to kiss her fingers. "That is no' me."

"I know that, too."

Hell, how did she manage to wind his heart so tightly around her delicate, callused fingers? He had indeed been a rogue, taking lasses to his bed from Skye to Inverness, taking what they offered without giving anything in return. Never, ever his heart. How could he give away what he did not feel? His heart had stopped beating for a single moment when he'd realized his uncle was never going to get up off the floor—and it was because of him that he was dead. When it began pumping again, it beat within the chest of someone different. He'd been changed, lost, and falling without an anchor, without knowing how to feel anything anymore. His father expected him to be strong—needed him to be strong for his mother's sake.

Life went on in Camlochlin, at least for most. The loss of her brother had forever changed Kate MacGregor also. Eventually, her laughter rang through the halls once again, but she saved her warmest smiles for Tristan. They had never spoken about why he had chosen such a reckless path. She knew it was easier to pretend.

"Ye've made me feel my heart again, Isobel."

"Tristan," his father called out as Tristan lowered his mouth to hers. "Bring her to the fire and come eat with us. Yer mother and Maggie have packed enough food fer an army."

His mother. How was he going to tell her about Isobel? And worse, the nettle that had been pricking his side all day, what if his father somehow discovered the Fergussons' secret? How far would he go to protect Cam—to protect Isobel? He looked at his father again. Would he have to protect them? He didn't know. He didn't know the man sitting a few feet away from him. "Come." He smiled at Isobel. "Before he sends Finn back."

"Is yer castle far?" Tamas asked him, pulling his teeth on a length of dried meat after everyone settled in.

"Aye, 'tis over the mountains, across deep lochs, and beyond the misty cliffs."

"Cliffs?" Tamas's sleepy eyes rounded with excitement.

"Narrow cliffs," Will answered him, tossing an apple stem over his shoulder. "The kind wee lads have trouble guiding their horses over and fall to their grisly death."

"Tell that to Cam." Tamas shrugged, unfazed. "He will be steering."

Tristan nodded when Will threw him a look filled with surprise, admiration, and pity. "We are workin' on it."

"'Tis like ye, Tristan."

They all turned to Callum MacGregor, peeling a pear with his dagger.

"What is like me, faither?" Tristan met his gleaming gaze over the flames when his father finally looked up from his work.

"Stayin' away fer almost a month. Never considerin' what ye put us through. I know ye are a man, but ye are a reckless one. We canna' help but worry that ye will get yerself killed by some enraged husband or faither—or brother. And Patrick Fergusson of all brothers. When Davina told Rob where ye might have gone, we…" He did not finish, but looked away into the darkness of the trees instead.

"Fergive me."

A twig snapped in the fire, the only sound that was heard as Callum turned back to his son.

Tristan almost smiled when his father blinked at him as if he didn't know the man sitting across the flames. He didn't, and Tristan hoped to right that, too. "Because of him"—he motioned to Tamas—"I know what I have put ye through all these years, and I ask yer fergiveness fer it."

"Granted," his father said, then cleared his throat to vanquish the tenderness softening his gaze. "Hell, the runt must be riotous indeed."

"Far worse than I ever was," Tristan said, tearing a chunk of black bread in half and handing a piece to Isobel.

"Worse than when ye put poison oak in Colin's bed?" Rob asked, then laughed with Will when their cousin remembered the incident and tossed his head back, howling.

Tristan gave Tamas a sinister smile. "And ye thought I wouldna' do it."

"It still would not have equaled what I did to ye," Tamas replied with another dismissive shrug.

"Och, hell, he's bold!" Will clapped the boy on the shoulder, almost driving him into Finn's lap. "Tell us what ye did to him, lad."

"Well," Tamas began, sparing Tristan a triumphant grin first. "I shot him in the forehead with my sling and knocked him out cold."

All four Highlanders turned to Tristan in unison, their mouths gaping open.

"There's more," Tristan told them, unashamed of his

suffering at the hands of such a wee opponent. He knew the warriors around him would not be angry with Tamas, but rather appreciative of his brash courage. He was, of course, correct, and he drew closer to Isobel while his kin laughed at the hornets and the broken walking stick. He would likely be teased about it for weeks to come, but he smiled and took Isobel's hand in the dim light of the fire.

"They like him. 'Tis a good beginnin'."

Isobel wished she was as optimistic as Tristan, but each time she looked at the MacGregor laird, she saw him burying his sword in her father—into Cam if he ever discovered the truth. How could she smile with him, laugh with him? She hadn't spoken the truth when she'd told him she wasn't afraid of him anymore. She was terrified of what he might still do.

His laughter drew her eyes to him. Dear Lord, but he was an imposing man. Even sitting, he towered over all the others, save for his son Rob. Where Tristan was built for speed and agility, both his father and his brother were built for combat. Their bare legs were long and muscular beneath the knee-length hem of their plaids. Their shoulders were wide and straightened with pride and confidence.

As if feeling her eyes on him, the Chief angled his head and looked directly at her. Isobel turned away.

"Are ye feelin' unwell again?"

He hadn't spared her a word on their journey so far, and Isobel did not want to talk to him now. She shook her head. "I am fine."

"Ye look as pale as the moon," he said, inviting the others to turn to her as well.

Isobel cringed. "I am weary, that is all." Briefly, she met the Chief's gaze again, meaning to give him her most resolute look. He smiled at her. It was neither pitying nor mocking. Nor was it the kind of lip-curling, heart-stopping smirk that Tristan possessed, but it softened the uncompromising angles of his face just enough to reveal another man hidden behind the gruffness.

"Ye better sleep then, Bel." She blinked and turned to Tamas when he spoke. "Ye know how foul ye get in the morning when ye do not get enough sleep."

She was about to admonish him when Will clipped him on the shoulder. "Dinna' speak so to yer sister, runt."

Isobel clenched her jaw. Luckily for him, there was something about William MacGregor that she liked. He possessed the same carefree laughter as Tristan, only his was tinged with a bit of ruthlessness—as if he could laugh and sing a merry Highland ditty while he cut his enemy's throat. She should keep Tamas away from him for that reason alone, but if he struck her brother one more time, whether he was right to do so or not, she was going to crown him over the head with a stick.

On instinct, she reached out her hand to stop him when Tamas plucked a beetle from the ground and set it gingerly on Will's bread while the Highlander turned to agree with something Rob said. Tristan saw him do it and called out to Will when he brought the bread to his mouth, but it was too late. The beetle crunched, Will went three shades paler, and Tamas rolled over on his side laughing with glee.

"Aye, go on and laugh," Will told him, spitting a beetle leg out of his mouth. "Tomorrow ye ride wi' me." He turned to Tristan, a shadow of wicked intention darkening his diamond-colored eyes. "He rides wi' me."

"Aye," Tristan agreed easily, offering Tamas a pitying look.

Isobel glared at him. "What do ye mean, aye?" So was this how it was going to be then, with Tristan stepping aside and letting his family do as they pleased to hers? She fumed. She would protect them herself, as she always had.

Turning to Will, she gathered her courage around her like a mantle and spoke softly, meaningfully. "If ye dare harm a hair on my brother's head, I vow I will poison ye in—"

"Mayhap"—Will swung back to Tamas in the middle of Isobel's quiet tirade—"ye are no' so brave after all if ye need yer sister to protect ye."

Immediately, Tamas puffed up his chest. "I can take care of myself. I will ride with ye tomorrow and prove it."

Isobel wanted to shout at the both of them, especially Will. Her threats failed to impress or interest him in the slightest. And how clever of him to use her maternal instincts against her. And Tamas! Dear God, Tristan had warned her that he was headed down a dangerous path. He deliberately provoked men's anger. Someday it might get him killed.

"He is prideful!" she said quickly and with a bit more humility, hoping to annul the deal her brother had made.

"Too fearless fer his own safety," Tristan added promptly.

Isobel let out a surrendering sigh. She turned to Tristan knowing he was not trying to save Tamas from Will, but from himself. Behind him, Cam nodded.

"Yes," she finally admitted aloud. "He is."

Tristan smiled and pulled her in, resting his forehead

against hers and speaking low enough so that only she could hear. "He shall ride with Will."

It was one of the most difficult things she had ever done, but she nodded, completely trusting her brother's life in someone else's hands.

Luckily, Tristan wasn't just anyone. No man of honor ever was.

Chapter Thirty-six

They started out early the next morning, about a quarter of an hour after Will discovered his saddle had been loosened during the preparations. For Tamas's sake, no one remarked on the fall Will would have taken had he mounted.

Isobel gave them all that much.

The terrain was treacherous along the rocky coast of the Firth of Clyde, or at least it was to Isobel's rump. She was still sore from the day before. If it wasn't for Tristan's supple warmth against her back, she would have cringed the entire way. When she leaned against him, his arms enveloped her, making her smile despite what lay ahead. Soon, she would step into the MacGregors' lair, and she was bringing Cam with her.

"I dinna' like when ye go stiff in my arms." His voice, so close and coarse against her ear, sent a ripple up her spine. "I would have ye soft and willin' in them always."

"And ye will always have yer way." She closed her eyes and purred against him. How would she ever leave him?

"Aye."

She heard the smile in his voice and smiled with him. "Would ye vanquish all my dragons fer me, knight?"

"Aye, if ye let me, I would."

He would. Oh, how she wished they were alone so she could turn in her saddle and kiss him. For one mad moment, she wished Camlochlin were closer so they could get there and lock themselves away one last time.

A horse trotted beside her and she opened her eyes and smiled at Tamas as he and Will passed her.

"Tristan?"

"Aye, my love?"

"When did ye first begin to love me? I want to remember it always."

Tamas's shriek halted Tristan's reply and turned her blood cold. She bolted straight up and watched, horrified, as Will, having dismounted with Tamas dangling fitfully from his fist, strode to the water's edge and let him go.

"Tristan!" Isobel gasped, clutching his shirt. "He cannot swim!"

Terror drained the color from his face as he leaped from the horse. She was close behind him until his boots hit the ground and he took off running. He sprinted toward the shoreline, leaping over rocks and narrow inlets, leaving Isobel and his gaping relatives with nothing to do but watch. Without breaking stride, he dove into the water only inches from Tamas's flailing arms.

Isobel nearly fell to her knees with relief as Tristan clutched her brother to his chest and began to swim back to shore. She tried to hold back the spring of emotions rushing though her, but when she saw the way Tamas's little arms were coiled tightly around Tristan's neck, she had to let her tears come.

Someone stormed past her. She looked up to see MacGregor bend over the rocks and reach down to separate Tamas's dripping body from his son's. When he straightened, his eyes smoldered like deadly blue embers on Will.

"Let that be enough."

"Aye, Laird," Will answered without quarrel.

"D'ye hear me, boy?" Gripping Tamas by the forearms, the giant Chief held him up to his level gaze. "That is enough!"

"Yes, Laird."

Isobel blinked. Was that her brother's voice, trembling and obedient? She held out her arms to take him when the Chief reached her, but he stepped out of her path and swung Tamas over his shoulder.

"I have him," he said. And then he said nothing more as he leaped to his mount, set her brother upon his lap, and wrapped him in his plaid.

When Tristan reached her a moment later, she helped him out of his wet shirt and kissed his chest. He had saved Tamas's life, just as he'd saved John's and Patrick's when the Cunninghams attacked. "Thank ye." Oh, how she loved this man. "Let me get ye into yer dry plaid."

Will stopped them as they headed back to Tristan's horse. "I thought he could swim. I didna' know—"

"There's nae harm done, cousin," Tristan eased him quickly with a pat to his shoulder. "He is safe."

He is safe. Isobel looked to where Tamas sat nestled in the arms of one of the most dangerous men in Scotland, and something in her heart went soft. Mayhap the terrible MacGregor Chief was not so terrible after all.

They rode for many more hours, and by the time they

stopped to eat, Isobel wondered if she would ever see a bed again.

"Do ye have yer own room at Camlochlin?" she asked Tristan, rubbing her sore backside before he lifted her to his saddle when their quick rest was over.

"Of course. 'Tis a castle. There are many rooms."

"Do ye think I could have a bath when we arrive? Truly, I have never felt so grimy."

Vaulting up behind her, he dipped his mouth to her ear and sent hot tremors to her belly when he whispered, "Only if I can join ye."

"In the bath?" She turned in his arms, and his smile deepened at the flush creeping across the bridge of her nose. The color of his eyes changed from warm golden brown to smoky amber when he nodded.

"In the bath, on the floor, against the wall... wherever I can have ye."

Her muscles ached, but not for rest. She wanted to peel away his plaid and taste him with her tongue, her teeth. She wanted to see his lithe, naked body hard and ready for her, feel him sink deep inside her while his teeth raked across her pulse. She remembered to breathe, drawing in a deep gulp of air, only to have it snatched away again when he slipped his hand behind her nape and bent his lips to hers.

"Of course, we have to call the priest in first. I gave Cam my word we would be wed quickly."

Her heart sank to her feet. She broke their gaze. How would she tell him? How *could* she tell him? Mayhap it was better if she didn't. He would only try to persuade her that she was wrong, and he would easily succeed, for she wanted too desperately to believe that their love could conquer anything that came against them. It couldn't, of course. Tristan could never be happy with his family continuing to hate her. And if they ever hurt Cam...

"Isobel?" He spoke her name on a quiet breath and fit his fingers beneath her chin so she would look at him. "I know what it is that brings fear to ye. I—"

"It is a monumental quest," she agreed over him. "But I will do all I can to help ye see it through. If I have to smile at an army of MacGregors to make them like me, I will do it. I love ye and I want ye to be happy always."

His smile began slowly and then broke into a grin as wide and as dazzling as the vast, cloudless sky. He turned to the closest man who could hear him and said, "Did ye hear that?"

"I did," his father answered, but Tristan had already turned back to her.

"She loves me."

"Are ye so surprised, then?" She laughed softly against his lips.

"Aye, I am. Ye hold fast to yer convictions, lass. 'Twas somethin' that at first excited me but terrified me later. There were days I thought ye would always hate me."

"But ye did not give up." She kissed his mouth, so close to hers, loving him more than she ever dreamed possible. "Even when I treated ye poorly."

"How could I? 'Twould be givin' up my heart, my life. Fer they are both yers."

How easily he made her forget. How easily he persuaded her that she was all he needed in his life to truly be happy. She wanted to believe it. Oh, if only he didn't need to fix what he believed he'd wronged. If only she truly was all he needed to be happy.

Another rider passed them, the force of his presence upon his horse dragging Isobel's gaze to his intensely blue one. She smiled at the future leader of the MacGregor clan. "Did ye hear that?"

Rob looked at Tristan first and then back at her. "Aye." He offered her a smile that was every bit as warm as Tristan's. "I heard it." He drew his mount closer and leaned in toward his brother. "The punch is in makin' certain *they* hear it."

Isobel knew whom he meant. Callum and Kate MacGregor. Hadn't Rob recently returned to Camlochlin with a wife the laird did not favor? Suddenly, she saw him in a whole new light. "Did ye proclaim yer love fer yer wife before them?"

"I did, and she did fer me. 'Tis a force nae heart that has known love can withstand."

"He protects ye," Isobel said as Rob trotted on ahead without another word.

"He protects everyone he loves. 'Tis his passion."

"Then"—she smiled, turning forward in his lap and snuggling deep against him—"he is not so different from ye."

She remained quiet for the rest of the day, forgetting what lay ahead and enjoying the sights and sounds around her; the lilting pitch of the Highlanders' voices, their boisterous laughter reverberating through the trees, Tristan's heartbeat against her ear.

Cam seemed to take a liking to Finn, spending much of the day at his side. He listened mostly while the young Mister Grant told him everything there was to know about his family and about the MacGregors of Skye.

By the second day, it was Cam doing most of the talking, and since Finn always rode at Rob's side, Isobel's brother had an additional listener.

Judging from the bits and pieces she overheard when

she urged Tristan to ride closer to them, Cam spoke mainly of Patrick.

"He tills the land alone?" she heard Rob ask him.

"He does everything to make certain we are warm and fed."

"A good trait, that," Rob said thoughtfully. "Aye, a good one."

By the end of their third night together, everyone was still in good enough spirits to laugh around the fire about wounds they'd received in one battle or another. Tristan laughed about his many close calls with death with the same gusto as the rest of them, proving to Isobel, at least, that he possessed more warrior blood than he realized.

She looked across the fire to where Tristan's father sat patiently answering the whirlwind of questions Tamas threw at him. Emboldened by the laird's indulgent tone, Isobel rose from her place and went to them. She sat close to her brother and stroked his hair.

"How are ye faring?"

He sighed and rolled his eyes to the night sky. "Fine."

"It is hard fer me…" she lifted her gaze to MacGregor "…to let go of him."

"What is his age?" the laird surprised her by asking.

"He is one and ten."

His features were quite striking in the firelight, and easily read. Isobel watched him calculate the years in his mind. When he concluded, he dropped his gaze to the flames. "Ye raised him."

"My brother and I did." Her voice shook. Never in her life had she thought she would someday speak to him about what he had taken from her family. "There are seven of us. Patrick is the eldest." She grew quiet again.

Now that she had the chance to tell him, she found her venom had lost its sting. What could she say? That she hated him for killing her father, when it was her father's fault that the Earl of Argyll died? How could she tell him that her loss was worse than the loss *his* family had suffered? She couldn't, not anymore.

"Tristan has told us much about Robert Campbell," she said quietly, courageously. There were new things she wanted him to know. "Tristan loved him well. He loves him still."

"I know," his father said, looking to where his son sat.

"Whatever else is said between us from this night on," Isobel pressed forward, "I wish ye to know that my brothers and I are deeply sorry fer what happened."

He didn't look at her again when he spoke, his voice so raspy and low she wasn't certain if it was him speaking or the wind. "So am I."

Chapter Thirty-seven

Tristan had crossed the narrows into Kylerhea on the eastern coast of the Isle of Skye a dozen times before when he'd visited lasses on the mainland, but he'd never returned with a lass, and never one who would break his mother's heart. Each moment that brought him closer to Camlochlin set another stone on his chest. He told himself over and over again while they traveled toward the brae pass of Bealach Udal that all would be well. Things always worked out in his favor. What, after all, was so terrible about wanting to end a feud his uncle never would have approved of? As long as his parents never discovered the truth, his mother would come to accept the Fergussons, just as his father did. She had to.

He set his gaze on the laird riding a short distance ahead with wee Tamas still tucked neatly in his arm. He knew why such a sight had brought a smile to his face every time he looked their way over the past five days. Tamas had won his father's favor. And for Tristan, it was as if he were seeing Callum MacGregor for the very first time. Not as a teacher, though he was one of the best.

His children were testimony to that. Not as a leader, with more responsibilities piled on his sturdy shoulders than any common man could withstand. The MacGregors of Camlochlin, who bore their name proudly during the proscription because of him, could attest to that. But as a father, a shield against any danger that dared come close to his bairn. Tamas wasn't his, but the child had no father because of him. The Devil MacGregor was no vengeful, unforgiving savage. Savages were not men of honor, and Tristan's father was that.

"Ye must speak with him about it."

He looked down at Isobel to find her staring back at him. "Aboot what?"

"About whatever it is that created this rift between the two of ye. Ye conceal it well beneath yer blithe demeanor, but it was there when ye spoke of him. It is there when ye look at him, just beyond the glimmer in yer eyes, shaping yer smiles with a trace of something unguarded and raw, like a wound that will not be healed."

He had wanted Isobel to know who he was, but she had looked even deeper. "I dinna' know if it can be," he admitted to her.

"Of course it can, my love." Her smile was tender, as was her touch. "Whatever he did—"

"Nae, my wound is self-inflicted, Isobel. I didna' try to fit in. I didna' try to be his son. How could I be his when I thought we were so different? I didna' know who he wanted me to be because I couldna' see who *he* was. I wanted my uncle and he was gone because of me."

"No, not because of ye."

"I believed it to be so," he told her softly. "And that belief was the dagger that first made me bleed."

She traced his lips with her fingers and he kissed them

in return. "Then, my handsome, most noble knight, begin
there."

The treacherous cliffs of Elgol were no match for Tamas
Fergusson. He found so much delight in the roar of the
waves below the narrow precipice that he roared back. It
was jarring enough to hear him screeching at the top of
his lungs, but when he leaned over the side of the laird's
horse as far as he could to have a look down, everyone
behind them let out a shout. Either he had complete trust
in the man securing him by the wrist, or his fearlessness
went beyond anything the rest of them knew—especially
Will, who nearly passed out just peeking over the edge.

Topping the cliffs, they came to a high ridge overlooking a vast, heather-lined glen and a wide bay to the west.
Quaint, thatch-roofed bothies littered the landscape while
snowcapped mountain ranges cut across the northern sky.
In the center of it all, Camlochlin Castle rose out of the
dark curtain wall behind it, the Devil's fortress cupped in
God's glorious hand.

Isobel took a deep breath and found the air moist and
refreshing to her lungs. Now, if she could just get her
heart to slow down.

There were already a number of people spilling out of
the bothies, as well as the wide castle doors, eager to see
the approaching riders. Rob took off into the glen first, his
horse's hooves trampling the heather as he raced toward
a woman breaking from the small crowd to meet him. He
bounded from his horse before it came to a complete stop
and swept her off her feet and into his arms.

There were other women waiting, two in particular
who watched in silence as the remaining riders trotted
toward them. One woman, the taller of the two, fixed

her dark eyes on the laird and Tamas first and then on Isobel.

"Fergusson prisoners?" The smaller woman, standing a bit hunched beside the first, quirked a raven brow at Cameron.

"Just Fergussons, Maggie." Coiling his arm around Tamas's waist, the laird dismounted and deposited the boy at her feet. Maggie and Tamas gave each other a level stare before Maggie huffed and watched him run off.

"Tamas!" MacGregor called out after planting a kiss on the taller woman's mouth. "Stay oot of trouble!"

"Yes, Callum!" Tamas called back.

After a brief but frigid glare at her husband, the woman turned her eyes on Tristan. "It is good to see you alive, my son." She didn't wait for his response, or for introductions, while Tristan helped Isobel dismount, but turned on her heel and strode back to the castle without another word.

Watching her, Tristan's father ran his hand over his bristly jaw. "I will speak to her," he murmured, more to himself than to anyone else, and promptly followed her inside.

"What will yer father speak to her about?" Left alone with them, Maggie MacGregor fisted her small hands on her hips and narrowed her eyes at Isobel and Cameron. "What have ye done this time, Tristan?"

Isobel hadn't been around so many people inside one structure since Whitehall Palace. Camlochlin was not as grand as the king's place of residence, but it was big enough to house more MacGregors than she was comfortable with. The halls were cavernous, with thick iron candle stands and bracketed wall torches lighting the maze of corridors.

Isobel did not smile at the faces staring back at her but reached for Cam's hand instead. She should not have allowed him to come. Her fear about her error in judgment was validated when three enormous Highlanders sauntered toward her and halted in their tracks when Maggie spoke the word, "Fergussons."

"Hell," one of them growled deeply with disgust.

"Are we havin' them fer supper, then?" Another, with red bushy hair peppered with gray and a long scar running from ear to chin, snarled.

"Easy, Angus," Tristan warned him with a wry smile. "This bonnie lass will bite ye back."

Isobel wanted to smile at him for crediting her with more courage than she probably had, and for coming to her rescue nonetheless. No matter what they thought of him here, the man she knew would have made Arthur Pendragon proud.

"Angus! Brodie!" The laird called out brusquely from the top of the stairs. "See that Camlochlin's guests are treated well."

The threat in his command did not need to be spoken aloud. The two burly Highlanders stepped away without another word or glance in her direction.

"Jamie," he called to the third. "Bring Cameron oot to Finn and keep an eye on the wee one called Tamas. See that no harm comes to him."

"Aye, Laird."

For the first time since she stepped into the castle, Isobel breathed a sigh of relief. And she had him to thank. She looked up at Tristan's father with appreciation in her eyes instead of hatred. The images she had of him, created from the horror of her childhood, were slowly being replaced by merciful glances and the tenderness in his large, scarred hands as he closed his plaid around her smallest brother. Somehow, Tamas had won his favor. That alone said much about him.

"Ye two." There was nothing merciful in his eyes when he pointed down at her and Tristan. "Come with me."

They followed him down a softly lit corridor, lined with heavy tapestries and littered with laughing children running for the stairs. When he reached the door, Tristan's father did not pause in his stride but pushed open the thick doors and plunged inside.

"He is here. Speak to him."

Kate MacGregor offered her husband a scathing glare but turned to them when they entered the large private solar.

"Very well," she said, her stinging glance settling on Isobel. "Miss Fergusson, I am certain you are a lovely enough woman, but you do understand that your father coldly took my brother's life. You and your family will not be welcomed here by me."

Isobel nodded, having nothing to say. She felt as if she were looking into a pool, gazing at herself. Those were *her* eyes filled with anger, *her* unyielding lips, speaking unforgiving words she understood all too well. What could she say?

"Should they suffer fer the crimes of their faither?" Tristan said for her. "Mayhap we should ask Maggie and know her answer."

"Tristan," his father warned. "Mind what ye say."

"I'll mind what I say if I'm wrong, faither. Am I?"

"Nae, ye are no' wrong," the laird admitted even while his wife turned from him. "Katie," he said more gently than Isobel had heard him yet.

"No, Callum," she refused his unspoken plea. "You

should understand better than anyone else. Growing up, your sister was all you had. You did not let your enemies kill her." She turned again to Isobel and Tristan, this time with tears in her eyes. "We were orphans, left alone to be raised by a handful of old soldiers. Robert was the one who gave me courage. He was more than my brother. He was my playmate, my dearest friend, and the most chivalrous man I know. He did not deserve to be shot down in the dark by a madman whose pride was wounded."

"I dinna' dispute the truth of that," Tristan told her gently. "Ye know that I loved him." His gaze flickered to his father, then away again. "But Isobel lost much also. She and her brothers—"

"I do not wish to hear of it!" his mother's voice overrode his. "Yer uncle was a good man, a fair man. He—"

"Ye know what he was, but ye would no' have it of me," Tristan accused.

"Not for the Fergussons!"

"Then that is a pity," he countered meaningfully, "because I love her and I intend to make her my wife."

Isobel drew in a sharp breath and closed her eyes, not wishing to see or feel the pain they had caused. Oh, but they were fools to believe the past could be so easily forgotten. The hatred would never end, and Tristan was about to lose his family because of her.

"You have betrayed us, Tristan," she heard his mother say.

"So be it." He took Isobel's hand and led her toward the door. "I will nae longer betray my heart."

Cameron watched Isobel and Tristan leave the solar and disappear down the corridor. Stepping out of the shadows, he looked at the heavy doors separating him from the freedom of ten years of guilt and cowardice. Thanks to Tristan, he refused to be that man anymore. Girding up his courage, he lifted his hand to knock just as the door opened again.

"I heard everything," he admitted to the tall warlord hovering over him. "Yer wife is wrong about one thing. A madman did not kill her brother. I did."

Chapter Thirty-eight

Tristan's chambers were not what Isobel had expected. To start, she had imagined a bigger bed, one covered in furs or silks to provide more comfort to the ladies who'd visited in the past. She was surprised to find his bed only slightly larger than Alex's. There were no draperies covering the two deep windows on the western wall to offer warmth or silence from the whitecaps rolling in from Camas Fhionnairigh bay below. A worn chessboard rested uselessly on a table in the corner, many of its pieces missing.

At first glance, one might consider the man who slept here to be careless and inattentive. But crossing the room to the cooled, soot-stained hearth, Isobel noted the old swords hung with care above, the polished bookcase to her right, carved in rich walnut wood, each shelf neatly lined with books. She smiled. He took great care of the things that mattered to him.

"They are my uncle's swords," he said, coming up behind her.

"I thought as much." She took a step away from him and went to the window. She couldn't be near him. His warmth, his touch, his scent all worked diligently against her good sense. "Tristan, I...I cannot let ye lose yer family because of me."

He did not move to go to her but remained where he stood in the middle of the room, alone, as he had been for most of his life. "Ye are my family, Isobel. Ye and yer brothers. Ye are all I want."

"But we are not all ye need. Ye risked so much by trying to help my family because of who ye are...who ye have always been. But I fear yer purpose will fail. In the end, ye will only have us..."

"Then 'twill be enough."

"No." She turned to look at him, letting her tears fall freely. "Yer honor is what makes ye who ye are, Tristan. How will it be enough when ye must betray yer family? Ye heard what yer mother said—"

"It will be enough because 'twas their choice. No' mine." He went to her, shortening the distance between them in two long strides. "Isobel, ye are the one who makes me what I want to be. *Ye* are what I need."

"There is something else," she cried, looking away from his fervent gaze. "Something I have not told ye that will change everything."

"I already know 'twas Cameron who shot my uncle, Isobel." He took her in his arms when she looked up at him, stunned and terrified. "He told me at the inn, and I dinna' care." He withdrew just enough to cup her wet face in his hands and look deeply into her eyes. "It doesna' change how much I love ye. Nothin' ever will."

He knew and he didn't care. She smiled at his blurry face, certain that no lady from his books had ever loved her knight so well. But... "But if they find out and come against us again, how will ye stand on our side?"

"They will no' find out. They will no' come against ye. My faither is no' the man I thought him to be. But even if I am wrong, Isobel, I will stand happily at yer side, knowin' *I* have made the right choice."

He had promised to dash her fears to pieces and change the things that saddened her to things that give her heart joy, and he kept his word. Finally, she allowed herself to breathe freely, to love him without apprehension. She wasn't going to leave him, and she would battle anyone who tried to keep them apart.

"I will make ye happy, Tristan."

"Ye already do." He bent his face to hers and kissed her. She curled her arms around his neck, keeping him close even after he withdrew. "I should send word to fetch the priest," he whispered against her ear.

"The priest can wait."

He looked at her, his sexy dimple deepening, and then he kissed her again.

His breath was hot against her mouth, his kiss even hotter. She opened to his marauding tongue and moaned with pure pleasure at the feel of him against her, inside her. She missed the way he kissed her, but this was different. He took deliberate leisure with her mouth, taking what he wanted at his own pace, as if defying the world outside to stop him. He drove her mad, but she liked it. She was his, and he would let no one separate them.

"I cannot wait..." she moaned against his teeth.

He laughed and, snaking his arm around her waist, snatched her clear off the floor. Her breath quickened, and she smiled as he carried her to his bed.

He undressed her slowly, spreading his tongue over every inch of flesh he exposed, whispering of how fine she was, how sweet she tasted. Her muscles twitched beneath the mastery of his mouth. In the soft candlelight, his deft fingers explored her most sensitive creases, making her wild for him. She wanted to give him everything, everything he wanted until there was nothing left. The brush of his hair across her cheek as he kissed her eager mouth sent tantalizing quivers to the tips of her toes. Dear God, she wanted him, more of him, all of him. She told him so on a breathless sigh that pulled a groan from the back of his throat.

"How long will ye make me wait?"

He rose above her, smiling like a pagan prince ready to take what was rightfully his. "No' too much longer," he promised, unfastening his belt.

She watched him strip out of his clothes and ran her fingers down the ripples of his tight belly. The delicate brush of her palm over his swollen head both mortified and thrilled her. She'd never touched a man so intimately before. Emboldened by his husky groan, she stroked him from the tip of his head to the base of his shaft. He closed his eyes and leaned back on his thighs, his hands splayed behind him. At this angle, his stiff erection jutted upward like a lance, inviting her to take her pleasure. Visions of climbing atop him and straddling such a beast made the muscles between her legs tighten. She closed her fingers around him, astounded by such a mixture of satin and steel and that he fit entirely inside her. He was too big for one hand, so she used both to pet him gently.

He watched her with hooded, hungry eyes and covered her hands with one of his to guide her over him with more pressure. When a silken thread of moisture seeped from his tip, he stretched out his long legs and lay back.

"Come here." His voice was thick with desire as she climbed over him.

"Where, my love?"

"Right here." He spread his knees and cradled her between his thighs.

Isobel gazed down at him while he guided his passion into hers. She clutched at his chest as he took hold of her hips and thrust himself deeper. She delighted in the delicious tightening of her nipples and the wild hunger of his mouth as he sucked each in turn. He flicked his tongue over her and raked his teeth against her taut flesh while his hands directed her up and down over his long shaft. When he stretched beneath her, her eyes traveled over his lithe, muscular angles and she impaled him to the hilt. His body twitched with pleasure, and Isobel felt a hot spasm of satisfaction that he was hers to do with as she pleased. And she pleased him well. When she spread her tongue over his nipple, he smiled, tunneling his fingers through her hair. He pulled her closer to his mouth and branded her with a kiss. He held her tight against him, looking into her eyes while he slid his hand down her back and bent his knees to take her deeper.

Violent jolts of pure bliss scored her soul, her nerve endings, until she panted above him, her breath mingling with his. And still he drove into her harder, closer, grinding his hips with hers and watching her with his whole heart in his eyes while she found her release with his name on her lips.

"I love ye," she whispered while he threw back his head and clenched his jaw. She felt him fill her with his hot seed, over and over until nothing remained but his hard, heavy breath and his wickedly satiated smile.

Later, Tristan ordered a bath prepared for them in his room. As he had promised, he climbed inside behind her, settling her neatly between his legs.

She rested her head on his chest and traced her fingers over the shapely contours of his calves, remembering the time she had cut his boot to get to the arrow John had put there. The wound had healed nicely.

"Ye dreamed of me once," she told him, recalling how he had called out her name while he recovered from his head wound...er...wounds.

"I dream of ye often."

As he scooped her hair away from her neck, the husky pitch of his voice at her nape sent warm trickles along her spine.

"Tell me now why ye risked so much to go to my home?"

"'Twas yer ankles."

"My ankles?" She lifted one leg out of the water and held it up to look.

"Aye." He closed his arms around her and kissed her neck. "Whenever we spoke ye always ended up stormin' away from me, exposin' yer ankles to my admirin' eyes."

Isobel thought about it for a moment and then turned in the bath to lie atop him, her breasts pressed against his chest. "Are ye never serious, then?"

"Only in how much I love ye, Isobel."

"And I love ye, Tristan."

He rose out of the water with her in his arms, his big hands cupping her wet rump as he made his way to the bed. They never made it to the soft mattress. When she coiled her legs around his waist he hefted her higher over his sleek, hard belly and made love to her where they stood.

Isobel woke sometime later alone in Tristan's bed. The sun had gone down outside his window. She sat up, wondering where Tristan was and hoping he'd gone to fetch them some food. She was as hungry as a bear, but the idea of leaving the room and running into his kin alone—especially his mother—made her heart pound.

When another quarter of an hour passed without his return, she girded up her loins and left the bed. She hated the idea of dressing in her dusty kirtle, but when she looked for it, she found that it, too, was gone.

In its place, draped across the bottom of the bed, was a gown of undyed lambswool and matching leather slippers. She picked up the gown, instantly admiring the luxurious fluidity of the fibers. She held it close to one of the dozen candles Tristan must have lit before he left. The stitching was exquisite, done in gold to match the thick braided girdle that hung low on the hips. Who had left it for her? She didn't care. She had never owned anything so fine and quickly put it on. It fit, though a bit snugly around the waist. The fibers felt warm and wonderful against her skin, and her mood quickly lightened. She ran her fingers through her auburn locks, slipped her feet into the slippers, and left the room.

"Och, good eve, m'lady." A woman sitting in a grand chair outside her door rose to her feet. "I didna' know ye had awakened. I am Alice. I'm to show ye to the Great Hall."

The Great Hall. They would all be there. Dozens, mayhap hundreds of MacGregors. She could do it. For Tristan, she would do anything—and at least she wasn't dirty. "Thank ye, Alice. Did ye leave this gown for me?"

"Nae, m'lady. Maggie left it. She said 'twould look fine on ye, and she was correct."

Isobel didn't know what to make of Tristan's aunt's leaving the gown for her. It was a kind gesture, and she would make a point of thanking her later. She followed Alice down the stairs but stopped when she saw Tristan standing at the end of the long corridor with his father.

"Aye," Alice laughed softly beside her. "He steals the breath of many."

Isobel smiled, nodding in agreement. Whether garbed in English clothes or the Highland plaid and boots he wore now, Tristan oozed male sexual appeal.

"All the Chief's bairns are strikin' to behold," Alice went on with the slightest tremble in her voice. "Just like their faither." Catching herself, the middle-aged hand-maid tore her gaze away from the laird and smiled at Tristan. "That one just knows it better than the others."

Again, Isobel agreed. She was still thinking about asking Alice how many of Camlochlin's lasses might want to claw out her eyes, when Tristan and his father embraced.

"What's this?" Will's cheerful voice calling out from behind her shattered the tender moment.

Isobel blinked the moisture from her eyes as Tristan and Callum turned in her direction.

"Ye gather a man in yer arms while yer lass stands here as bonnie as the sun?"

Tristan's eyes settled on hers, distracting her from everyone else in the hall but him. They stared at each other across the sudden ringing silence, lost in what they had shared earlier, locked away in his room. His smile deepened as his smoky gaze roved boldly over her curves, so well defined in her new gown.

"My son has returned to me, Will," the Chief said, curling his arm around Tristan's shoulder. "Alice, tell Cook to break open another cask of ale. We have double cause to celebrate."

Taking Isobel's arm, Will led her the rest of the way and handed her over to Tristan with a sly wink.

"The sun is drab and dull compared to ye, my love." Tristan lifted her hand and brushed a tender kiss against the underside of her wrist.

She blushed beneath the veil of her lashes, afraid to look at him, afraid that she might fling herself into his arms and to hell with anyone watching.

"It seems I have been dressed fer a celebration," she said, willing herself not to tremble at his nearness.

"Aye, the celebration of our betrothal. Father O'Donnell will be here tomorrow."

Her eyes darted up to his. "But yer mother…"

"She awaits ye at our table." It was the laird who spoke. "After speakin' with yer brother, we—"

"My brother?" Isobel smiled at him. "Whatever could Tamas have said to—"

"'Twas Cameron, no' Tamas," the laird corrected. "He told us what happened that night, Miss Fergusson. Katie wept, but…"

He went on, but his words were drowned out by the crashing drumbeat of Isobel's heart in her ears. She could not breathe. Cam told them the truth? He told them what he did? Was he still alive? She turned to Tristan and promptly fainted.

Chapter Thirty-nine

Isobel awoke in Tristan's bed with the chilling memory of Cameron's confession blaring through her thoughts. He told them! No! He could not have told them! She opened her eyes and pushed against the hands that tried to hold her still.

"'Tis all right, my love," Tristan's voice soothed above her.

Was he mad? How could anything ever be all right again? For ten long years she had guarded her brother's secret with her life, afraid—oh, so afraid—that if the MacGregors ever discovered the truth, they would come for Cam and kill him.

"Where is he?" she cried. "Where is Cameron?"

"Let me speak to her," a woman's voice said somewhere behind Tristan. "Leave us."

With a strangled sob, Isobel watched Tristan leave the room. She wanted to call out to him and beg him to take her and her brothers home. When the door closed after him, she set her tearful gaze on his mother, sitting on the bed beside her, and then covered her face with her hands.

"He was a babe," she cried. "He was trying to protect my father. He did not even know what or who he was shooting his arrow at."

"I know."

"Please, I beg ye, do not harm him. I would die if—"

"There now, my dear," Kate MacGregor pulled her hands away from her face and smiled tenderly at her. "No harm will come to him."

Isobel wanted to believe her more than she wanted anything in the world. But how? How could she when just a few hours ago this woman had practically spat her hatred at her?

"Your brother," the laird's wife said quietly, the past haunting her gaze, "told us that you both witnessed Callum killing your father. You were ten years of age. Orphaned even younger than I."

"Cam was only eight summers," Isobel told her, praying his age would be enough to pardon him.

"I can understand what you think of my husband, but he is no monster. He will not take revenge on a boy over something he did as a babe. No matter how tragic it was. Nor would I have him do so."

Isobel wanted to shout from the battlements. Was it true? They knew the truth and Cam was safe? She wept, as a decade of worry slipped from her heart.

"It does not lessen the pain of losing my brother," Kate continued, tears streaming down her cheeks now, as well. "But it eases my soul to know that it was not done with unfounded malice. You would understand the importance of that if you had known Robert."

"I feel as if I do know him," Isobel told her softly, sitting up in the bed. "And from all that I have been told, Tristan is verra much like him."

"I know," his mother agreed. "I have always known. The problem was, he did not." Kate took both her hands and squeezed. "Please forgive me for being cruel to you earlier and for making you feel unwelcome here. Ye must be an extraordinary woman to have won my son. Many have tried before you and failed."

"I did not want to win him," Isobel told her honestly. "He won me. He worked with steady determination to rid my heart of fear, and anger, and mistrust and won me with humility, and humor, and honesty. My lady, yer son is the most chivalrous man I know."

Kate stared at her for a moment and wiped a tear from her eye. "Most would not agree with you."

"They do not know him, then, and it is their misfortune."

"Aye," his mother agreed softly, "aye, it is."

The door swung open, pulling both their smiles to Maggie, entering the room with a delicate little fairy-looking woman behind her.

"Ye're awake then." Maggie sized her up with a sharp eye as she came around the side of the bed. "Tristan was afraid 'twas yer breathing affliction, but I assured him ye had only fainted. Are ye pleased with the gown, then?"

"Aye, did ye make it?"

"'Tis just something I worked on when I had the time. I made it fer Davina here, but she wanted ye to have it."

Isobel looked up and smiled at the most sweetly beautiful woman she had ever seen. Her hair was the oddest shade of pearly blond, instantly reminding Isobel of angels and halos. Her eyes were wide-set and almost too large for the rest of her diminutive features. If Isobel hadn't seen Tristan's brother Rob sweep her cleanly off her feet when he'd returned home, she would not have believed this wisp of a woman belonged to him.

"I hope you will be able to join us in the Great Hall tonight so that I might see how lovely the gown looks on you."

"That is verra kind—"

"Davina, my love, where are ye!" Rob called from somewhere below stairs.

Davina squeaked with something that sounded like glee and laughed, rushing out of the room. "Do not tell him you have seen me."

Kate smiled, waving her off. Maggie rolled her eyes heavenward.

"She is...playful," Kate explained to Isobel. "Something my eldest son has needed sorely in his life for a long time."

"She is lovely," Isobel told them.

"As are ye, daughter. Now, come, let's join the others for our celebration."

Isobel took Kate MacGregor's hand and let her lead her out of the room. No one had called her daughter in ten years.

The Great Hall was loud. That was the first thing Isobel would always remember about it...and what she came to love most about Camlochlin. Whitehall's Banqueting House might have housed more people, but most of them were not Highlanders with a love of strong whisky and song. Most of the men seated at or standing on the tables were well mannered, unless one of their comrades made an offhanded remark.

Wine, whisky, and ale flowed as freely as conversations—although one usually had to shout to be heard.

Isobel sat with Tristan at the Chief's table and was happy to see her brothers seated there as well. She was not surprised to find Tamas fitting in so comfortably among the MacGregors. He was like them, defiant, tough, and fearless. But Cam seemed equally at ease. Though his eyes still looked up warily from beneath his lashes when the Chief introduced him to his rowdy clan, Cam's smile grew wider and his laughter more genuine as the night wore on. He had been forgiven. It was what he had always needed. Isobel would always be grateful to the MacGregors for such a kindness.

She was carted off twice, once by Maggie to be formally introduced to a few of Maggie's closest friends, and then again by Davina to meet the castle dressmaker. While she listened to the names of fifty different colors most wool could be dyed to be, Isobel watched Tristan make his way over to a pretty girl with dark hair and a sulky mouth.

"That is Caitlin MacKinnon," Davina told her, following her gaze. "You need not worry over her. Tristan barely exchanged a word with her when he returned from England. It was you he spoke of."

"Me?"

"Aye, he told me about you and said he preferred wild flowers over the delicate ones."

Isobel laughed. That was something he would say. She looked at Caitlin again and felt sorry for her—to lose him...

"Did she care fer him?"

"I think so," Davina told her truthfully.

"Then it is good that he speaks with her now." She turned back to the dressmaker. "The emerald green sounds perfect."

Tristan broke away from Caitlin as Isobel began making her way back to the table. They met in the center of the hall, his smile wide and his eyes lit with the dangerous gleam of a wolf about to pounce.

"How many of them do ye have to apologize to?"

He threw his head back and laughed and then swooped back with fluid grace to plant a kiss on her neck. "Only to the ones I think might try to trip ye into the hearth fire."

"Ah, my knight in shining armor."

Sweeping his hand behind his back, he bowed. "I live only to serve ye, my lady."

When she kept walking, he quickened his pace and slipped his arm around her back, pulling her closer to whisper against her ear. "How might I serve ye, with my tongue or somethin' harder?"

"Tristan!" She pinched his side and blushed, smiling when Kate caught her eye from the table. "Yer family is but a few feet away."

"Let's go to bed, then, fer I canna' wait to have ye."

Isobel cleared her throat and cut her gaze to Davina only inches away. "What of yer word to Cameron about waiting for a priest?"

"I gave him my word to find a priest as quickly as I could. That word I have kept." He smiled rather wickedly. "I did try to wait until the priest arrived, but ye, my lovely, would no' have it."

She blushed, knowing he spoke the truth. She turned back to him only to find his mouth closer to hers. "Well, ye will have to wait now."

"Ye enjoy torturin' me."

"Only a little," she admitted with a playful smile and a provocative wink. "Not too much longer, though."

He drew his bottom lip between his teeth and gave her rump a squeeze as she stepped away from him.

Tristan watched the gentle sway of Isobel's backside while she walked away. He smiled, eager to get his hands on it. Hell, but she looked fine in that gown. The creamy color suited her complexion and the snug fit accentuated all her womanly curves. Still, it didn't stop him from wanting to peel her out of it and taste every inch of her.

Drawn by desire and the need to be near her, he made his way to the family table and took his seat beside her. He leaned closer to inhale the sensual curve of her neck while she shared a word with Finn. She still smelled fresh from their bath, with a hint of his own scent still lingering on her skin from their lovemaking. He straightened, doing all in his power not to haul her into his arms and carry her up the stairs to his bed.

The celebration was finally winding down, with many of the men in the hall too drunk to do anything more than slump over their chairs. At Tristan's table, though, his kin showed no signs of growing weary from their laughter and drinking. Of course, Angus and Brodie MacGregor could have consumed every last drop of whisky in Camlochlin and still found their way to the victorious side of a battlefield.

As it grew somewhat quieter in the hall, the women at his table, including Isobel, found it easier to talk about everything from sewing to babes, while the men's conversations turned inevitably to fighting. Tristan shifted in his chair, not quite interested in any opinion but one about the fastest way to get his betrothed into bed. And no one was offering *that* discussion.

"Isobel, tell us about your home."

Tristan cut his mother a dismal glance, which she completely missed, and reached over to swipe Angus's cup and empty its contents before the brute had time to take a swing at him.

"So 'tis just the seven of ye who do all the work, then?" his father asked. "Ye have nae tenants to help?"

Tristan looked at him through watery eyes, thanks to the potency of Angus's brew, and couldn't help smiling at Tamas, the youngest warrior at the table, leaning against his father's strong arm, trying to stay awake.

"They all left us after..." Isobel didn't finish. She didn't have to. Everyone at the table suspected the reason and grew quiet.

"Patrick could use some aid, faither," Tristan told him. "Now that we're all kin..."

"Of course," Callum agreed easily. "Take with ye as many men as ye need."

Isobel turned to further muddle Tristan's head with her most radiant, grateful smile. He leaned in to kiss her but missed when she turned back to his father.

"That is most kind. And let me also thank ye fer the goods ye have sent over the years. I did not know they were from ye, but they helped in some of our most difficult times."

The laird nodded, looking a bit uncomfortable, as though he'd been caught being soft. Not that everyone didn't already know, but none would dare accuse the mighty Devil MacGregor of having a heart. Tristan was glad he saw it now. He was glad they had finally spoken about things that had been hidden for so long. Mostly, he was glad that he had room in his heart to love with equal measure the two men who raised him. He had dressed himself as the fool for so long, always afraid of never being the man his uncle was, afraid he could never be the warrior he thought his father wanted him to be.

But even warriors had honor.

His wound had been healed. And he had Isobel to thank for it.

"Tamas sleeps," he noted with enough enthusiasm in his voice to give him away—at least to Isobel. "Isobel and I will bring him to his bed."

The blush that stole over her cheeks as Tristan stood to his feet, pulling her along with him, drew the attention of one other Highlander at the table.

"Since when," Will asked him with a teasing quirk of his brow when Tristan rounded the table to gather Tamas into his arms, "d'ye need an excuse to leave the table fer other pursuits?"

The challenge that sparked Tristan's eyes drew a rueful smile from Rob, who knew all too well what was coming. Tristan might have set his feet on the right path, but he was still Tristan.

"Mayhap the question ye should be askin' is why my pursuits have always left ye as ye are now, Will, caressin' a drink rather than a lass." He offered his cousin a rapier-sharp smirk and a slight bow. "Dinna' fear, with me gone and a wee bit of fortune on yer side, what I leave behind can be yers."

"Ye are a devil!" Isobel told him as they left the hall.

"Nae, my lovely, I am the Devil's son." He looked down at Tamas, asleep in his arms, and kissed the boy's forehead. "And if good fortune still loves me, we shall take great pleasure in tryin' to make one of our own."

Chapter Forty

After putting Tamas into bed, Tristan waited by the open door while Isobel tucked her brother in. He held his hand out to her when she was done and waited for her to take it. When she did, he swept her into the hall and waved his other arm across his waist, offering her the path to his room.

"So gallant are we about it, then?" Isobel cut him a hooded glance.

"Is it gallant to admit that all I want to do right now"—with a flick of his wrist, he twirled her on her slippers, gracefully ending up behind her—"is look at ye from this angle?"

He felt himself go hard at the perfect roundness of her bottom. It wasn't a good condition to be caught in, standing in the corridor, wearing a plaid with no breeches beneath. He didn't help matters by imagining himself bending her over his bed and taking her from behind. She turned to look at him just as he tucked his erection beneath his belt.

"Trust me when I tell ye, lass"—his smoldering gaze

captured hers when she lifted it from his hands—"there's nothin' gallant aboot what I want to do to ye."

"Then perhaps I should quicken my pace," she replied in a sultry tone that snapped across his back like a whip.

He lunged for her and the nearest door. He was done waiting.

"This is the solar! Tristan!" She gasped when he slammed the bolt home. "What are ye doing?"

"I'm lockin' ye in," he said, rounding on her.

She giggled, but he could detect the thread of fear in her voice. "Still, someone might come."

He stalked her around a chair. "The danger makes yer blood run quicker, does it no'?" 'Tis a wee bit more thrillin', aye?"

"Should I be afraid of ye, then?"

"Aye." He tossed his belt to the floor and shrugged out of his plaid. "Ye should."

She made a dash for the other side of the solar, but he caught her and held her flat against the wall. "I will have ye here, Isobel." He locked her wrists over her head with one hand. "Right now."

"Ye will force me to scream." She closed her eyes, exposing her throat to his sensual bite. Her bosom heaved against his chest.

"I intend to make ye scream mightily." Dipping low, he molded his thighs to the hollow curve between her legs. He pressed the flagrant hardness of his body against her and pulled the neckline of her gown down to expose the fullness of her breasts. He bent his knees, careful to keep his weight against her, and licked a fiery path to her nipple. He spent little time there, though, too eager to have her.

Grasping handfuls of her gown, he yanked the wool up over her hips, rising with it to impale her against the wall.

He paused for a brief moment to bask in her quick surrender, and then he drove himself into her with such force her feet left the floor.

"Who says ye are not a warrior?" she grunted with him as he tore himself into her.

"Hell, woman, ye drive me mad." He bore her against the wall with the strength of his kiss and the hard thrusts of his body, lifting her legs around his waist to deepen his powerful lunges.

"I meant to take ye from another direction," he breathed into her mouth, then laughed softly against it. "Later." He filled her to her womb with his torrential release and then plundered her further, until she screamed his name and shook in his arms with her rapture.

A shout from the battlements pulled Isobel from her slumber the next day. She opened her eyes, blissfully aware of every part of her body and nothing else. After Tristan had made love to her in the solar, he carried her to his bed and made love to her all night until they finally fell asleep locked in each other's arms, too exhausted to move. She spread her palm over his pillow now and wondered where he was. The sunlight glaring through the windows told her it was midmorning.

Midmorning? She sat up. Dear God, she was getting married today! She swung her legs over the side of the bed and reached for her kirtle and shift. Her eyes widened at the sight of the emerald gown laid neatly over a chair in the corner. She rose and went to it slowly. It was the most exquisitely beautiful gown she had ever laid eyes on. She reached for it, but a sharp knock on the door startled her.

"Isobel!" Cameron called from the other side.

"A moment!" She rushed back to the bed and dressed

as quickly as she could in her shift and kirtle. "Come in, Cam."

The door burst open and her brother's face broke into a wide grin. "Isobel, a boat approaches. It is our brothers! Make haste! They were about to dock when I came to fetch ye." He raced back out of the room, leaving her there, stunned.

Patrick was here? Lachlan and John? Oh, how she missed them! Without bothering to slip into her shoes, she hiked up her skirts and ran out of the room and down the stairs.

She reached the shoreline of the nearby bay just as the small boat docked.

"That's John MacGregor of Stronachlacher rowin'," Angus told the Chief beside him. "Fool ought to know no' to come in this way wi'oot a banner."

Isobel didn't hear the rest of the conversation, but followed Tamas into the water and practically leaped into Patrick's arms as he stepped out. Oh, it was so good to see them again! Lachlan and John looked a bit pale, what with the row of Highlanders staring at them, all bearing weapons, but their fears subsided when they saw that their sister was well. Alex was with them, and Isobel embraced him next.

"When did ye return from England?" she asked him. He didn't answer but glared over her shoulder.

"Patrick!" Tristan joined them with a wide grin and took his arm. "What are ye doin' here?"

"The better question," Alex snarled, "is what is *she* doing here?"

Isobel was thankful that Tristan kept his smile intact while he scooped John up in his arms. "Did ye miss me, then, John?"

John's grin was so wide even the dangerous warriors behind them had to smile.

"Isobel," Alex snapped at her. "I wish to have a word with ye in private."

"The solar mayhap?" Tristan offered glibly.

Goodness, but he made her blush at the worst times! "Of course, Alex," she said, holding out her hand to him. "There is much we have to discuss. We will go to the Great Hall."

"How's my brother Colin?" Tristan asked him as Alex passed.

"He split my lip."

"I feared he might. I hated leavin' ye with him."

Isobel yanked her brother's arm when he moved toward Tristan. "Are ye that much of a fool?" she hissed. "Look around ye. Lift yer hand to him and ye will be minus an arm."

Alex let her pull him toward the castle, looking over his shoulder a few times as they went. "What the hell have ye done, Isobel?"

"Hush, Alex. Have the control to at least wait until we get inside. Ye are reckless and will get yerself killed one of these days. And it is mine and Patrick's fault fer being too lenient with ye."

"Patrick was worried sick over ye."

"Well, as ye can see, I am fine."

"Did they force ye to come here with them?"

"No," she told him, leading him into the castle. "Cam, Tamas, and I came willingly."

"Have they treated ye poorly?"

"They have treated me like a queen."

"They killed our father, Isobel. Have ye fergotten that?"

She stopped and looked at him, shaking her head. "No, but I have put the past behind me where it belongs, as have they. Ye must do the same."

"I never will," he vowed, and then turned to the men entering the castle. His eyes hardened on Tristan. The laird's eyes hardened on him.

"This is good fortune!" Tristan's ever-joyful smile lit the halls. "Ye have all arrived in time fer our weddin'. Where the hell is Father O'Donnell?"

John, perched on his shoulder, laughed into his hand at Tristan's expletive.

"Yer wedding?" Alex glared at Tristan first and then at Isobel. "How can ye mean to—" His words ceased abruptly when Callum MacGregor appeared at his side.

"Alex Fergusson," the Chief said quietly, dangerously.

Alex swallowed audibly and tilted his face up to meet Callum's lethal gaze. Patrick took a tentative step forward, but Tristan stopped him.

"Ye are sorely in need of some guidance. Ye will stay here."

"What?" Alex looked ill.

"With him," the laird pointed to Tamas. "Ye will both remain at Camlochlin under my command."

Tamas grinned. Alex balked. "I am not a child to be—"

"Ye behave like one." The raw power in Callum's voice quieted everyone around them. "'Tis time ye became a man, and ye will do that under my direction if ye ever want to leave here alive."

He flicked his gaze to Isobel when she made a frightened sound. "Will ye trust me with them, then? I didna' do poorly with my own sons, aye?"

"Aye," she agreed quietly.

He turned to Patrick next, and when he, too, nodded, Callum scooped up Tamas in his arms and called over his shoulder, "Come, Patrick, we have much to discuss aboot yer land and how many men ye think ye will need to aid ye with it. Brodie," he said, entering the Great Hall, "Alex is now yer charge."

Tristan spared Alex a genuinely pitying smile as Camlochlin's sourest warrior hauled him into the Great Hall behind the others.

"I like all the mountains," John said, looking up at Tristan after he plucked him off his shoulder and set him on his feet.

"Is that so?" Tristan smiled at him and mussed his crown of orange hair. "Well, we shall have to climb one of them, then."

John's eyes opened wide. "Can we?"

"Of course, that is what they are there fer. But later. Now, go with the others and let me have a word with yer sister."

When they were alone, Tristan took her hand and kissed it. "Have I thanked ye, fair lady?"

"Fer what, gallant knight?" She looked lovingly into his eyes.

"Fer rescuin' me."

She crooked her smile at him. "It is what I do best."

He laughed and looked inside the Great Hall at their two families sharing drinks and discussing their future. Hell, it was a good moment. A good day, to be followed by many more if he had his way about it. And as most already knew, Tristan MacGregor almost always had his way.

"Now." He took Isobel in his arms and bent to kiss her. "Where the hell is that priest?"

Mairi MacGregor is a
loyal Scotswoman.
Connor Grant couldn't be more
loyal to the British crown.
To fall in love would be
unthinkable . . .

Please turn this page for
a preview of

Tamed by a Highlander

Available in mass market
in September 2011.

Chapter One

Mairi MacGregor sat in a chair in her father's guest chambers at Whitehall Palace waiting for the door to open. In her lap, her fingers twisted a loose thread in her kirtle, over and over, until the coarse wool made her flesh raw. But that was the only outward sign of the turmoil within her. He was coming, likely walking up the stairs at this very moment. She breathed steadily, even offering a temperate smile to her mother pacing before her.

"I'm certain there is a good reason fer Rob to have gone home. Ye must not worry so."

"What is taking them so long?" Her mother wrung her hands as she proceeded on her steady march. "You do not think your father brought Captain Grant and Colin to the king first, do you?"

"Callum would not keep our sons away from us a moment longer than he has to, Kate," Lady Claire Stuart reassured her from her seat beside the hearth fire. "We will find out soon enough why they have returned to the palace without their brothers. If it was something dire,

Connor would have told us the moment he arrived. Now sit down. You are making me fidget."

Kate continued to pace. As a mother, she had every reason to fret. Mairi's eldest brother, Rob, had taken a detour along the Scottish border on their way to England. With him rode the youngest of the MacGregor brood, Colin, their cousins Will and Angus, and Finlay Grant, Graham and Claire's son. They had not arrived at Whitehall the day after the rest of their kin, as planned, but had sent Angus back with news of an attack on an abbey and a lass Rob had rescued from the flames.

The MacGregors and the Grants knew nothing more until today, when Colin arrived with Captain Connor Grant.

He was here. Connor was here.

The knot in Mairi's stomach grew tighter than the one in her fingers. It had been three years since she told him she hoped never to see him alive again. Seven years since the last time he told her he loved her and then rode out of Camlochlin to join the king's Royal Army. She had never forgotten the way he looked that day—resolved, despite the tears she foolishly shed for him.

He never saw her weep again after that.

"Try no' to bite off his head this time, aye, Mairi?"

She turned to her brother, lounging in a high-backed chair, his boots dangling over the side. "Whatever d'ye mean, Tristan?" She did her best to sound unfazed. "I have nothing at all to say to him."

His quick eyes dipped to her fingers coiling her thread. She ceased instantly. He said nothing more and Mairi was grateful. She usually enjoyed sharpening her tongue on Tristan's lightning wit, but when it came to Connor she would lose.

The three of them had grown up together. Tristan

knew she had fallen in love with his best friend when she was six summers old. She had followed them everywhere, much to their disgust, until she finally proved she could climb any tree they could and get into the same trouble they did without crying like a babe when they got caught. Tristan was with them as they grew older and Connor grew more aware of her, and fonder of her, until he finally kissed her beneath the shadow of Bla Bheinn. Connor was twelve when he first promised that one day he would wed her and build her a home in her beloved Highlands. He was seven and ten when he left.

Connor had always been a part of her life. A part she cursed and cherished in equal measure. If she hadn't fallen in love with his broad, sweeping smiles, or seen her future in the fathomless depths of his sapphire eyes, she never would have learned how false a man's heart could truly be.

She hated him.

The door opened. Her breath paused when her father stepped into the chamber. Behind him, Graham Grant entered the room with Colin. Mairi was happy to see her youngest, dearest brother alive and looking well, but her eyes were already moving toward the tall, elegant captain framing the door. Dear God, how was it possible that he had grown even more handsome than the last time she saw him? She hated the royal uniform that stretched across his broad shoulders, but she could not deny that he looked more imposing in it than in the Highland plaid he used to wear.

He entered the room, sparing her only a brief glance behind silken strands of pale gold eclipsing his vision.

The thread in her fingers popped.

"Colin!" Her mother hurried forward and gathered her son in her arms. "You look dreadful. When is the last time you ate? Where is Rob? Why is he not with you?"

After assuring her that both he and Rob—and Finn, he added for Claire's benefit—were well, Colin broke away from his mother's grasping hands and crooked his mouth at Mairi when she caught his eye. It was all she would get from him for now, and all the reassurance she needed to know he was unharmed. He'd passed her the very same look many times before, after one of their "skirmishes" with the Covenanters and Cameronians who were foolish enough to find themselves on or near Skye.

"I want a full account of what happened since ye left us." Callum MacGregor sat calmly, but his voice held the authority of a king.

Mairi listened while her brother recounted the Dutch attack on Saint Christopher's Abbey with less interest than she would have had on any other day. She could feel Connor in the room. His very presence made her burn with so many emotions she feared that if she looked at him, she might be tempted to stare at him forever, or leap from her chair and claw his eyes out of his head.

She closed her eyes and drew in a deep, silent breath. She didn't need to look at him to see his face. It haunted her daily. His eyes were the same color as the vast heavens over Skye on both summer days and stormy ones. His lips were full and straight, save when they curled into a slow, sensual grin adorned by a dimple on either side of his gold-dusted cheeks, the right dimple deeper than the left and needing only the slightest encouragement to appear.

She couldn't think. She couldn't breathe with him

there. She kept her legs from moving by finding another thread in her kirtle and knotting it.

"What do the king of England's enemies care aboot a novice of the order," her father asked, "that they would burn doun Miss Montgomery's abbey and pursue her across the braes?"

"I gave Rob my word to tell no one here who she is, including the king," Connor finally spoke, his deep, drawling voice like a balmy breeze over the moors. "But ye are his kin, and ye should know the danger he is in."

His words, not his voice, pulled Mairi's gaze to him.

"The danger I fear he may be bringing on Camlochlin."

What was he saying? Rob...everyone at Camlochlin was in danger? Why? Who was this lass whose life her brother had saved? When Connor told them all a moment later, she sat stunned in her seat and then blinked when her father told them all to pack. They were going home in the morning.

"Faither," she interrupted him as Connor and Colin left the chamber on their way to tell the king, who had led the attack on the abbey, "if this Dutch admiral attacks Camlochlin, I would like to fight."

He gave her a horrified look that changed with her next heartbeat to one rife with warning. "Never suggest that to me again."

"But ye know I can wield a sword!" she argued, blocking his path when he moved to pass her. He had no idea how often she had done so in real combat. It was better for her parents never to discover that she and Colin had joined the rebel militia formed to save their country from the political and religious zealots bent on promoting Presbyterianism. "Ye refuse me because I am a woman!"

"Ye're damned right!" He cut his molten gaze to Claire first, for teaching her how to use a sword as skillfully as her brothers, and then to his wife for helping. "Ye will remain here," he told her. "And now that I think better on it, Connor will remain with ye. I dinna' know where ye and he sneak off to at home, but ye willna' be doin' it this time."

Here? She couldn't stay here! Not with Connor! The king certainly wouldn't let his captain go running off to Skye to fight in a battle they weren't even sure was going to happen. Mairi opened her mouth to protest further, but her father stopped her with a stern look.

"I willna' be persuaded, Mairi." His tone softened a bit. "Ye are my daughter and ye will obey me in this. I love ye, and I will do whatever I need to do in order to keep ye safe."

Her eyes opened wide with pleading. "But—"

"Graham," he said, cutting her off and turning to Connor's father. "Ye and Claire will stay, as well. If Rob is correct and Miss Montgomery's enemies are here, we dinna' want to arouse their suspicions by all of us rushing home."

Graham agreed and left the chamber with the rest of her kin, leaving Mairi alone with a dozen curses spilling from her lips.

She was still fuming when she entered the Banqueting House and was greeted by Henry de Vere, the Protestant son of the Earl of Oxford. Damnation, she wasn't in the frame of mind to be polite to him now.

Nae, she couldn't let the idea of being trapped in the palace with Connor for God knows how long distract her from her original plan. She wished she had Tristan's knack for looking on the brighter side when all was going to hell. She was staying, and it would give her more time to discover if the scar running down Oxford's face had been put there by her own dagger last spring when the militia raided a secret meeting of Covenanters.

"I was looking for you." He smiled and brought her hand to his mouth for a kiss. "Forgive me for being so anxious at the thought of seeing you again. I—"

"I am flattered, m'lord." Despite the urge to wipe her hand on her kirtle, she managed a smile. If he was a Covenanter, she would have to kill him, but it could wait. "What lady wouldna' be pleased to find herself admired by so fine a gentleman?"

"You honor me." The flush across his jaw convinced Mairi that not too many women did.

Good Lord, but why did English men insist on wearing those hideous periwigs on their heads? It gave them the same look as the sheep that grazed on the hills of Camlochlin.

"Come, I want you to meet my sister Elizabeth. She just arrived from visiting our relatives in Somerset and is anxious to meet you. I told her all about you. I do hope you don't mind."

Not *all* about her, Mairi hoped, and almost smiled genuinely for the first time that day.

Davina Montgomery is
the Crown's greatest secret.
But when a powerful warrior
steals her heart,
their passion may destroy
the English throne.

Please turn this page for
a preview of

Ravished by a Highlander

Available now.

Chapter One

*H*igh atop Saint Christopher's Abbey, Davina Montgomery stood alone in the bell tower, cloaked in the silence of a world she did not know. Darkness had fallen hours ago, and below her the sisters slept peacefully in their beds, thanks to the men who had been sent here to guard them. But there was little peace for Davina. The vast indigo sky filling her vision was littered with stars that seemed close enough to touch should she reach out her hand. What would she wish for? Her haunted gaze slipped southward toward England, and then with a longing just as powerful, toward the moonlit mountain peaks of the north. Which life would she choose if the choice were hers to make? A world where she'd been forgotten, or one where no one knew her? She smiled sadly against the wind that whipped her woolen novice robes around her. What good was it to ponder when her future had already been decreed? She knew what was to come. There were no variations. That is, if she lived beyond the next year.

She looked away from the place she could never go and the person she could never be.

She heard the soft fall of footsteps behind her but did not turn. She knew who it was.

"Poor Edward. I imagine your heart must have failed you when you did not find me in my bed."

When he remained quiet, she felt sorry for teasing him about the seriousness of his duty. Captain Edward Asher had been sent here to protect her four years ago, after Captain Geoffries had taken ill and was relieved of his command. Edward had become more than her guardian. He was her dearest friend, someone she could confide in here within the thick walls that sheltered her from the schemes of her enemies. Edward knew her fears and accepted her faults.

"I knew where to find you," he finally said, his voice just above a whisper.

He always did know. Not that there were many places to look. Davina was not allowed to venture outside the Abbey gates, so she came to the bell tower often to let her thoughts roam free.

"My lady—"

She turned at his soft call, putting away her dreams and desires behind a tender smile. Those she kept to herself and did not share, even with him.

"Please, I…" he began, meeting her gaze and then stumbling through the rest as if the face he looked upon every day still struck him as hard as it had the first time he'd seen her. He was in love with her, and though he'd never spoken his heart openly, he did not conceal how he felt. Everything was there in his eyes, his deeds, his devotion—and a deep regret that Davina suspected had more to do with her than he would ever have the boldness to admit. Her path had been charted for another course, and she could never be his. "Lady Montgomery, come away from here, I beg you. It is not good to be alone."

He worried for her so, and she wished he wouldn't. "I'm not alone, Edward," she reassured him. If her life remained as it was now, she would find a way to be happy. She always did. "I have been given much."

"It's true," he agreed, moving closer to her and then stopping himself, knowing what she knew. "You have been taught to fear the Lord and love your king. The sisters love you, as do my men. It will always be so. We are your family. But it is not enough." He knew she would never admit it, so he said it for her.

It had to be enough. It was safer this way, cloistered away from those who would harm her if ever they discovered her after the appointed time.

That time had come.

Davina knew that Edward would do anything to save her. He told her often, each time he warned her of her peril. Diligently, he taught her to trust no one, not even those who claimed to love her. His lessons often left her feeling a bit hopeless, though she never told him that, either.

"Would that I could slay your enemies," he swore to her now, "and your fears along with them."

He meant to comfort her, but good heavens, she didn't want to discuss the future on such a breathtaking night. "Thanks to you and God," she said, leaving the wall to go to him and tossing him a playful smile, "I can slay them myself."

"I agree," he surrendered, his good mood restored by the time she reached him. "You've learned your lessons in defense well."

She rested her hand on his arm and gave it a soft pat.

"How could I disappoint you when you risked the Abbess's consternation to teach me?"

He laughed with her, both of them comfortable in their familiarity. But too soon he grew serious again.

"James is to be crowned in less than a se'nnight."

"I know." Davina nodded and turned toward England again. She refused to let her fears control her. "Mayhap," she said with a bit of defiance sparking her doleful gaze, "we should attend the coronation, Edward. Who would think to look for me at Westminster?"

"My lady..." He reached for her. "We cannot. You know—"

"I jest, dear friend." She angled her head to speak to him over her shoulder, carefully cloaking the struggle that weighed heaviest upon her heart, a struggle that had nothing to do with fear. "Really, Edward, must we speak of this?"

"Yes, I think we should," he answered earnestly, then went on swiftly, before she could argue, "I've asked the Abbess if we can move you to Courlochcraig Abbey in Ayr. I've already sent word to—"

"Absolutely not," she stopped him. "I will not leave my home. Besides, we have no reason to believe that my enemies know of me at all."

"Just for a year or two. Until we're certain—"

"No," she told him again, this time turning to face him fully. "Edward, would you have us leave the sisters here alone to face our enemies should they come seeking me? What defense would they have without the strong arms of you and your men? They will not leave St. Christopher's, nor will I."

He sighed and shook his head at her. "I cannot argue when you prove yourself more courageous than I. I pray

I do not live to regret it. Very well, then." The lines of his handsome face relaxed. "I shall do as you ask. For now, though," he added, offering her his arm, "allow me to escort you to your chamber. The hour is late, and the Reverend Mother will show you no mercy when the cock crows."

Davina rested one hand in the crook of his arm and waved away his concern with the other. "I don't mind waking with the sun."

"Why would you," he replied, his voice as light now as hers as he led her out of the belfry, "when you can just fall back to sleep in the Study Hall."

"It was only the one time that I actually slept," she defended, slapping his arm softly. "And don't you have more important things to do with your day than follow me around?"

"Three times," he corrected, ignoring the frown he knew was false. "Once, you even snored."

Her eyes, as they descended the stairs, were as wide as her mouth. "I have never snored in my life!"

"Save for that one time, then?"

She looked about to deny his charge again, but bit her curling lip instead. "And once during Sister Bernadette's piano recital. I had penance for a week. Do you remember?"

"How could I forget?" he laughed. "My men did no chores the entire time, preferring to listen at your door while you spoke aloud to God about everything but your transgression."

"God already knew why I fell asleep," she explained, smiling at his grin. "I did not wish to speak poorly of Sister Bernadette's talent, or lack of it, even in my own defense."

His laughter faded, leaving only a smile that looked to

be painful as their walk ended and they stood at her door. When he reached out to take her hand, Davina did her best not to let the surprise in her eyes dissuade him from touching her. "Forgive my boldness, but there is something I must tell you. Something I should have told you long ago."

"Of course, Edward," she said softly, keeping her hand in his. "You know you may always speak freely to me."

"First, I would have you know that you have come to mean—"

"Captain!"

Davina leaned over the stairwell to see Harry Barns, Edward's second in command, plunge through the Abbey doors. "Captain!" Harry shouted up at them, his face pale and his breath heavy from running. "They are coming!"

For one paralyzing moment, Davina doubted the good of her ears. She'd been warned of this day for four years but had always prayed it would not come. "Edward," she asked hollowly, on the verge of sheer panic, "how did they find us so soon after King Charles's death?"

He squeezed his eyes shut and shook his head back and forth as if he, too, refused to believe what he was hearing. But there was no time for doubt. Spinning on his heel, he gripped her arm and hauled her into her room. "Stay here! Lock your door!"

"What good will that do us?" She sprang for her quiver and bow and headed back to the door, and to Edward blocking it. "Please, dear friend. I do not want to cower alone in my room. I will fire from the bell tower until it is no longer safe to do so."

"Captain!" Barns raced up the stairs, taking three at a time. "We need to prepare. Now!"

"Edward"—Davina's voice pulled him back to her—"you trained me for this. We need every arm available. You will not stop me from fighting for my home."

"Orders, Captain, please!"

Davina looked back once as she raced toward the narrow steps leading back to the tower.

"Harry!" She heard Edward shout behind her. "Prepare the vats and boil the tar. I want every man alert and ready at my command. And Harry..."

"Captain?"

"Wake the sisters and tell them to pray."

In the early morning hours that passed after the massacre at St. Christopher's, Edward's men had managed to kill half of the enemy's army. But the Abbey's losses were greater. Far greater.

Alone in the bell tower, Davina stared down at the bodies strewn across the large courtyard. The stench of burning tar and seared flesh stung her nostrils and burned her eyes as she set them beyond the gates to the meadow where men on horseback still hacked away at each other as if their hatred could never be satisfied. But there was no hatred. They fought because of her, though none of them knew her. But she knew them. Her dreams had been plagued with her faceless assassins since the day Edward had first told her of them.

Tears brought on by the pungent air slipped down her cheeks, falling far below to where her friends...her family lay dead or dying. Dragging her palm across her eyes, she searched the bodies for Edward. He'd returned to her an hour after the fighting had begun and ordered her into the chapel with the sisters. When she'd refused, he'd tossed her over his shoulder like a sack of grain and brought her there himself. But she did not remain hidden. She couldn't, so she'd returned to the tower and her bow and sent more than a dozen of her enemies to meet their Maker. But there were too many—or mayhap God didn't want the rest, for they slew the men she ate with, laughed with, before her eyes.

She had feared this day for so long that it had become a part of her. She thought she had prepared. At least, for her own death. But not for the Abbess's. Not for Edward's. How could anyone prepare to lose those they loved?

Despair ravaged her, and for a moment she considered stepping over the wall. If she was dead they would stop. But she had prayed for courage too many times to let God or Edward down now. Reaching into the quiver on her back, she plucked out an arrow, cocked her bow, and closed one eye to aim.

Below her and out of her line of vision, a soldier garbed in military regalia not belonging to England crept along the chapel wall with a torch clutched in one fist and a sword in the other.

THE DISH

Where authors give you the inside scoop!

♥ ♥ ♥ ♥ ♥ ♥ ♥ ♥ ♥ ♥ ♥ ♥ ♥ ♥

From the desk of Kate Brady

Dear Reader,

I first met the hero in LAST TO DIE (on sale now) several years ago. His name was Mitch Sheridan, and I got to know him long before his brother, Neil, came around and launched the Sheridan series. Mitch was the hero of my first foray into contemporary stories, and toward the end of that manuscript, I learned he had a brother and a sister. I knew nothing about either one, but became fascinated by all three Sheridans. I went on to write Neil's story and later to sell it.

That's when I came full circle back to Mitch. His original story didn't involve the maniacal murder plot expected in romantic thrillers, but Mitch himself was a character I'd always loved. Gorgeous, famous, sexy, and driven by a deep-seated need to save the world in order to redeem his own failures, Mitch required a heroine who would take the blinders from his eyes and make him face the truth instead of running from it. Someone undaunted by his fortune and fame.

Dani Cole seemed right for the job. A cop with a hard life, Dani emerged in the story as tough as the pit bull she'd once rescued. She was stubborn, independent, resilient. And she made it clear to Mitch when they were just teenagers that she could manage life's challenges without him. In fact, she preferred it that way.

Eighteen years later, when their story opens, sexual sparks fly, but Dani still refuses to let herself lean on Mitch. Now, here's where I—as a modern female author— encounter a dichotomy that's always hard to handle. I'm an educated and progressive woman perfectly capable of taking care of myself. But I'm also a sucker for a man who knows what he wants. And when what he wants is a specific woman—whom he's wanted for eighteen years—I have to admit I find that pretty darn sexy. I'm not talking about anything brutish, mind you. But watching Mitch charm his way back into Dani's life, and then seeing him fear she was in danger, reminded me of why I fell in love with him and his brother in the first place. It may not be very liberated of me, but there it is.

Of course, before they come around to bliss, they'll have to track down a diabolical murderer and unravel a hair-raising plot that's motivated by far more than money or vengeance.

People continually ask how I come up with such warped psyches. I can only say that somewhere between grading papers and conducting church choirs and doing laundry and running kids around and cooking meals and cleaning up after pets—twisted little thoughts sometimes niggle. It's great fun to put pen to paper (or finger to keyboard) and flesh them out!

I hope you enjoy going along with Mitch and Dani to conquer that evil killer and find true love.

Happy Reading!

Kate Brady

From the desk of Paula Quinn

Dear Reader,

When I was given the opportunity to write "The Children of the Mist" series, I was overjoyed. I couldn't wait to begin and to be reunited with my two favorite characters, Kate and Callum MacGregor, from LAIRD OF THE MIST. How exciting to meet their sons and their daughter, to fill over twenty years of time in my head discovering who my new heroes and heroines were, and who they were to become. You already met the devoted, uncompromisingly stubborn firstborn, Rob MacGregor, in the first book in the series, RAVISHED BY A HIGHLANDER. His brother Tristan, the hero (and I breathe a little sigh as I type that particular word for this particular man) in my brand new book SEDUCED BY A HIGHLANDER, is nothing at all like him. In fact, Tristan is nothing like anyone in his family. Or so everyone, including him, believes. Up until my revisions for this book, even I didn't know who Tristan truly was.

He had us all fooled.

Like every other woman who meets him, I quickly fell in love with his natural charm and vibrant smiles. But it was a facade, and it took me some time before I realized it. Me, his author. Even after I did, breaking through the barrier he'd built between himself and the rest of the world made him the most challenging and ultimately gratifying hero I've ever written.

You see, Tristan had been wounded as a boy. Not physically, but it's the scars on one's heart that take the longest to heal...so they say. Being privy to his entire life, I knew the event that had changed him, but I didn't want to go back and examine how it had. Honestly, it was too painful for me. Thank God my editor is brilliant and told me I needed to go back and see the event through my young hero's eyes and then write it into the Prologue.

If you've read it, then some of you might already hate me for the death of Robert Campbell, beloved Galahad in A HIGHLANDER NEVER SURRENDERS. It's okay; I hated myself for a while for writing it. But it was in the moment of the earl's death that I finally saw who Tristan truly was—the man he had wanted to become. My carefree, reckless rogue was really a knight in shin...ok, well, rusty armor. But as the fair, feisty damsel Isobel Fergusson assures him, armor can be polished.

Pick up a copy of SEDUCED BY A HIGHLANDER and follow a knight's quest for honor as it leads him to the arms of his ladylove...even if she does hate him.

Enjoy!

Paula Quinn